# MOONS' KISS

Kimberly K. Comeau

FIRST EDITION
First Printing, 2012



This is a work of fiction. Any similarity to real persons, living or dead, is coincidental and not intended by the author.

ISBN-13: 978-0-615-62998-8
ISBN-10: 0615629989

Printed in the United States

To Harold,
without whom I would not be as strong.

## Acknowledgements

"Thanks" are insufficient to express my gratitude to the members of PC Quill. Lauren, Ted, Shawn, Sherri, Diane, Wilma, Bill, Charlie, you folks are critique partners extraordinaire.

To Melissa Alvarez at Book Covers Galore, who captured the soul of Axxord, thank you a hundred times over.

Without external confirmation, it's hard for a writer to focus, improve, and keep going. Shawn, your passion for *Moons' Kiss* bolstered my confidence while others tore it apart. When you gushed over story elements and characters, your excitement helped me overlook rejections and others' criticisms. This book is as much your bright star as mine. Thank you for all you've done. You embody and go beyond the term "friendship."

# YATREN LANGUAGE DICTIONARY

**abbah** – A daily religious ritual performed by the devout at dawn and sunset.

**arenta** – Any child born to one of the Chosen of Acrahh following a shecaren birth. According to Hyranian edict, arenta means "blessed child."

**Chosen of Acrahh** – Any woman who gives birth to a shecaren.

**cor-anda** – "man-thing."

**ilan** – **"lady."** A woman's title that reflects either political position or educational achievement.

**janquer** – The shon regis's advisory council, composed of one representative from each tribe, with the exception of the Manteen. Also denotes a member of that council. Only the shon regis may administer the unification prayer or divest a janquer member.

**Kitarin** – The tribe occupying the forestlands north of Ayahn Rahh and the Tydonddy Mountains. Their isolation has evoked rumors of an unnatural ability to see into men's souls, which exaggerates a taught ability to interpret body language. They are also renown for animal husbandry and their knowledge of plants. Their capitol is Kaytron.

**Manteen** – Descendants of the followers of Mante, who fled Ringgal during civil war. Cut off from the ocean, they resorted to cannibalism before learning to survive in the arid canyonlands northeast of the Rahhe Mountains. Their language evolved autonomously from that of other tribes. They are considered by the shecarens to be a tribe of Yatra, although Yatren laws are rarely enforced in their protection. They have no known capitol.

**mia** – Horned sheep valued for their wool and milk. The Ofrann consider their lives linked to the survival of their mian flocks.

**Ofrann** – The tribe that occupies the Ofrann desert, sometimes self-referred to as "The Blessed of Acrahh" because of their large nomadic population. Nomads are thought less likely to deplete or pollute natural resources than are stationary populations. The Shangren Oasis is the Ofrann capitol.

**Ringgangley** – A sea-faring tribe whose major population centers are located along the coastal regions of the Rahhe Mountains. Their major trade exports are fish, ocean products, rare woods, wool, and textiles. Their capitol is Tes-Raly.

**shecaren** – "child of god." Used as a title of respect when addressing one of Acrahh's sons/daughters. When used by one shecaren to another, means "brother"/"sister."

**shon regis** – The ruling shecaren, typically the eldest. A shecaren may not swear the Oath of Yatra before his/her 16th sun year (second moon year).

**shuren** – A camel-like desert animal domesticated for use as a pack animal.

**Thurrang** – The tribe occupying the grassland plains and mountains along the Ofrann Desert's southern border. The Thurrang are skilled craftsmen whose prized exports include metal implements and glassware. Internal and border disputes, along with their ill treatment of women, discourages free commerce. Their capitol is Zarthon.

# CHAPTER 1

The desert's largest predator did not hunt during sunlit hours, but in this part of the desert, not all predators were animal. Thus Manerra rode armed while searching rock and scrub shadows for a pregnant mia. A wadi halted his search. He tugged his mount's reins and scrutinized the rugged drop-off. Amid the jumbled rocks that littered the wadi floor, foot-high scrub bobbed in the breeze. The growth assured him that more than a year had passed since this dry riverbed had channeled a flood.

Ridges scoured into the sandstone walls by centuries of floods permitted a safe descent without dismounting, but a lone traveler was prudent who considered any wadi crossing dangerous.

Dangerous. He snorted. His uncle Hyran had demonstrated *dangerous*. Survivors of the fighting at Varaar field had described how Hyran stabbed his attackers with an arrow pulled from his body even as they killed him.

Manerra slapped the shuren's neck in anger and tightened his knees as she plunged down the slope. Damn Hyran's soul for the timing of his death.

A distant scream caused Manerra to jerk. Startled by his reaction, the shuren leapt the final feet to the wadi floor and landed with a jar that threw him against her neck. He barely retained his balance during her momentum-driven run toward the mouth of a canyon.

Direction of the scream was difficult to determine this close to the canyon walls. Manerra thought it came from the canyon itself, and his anxiety increased as cliffs loomed on either side, limiting view, maneuverability and escape options.

Two fur-clad figures atop the western wall pointed and shouted. Only then did Manerra spot their companions: little more than shadows clinging to the cliff face, their movements betraying their locations. And he spotted their prey: a white-clad body lying atop stone rubble at the base of the cliff.

Farmers and herders did not wear white, and the stupidity of pursuing the illegal sport of hunting Manteen—especially alone—fit the mentality of Thurra's young nobles. Stupidity should not expect rescue. Besides, the fool might already be dead. Enough time remained to escape without endangering his own life.

But the Manteen were cannibals. Better to die here than live with the guilt of yet another Yatren death.

Manerra directed the shuren toward the eastern canyon wall, looped the reins over his pack and nocked an arrow. The Manteen lowest on the cliff wall were his greatest threat. As long as they clung to the cliff face they were easy targets, but on rocky ground, no hunter was to be engaged carelessly. Manerra's advantages of shuren and bow were slight. The Manteen hunted wild shuren.

Manerra aimed for the man lowest on the cliff wall and released the bow cord just as the shuren sidestepped. He didn't wait to see his arrow shatter on stone. He swore, grabbed the quiver, and slid off the shuren's back, raising dust as he landed. Nine remaining arrows against seven moving targets were grossly uncomfortable odds.

His second shot brought down the man lowest on the cliff face. That one's abruptly silenced scream sent a ripple of activity through the remaining climbers. The one highest on the cliff wall reversed his direction of climb while the one lowest rushed to reach the scree slope. He jumped just as Manerra took aim and did not rise after hitting the rubble. Whether his fall behind a rock large enough to conceal him was coincidental or planned, and whether the Manteen remained conscious, Manerra had no way of knowing. Almost without hesitation, he violated training and shifted his attention to the next highest climber.

As he brought the arrow tip up, a flash in his peripheral vision sent him leaping sideways. His arrow shot wobbling through the air while a thrown ax dented the nearby ground with killing force.

Manerra nocked another arrow.

The climbers had abandoned caution in their attempts to reach their companions atop the plateau. Manerra's target jerked and yelled when his arrow struck, but kept his grip and, thigh-pierced, continued climbing.

As Manerra drew back on the bow cord, a nearby clink of stone caused him to whirl. He stared into a red skinned face with brown eyes and black hair. He could have been looking at himself two years earlier, except the snarl of hatred on the boy's bloodied face shocked him.

The Manteen's upraised arm descended. Manerra released the bow cord and leapt aside. The dull thunk as his arrow hit target lost significance beside his own startled cry. The Manteen's knife had cut through two robes and a loincloth before clanking on stone somewhere behind him.

The boy fell, still alive, with a punctured lung.

Manerra nocked another arrow, shot at those on the cliff edge, then dashed toward the base of the cliff. He hoped his shot drove the Manteen back from the edge, but he didn't expect such luck.

He ran a broken course, untouched by the hail of rocks that cracked and ricocheted off the rocks around him. The dash in was foolishly risky, but escaping weapons' range carrying a man's dead weight was his opportunity to die.

Death guaranteed his escape from succession.

Not this way! Not desecrated.

Manerra bent to grab the white-clad body and very nearly tripped in shock. What in the gods' known world was neither Yatren nor Manteen?

A rock hit his shoulder. Manerra screamed and jerked, grabbed the man-thing by its armpits and ran, half-carrying, half-dragging the body, moving faster than he thought possible carrying such weight.

A triumphant shout and staccato of rocks accompanied his retreat. Screams of outrage followed his escape from weapons' range, hatred translating where words did not.

The shuren, spooked, shied from the strange scent Manerra carried and evaded his grab for the reins. "Shuren, now!" Manerra yelled, which neither calmed the nervous beast nor eased his own desperate anxiety. He dropped the man-creature and approached the shuren with a hand extended, all the while fighting an urge to lunge for her trailing reins. In the end, with his hand less than a foot from one rein and the animal's massive head turning aside, Manerra did lunge. Leather brushed his palm then burned his fist as the shuren leapt away. A fast grab with his free hand halted the slipping rein.

Manerra forced her to stand beside the man-creature, looped both reins around his forearm, then lifted the man-creature and shoved it over her withers. The shove sent his pack to the ground, but its retrieval meant a momentary delay. A standing leap got him far enough over the shuren's back to swing a leg up and over, but before he straightened, she broke for the mouth of the canyon. Manerra panicked before a hand-grab in her fur gave him the stability to recover his balance.

A fistful of shirt fabric prevented the heavy body across his knees from shifting on the wadi's up-slope. Manerra's concentration didn't leave the bunch, pull and stretch of the shuren's muscles as she climbed the ridge. He remained tensed to jump and take the man-thing with him if the shuren's footpads slipped on the sandy rock, but the shuren gained the crest without mishap.

Manerra halted the heaving beast on level ground and twisted to assess their escape. He could detect no movement at the canyon mouth or along either ridge, but stillness and silence did not alleviate his fear. As long as he tarried in this damnable region, he trusted neither his safety nor his luck. "Acrahh, look to your son," he pleaded with passion, turned the shuren's nose eastward, and slapped her hard.

Well away from the canyon and wadi, Manerra investigated the body across his knees. It lived. Its clothing and short, straw-colored hair were its obvious oddities. The line from cheek to chin angled unusually sharp, and there appeared a heftiness in the underlying bones uncommon among Yatren. Even the skin, although red, was brighter red than his own, and hot to the touch. Either the man-thing had been held among the Manteen long enough to develop a fever, or the fever had made it careless enough to become Manteen prey.

Fever. Illness.

Manerra grabbed two fistfuls of shirt fabric, but froze without flinging the man-thing to the ground. Yutrenta and Denassa were physicians.

So what? Except for the blood on his robe, who would know what he had found if he shoved it off and rode away?

He would know. If he rode away, he could never mention the killing of the young Manteen, because that death would raise questions leading to the other killings, and lying, for a son of Acrahh, was a worse offense than murder.

A memory image of the Manteen boy returned with force. The Manteen were Ringgangley descendants, protected by the Oath of Yatra: his brother Aya's stewardship, and soon to be his. It was the man-thing that was not-Yatren.

*Two Yatren lives exchanged for . . . what?*

*Decisions of life and death are Aya's alone.*

*But I've already killed. Not once, but twice.*

He had to deliver the man-thing to Aya, even if it became a cadaver.

Pray Acrahh it died before he reached camp.

Shaken, he pulled the shuren to a halt but sat for a moment before trusting his knees to take his weight. The man-thing he laid on the ground, then returned to the shuren for his pack.

Opening the pack, he froze, suddenly afraid to touch its contents. In his early morning anger and haste to leave camp, he'd taken Yutrenta's pack, not his. What had it been doing on the communal side of the tent?

The spring birthing. Aya had ordered him to find the lost mia because the women were occupied with the birthing. It was the order that had sparked their pre-dawn argument.

Manerra resisted an impulse to throw the pack on the ground. Nothing was going right. Nothing.

He had no choice. He had to use Yutrenta's supplies. He rummaged through her pack until he found enough boiled rags to bind the man-thing's wounds.

He had no interest in parting the blood-matted hair to inspect the head injury while the thigh wound saturated the leggings. He cut through the form-fitting fabric, but jerked away when the material parted. The flesh beneath lay pinkish-white, as though it sickened beneath the foreign covering. Manerra dropped his knife and scrubbed his hands in the sand, as though removing blood could save him from the unknown illness. He might have laughed at himself had the situation not felt life threatening. He hesitated so long, a drop of blood dripped onto the sand from the thigh wound. Only then did he rouse enough to fold a rag the size of the wound and tie that pad into place.

Blistered flesh on the man-thing's hands and wrists made Manerra believe the creature had burned through wrist cords in his determination to escape the Manteen. The burns made Manerra wonder whether the creature had had companions, but he shuddered away from that speculation. He did not want to know what this creature had seen.

He found burn salve in Yutrenta's pack and applied it with a cloth-covered fingertip, then wrapped the hands and wrists with cloth. After that, there was nothing to do except dribble water into the man-thing's mouth until he was confident the wind and sun would not steal from it that which the Manteen and the fall had failed to take.

Manerra poured water into a bowl for the shuren, then quenched some of his own thirst. He inspected, treated, and bound his hip wound, then readjusted his veil over his nose and mouth and packed away the items he'd used. He no longer wanted to think. He wanted to be home. Even Aya's disapproval seemed more appealing than being alone with insecurities and foreboding and whatever kind of creature it is he'd found.

Manerra stole a moment's rest leaning against the shuren's side while he scrutinized the hard-baked landscape. Only the air moved, a shimmer of heat under the approaching midday sun. Normally, he would not travel during this part of the day, but this day was no longer normal and the region in which he paused, far too hostile. He bent, gained a purchase on the unconscious man-thing, hoisted it to his shoulder, then heaved it across the shuren's back, crying out with a pain that shot down his back and up his arm from the rock-bruised shoulder. The creature groaned during this handling, its first sound since the scream.

"Sleep, man-thing," Manerra gasped, not wishing to deal with more this day. When the sharp pain in his shoulder eased, he drew a blanket from the pack, flung it over the stranger's body, then shook back his braids and lifted his robe's hood over his head. With that protection from the sun and none from the heat, he checked his weapons, then led the shuren beside a low rock and mounted from its summit. Finally, he urged the shuren home in as direct a route as he could guess.

# CHAPTER 2

Sand deposited leeward of rocks and flora provided a directional reading while the sun rode its zenith, but Manerra relied upon sand and wind direction only until he found a narrow patch of shade cast by a rock bridge and halted the shuren within its shadow. The shuren, surly from hard use, was content to stop, and Manerra used the rest time to examine the man-thing. It clung to life as tenaciously as any dune grass, its skin damp and hot.

He would not easily lift the man-thing again if he lowered it to the ground, so he soaked a blanket corner in water and forced the fabric into the man-thing's mouth. It did not suck.

Manerra hesitated overlong, but finally took water into his mouth, supported the other's head, and forced water past its cracked lips. He felt a swallow against his fingertips and broke the kiss so rapidly, excess water ran across his hand to the ground. A shameful waste. He shuddered, wiped his mouth on a sleeve, and could not bring himself to repeat the sacrifice. Instead, he wiped the man-thing's face and neck with the blanket's wet corner. As an additional precaution, he covered its nose and mouth with a makeshift veil, wrapping the rag's points around its head and tucking the loose ends behind each ear.

Manerra sank to the ground, back and head resting against the stone bridge, and closed his eyes. Would the creature's presence assuage his return or heighten his brother's anger?

He'd accused Aya of capriciousness! Something even the janquer—the tribal representatives who advised Aya—didn't dare. "Tradition can be forgotten if you decree it!" he'd yelled.

Manerra stretched his arms, trying to relieve tension in neck and shoulders. Hyran's murder hadn't been the only topic-turned-weapon in this morning's argument. Hyran's murder, Vantrann's appointment to oversee the intertribal settlement of that murder, and Manerra's upcoming succession confirmation were so jumbled that he could not think clearly. He felt betrayed by Vantrann's acceptance of Aya's appointment, and the gods could spit on him, but he didn't want any reminder about the succession. And all other issues aside, Hyran had been a criminal for as long as Manerra could remember. So why was his uncle's murder suddenly so awful?

Manerra started traveling again before midday passed, angling toward the butte that Aya had used as a landmark during the previous day's travel. When he recognized no smaller landmarks, he turned the shuren's head southeast and rode until he spotted their tent.

They traveled north not by the established trade route, but by an overland trek of Aya's choosing. The harder journey, intended to safeguard the nation's unescorted leaders, ritualistically duplicated Yatra's historically significant return to Ayahn Rahh. The journey formally established Manerra's succession. It was only bitter to realize how little he was seen to have matured by his brother and erstwhile guardians. Recalling the eagerness with which he had anticipated Aya's arrival in Thurra only left him resenting the reality of their reunion. Of all the changes over the last four years, how had a deterioration of their relationship become one of the greatest?

"Mana!"

His arm jerked, halting the shuren. Blushing over his reaction to Shurna's hail, Manerra slapped the shuren once, then harder, before she moved.

Camp now alerted, the three women converged to meet him, Shurna and Yutrenta leaving the flock, Denassa angling from the fire pit. Hurried walks became runs when they spotted the body crushing his knees.

Denassa arrived first. She reached toward the man-thing, then gasped and jerked back. Her reaction made him realize that she, too, had been fooled by the white clothing. Then Yutrenta and Shurna arrived, Shurna grabbing the shuren's cheek strap while Yutrenta laid hands on the man-thing.

Yutrenta's, "What happened?" overrode Denassa's, "What is that?"

Manerra dropped the reins and swung a leg over the shuren's croup. He intended to dismount while the women were distracted, but Shurna's, "You're hurt!" dashed that hope. He turned toward Shurna, who stared at the gap where the knife had cut his robes. Too much dried blood stiffened the fabric to belittle the injury.

"Manerra!"

All attention jerked toward that horror-filled cry. Aya ran toward them. He slowed to a rapid walk only after his attention locked onto Manerra's face.

"Shon regis," Manerra answered, his throat clamping down so hard on the formal title that it emerged as little more than a whisper.

"Take the shuren to the tent," Yutrenta ordered Shurna. A stained cloth fluttered from Yutrenta's hand. She had removed the head bandage in the few moments Manerra's attention had been diverted.

The shuren stepped forward, blocking Manerra's view of his brother. He started to follow, but Aya's, "Manerra, wait!" stopped him.

He obediently waited while Aya approached, helpless to control the hope and resentment that shredded his emotions. More than anything, he wanted assurance that Aya's fear for his safety came from love and not from an obligatory duty to safeguard Acrahh's son.

"Remove your robes."

That order came before Aya stopped walking. It was a parent's order to a child, or a husband's order to his wife, not one of respect between men. Manerra blushed hotly and started toward the tent.

Aya grabbed Manerra's shoulder.

Manerra yelled, twisted in Aya's grip and went to his knees, tear-blinded, left arm cradled in the right.

"Manerra!" Aya dropped to his knees beside him and began tugging the cords that laced the front of his travel robe. Manerra tried to twist away, which only got him a terse, "Stop!"

Denassa was suddenly on her knees in front of him, gripping his arm and demanding, "What's wrong?" then untying the laces of the dress robe Aya's efforts uncovered.

"I got hit by a rock," he confessed before their combined efforts succeeded in uncovering the bruise.

"Thrown by that one?" Aya jerked his head in the direction of the retreating shuren.

"No. The man-thing was to have been their supper."

Aya stopped unlacing his travel robe.

"Manteen?" Denassa gasped.

"How many?" Aya's voice went cold. Manerra resisted an urge to look into Aya's face, not wanting to see his disapproval. He was shecaren. There was no other. His death could plunge the nation into a power struggle that the janquer might not be able to contain. He'd heard it all. He didn't want to hear it again. He had trained in weaponry for . . . the efficient butcher of cacti? As a topic for conversation?

"Seven."

Aya pulled the dress robe off his shoulder just then, so Manerra did not know whether Denassa's gasp came in response to the number or the injury. Manerra did not crane his neck to look at the bruise. It was enough that he knew its ache. He flinched when Denassa reached for his shoulder, but she only lifted his veil off his neck.

"That was an irresponsible risk."

Manerra stood up so quickly that Denassa's fingernails scraped his chest. "Damn it, Aya!" He stumbled back a step, choked into silence by a flood of protests that wouldn't sort themselves. The single, blasphemous curse hung between them like a wall; Tackta's legacy—a thing Aya despised.

Manerra slammed the air with his fist. "I knew they were hunters. I'm not so stupid that I challenged them on the ground. I thought that thing," he stabbed a finger toward the tent, "was Thurrang. Don't you tell me to wear the mantle of stewardship? Today, I did. But even when I do what you want, I'm wrong." He took half a step toward Aya, rocked from heel to ball, then whirled and headed toward the tent. Why had he returned? Why couldn't he have kept going?

Because no man would harbor a shecaren without strong persuasion.

Why did Tackta not kill me when he had the chance?

*Manerra, run!*

With his mother's scream ringing in memory, Manerra veered away from the trap the tent represented. How old was he then? Three sun years? Four? Regardless, he had needed no second urging. He singed his hand on the hot rock behind which he'd crouched in his haste to comply. Terror was his goad, fed as much by Matera's hysteria as by knowledge of Tackta's intentions should he be caught. But an unexpected awareness that the desert toward which he ran was a danger he couldn't survive made him stumble, and a fist closed upon the fabric covering his shoulder. He twisted and bit like a snake and Tackta released him with a curse.

"No!" Matera jumped on Tackta's back trying to stop him. "No!" But Tackta shook her off like so much of a nuisance and his foot in her face ended her interference.

Manerra watched, too terrified to scream. He bolted, while tears distorted the desert growth. He only wished Tackta to follow him and leave his mother alone. There was no real hope of escape. There never was. His legs were too short and Tackta's, too long. Tackta caught the back of his robe and hit him close-fisted when he slued about. Manerra remembered Tackta's grunts as he swung and the acrid stench of Tackta's sweat, but not the pain of the blows.

After the beating, Tackta staggered away, leaving him curled on his side with his face in the sand. Matera crept to him and with a tentative hand, wiped blood-adhered sand from his brow and cheek. Her expression, her blood, terrified him. He sniffled and she lifted him from the ground, clutched him to her breast and rocked—without words and without tears—as if shock were communication and empathy enough. Only then did he feel pain: an excruciating hurt.

Odd that love and protection hurt so much when terror and hatred were so numbing.

There had been no explanation for Tackta's rage that day, just as there had been no explanations for prior and subsequent beatings. Manerra could recall vague episodes of disappointment, where Tackta demanded answers to questions Manerra did not understand. But then, he had been a child—a babe!—and lacked the coordination and understanding to please his mother's mate, where even the nature of Tackta's tests were lost beneath the burden of more searing recollections.

Would those who envied him envy him still if they knew the price he had paid for being what he was? Every one of them, including Aya, would be shocked to know how desperately he yearned to avoid succession.

"Please bring forth a shecaren," that plea-whisper broke, backed by the full weight of his desperation. He was running out of time. If a sibling wasn't born at this year's Ingathering, he would lose his chance to abdicate.

"Shecaren."

Manerra startled and whirled. He had not heard Denassa approach. He had not been aware that he'd stopped walking. His first wonder was whether she'd overheard his plea, but she stood, head bowed, in a deference they rarely used privately. Her formality reminded him of how deeply the janquer were affected by shecaren arguments.

"What does he want from me, Dee?" Manerra bypassed the expected acknowledgment.

Denassa's head lifted.

"Is he afraid I'll challenge his decisions? Or challenge his rule?"

Discomfort overcame her surprise. "He's not confided in me."

He interpreted that as a plea not to compromise her position. "Then tell me what I've missed these last four years. What happened to him?"

"After leaving Kita, we returned to Ayahn Rahh—"

"I know where you went!"

She stopped talking, her frustration evident.

"Dee . . ." he floundered in his search for the one question that would make sense of their arguments. Then suddenly, "Did he want me back?"

Her composure dissolved. "All the years you were gone, he did little more than talk about your return and relate stories of his own tribal years. He planned our arrival in Thurra to coincide with the completion of your training."

Manerra flushed hotly. "Then why can't we talk? Did he have feelings for Hyran he's never mentioned? Have I failed him?"

Denassa was shocked again. "It's only been a day. Give—"

"No. No, it's not," he cut her short. "We only spoke of it today. Whatever's been wrong has been wrong since Thurra." But because Hyran's death was the obvious answer, Manerra asked, "What, in my father's name, is that thing I risked my life to save?"

"Shecaren . . ." she pleaded as though she could not possibly know any of the answers he wanted. "Is your shoulder broken?"

He blushed. He had tried to hide an injury. "I don't think so."

"May I examine it?"

He choked on a laugh of dismay, but sank to his knees in silent submission. "You could as easily have asked to cut off my leg," he offered as she approached, then flinched when she shifted aside fabric and her fingertips brushed skin.

"I can't examine the bone without touching you," she said.

"I know." And although he steeled himself, her probing fingers wrenched out cries of pain. He sat slumped upon his heels and gasping by the time she was certain his bones weren't broken.

Denassa stroked his temple, then his braids. "I need to look at your hip," she said, "but that can wait until you've taken willow bark tea."

He tilted his head in agreement, needing that relief from pain even though getting it meant returning to the tent. Avoiding Aya even for a day was impossible. Sleeping in the desert would not succeed for long.

"I have not seen a man like the one you brought back," Denassa said. "The founding stories describe the division of the tribes and the existence of the Laytose, and Ringgangley histories explain the creation of the Manteen, but no history describes other Yatren-like men."

"Except demons," he reminded her.

She hesitated before answering, "And the gods."

# CHAPTER 3

In a rare breach of custom, the black curtain that separated the women's quarters from the tent's communal area had been drawn aside to allow Yutrenta ample room to work. But sight of the man-thing, lacking even the cover of bandages, halted Manerra inside the tent flap. The large amount of pale skin assaulted his senses. Denassa paused beside him and stared, seeing what? Surely not a god.

Aya crouched between Yutrenta and the man-thing as though, even unconscious, the creature might harm her. At Aya's back, Yutrenta blew on a brazier's coals. The tiny three-legged pot straddling the flames was used exclusively in the preparation of dayflower, a poison or a painkiller stronger than willow bark, depending upon how one prepared it.

Aya started to look up and Manerra turned away. He crossed to the only pallet half concealed by the drawn curtain while Denassa passed into the women's quarters.

"Not broken," he heard Denassa murmur, then heard the dragging of baggage, during which he imagined a flutter of hands in silent speech.

Denassa returned carrying her physician's bag and settled on the mat beside his pallet.

He gulped down the tepid, bitter tea she offered, then sipped on the water she used to refill the bowl.

"How did you find him?" she asked while he drank.

She intended that Yutrenta and Aya should hear her. Manerra was certain of that. He assumed her interrogation to be his reckoning.

"The Manteen had him atop a plateau. I heard him scream when he fell." He hesitated. "I got to the place he fell before the first Manteen reached the canyon floor. I swear it, Aya. I thought he was Yatren or I would not have tried for him."

"We steward all living," Aya answered in that infuriating, noncommittal way he had of concealing emotional reactions.

Manerra's brow creased in grief. "Two fewer."

Heavy silence followed. Manerra saw again the Manteen boy—so young—with the arrow point buried in his chest. His arrow. His murder.

Aya left the tent when Shurna began shaving the man-thing's head, still without speaking or glancing in Manerra's direction.

* * * * *

A stitched wound did not amount to surgery as physicians defined it, so Manerra was not offered dayflower for the pain. It was an irony not lost on him as he watched Yutrenta and Shurna, later assisted by Denassa, peel back a portion of the man-thing's scalp and remove a square of bone from the exposed skull.

He did not watch long. The violence of the morning commingled with the intimate violence of the surgery. Manerra's hair rose and his scalp ached. Even with eyes closed he could not escape the sounds of the surgery or the heavy smell of burning oil mingled with the scent of blood and the pungent-sweet aroma of dayflower. He envisioned Yutrenta smoothing the scalp flap over the living brain and stitching the wound closed, but in his too-vivid imagination, the center of that skin flap rose and fell with the pulse of a heartbeat until he moaned and shifted in an effort to escape that image.

How could any living thing survive the violence of that intrusion?

The same way a seed falling into a rock crack grew into a tree. But such hearty seeds were few, and perhaps this demon seed would not survive Yutrenta's efforts to save it. If it survived and harm befell the nation through it, he would bear blame for bringing a demon into the heart of Yatra's nation. That legacy scared him far more than the anticipation of Aya's reprisal. This complication confounded his abdication. He already bore blame for Hyran's murder. He could not passively accept responsibility for the demon, as well.

He wished the man-thing had not survived its fall. Then he fervently wished someone other than Yutrenta performed the surgery.

* * * * *

Physical ache and bloody images drove Manerra to sit up with the hope of pacing away his discomfort. But when he sat up, he realized he had dozed. A single lantern burned where four had poured hot light throughout the tent. Amid the flickering shadows, he misinterpreted Denassa's hunched form. He blushed even as he realized the significance of her tongue cleaning of the creature's wounds. The nearest water source lay a day and a half's travel north; farther in any other direction.

Yutrenta slept on a pallet within easy reach of the man-thing. Aya and Shurna were gone.

Denassa straightened, sipped from a bowl, then spit the water back into the bowl.

"Does he taste so bad?" Manerra asked and saw the hand holding the bowl jerk.

"Mana!" She looked back. "You startled me."

"Your licking him frightens me."

"He may be Yatren in the same way our flock are mian."

Their flock were rare animals—white, not albino. Denassa's remark only reminded him that the loss of the pregnant female impacted their wool trade.

"Don't close your eyes when you lick him, then tell me how he's as Yatren as the mia."

"You would do well to keep Ofrann manners. No one's slept—"

Manerra straightened. "Is that it, Dee?" He flushed. "Three years among the civilized tribes undone by a year among the Thurrang?" Yutrenta's head came up, eyes squinting and brow furrowed. "Maybe Vantrann should hear this." He got to his feet, stiff and hurting. Eighteen-year-old Vantrann, three years his senior, had been closer to him than any other janquer member before Aya's appointment drove a wedge between them.

"That is not what I meant," Denassa protested.

"At least the Thurrang admit their faults."

"What are you talking about?" Yutrenta's speech came slurred.

Manerra whirled and headed for the tent flap.

"Manerra!" Denassa was shocked.

"Manerra," Yutrenta said, but he did not stop. He refused to stand for another lecture.

Manerra paused outside the tent flap until breathing slowed and eyesight adjusted to Ryna's dim light. In a region where only an occasional cactus stood taller than the scrub, Aya and Shurna loomed above the dozing mia like apparitions from a mist. Manerra started toward them.

The nearest mia roused at Manerra's approach, bleated, and shuffled aside before they caught his scent. Aya whirled at the disturbance. Manerra immediately stopped walking and bowed his head. "Shon regis," he said.

"Shecaren."

'Brother,' that recognition meant when Aya said it, but in a rare failure of reaction, the endearment generated no corresponding warmth. Manerra brought his head up. "We must move camp," he said.

"Shon regis." Shurna dipped her head toward Aya and started away, but paused long enough to pass Manerra her bow, quiver, and crook.

"The mia is lost," he whispered as he accepted the weapons.

"We lost another tonight."

He looked the direction she jerked her head and saw a mia lying on its side, separate from the other animals. It took a moment to realize that the dark shadows near head and tail were bloodstains.

"Why hasn't the body been moved?" he asked with alarm.

“It just happened.” Shurna offered veneration and left.

"Why move camp?" Aya asked.

"Predators!"

"Kayarra sacrificed for the flock? Yutrenta will not be pleased. But you said that before you knew about the mia."

Kayarra: "the lost one." Manerra made the connection immediately. "'Cor-anda' suits him better."

"He's not an animal to go unnamed."

"Then name his tribe," came out of Manerra's surprise.

"Hyranian rumors don't explain the truth, only exploit it."

Manerra's heart pounded. He knew those tales. They warned of living demons who flew and wove metal into cloth and captured the spirits of living men to use as lights in night camps. He thought the rumors were intended to frighten the devout and young. No part of them was supposed to be true.

Why not? He had made the connection between the cor-anda and the demons in the founding stories.

Suddenly chilled, Manerra shifted weight. "What will you do with him?" he asked his brother.

"Ask our father to spare his life. Yutrenta will be hard-pressed to forgive you if he dies during the move."

Manerra's head snapped around. "What?" he demanded, disbelieving.

"You said we must move camp."

Sight and awareness hazed.

". . . the janquer know so they can plan for the move," Aya was saying when awareness returned.

"I was not making your decisions," Manerra protested.

"No shecaren has the luxury of speaking without forethought."

"I'm sorry! It won't happen again."

"Regrets do not change decisions."

"Whose decision?" Manerra reeled with an anger he'd only felt toward Tackta until now. "Yours, to have me kill him? Yours, to turn the janquer against me? Yutrenta is yours. She will always be yours."

"She serves us both."

*Do you mean 'services'?* Manerra came dangerously close to demanding, although he knew it wasn't true. He wanted to hurt Aya as badly as Aya had hurt him.

"Do not divide the janquer," Aya's warning was forceful. "If you love the nation, do not make them choose between us."

"You can not imagine my love."

Aya took a step forward but Manerra stepped back.

"Explain," Aya demanded.

Manerra lost his nerve. Admit his intention to abdicate? Not here. There was no escaping who he was—who his father was—and the god fear. There was no place for him beyond the janquer and the House of Moons, and no place for a child of his issue even on the janquer. "I can't talk. I can't think." He whirled and headed toward the tent without caring whether Aya stayed or followed.

The women looked up when he came through the tent flap. Their faces registered shock when he threw the crook on the mats with a clatter. "We move camp in the morning," he announced without meeting their eyes.

Aya came through the door flap behind him and stopped.

"Why?" Yutrenta recovered first.

Manerra stabbed a finger in the cor-anda's direction. "For the blame of that one's death."

"I gave Manerra this decision," Aya's statement was unbelievably calm.

"The choice wasn't offered!" Manerra shouted.

"Shecarens, is there some way—" Shurna did not complete the question. Manerra suspected that a signal from Aya accounted for her abrupt silence.

He had no chance against such blatant control. He pivoted in a backward step and headed for the door flap, expecting Aya to block his departure. He passed so close to his brother their robes brushed. Yet even as his foot contacted the ground outside the tent, he did not believe that Aya had let him go.

# CHAPTER 4

Aya stood for a long moment after Manerra's angry departure, head bowed and eyes closed, struggling for control of emotions that must be kept from the janquer. When, at last, he opened his eyes, he could not hold Yutrenta's gaze. Her anger did not disguise the hurt of her betrayal.

"Shon regis," Shurna's audible concern provided a welcome diversion. "Shall I talk with him?"

"And tell him what?" Aya demanded. Even knowing her love for Manerra, he could not allow her intervention. The entire council could not veto a shecaren's decision. If a sacrifice must be made, better it be Kayarra than the nation. Although, awareness of an increasing number of consequences associated with Kayarra's death came close to destroying his nerve. He waved a hand to stop Shurna from answering. "Leave him." He took a difficult breath. "Yutrenta, will Kayarra survive a move?"

"He has survived the Manteen, a fall, and trepanation. Ask your father how much more we can demand of him." Her tone seared him, and yet her hand shook as she trickled drops of infusion from a spoon into Kayarra's slack mouth.

"What is the reason for the move?" Denassa asked.

"To safeguard the remaining flock, which even now stands unprotected . . ."

Shurna started to rise.

" . . . and because we need water."

Shurna crossed to the crook that lay on the mats.

"Neither justifies the decision," Yutrenta retorted. The tears in her eyes contrasted her clenched jaw. "This argument is about lessons, isn't it?" she guessed. "So tell us. Which lesson of shecaren training justifies a man's death?"

"His choices are not personal. What he does affects the nation."

Lord Razon's private warning returned with force. His son and Manerra spent nights together in each other's rooms during the final two moons of Manerra's placement.

What had Manerra and Vantrann been thinking? Had they believed their escorts blind and dumb?

Vantrann claimed nothing had happened between them, that their rooming together had been innocent, and yet Vantrann had paled when

Aya assigned him oversight of the Hyranian murders. If Vantrann did not understand the appearance of crimes committed, he understood fully the impact his appointment would have on Manerra.

That Razon did nothing to stop the boys once he learned of their transgressions did not surprise Aya after the initial shock of the revelation. Not only was Razon's knowledge a useful threat, but any bond that developed between Manerra and Vantrann could influence shecaren decisions in favor of the Thurrang. It was exactly why shecarens and janquer were forbidden intimate involvements with anyone. Manerra knew this and ignored his training, to Aya's everlasting shame.

Aya was surprised only that Manerra had waited so long to express his resentment over Vantrann's appointment.

"And nothing less than murder will teach that?" Tears spilled down Yutrenta's cheeks. "So, when I am sacrificed in some shecaren lesson of rule, I should not be surprised?" She gasped sobs by the time she finished the question, but still she did not look away.

"Yutrenta!" Her logic shocked him back into the present. "I could not—" do to her what he was doing to Manerra, whom he loved just as much? His actions made that a lie before the words were said. That's why she suddenly feared him. His voice went husky, "I don't have a choice."

"Even saying that is a choice." She turned away.

Denassa slipped an arm around Yutrenta's waist, which struck as a consolidation of the janquer against him. He turned and stared at Shurna, who alone stood beside him, gripping the crook she'd picked up from the mat.

"I want your opinion," he demanded, trying unsuccessfully to keep his voice steady. "Do you fear my use of you?"

"It is a fact of being janquer that we will be used in matters of state, including the shecaren's training; otherwise, we are little more than escorts," Shurna's matter-of-fact calm steadied him.

"Denassa?"

"It is hard to accept an unthreatened move."

"Can you tell me he will live if we stay?"

She stared down at Kayarra before answering, "No, shon regis."

"Then the shecaren's decision stands." Aya turned, stepped through the door flap, and a moment later, heard someone come through behind him. He stepped aside to allow Shurna passage.

"Not one of us envies your decisions," she murmured and touched his sleeve in passing.

His frustration peaked. If they did not want his decisions, why did they dispute them?

Aya scanned the desert for Manerra. When he failed to spot him, he counted the shuren. Three. That all the animals were accounted for did not relieve his anxiety. Manerra was armed only with a belt knife.

Was Manerra angry enough to attack him?

That bit of paranoia sprang from Tackta's influence; tortuous memories reawakened by the recent and stunning circumstances surrounding his and Manerra's reunion. Aya didn't have to close his eyes to see the thin, bruised child who screamed as he was pulled from Matera's arms; the child who cowered from an upraised hand and cried from the terror of night visions. Even Tackta's death by Aya's own hand had not assuaged the helpless rage that sickened him with every recollection of the shecaren's abuse. Manerra's childhood—his innocence—had been stolen by one man's obsession with power.

"Manerra," Aya groaned, helpless to remove that pain from either of them, certain that Manerra's feelings for Vantrann—strong enough that he violated divine law—had much to do with the repeated losses Manerra had suffered as a child. Their four-year separation had exacerbated those losses. Nevertheless, Manerra's traumatic past did not excuse his behavior. To forgive him without remorse risked Tackta's influence gaining power when the shecaren swore the Oath of Yatra at an ingathering less than five moons away.

# CHAPTER 5

"Aya."

Shurna's quiet call came as Aya reached for the strap of the temple stone's leather case. She stood momentarily visible in the doorway before fabric shushed across the opening, separating them and locking in the lamplight.

Aya glanced around. All small supplies were packed. Only the bedding Kayarra occupied and the tent remained unsecured. Yutrenta, hunched over Kayarra in an attitude of prayer, prompted Aya to murmur, "Father, spare his life," before he left the tent.

The predawn breeze chilled and stopped him as he stepped through the flap. In that pause, Aya spotted Manerra. His brother supported his left wrist in his right hand and walked with a perceptible limp.

Long ago, a lap cradle might have eased Manerra's pain, but such intimacy—rare even then, so fearful was Manerra of a hug's constraint—was irretrievable now. This journey was one of losses and gains, with gains possible only if sacrifices were made.

Aya started forward to intercept Manerra before he reached camp.

Manerra slowed, then stopped, and Aya took the opportunity of Manerra's bowed head to locate the dust discoloring his brother's robe. Manerra had been kneeling and sitting but not lying down; another who had not slept last night.

"Join me in abbah," Aya invited and continued away, but not before he glimpsed Manerra's deeply creased brow as his brother looked up.

Without any sign of acquiescence that Aya noticed, Manerra followed. When Aya mounted a low, flat boulder, Manerra paused to remove his weapons belt. When Manerra looked up, Aya extended a hand to him.

Manerra hesitated before gripping it.

Manerra's gasp as he cleared the rock edge came as much from emotional as physical pain. "One of the Manteen I killed yesterday was younger than me," he said, unable to control the wobble in his voice. He stopped talking and glanced away.

"The innocence you lost and gained yesterday is only the beginning," Aya's tone was gruffly conciliatory, as it hadn't been since their reunion.

Manerra looked back, perplexed. He knew too well the innocence he had lost. But innocence gained?

Innocence by law, the sudden realization left him numb. Aya forgave the murders he committed during the rescue. But " . . . only the beginning" was a stunning reminder that a shon regis—only the shon regis—held the decision of life and death over any criminal, and a death decree—its execution—could not be delegated. Yesterday, he learned what that decree meant personally, intimately, and the remembrance sickened him.

Rumor claimed that Aya had been so enraged by Tackta's mistreatment of the shecaren that his knife blade broke in Tackta's chest from the force of his killing blow. Manerra had never asked whether the rumor was true. He had never wanted that knowledge of his brother, but now the image of a killer was reflected in any pool of water.

Aya indicated the place he should stand and Manerra shifted to face the brightening east. Aya did not move into position opposite him.

"This journey is a passage for you. Do you understand that?"

Manerra pressed a hand against his thigh. "Yes." He avoided Aya's eyes.

"How is it so?"

Manerra forced thoughts past distractions. "When we reach Ayahn Rahh, I will be confirmed as your successor," he answered.

"There is more," Aya said without elaboration.

Manerra glanced toward camp and saw that the tent had been dismantled.

"Don't walk away from disagreements," Aya told him. "You lose the respect of your adversaries and weaken the janquer by your actions."

That brought his attention back. "I don't challenge you."

"My concern is for your future, not mine."

That statement brought overwhelming distress. "The cor-anda determines my future."

"Your attitude determines outcomes."

"Not if he's evil."

"Then you believe our father is dead?"

The hairs on Manerra's neck rose. For a demon to be found on Axxord, their father had to be dead.

"Beware speculation," Aya's demand was urgent, forceful. "Implications can cause irreparable harm."

Manerra whispered, "Denassa could not explain him," which was dire. She was their historian.

"Do not speculate."

Manerra met Aya's eyes and saw a hostility that endangered him.

Aya closed the gap between them with a step and Manerra flinched in anticipation of a strike. But Aya turned toward the breaking dawn and extended his right hand at waist level. Manerra inhaled sharply through a pounding heartbeat before he placed his cupped hand beside Aya's.

The rest of the ritual blurred. Manerra closed his eyes on cue, although for years he had performed this ritual with a firebrand and open eyes. The weight that settled onto their conjoined hands exceeded the weight of any identically sized stone, and the flare of light that penetrated his eyelids appeared dazzlingly blood red.

During past personal crises, the ritual of abbah had steadied him, but this morning Manerra lost the sense of the words Aya intoned and could not recover them.

"Peace to all the nation through eternity," Manerra spoke the final refrain in unison, not completely failing his duty, but questioning it, and doubting national peace if the cor-anda reached the Shangren Oasis alive.

Aya extinguished the temple stone's harsh light and Manerra, blinking, averted his gaze from the breaking dawn.

"He's not alone, Manerra," Aya said as he returned the cloaked stone to its pouch.

"I know," he answered automatically, although he hadn't consciously linked the cor-anda to a mother, family, and tribe before Aya said that. What did a sixth tribe mean for a nation that had no explanation for men who were not Yatren?

"Did you notice his hands and feet? He did not grow the food that fed him. Nor did he walk to the place you found him."

Manerra walked to the edge of the rock, stepped down hard, and stiffly knelt to pick up his belt. He didn't want to talk about the cor-anda. He didn't want to talk to Aya. He didn't want to talk at all. "I know he held his hands in fire to escape the Manteen."

"Lead today."

Manerra dipped his head sideways, and Aya started back to camp before Manerra finished adjusting his weapons belt.

*****

Yatren robes were shockingly incongruous on the cor-anda. The women had not redressed it in white, but the short, dune-colored hair would never confuse it for a Yatren elder. Staring at the creature lying on the pallet surrounded by sand, stone, and prickly flora, Manerra imagined walking away and leaving it beside the midden pit, but knew there was no chance of that happening. The creature's life or death had passed from his control the moment Shurna hailed him upon his return. Whatever happened from this moment on lay in Yutrenta's skill and Acrahh's intentions. Which in no way relieved either his guilt or his fear.

Manerra dutifully helped Aya, Denassa, and Shurna lift the rolled tent onto a waiting shuren and secure it, then helped Aya lift Kayarra onto the same animal, where Yutrenta, by this time mounted, clamped her knees and lifted while the shecarens shoved. Manerra alone cried out in pain during this handling, and stood aside when they finished, gripping his arm, while his companions scooped up bedding, distributed carry baggage, and took up reins or a driver's crook for the imminent departure.

"Drink this." Denassa approached with a bowl and lifted it toward his mouth.

Manerra jerked his head back and took the bowl from her, resenting the suggestion of his helplessness. Denassa wordlessly set a sack on the ground and left. He took a mouthful of tea, expecting willow bark, and was so startled by the bitter, slow heat across his tongue he didn't swallow. The bowl contained willow bark tea—mostly willow bark, true—but it held dayflower before Denassa poured the infusion. His first thought was to spit the tea back into the bowl; his second thought was to swallow. He swallowed, with his tongue and lips going numb. Denassa would not have dared such a stretch of code if she'd known about the bowl's prior use. Which meant there had been a silent collusion among physicians, possibly including Aya, or a genuine mistake made amid the turmoil of resentful silences and hectic packing. Whatever the reason, Manerra swirled the tea to rinse the sides of the bowl then gratefully drank it down. The toll of a sleepless night discouraged the prospect of a burdensome trek. Constant, even intermittent, pain would neither improve his disposition nor help relieve communal tensions.

Manerra packed the bowl, hefted the sack, and went to take the reins of Yutrenta's mount. Was this more deliberation, that he should be left with responsibility for the creature he'd brought among them? He would never escape that fact even without another reminder.

If his attitude really did influence outcomes, then the cor-andan tribe beware, because he safeguarded Yatren life and none other.

* * * * *

Aya had been paralleling the Shangren trade road for the sources of water that supplied travelers along that route. But even if Manerra had not known that, he could not have led the company far astray. The Rahhe Mountains formed the distant, saw-toothed horizon to his left and the low sun dazzled his eyes when he glanced right. Somewhere beyond the northern horizon lay the Shangren Oasis, the seat of wealth and power of the Ofrann tribe and the desert that shared its name.

Reaching the Shangren Oasis meant an opportunity to replenish their supplies, although Manerra dreaded their arrival. Hyran had been Ofrann. His murder would add fuel to longstanding Ofrann complaints against the Thurrang. Combining that news with the discovery of the cor-anda meant a stopover full of negotiations, strategy sessions, and armed escorts. They would leave the Shangren more tired than they arrived.

Visions of Ofrann violence cycled through Manerra's head until the dayflower-laced willow bark wore off and pain replaced even his most horrific imaginings. As he limped, he kept watch on his shadow, determined to walk until midday forced their halt, certain he'd have to swallow pride and ride during their evening march.

A shriek brought the shuren's head up with a jerk. Manerra's arm was wrenched backward by that jerk. Whirling, he grabbed for the reins with his weak left hand, fearing the animal's bolt. His grab missed when he saw Yutrenta fall, and in startled confusion, he released the reins, thinking to catch her. The shuren hadn't reared. How had she fallen?

Yutrenta landed on her feet, but fell to her knees under the cor-anda's weight. Kayarra hit the ground hard enough to knock the breath from it and Yutrenta collapsed over its body. Manerra reached her as her head came up and she gasped. Then her head plunged forward again and her mouth encircled the cor-anda's lips while her thumb and forefinger pinched its nostrils shut. Manerra froze in horrified understanding.

Denassa dropped down on the cor-anda's far side and reached for its neck. Yutrenta gasped again, and again forced air into the creature's mouth.

Aya and Shurna arrived at a run. Aya went to his knees beside Yutrenta, and Shurna circled to Denassa's side. Only Manerra hung back, paralyzed with guilt, while the physicians fought to revive the thing he despised.

"He's breathing!" Denassa shouted, gripped Yutrenta's shoulders, and shoved her away. "Trenta, he's breathing."

Yutrenta resisted Denassa's shove for one moment of assurance, then brought her hands to her face in an unsuccessful attempt to stifle gasping sobs. When Aya placed an arm around her shoulders, she flinched away, then bent at the waist until her braids lay in the dust. "Shon regis," she pleaded, "I beg for a canopy and your leave. I would stay with this man." She burst into tears.

Aya pulled back, his face maroon with embarrassment and dismay. Denassa and Shurna stared before Aya finally said, "We camp here."

Aya stood and Manerra shifted uncomfortably under his brother's scrutiny before Aya looked away.

The shuren! Manerra followed his brother's gaze. Weighted with baggage, the animal had not run far, but capturing that one, unfettered, was a patience-trying game of keep away and tag.

"I'll get her," Manerra offered, but Aya's "No!" stopped him in mid-turn. He stood in frustration and watched his brother leave to retrieve the animal that bore their tent.

Manerra looked around. This was not an ideal campsite. Rocks would have to be moved to accommodate their tent. While that wasn't an overwhelming chore, snakes, rodents, and venomous insects found moisture as well as protection from sun and wind-driven sand under and amid rock piles. It was a risk they should not be taking, especially with the cor-anda's blood scent on the wind. But Aya had decided, and so they must make the best of a worsening situation.

Manerra searched for level ground containing the fewest rocks and cacti, and finally settled upon a less-than-perfect patch of ground littered with the smallest rocks. While Denassa and Yutrenta, still wet-faced and distressed, inspected the cor-anda's bandages for bleeding, Manerra paced off the diameter of the tent and began removing rocks from his imaginary circle.

"Not much difference in choices, is there?"

Manerra straightened with a rock gripped in each hand and looked over his shoulder at Shurna. What was he to answer? 'You're right, but this is what we get when decisions are forced upon us. Take your pick of the rock you will sleep on'? Aya would hardly approve.

His gasp came so quickly, Manerra had time only to turn his head before his determination dropped away like the rocks from his hands.

"Mana!" Shurna rushed forward and touched his back. He recoiled before he remembered she would never intentionally hurt him. "What's wrong?" Despite the fear and confusion in her voice, he could neither look at her nor answer.

It was Aya's approval he wanted—still—more than anything else. It was Aya who had rescued him and Matera from Tackta. It was Aya's wisdom that exposed most wants of the tribal leaders as petty, selfish, or shortsighted. How could he learn Aya's ability to see past demands to underlying issues? How did he decide matters of justice when compassion lay dead in him? How, how, how could he face any comparison with his brother?

"Manerra!"

He turned to face Shurna's rising alarm before she called for one of the physicians.

"Don't, Shurna," he pleaded as though she could read his thoughts. "It's only . . . everything. Everything suddenly hit me at once. I will be all right."

She stared at him . . . studied him . . . her breath coming quickly, but she did not reach for him again. He locked eyes with her but broke that contact first, suddenly doubting his own insistence. A witch, she had been called to his face, by men who forgot that he and Aya had Kitarin training; that all janquer members could read the minute flinches and glance-aways that revealed so much about an individual's inner thoughts.

"You are not alone," she reminded him.

That offer to listen both wrenched at his heart and scared him. He wanted nothing more than to unburden mind and soul, but the words that could achieve a catharsis would irreparably damage his relationship with the individuals he most loved and trusted. She could not listen to him without acting. Her duty, which must be greater than her love for him, was to protect national unity and serve the shon regis to that end.

"I can never be alone," he replied, but bitterness failed to make that statement the agreeable acknowledgment he intended it to be.

*****

They labored in silence, intent upon completing the all too familiar chores of establishing camp. Rocks removed from the tent site were stacked to create a windbreak for the fire pit Denassa dug, as if this inhospitable place might be their home for a fortnight or more. When midday heat halted their work, they constructed canopies instead of the tent. Yutrenta had already raised one atop the cor-anda. A second was constructed where Shurna and Denassa could watch the flock, and a third provided shade for the shecarens.

Manerra located bedding and made pallets for himself and Aya beneath their canopy. When he finished, he lay down in the shade and watched Aya, who knelt beside Yutrenta. Not in his memory could he recall Aya being so rattled by anyone or anything as by Yutrenta's request for leave. Aya's order that they make camp had postponed his answer, not been his answer.

Manerra lay back upon the mat and stared at the red- and white-stripped fabric of the canopy's roof. Only the warp threads were red in the colored stripes. The white weft threads made tiny, alternating dashes across the red strands.

"Manerra."

Manerra opened his eyes and shut them against sunlight. He had fallen asleep despite the discomfort of pebbles beneath the mat.

"Drink this." Aya forced a hand between his back and the mat and lifted him toward sitting. Manerra braced a hand on the ground in order to support his own weight and steadied the bowl at his mouth with the other, eyes still closed. He swallowed a mouthful of willow bark tea mixed with something else—not dayflower, this time. He remained too groggy to puzzle it out. He finished the liquid, or assumed he had, because Aya took the bowl away and let him lie down again.

"You and I will ride for water," Aya said as if in a bad dream. "The janquer will stay here with Kayarra."

"When?" Manerra slurred the word.

"After midday."

Manerra passed into oblivion on a wave of dismay.

*****

Aya had not awakened him; neither had the sounds of his companions' resumed chores. Manerra woke to the sight of a standing tent, a waist-high windbreak, the scent of the evening meal cooking over coals in a fire pit, and the suspicion that Yutrenta's infusion was partially responsible for his unusually deep sleep. He felt shame that others had completed his chores.

Denassa looked up as he approached the fire pit. "How do you feel?" Her tone held genuine concern.

"Better. A little stiff. Where's Aya?"

"In the tent."

He started away.

"He speaks with Yutrenta," she called.

He circled back and again stopped beside the fire.

"Your supplies and Aya's have been separated," she said. "Shurna did that before she left with the flock."

"Has Aya answered Yutrenta's request for leave?" he asked.

"Yutrenta withdrew it."

Manerra wasn't certain that he believed Yutrenta would have left their company and the janquer to save the life of something not-Yatren. Her vow of the unification prayer safeguarded that which was Yatren. Was choosing the cor-anda's life over shecaren orders a violation of her covenant? He honestly did not know. He only knew the turmoil the creature brought with it, not by intention, because it remained unconscious, but simply because it existed. Aya had to understand that, and yet Yutrenta was allowed to treat it—which implied a decision on Aya's part.

"Thank you," he said with feeling.

"I did nothing. The decision was Yutrenta's."

"Thank you for telling me."

Denassa stopped stirring the cook pot and regarded him. "Sometimes I have to remember what it is like not to be janquer. It is odd that I no longer think a statement has only one meaning, even when spoken by a shecaren."

"My mother was mortal, Dee. My father—" *did not save us from Tackta!* He lost his thought's direction. ". . . you know," he finished lamely. "I can mistaken what I see. As Aya is so fond of telling me, it is the lesson of the mirage."

* * * * *

Silence was customary during mealtime, but Yutrenta's silence included slumped shoulders and an unnatural attention to her supper bowl, as if exhaustion or depression formed a lump she couldn't swallow. After Aya finished eating, he broke the obligatory silence with a signal to remain seated.

"While Manerra and I are gone," he said, "do not permit the approach of anyone, not even kin. I suggest use of the death flag, with illness, its explanation. Do not, if Kayarra wakes, let him be seen."

Manerra was astonished to hear Aya acknowledge even that much danger associated with the cor-anda. He stared at his hands, clenched in his lap.

"But most importantly, do not allow assumptions that the danger is to Manerra or I. Although I expect no encounters, I must know of any exchange that occurs while we are gone.

"Yutrenta knows of no well or cistern closer than Rajma's Head, so we go there. I leave you with the flock, two shuren, and the expectation that you keep the gods' rites. If all goes well, we will return before the moon changes. If it does not . . ." his hand slipped sideways, fingers flat, palm up. That hand returned to his thigh. "The tribal leaders know what is expected of them. You know the resources at your command. Do not hesitate to use either."

Yutrenta's posture tensed, her face pale. "What of Kayarra?" she asked.

"Will he live?" Aya countered.

Her hand lifted from her knee and fell back.

Aya sat silent a moment. "I do not have the knowledge I must have to make a decision. If Kayarra lives, you have the gratitude of one whose life you saved. If he dies, discover his tribe's location and its intentions, but not by sacrificing the rites of the Ingathering. That, most important of all, or there will be no shecaren to follow us."

There might not be anyway, Manerra thought, but did not say so. The janquer knew. Not every Ingathering saw the birth of a shecaren. Not every shecaren born survived infancy.

"And we do what, with an unknown tribe?" Denassa asked.

Aya looked pained. "Peace to all the nation through eternity," he recited with emotional gravity the one line in abbah that never changed. "It is your covenant. Do not fail me—I beg you—however you keep it." He stood, signaled Manerra to follow, and started toward the tent, where separated supplies awaited their departure.

# CHAPTER 6

Ryna alone rode the gem-studded sky. Trys, her shy and stealthy lover, hid behind cloud cover low on the northern horizon. At three-quarters full, Ryna bathed the desert with enough light to spare travelers mishap with cacti and the stone rubble that littered this part of the desert. Aya stopped to rest only once before moonset, although Manerra could not guess the last time Aya had slept through a night. When Ryna set, they erected a canopy and slept until the raucous calls of barra birds announced dawn's approach.

Breakfast consisted of crumbled flatcakes cooked over last night's supper fire and dried dates washed down with precious water. Aya had had the women combine water from partially full skins so they could take as many empty skins with them as possible. The water they carried was enough to reach Rajma's Head, although, in truth, their water was likely to run out before they reached the rock that marked the cistern. If an accident prevented their return, the janquer lacked sufficient water containers to reach either the Shangren Oasis in the north or Ringgal in the southeast.

This was the kind of situation that wise men avoided if they valued their lives and those of their companions.

They began walking before the sun broke the eastern horizon, stopped at dawn to perform abbah, then pressed ahead toward midday, pushing against weariness so intense it precluded talk.

Manerra spotted the lone rock jutting above the scrub when they crested yet another sand-scoured hill. The rock jutted from the adjacent hill, twice the height of a man and so shaped like a face that some long-dead man had named it for a much longer-dead shon regis. Manerra thought it ironic that two living shecarens turned to the effigy of an ancestor in their time of need. Reaching the cistern meant not only water but rest, and the wound on his hip had been aching since mid morning. The willow in their packs was ground bark, which needed water they didn't have to make an infusion that could relieve his pain. He clamped his jaw, returned his gaze to the ground, and steadfastly followed Aya's heels and robe hem down the slope.

Aya's abrupt halt caused Manerra to swerve rapidly to avoid collision. Not until Aya started walking again, more rapidly than before, did Manerra spot what Aya had seen. Only for a breath did he believe that the sunken trench marring a third of the opposing hill was a natural part of the terrain. He stood frozen in shock while the shuren nudged his arm and then sniffed the ground. Finally, Manerra took a hesitant step forward, dropped the shuren's lead, and ran down the slope after his brother.

When Manerra reached him, Aya stood on the rim of the collapsed tunnel, staring at the broken ground. Manerra stared too, still denying what he saw. The cistern's entrance was a flat scattering of soil and rocks down the hill's slope to his right. Left, where the underground pool had ended the tunnel, a dimple of soil, stone and displaced vegetation marred the slope. Only the presence of corriah trees, their branches violently thrust together or snapped off during the cave-in, gave any hint of the water buried beneath.

"How?" Manerra shook his head, his brain racing through possibilities. Digging down to the water was his first impulse, but only the tunnel entrance had been shallow. The cistern now lay under twenty feet of clay and stone.

Aya turned, his eyes as hard and cold as Rajma's behind him. "Do you have any water left?" he asked, his voice unrecognizable in its harshness.

"A little."

"Drink it," Aya ordered. "All of it."

Manerra froze, unsure whether Aya realized what he ordered.

"Now!" Aya shouted, hands clenched.

Manerra fumbled at the cord that fastened the flat water skin to his belt. His hands were clumsy as he removed the stopper and lifted the container to his lips. When he swallowed, his throat knotted so painfully that he might as well have swallowed a stone rather than the single mouthful of warm water he managed to get down.

"Give it here," Aya demanded when he lowered the skin from his lips.

He handed it to his brother, who ignored the offered stopper and upended the skin. Two drops hit the dirt between them and evaporated. "You will regret those drops," Aya said and returned the empty skin.

"Why did you do that?" Manerra asked, his emotions indecipherable from the fatalism that wrapped him.

"The skins sweat."

Manerra glanced at the broken corriah trees and away. Not all indicators of ground water provided accessible water. He looked for barrel cacti and saw none. He thought of Denassa, Yutrenta, and Shurna, but flinched away from those thoughts.

"Help make camp," Aya said and passed him, headed back up the adjacent hill toward the shuren who bore their supplies.

Aya was drawing near to them everything and anything that could extend their survival, while Manerra battled panic. Stay here? A feeling of residual evil gripped Manerra with such strength it drove him to flee this place, not stay.

He turned and followed Aya down the hill of Rajma's Head with legs so stiff from tension it hurt to walk.

# CHAPTER 7

Aya and Manerra rode after breaking midday camp, then walked when their shuren's gait slowed to a listless plod. Their destination was wadi Helturaan, the closest water source either of them knew.

Beyond nomads and a few others born to the desert, the knowledge, skills, and means necessary to achieve a desert crossing were largely the providence of caravan drivers and guides, who amassed wealth from their guarded knowledge. Manerra and Aya were more likely to reach wadi Helturaan unaided than to gain assistance from travelers, but the chance, however slim, was a risk Aya took by traveling the trade road.

Aya assumed the cave-in at Rajma's Head was either a strike against the Ofrann tribe that controlled the desert's north-south trade, or an attempt to discourage the Thurrang-Ringgangley pilgrimages to Ayahn Rahh. Without convincing proof, he refused to assume that Hyranians had carried out the devastation, although wanton destruction was their typical method of attack.

Aya doubted that Thurra's Lord Razon was involved in the destruction of Ofrann property. So far, Thurrang borders had contained Razon's power grabs, and as long as Thurrangy lords bickered among themselves, Razon was not strong enough to risk Ofrann ire.

Unless he hoped to consolidate his fragmented rule against the onslaught of an Ofrann threat.

Manerra cried out.

Aya whirled. "What's wrong?" He backtracked the few steps to where Manerra stood in obvious pain.

Manerra took a tentative step—a definite limp. "I will be all right."

"Is it your ankle?"

"My hip. I stumbled. I'll be all right."

"Show me the wound," Aya ordered, regretting his failure to act upon a midday impulse to inspect Manerra's injury. He blamed the turmoil over the discovery at Rajma's Head for the flittering away of that thought. Another excuse was the resistance he hadn't had the fortitude to face, which, right now, hardened the eyes staring back at him. 'If you can trust no one else, trust me,' he nearly blurted, but stopped himself in time. There existed too great a chance he must one day decide his brother's life.

Manerra reluctantly lifted the hems of his robes.

Aya waited while Manerra removed his loincloth, then dropped to one knee and removed the bandage that bound the wound. There were stains on the cloth, not of blood, that momentarily stole his breath.

"Aya?" alarm was audible in Manerra's voice. The boy bent for a look at his injury.

The wound was swollen and hot to the touch. Pressing along the seam produced blood-streaked pus in one area near the end of the gash. The poison might still be controlled. The wound might still heal.

If they had water.

"I was a fool to have brought you," Aya said, his throat constricting. He had risked his brother's life for what? A chance to spend time alone with him after their too-long separation? Facing a several-moons-long journey with only janquer escorts, ample opportunities existed to relearn each other without unnecessary risk to Manerra's life and the succession.

Manerra must never accompany him into another dangerous situation. The discovery of Kayarra made that crucial.

"Suck clean the tip of your knife," Aya said, finally looking up into the fearful brown eyes staring down at him. A ridge had risen between those brows. "You should lay down for this."

# CHAPTER 8

Wind violently flapped his clothes and beat hair around his ears as he fell, the wind's rush, deafening. He spread his arms in an effort to slow, then frantically back swam as the ground rushed up.

He jerked awake.

Despite his gasping breaths, he still heard the slap and drag of cloth against cloth. He jerked his head toward the sound and watched a flap of black and white striped cloth billow inward, then strike and grate along fabric as it was sucked out through the doorway. His eyes followed the stripped wall fabric to the ceiling, then continued along that conical slope to a central pole. The base of that pole rested somewhere on the ground near his head. A black curtain divided the tent and rippled in the same gusts that blew the door flap. He lay at the base of that curtain, on a blanket peppered with sand. The grains pressed like needles into the naked flesh of shoulder blades and buttocks.

He swung his left hand over his body, intending to use momentum to roll onto his side, but cried out in pain as his arm dropped like a log onto his chest. He arched backward into blackness.

* * * * *

He realized he was awake again when he blinked. The tent held shadows. The slap of cloth against cloth had stopped, but sand grains still needled and numbed all the flesh that covered weight-bearing bones.

He lay on his back, head elevated, arms atop the blanket that covered him. Someone had arranged him that way. Who? Why? Where was he?

His only memories were vague impressions of severe illness. He remembered throwing up. And glimpsing rocks and sand and a dead bush from the height of an animal's back. That he didn't remember eating and he didn't know what animal he had straddled paled beside the fact he couldn't remember a time when he wasn't sick.

He lifted a hand into his field of vision.

Most of the skin was gone.

A tingle shot down both legs.

The flesh—mottled pink, white and red—glistened as if wet. He lifted his left hand. It wasn't as raw, but the sight still sickened him.

Scabs encircled each wrist and crusted the edges of raw flesh. Someone had curled his fingers loosely around wads of cloth. He attempted to drop one of the wads but the resulting pain stopped him.

He lowered his hands to his heaving chest and searched the tent. Grass mats covered the ground: blue and yellow woven into geometric patterns. Nearby lay a folded red and gray blanket, flattened in the center as if someone had used it as a seat.

If people he knew cared for him, shouldn't he recognize something?

He craned his neck in order to see the door flap. A small breeze nudged the fabric, filling its center. Suddenly, an edge flipped and spilled the cool volume into the tent. He caught no more than a fleeting glimpse of dim sunlight beyond. He straightened his head and raised a hand to press away the new pain creeping into his temples. Fingertips touched scabs where hair should have been. He followed the line of scabs. When he felt past them, his fingers dipped into a bowl of soft flesh.

That couldn't be.

He returned to the scabs and bore intense pain to press their edges. He felt skull bone on one side of the scab and that frighteningly spongy give on the other. He fought down a scream, and for a moment couldn't breathe. Eyesight dimmed before he managed a swallow and drew another breath, his heart hammering against his chest.

He hooked a thumb over the edge of the blanket, threw it back, and scanned his body. Badly bruised, but in better shape than his hands.

His head dropped onto the pillow, the burst of panic-driven strength vanishing as fast as it came. The jar to his head increased the pain in his temples, and the movement of his hand awakened excruciating pain. He rested his hand on his chest and squeezed his eyes shut in order to assess the remembered image of his body. A bandage covered his right leg from groin to calf. His forearms, ribs and hip were yellow and purple.

He brought the hand that didn't hurt so much to his head, desperate to know the size of the missing bone.

Laughter bubbled in his throat and only panic kept it down.

The hole in his head was the size of his eye socket.

Bruises could be accidental; missing bone was deliberate. He questioned the injuries to his hands and leg and hoped the person or people who had done this to him had died in the doing of it.

Light fell across his eyelids and he jerked his head aside. Gloom returned as the door flap struck cloth. He strained to make out the figure standing inside the doorway holding a wooden bowl. He or she made no move to approach.

Black cloth encircled the head, leaving only an eye slit: a dark hollow of shadow. The "dress," laced at the neck, fell in loose gray folds from shoulder to mats and concealed any distinguishing body curves.

He startled when the person shouted, and then winced at the

reactive throb in his head. His first impression was right. A man could not achieve that pitch of sound.

The door flap burst open behind the woman and another figure entered, this one a head taller. The breasts were definitely a woman's. The newcomer rushed past the girl and dropped to her knees beside him. His attention shot to her eyes. A physical jolt ground his shoulders into the sandy blanket. An animal's eyes stared down at him. He brought his good hand up to ward her off. She grabbed his forearm. He screamed.

Startled, she released him, and garbled sounds came through her veil.

The girl by the entrance answered.

"You're not real," he told them, although the throbbing in his arm refuted that claim. The headache was jumbling his perceptions. Something they'd done to his brain had damaged his hearing. He swallowed down a scream of terror.

"Tell me you didn't do this to me." Words poured out faster than he could track. "Fuck you!" he heard himself say when awareness rejoined. "Kill me, if you're going to. Do it!" He choked on tears, then started laughing, which hurt both stomach and head. He clutched his middle, brought his knees and head off the blanket in a curl of agony, and rolled onto his side, his back to his captors. In this false privacy, he sobbed until his nose and throat clogged—until he couldn't draw breath—and consciousness slipped away.

# CHAPTER 9

Aya watched Manerra, who lay curled on his side under the canopy, eyes closed, brow furrowed. Manerra's earlier, hard panting had relaxed toward the slow rhythms of sleep, but Aya doubted that Manerra had lost awareness despite his shallow breaths. With any luck, the dry willow bark Manerra held in his cheek provided some relief from pain, although Aya's mouth was so dry it had become painful to swallow. He assumed Manerra fared no better.

The gravest drawback of the trade route was the scarcity of edible flora. The water-hoarding cacti that could sustain a man also provided fodder for shuren and mia. Aya did not wander far from the canopy in his search of the area, only far enough to assure himself that nothing edible grew in their immediate vicinity.

He returned to camp, knelt in the dust, and scraped out a hollow, which he lined with a slit water skin. He positioned rocks around the skin's rim to hold it flat, then carefully added rock layers atop rock layers until his hollow construction stood hip high. By the time he closed the tower's neck with a capstone, he was too weak to build another.

Before performing abbah, he hobbled the shuren on the far side of the canopy, well away from his stone structure, and weighed her lead with the heaviest rock he could shift. The weighted lead would not prevent her from breaking free if she caught scent of a predator, but it would discourage her casual wandering and the danger she posed to his fragile structure. If the stones fell before morning, the shuren assured their survival for another day—but they had a better chance of reaching a well and rejoining the janquer with the animal alive. Nevertheless, he would not hesitate to bleed her if she became their only means of survival.

He performed abbah facing west and the setting sun, standing beside the canopy that sheltered Manerra, with a whisper of a voice that soon failed completely. Doggedly, he mouthed the words that welled, emotion-laden, inside his head, and surrendered his trust to their father for protection through the night. After the final affirmation was sworn and the temple stone returned to its pouch, Aya looked down. His brother slept. He was sure of it, although Manerra's brow remained creased in sleep.

Aya knelt and studied the face of the man emerging from the child he loved. Manerra's veil had slipped, exposing a ruddy cheek as sparse of facial hair as his palm, a cheek randomly criss-crossed by disheveled strands of narrowly braided, jet-black hair. Even in sleep, Manerra's eyes drew Aya's attention. Their lashes followed the curve of cheekbones delicately shaped and strong. Manerra resembled his mother. Relentless work and Tackta's fists had battered Matera's beauty but not destroyed it. And although Tackta had tried to break Matera's will and faith, it was his failure to succeed that had hastened his capture.

Aya jerked upright, awash in the rage and horror that came with memories of Tackta. He turned toward the small mound of their supplies, yanked out blankets, and dropped down beside Manerra to keep watch. Anger kept him company through the fading dusk and rapidly increasing chill—until, finally, even memories could not prevent his eyes from closing.

# CHAPTER 10

He heard humming and looked around for its source. An animal's head rounded on him and its black lips lifted away from finger-length canines. He gasped, jerked, and stumbled backward. The humming remained with him when he opened his eyes. He blinked in the light that penetrated the ceiling fabric and rolled his head toward the source of the sound. The humming stopped as soon as he moved.

The girl dropped a cloth and shot a hand to the mat, but froze without fleeing.

"Puh—" He cleared his throat and swallowed with difficulty. His throat was dry. "Please don't stop."

She remained poised to bolt.

"If you're so fucking scared of me, why are you always here?" he demanded. "What have I done to you?" When she didn't answer, he asked, "Don't you understand me?" and knew by her unaltered expression that she didn't. "Who am I?"

That was more honesty than he could handle. He looked at the cloth ceiling and blinked burning eyes.

She said something in a rush that might have been a single word for all he knew.

He stared at the ceiling. "I can't— I can't understand a goddamn thing you said."

"Kayarra."

He looked at her then. She used that word when she wanted his attention. It might even be his name, although it held no meaning, no connotation of self. His past encapsulated his illness. Instead of childhood, he remembered vomiting. Instead of parents, he remembered sand grating raw the flesh over shoulder blades, and being held down while this girl did things to his hands that left him screaming and sweat-soaked.

He returned to the present with a shudder and flexed a hand as if to assure himself the worst was over. The resulting pain did not reassure him. He wasn't sure of anything.

She lifted her hand from the mat, tapped her forearm, and said something.

He looked down at his own forearm, at still-ugly bruises and peeling scabs.

She tapped her forearm again and repeated the sound.

He studied her a moment, then attempted the word.

Her lips quivered toward a smile.

"So what the hell did I say?" he demanded. "'Arm?' 'Sleeve?' 'Gray?' With everything I can't say, why the hell 'arm'? You want something useful? Say 'fuck.' Fuck, fuck, fuck." The final repetition came out as a whoosh, as if the breath had been knocked from his chest. He desperately wished her gone.

She said something, so heavily slurred that it took a minute to realize she'd spoken in his language.

He threw an arm over his eyes to hide the tears that broke free even as he choked with laughter. It was a frightening sensation, as though the final strings of sanity had snapped. By the time she touched his shoulder, pain, mirth, and hope all felt like despair and her touch had no power to draw him back.

# CHAPTER 11

The sun hung low on the horizon. Denassa interrupted supper making to locate a choice stick from the deadwood, dried dung and grasses that Shurna had dropped beside the fire pit. When she straightened, she noticed Yutrenta still standing north of camp, arms folded close as if chilled by the anticipation of nightfall. Denassa set the stick aside, stirred the contents of the cook pot, then walked out to where Yutrenta stood.

"Trenta," she called softly as she approached and saw Yutrenta startle.

"There's no sign of them, Dee."

"The evening's early. They would be preparing for abbah, not traveling."

"They should have rejoined us at midday."

"Manerra might have struggled to maintain the pace," she said, then hastily added, "They are both physician's assistants. Aya will not let him come to harm."

"At risk to his own life!" Yutrenta snapped and looked away. Eventually, she looked back. "Forgive me, Dee. Lack of sleep does not excuse rudeness."

"None of us has slept much."

"Can I help with supper?"

Denassa chuckled. "One of us better stir the pot."

Matching step, they returned to camp.

"Do you fear Kayarra?" Yutrenta asked before they reached the fire pit.

"I am wary of him."

"Shurna offered to assist me if you prefer not to treat him."

Denassa blushed. They reached the fire pit and Yutrenta removed the pot lid.

"There is no reason to endanger her life." With a wooden spoon, Denassa scraped scorched food off the bottom of the pot, grateful for the opportunity to avert her face from Yutrenta's scrutiny.

"Your life is no less valuable than hers or mine."

Denassa faced Yutrenta even though her cheeks still burned. "If I fail you, I fail the shecarens," she said.

Yutrenta turned away and Denassa despaired of saying anything that did not increase Yutrenta's anxiety. The janquer failed their primary duty if harm befell either shecaren. This journey was the only time covenanted escorts were forbidden from accompanying them. For the first time in her seven years of service, adherence to divine law threatened their safety. And yet, ironically, if Aya or Manerra died, Kayarra and his tribe, not the janquer, would bear blame for their deaths.

Yutrenta held out bowls and Denassa filled them with rice stew, then moved the heavy pot off the fire and thrust her deadwood branch into the coals. When the stick caught fire, she handed it to Yutrenta and followed the Ofrann into the desert. Shurna noticed their departure and joined them for abbah.

The silence during supper merely continued a silence that had held since abbah, the same silence that had ended so many of their earlier attempts at conversation. Yutrenta signaled the end-of-meal by asking Denassa to feed Kayarra. Denassa signaled acquiescence and left. She hobbled one of the mia, filled her empty supper bowl with steaming milk, and carried the bowl to the tent.

She ducked through the door flap and paused while her eyes adjusted to the gloom. Kayarra sat, legs splayed, slouched like an infant, an elbow braced on his uninjured thigh, the other hand braced on a mat. Denassa's gasp brought his head up in slow motion. When he squinted at her with his spirit's eyes, the hairs on the back of her neck rose.

"Supper," she said and lifted the bowl, relieved when his eyes followed the bowl's motion. Hesitantly, she approached and knelt, and touched his goose-fleshed arm when she saw that he'd closed his eyes. Those eyes opened: white, with a winter-blue iris encircling a liquid-black center. So unlike Yatren or animal eyes that they unnerved her still. She raised the bowl to his lips and his hand intercepted it. He tried to guide the rim to his mouth, but his shaking hand caused milk to slosh over the rim. Denassa pulled the bowl back, snatched up a nearby rag, and blotted milk from the red and gray blanket bunched in his lap. She left the rag lying atop the blanket and waved him to keep his hands down. "Drink," she urged .

"Tahh," he said . . . "drink," as an infant would say it, with an inflection never before heard. "Tahh," he repeated before she recovered from her surprise.

"Who are you?" she demanded.

"Tahh."

She set the bowl aside. "Who are you?"

His explosive answer caused her to jerk back. She doubted her ability to interpret his facial expressions. She patted her chest. "Denassa," she said. "You." She stopped short of touching his shoulder.

"D'assa," he said, omitting sounds from her name.

"Denassa," she repeated. "Denassa. You," she touched his shoulder.

"D'assa."

A chill prickled her scalp and rose gooseflesh on her arms. "Trenta!" she yelled, not knowing whether the Ofrann was close enough to hear her shout.

Kayarra winced.

"Dee?" Yutrenta burst through the tent flap and halted as suddenly as she arrived.

"He talks."

"He's been talking."

"Yatren."

Yutrenta released the tent flap and crossed to Denassa's side.

"He said my name," Denassa continued as Yutrenta knelt. "And drink. He said drink. But when I asked his name, he said mine."

"How are you called?" Yutrenta asked Kayarra.

Nothing in Kayarra's expression indicated understanding. After a long silence, he slumped sideways onto an elbow, then half rolled, half fell onto his back with a grunt. His next breath was a single, sharp word.

"*Shii*," Denassa repeated.

"Stop!" Yutrenta snapped and Denassa started.

Yutrenta leaned forward, caught her weight on both hands, and in the heavy silence, broken only by Kayarra's moaning breaths, sat with head hung. When finally the curtain of her braids parted, her expression was grim. "Forgive me, janquer lady Denassa," she said.

"What did I say?"

"His word sounded like a curse." She shook her head in dismay. "I won't think clearly until the shecarens return. Please forgive me." Yutrenta jerked upright and hurried from the tent.

When Denassa stirred, it was to search for a utensil with which to dribble milk into Kayarra's mouth.

* * * * *

Supper the next evening was a depressing affair. For Aya and Manerra to be dead placed the nation's welfare in janquer hands and eliminated any future Denassa had beyond janquer rule. At least, until a shecaren was born, trained, and sworn to the Oath of Yatra, and sixteen years stretched the limit of her childbearing years.

Her father's lineage ended if the rule of Ringgal passed to her mother's brother's son. For the first time in her life, she considered breaking a covenant in order to provide Ringgal with an heir. To do so would not be her first public humiliation, only the first to be based upon fact.

Shurna touched her knee, shifting Denassa's attention from the bowl of food gone cold in her lap. Yutrenta signed *ready* and *question*, large enough to make Denassa realize she'd missed an earlier, less blatant query.

"Our only duty is to the shecarens," she said and set her bowl aside.

"We lack the resources to follow them," Yutrenta stunned her by opposing the intimation that they move camp.

"The mia can carry supplies," Shurna said.

Yutrenta shifted her attention to the heart of the fire around which they sat. "The shecarens have a nomad's knowledge of the Ofrann. And skills many nomads lack."

"And Aya was the only one fit enough to travel," Denassa said, while an ugly wonder rattled her. Did Yutrenta want the power that shecaren deaths gave the janquer? She flushed. She could believe that of Vantrann, not Yutrenta. Denassa rubbed her face. She felt grossly unprepared for the position she held. Even Vantrann, four years younger, seemed worldlier. He sat in judgment of Hyran's killers, prepared to make an offer to the Ofrann tribe on behalf of the Thurrang.

"For that matter, we could cache our trade supplies," Yutrenta replied, "but Kayarra cannot travel, and it was Aya's order that we stay here until his return."

"One of us could go after them," Shurna suggested.

"No!" Yutrenta replied. "No. Already, we haven't enough water skins to travel between wells."

Denassa clutched her hands in her lap.

"We have the flock," Shurna said.

"We need the supplies they carried," Denassa stated. "And the temple stone." That addendum brought her close to tears. The temple stone was not intended for mortal hands. It had been Acrahh's gift to shon regis Yatra, for shecaren use only. She had handled the temple stone—each of them had—because Aya had insisted they know how to handle it safely. But they weren't supposed to have an actual use for that knowledge.

Shurna gasped and gripped Denassa's knee. Denassa jerked her head around. On elbows and knees, naked, Kayarra crawled, halfway in, halfway out of the tent. Yutrenta rushed past, leaving Shurna and Denassa to scramble after.

"Back!" Yutrenta warned. She crouched beside Kayarra, a hand in the center of his back. While Denassa watched, she lifted the tent flap and peered inside. "We must clean a mat. Shurna, help me lift him."

Together, Yutrenta and Shurna raised Kayarra to his knees, then to his feet. Denassa watched his face until Yutrenta's urgent, "Dee, please remove the mat," sent her hurrying to help.

The tent smelled of urine, but only the mat nearest the door flap appeared wet. She dragged it from the tent and away from camp, stamped sand through the fibers, then left it weighted with rocks to dry in the morning sun.

Shurna stood warming herself beside the fire pit when Denassa returned. Denassa halted beside the Kitarin and reached out to the fire's warmth. "Shurna, why would Kayarra be confused by the desert? He was found here."

Shurna looked up, not as amused by the question as Denassa expected. "Kayarra was taken in the canyonlands. We are well beyond them. I think he would wonder how he arrived here."

Denassa blushed. "You're right. I'm too ready to believe Mana's theory of him."

Shurna grinned. "If Kayarra could fly, I think he would not have fallen from the cliff face."

Denassa blushed deeper, realizing how little she had thought through the details of Kayarra's founding as they related to Hyranian rumors. "How did Hyran know about a sixth tribe before we did?"

"I wonder that myself. I sincerely hope he had no hand in Kayarra's capture." She rocked for a moment, as if the windbreak and fire's heat failed to stave off the evening's chill. "But I will not guess what the shecarens know or don't know."

"Aya says he keeps no secrets."

"Aya does not share rumors."

Some rumors, Denassa heard herself—multiple times—and not only from Thurrang lords. Anything related to Hyran's bid for power affected their decisions.

Hyran had called himself arenta, meaning "blessed child." According to Hyran, the title was bestowed upon any child born to the Chosen of Acrahh after a shecaren birth. He claimed that Acrahh wished the shecarens to accept the counsel of their half-blood siblings. Soon after Hyran's self-titling, he scandalously married the only other living "arenta," a Kitarin woman named Myra who was nearly as old as his mother.

"Hyran traded along the eastern route," Denassa mused. "If Kayarra came through the Smoking Mountains, or north, through Thurra's forests, I could believe it. But to be found in the canyonlands . . . . It makes no sense."

"The Manteen explain why he was alone. I suspect he knew his fate if he failed to escape."

Denassa glanced away, facing into the cold wind that was as much a part of the desert as the sand. The dust-filtering veil hid the grim purse of her lips. "Please, Shurna." She would have nightmares before morning if Shurna said another word; would likely have nightmares anyway.

"I saw dysie today. It wasn't ripe, but tomorrow I'll gather it."

"How long must we wait before we move camp?" Denassa demanded. If Shurna changed the subject, she wanted a subject that supplied answers.

"The shecarens will return here. If Manerra is the reason for their delay, time spent searching for us could be fatal."

"Eventually, not moving will be fatal for us. Fatal for the animals."

"I trust Yutrenta's knowledge. I see no fatalism in her choices."

Denassa clapped a hand over her mouth, but not fast enough to muffle a cry of dismay. *How will we know if she's chosen death?* Denassa couldn't ask. She jerked out of Shurna's sudden grip and bumped into the windbreak. One of the rocks fell and others shifted. She jerked away as if singed.

"Denassa!" Shurna cried. "We are not in danger."

Perhaps Shurna realized the ludicrousness of her declaration, because she stopped following after a few steps.

*****

They were three. Denassa found that reassurance before she returned to camp, shivering in the night wind. No one janquer preference counted for more than another. Yutrenta was to be heeded because she was Ofrann-born, just as Denassa's companions would look to her for guidance if danger threatened them at sea. What if's and what might's had no place in the decisions they faced. If Acrahh intended to sacrifice them on the altar of his sons, that calamity would happen no matter the choices they made. Denassa had accepted that truth before she accepted the unification prayer, although, in reality, she never expected disaster to occur.

# CHAPTER 12

Aya opened his eyes to stars: a glittering expanse partially obscured by the puffing billow of a canopy's roof. His feet were cold and his muscles stiff where he had shifted off the thin insulation of the mat in his sleep.

Manerra's blanket covered his head. Aya listened for the shecaren's breathing, found the reassurance he wanted, then crawled on hands and knees to the nearest rock and began licking off the dew.

When finally he could swallow without pain, he picked up a rock and carried it back to the canopy. A touch on an arm aroused Manerra, who obligingly rolled onto his back in response to Aya's pull. Aya tugged off his brother's veil and tipped the rock over Manerra's mouth. Drops of water struck Manerra's lips and were licked away by a questing tongue. Aya held the rock close enough for Manerra to lick while he stroked braids from the boy's forehead.

He felt no fever.

Manerra tried to speak, but the word came out as a rasp. He pushed Aya's hand away, struggled to sit, then crept away in search of more rocks and the thin covering of water they held.

Through moon set and the dark before dawn they gathered dew, first with tongues to sate dangerous thirsts, then with rags, squeezing drops into empty water skins. Finally, damp and shivering, with barra birds trilling dawn's approach, Manerra helped Aya dismantle the hollow stone tower, tediously collecting dew from each rock until they reached the shallow waterskin-lined pool at the bottom. With Manerra holding a water skin over the pool to catch every drop, Aya repeatedly dipped his rag into the water and squeezed it over the mouth of the skin. After he emptied the pool, he gave Manerra the rag to suck dry.

Between them, they had collected nearly half a skin of water. Aya assumed it would be the last water they found until next dewfall.

# CHAPTER 13

"Kayarra stood unaided," Yutrenta announced before Denassa reached the cold fire pit.

"Good news," Denassa answered, trying to draw pleasure from the announcement. Impossible. If not for Kayarra, Aya and Manerra would not have left camp eight nights ago. She poured the milk she carried over the dry beans in the cook pot and reached for the lid.

"I want to move camp tomorrow."

Denassa froze before her fingers touched the lid. She straightened and stared at Yutrenta as if at a stranger. "He hasn't taken his first unaided step."

"He will ride."

"Alone?" Five nights ago, Denassa would have rushed to pack. Now, breaking camp and traveling felt like folly. Kayarra's fall from shurenback would be as dangerous as . . . . She shied from that thought, keenly aware of the grief that lay like an ocean's tide beneath her depression. Time for action, if there had ever been an optimum one, was past. Here, at least, they had the dew mounds and the windbreak and most of the foodstuff that was to have carried them to the Shangren.

And the animals had twice broken dew mounds to reach the water, and Shurna was having to take them farther afield for grazing than was safe. Milk production had decreased even among not-nursing females. They would lose young if fresh grazing wasn't found soon.

"We will cache our trade goods. If you or Shurna will support Kayarra, I will herd the flock."

"I'd not be able to see past his shoulder," she said before she realized the implicit agreement in that statement. But it no longer mattered. Moving or staying affected her critical choices only insofar as it affected her life or death. With no imminent threat to her life, the unresolved question of Ringgal's heir remained.

* * * * *

They lashed supplies onto animal backs by lantern light. By the time the brightening sky sent Night fleeing into the shadow of plants, they traveled. When the sun broke the horizon, they paused for abbah.

Kayarra, left alone on shuren back, gripped the animal's fur so hard it sent annoyance shivers along her neck. For his safety, Denassa hobbled the animal through the blessing of the sunrise, and through the sharing of milk and broken flatcakes afterwards, eaten where they stood.

With breakfast finished, Yutrenta mounted behind Kayarra and Denassa slapped the shuren into motion. Their second animal followed, its lead tied to the baggage of Yutrenta's mount. Shurna trailed with the flock.

By mid morning, Kayarra's head lulled on his chest, but it wasn't until he stopped moaning that Yutrenta called a halt. Denassa retreated to Kayarra's leg and gripped his ankle. "Are we to camp?" she asked Yutrenta.

"We're more than a day from Rajma's Head," Yutrenta evaded her question. "At this pace, it will take us three days to reach it."

"They ran—" Denassa stopped herself in time. The shecarens had run out of food four days ago. With this added complication, it wasn't something that needed to be said. "We can use the canopies through midday. Maybe after resting, Kayarra will be able to travel." But Kayarra was sickly pale and his eyelids did not even flutter when the shuren stopped walking. Dangerous or not, she wanted to leave him and go on, or keep walking now. It was still well before midday, and their sacred duty—

She dipped her head, ashamed of her selfishness. The shecarens should not have gone for water. It was a risk the janquer should have taken. Never should both have gone together. Manerra had not been fit enough for such effort.

"Hold him," Yutrenta said.

Denassa gripped Kayarra's leg with both hands while Yutrenta lowered him along the shuren's neck. She dismounted quickly, circled Denassa, reached up, and pulled him from shurenback. Denassa helped break his fall, then lead the shuren away.

"Are we resting or raising canopies?" Shurna came up while Denassa tied the shuren's lead to scrub.

"I think we're camping." She finished the knot and turned as she straightened, seeking Shurna's eyes. "We need to talk." She shrank from that necessity, but too much had gone unsaid for too long. "I ask for counsel."

"Can Kayarra be left alone?"

"He's unconscious."

"Then let's talk." She turned and led the way to Yutrenta's side.

Yutrenta looked up when they approached but did not remove her hand from Kayarra's temple.

"Denassa asks for counsel," Shurna said before Denassa could draw breath enough to speak.

Yutrenta's startled attention shifted to Denassa. "How urgent is your need? I wish for a mat, blankets and canopy for Kayarra."

"I'll get them." Denassa returned to the shuren, and was reaching for canopy poles before she realized Shurna had followed her.

"Have I time to unburden the mia?" the Kitarin asked. "I'll concentrate better knowing the beasts won't eat the mats or leave with our supplies."

"It will take me that long to set up a canopy," Denassa answered.

Shurna left to attend to the chore. When Denassa returned with her arms full, she was surprised that Yutrenta left Kayarra's side to help her raise the canopy.

"Will he be all right?" Denassa asked while they worked.

Yutrenta tilted her head. "Beyond making him comfortable, there's little we can do for him."

"His headaches concern me."

"Me, too."

Their conversation lapsed. In fairness to Shurna, Denassa could not address her concerns with Yutrenta. They worked without speaking.

"I brought a mat and blankets," Shurna announced upon her return.

Yutrenta helped her make a pallet. By the time they'd finished, Kayarra had not regained consciousness. It took all of them to shift him.

Yutrenta knelt on the edge of Kayarra's blanket, reached across his body, and gripped the hands Shurna and Denassa extended. "Let our wisdom recognize the value of compromise, and our love for one another and the nation prevail," she said, squeezing Denassa's hand before releasing it.

Denassa and Shurna settled on the ground opposite her in the shade cast by the canopy.

"I have been imagining terrible fates for the shecarens," Denassa began. "I can't help it. I've wondered over and over whether we could have stopped Aya from leaving."

"Regrets won't change the past," Shurna said.

"I know." Denassa paused, hoping to speak with less strain when she continued. "We know something has happened. I only ask that we stop speculating and assume the worst. Not because I can believe they won't return, but because ambivalence is our undoing. That's why I ask to know what your expectations are; what we must do now." She stopped talking. Grief distracted her from the objectivity she needed.

"Do you question the breaking of camp or our destination?" Yutrenta asked.

"Neither. I know we have to reach water. But the mia won't find grazing along the trade route, and it's obvious that Kayarra is not well enough to travel."

"We're not dividing the company," Yutrenta stated.

"You were ready to leave the janquer because of Kayarra, but I serve shon regis Aya and no other."

"We all serve shon regis Aya," Shurna interceded.

"Aya's last command was for Kayarra's care," Yutrenta defended her decisions.

"But if he's dead—if both shecarens are dead—" tears spilled, but she kept on stubbornly, "we must make decisions for ourselves. That you've moved camp tells me you've reached the same conclusion. Am I wrong?"

"No," Yutrenta answered grimly.

"One of us on shuren back can reach Rajma's Head and return by tomorrow."

"With what water?" Yutrenta asked.

"With milk before I leave and the water at Rajma's Head."

"No," again Yutrenta refused. "If it were that simple, the shecarens would have returned. If Manerra developed fever, Aya would have gotten him back to camp even if it meant tying him to shuren back. My sense—" She glanced away. "My sense is," her voice went husky, "something worse has happened."

Yutrenta's admission confirmed her dread. Although Denassa had anticipated agreement, hearing the words was a harsher blow than she expected. She couldn't speak until her throat stopped hurting. "I wish to hear Shurna's choice," she said, resolution hardening her will. Her request took the final decision away from Yutrenta.

Shurna did not answer immediately, although she must have considered their options before now. "My desire is to reach Rajma's Head as quickly as possible," Shurna spoke slowly. "However, the shecarens' enemies are necessarily our own. If Hyran's followers have avenged his murder, we've greater safety in numbers. I cannot risk more lives. My decision must be to stay together."

Desperation replaced Denassa's dismay. "We can leave Kayarra at camp, go on to Rajma's Head ourselves—tonight—and be back before midday."

"No, Denassa," Yutrenta said quietly.

Denassa struck the ground with her fist. "I don't serve Kayarra!" she shouted. "If the shecarens have died through our inactions, who will follow us? Who will dare to?"

"Those who respect the gods' laws," Shurna answered.

Denassa fell forward, caught her face in her hands, and cried.

"My vow is the same as yours," Yutrenta objected, "and Aya's last order was for Kayarra's care."

"When do we make decisions for ourselves?" Denassa demanded through tear-wet hands. "How long do we live on prayers rather than action?"

"We are acting," Shurna objected.

"I don't mean for the well-being of—" Denassa broke off, fumbling for a word to describe her loathing, "some creature."

"*Kayarra*," Yutrenta's tone was stern, "may help assure our well-being."

"How?"

"He knows what his tribe wants and where they are."

"And you understand him?"

"A few words."

"The mia understand more commands than he does."

"This exchange is not helpful," Shurna broke in.

"You're scared of him," Yutrenta said.

"His presence violates the laws of this journey."

"The gods' laws make exceptions for life and death situations."

"Not when the life of an animal is held dearer than Acrahh's own sons."

In Yutrenta's stunned silence, her face went grim. "I was midwife at Manerra's birth," she said at last, her voice strained. "I love Aya as I love no other. But we rule the nation if they die, and I will not give that power to a single tribe by foolishly losing our lives."

It was Denassa's turn to be stunned. Vantrann, alone among the janquer, remained in Thurra. "I don't question your love," Denassa said, but that was close to a lie. She had questioned Yutrenta's loyalty. She had been confused by Yutrenta's inaction, then by her haste, and throughout, frustrated by her silence. Denassa ducked her head. "Yes, I'm scared, but not of Kayarra."

Kayarra groaned. Yutrenta touched his shoulder, then reached for her physician's bag.

"You know Ringgangley rule," Yutrenta stated as she withdrew the horn peg that secured her bag's leather flap. "You can do this."

"We need the temple stone."

"We will find it. You know its danger in untrained hands." She uncorked a vial and brought it toward Kayarra's mouth.

Kayarra shouted, startling them all, and slapped Yutrenta's hand away. Yutrenta lunged for the vial that flew from her hand and hit the ground, snatching it up before all its contents spilled.

Shurna, closest to Kayarra's shoulder, grabbed his wrist. He screamed and slammed a fist against her forearm.

"Leave him!" Yutrenta scrambled away. "Leave him." She snatched her bag away while Denassa and Shurna scrambled out of reach.

He writhed onto his side, arched backward, wailed, and pressed a palm against each eye.

"Are you all right?" Yutrenta called to Shurna.

Kayarra began a desperate tirade, broken by sobs and shouted cries.

Shurna removed her hand from her arm. "I'm all right."

Denassa turned away from Kayarra's pain. "I'll get another canopy," she said.

Shurna sank to her knees and began a soft, wordless throat song—a

Kitarin lullaby. Yutrenta joined Denassa at the shuren. Instead of reaching for canopy poles, though, Yutrenta grabbed the end of the rope that secured the tent.

Shurna throat sang until she grew hoarse, a song of innocence that did little to assuage Denassa's dismay while she helped Yutrenta raise the tent. They had been packed and traveling. She didn't want to camp yet. But did another day's delay—or another eight days' delay—matter anymore?

Tears started anew, a silent, steady trickle that made her veil cling to her face. When Yutrenta slipped an arm around her shoulder, Denassa stiffened, then dropped the tent fabric, clung to Yutrenta, and sobbed, her forehead pressed into the juncture of Yutrenta's neck and shoulder. "I'm sorry, Trenta," she gasped when she could speak, "I can't give them up."

"He is not gone," Yutrenta whispered as though her conviction were badly shaken.

*He*, she'd said. Not *they*. Had she abandoned hope of Manerra's survival? That Yutrenta loved Aya, Denassa had known for years. That there could never be a consummation, they all knew.

"Have you any willow infusion?" Yutrenta asked.

Denassa pulled back and looked up into Yutrenta's red-rimmed eyes. "In my bag."

"I had only what was spilled." Yutrenta brushed Denassa's cheek with fingertips. "No more spilled water," her sternness held grief. "Look on Kayarra for me?"

Denassa tilted her head.

"Be careful." Yutrenta turned away, back to the stake she'd been pounding.

That was Aya's habit, Denassa realized, to order adversaries to a common task. Maybe it was Yutrenta's wordless acceptance of her apology.

She returned to the small pile of baggage she had carried during their short journey and withdrew her physician's bag.

# CHAPTER 14

Distant bleating distracted Denassa from the frustrating, grief-filled task of repairing Manerra's dress robe. She'd already set the robe aside two earlier days because of inability to concentrate. Sand rubbing had removed the bloodstains, but she'd had to remove an earlier needle-weaving attempt when she'd misaligned enough threads that the fabric puckered.

Hope and futility complicated the task. Privately, she believed, if she completed the repair, the owner of the robe would return to fill it, but logic warred with hope. The twin abalone crescents on the robe's shoulder meant that no one but a shecaren could wear it. A tribal symbol centered on the chest would permit a janquer member to wear it, but adapting the robe for anyone else's use was not something she could consider.

Denassa assumed the approaching flock was theirs, but Aya's order that Kayarra be concealed caused Denassa to set aside the unfinished robe and stand up in the long shadow of the tent. The white mia were unmistakably theirs.

She watched Shurna approach with the flock and waved a greeting. Shurna pointed northwest. Denassa stepped around the curve of the tent. Two gray-robed figures approached, trailed by a single shuren. At this distance, the newcomers were as anonymous as any Ofrann travelers . . . until she glimpsed the blue and yellow strap that crossed one traveler's chest.

"Trenta!" Tears sprang as she screamed, "They're home!" She stumbled forward, then snatched up handfuls of robe and ran.

Three body lengths away from them she staggered to a panting halt and bowed her head, only to find herself in an embrace that took her breath away. "Lady Dee," Aya murmured into her hair. She laughed through the tears that wet his robe. And clung to him, and he to her, until the gradual realization of his weight loss penetrated her painful joy.

"Shon regis." Shurna's heartfelt greeting sounded behind her, more controlled than anything she could manage. "Shecaren."

Aya released Denassa and stepped into Shurna's embrace, and Denassa wiped her eyes with the back of a hand. Then Manerra stepped into the spot Aya had vacated and Denassa reached for him. The shecaren's brief hug held all the awkwardness that was Manerra, while the protrusion of his ribs and shoulder blades told of his own privation.

"What happened?" she ignored custom to demand.

"The cistern at Rajma's Head is no more."

Shurna's gasp echoed Denassa's.

"Enough," Aya intervened. "Stories can wait."

Denassa took the shuren's lead from Manerra's hand, turned, and only then noticed Yutrenta. The Ofrann, still a distance away, knelt on the ground, bowed in what Denassa mistook as Thurrang obeisance. Except Yutrenta was not leaning far enough forward to touch her forehead to the ground. As Denassa stared, Yutrenta's shoulders shook and the sound of her sobs came through the sand-grating shuffle of the shuren's restlessness, the flap of robes, and the sharp, excited breaths of those around her.

Aya started forward then, and Denassa tugged on the lead of a beast that refused movement. It took several slaps of the reins across the shuren's leg before she stepped forward, and by that time, Aya had reached Yutrenta. He knelt in front of her, lifted her face in both hands, and pressed his forehead to hers.

* * * * *

Manerra spotted their black and white striped tent and the willpower that kept him walking drained away so suddenly, he staggered and braced for a fall. Only his grip on the shuren's reins kept him upright. When vertigo passed, he glanced at Aya, but Aya had not noticed his difficulty. If the janquer had not moved camp, he was certain he would have arrived across shuren back, not walking. Even this close to home, a faint was possible.

All he wanted was sleep, even more so than food.

Shurna spotted them, alerted camp, and Denassa reached them first, running and out of breath with crying. Thankfully, she expended most of her emotion in Aya's arms. Manerra wasn't certain how much hugging and weeping he could withstand without falling, even while relief brought tears to his own eyes. He relinquished his grip on the shuren's reins to Denassa with reluctance. That grip had helped him maintain his balance. But Shurna embraced him and kept an arm around his waist, and he remembered very little of those final steps home until he glanced back and saw Aya and Yutrenta trailing in a half embrace close behind.

He pulled free of Shurna's support, reached for the tent flap and halted, stopped short by a urine odor that made him gasp. "What is this?" he demanded out of surprise and stepped away from the tent.

"Kayarra lives," Shurna answered.

Anger made his hands shake. "Is he not civilized?"

"He can't walk unaided."

"Neither can—" He clamped his teeth shut on the tirade behind that opening, pivoted, stumbled, and brushed between Shurna and Aya as he passed them. He collapsed on a mat beside the cold fire pit, sucked a ragged breath, and remembered nothing else until Yutrenta woke him—maybe moments, maybe hours later—with a warm tea she urged him to drink.

* * * * *

Denassa's shouts outside the tent brought his head up with a jerk and made his heart pound. A peculiar gasping cry came from the other side of the black curtain, then Yutrenta burst through, skirts lifted to calves, and plunged through the tent's door flap. He squinted into the flare of sunlight that accompanied her exit but caught no more than a glimpse of sky, sandy ground, and gray-green brush before the flap fell closed.

He blinked in the weak light of the tent and crept toward the central support pole, making progress by pulling himself along on one elbow and pushing with his uninjured leg. When he reached the pole, he hooked an elbow around it, drew his good leg under him, and slid a shoulder along the pole as he stood. He swayed unsteadily until a fog of vertigo passed. Then he studied the distance to the doorway. The fabric walls weren't likely to support his weight if he fell. He waited for the outside commotion to reach the tent.

A hand—its back covered with a fine down of black hair, fingers thicker than a woman's—started to push the door flap aside, stopped, then abruptly withdrew. A man's voice erupted: startled, disgusted. A woman protested. Sand crunched as someone left.

The door flap bulged inward again. This time, the top of a cloth-covered head appeared. The person cleared the doorway and straightened before their eyes locked. The man halted.

Behind the stranger, Yutrenta entered, sliding past in the narrow gap between his shoulder and the wall. Her eyes were red-rimmed, her lashes wet. She'd been crying.

The newcomer reached up, loosened his veil, and let the fabric fall across his chest.

He stared at a gaunt face full of lines and folds, with facial hair peppered more gray than black. The animal eyes that held his were steady, curious, unafraid.

Shurna crowded in beside Yutrenta, and Yutrenta began something that sounded like an introduction. He heard his name spoken, but what the stranger's name was, he didn't know. She used too many words, and he didn't understand the protocol—where a name fell amid everything else she said.

When she finished talking, the man spoke, but he understood none of the reply. Unlike Dee, the stranger used no hand signals when he spoke.

"So much for a fucking arm, huh?" he said, using their word for arm, and saw the man glance down at his forearm. A peculiar thrill ran down both arms and tingled his fingertips. The stranger had understood him.

The man said something and lifted a tooled leather strap from his shoulder. Yutrenta reached for the strap, and Kayarra followed the leather case that cleared the man's robe. The heavily tooled case depicted a slender, hoofed creature rearing up from lush vegetation. Between its forelimbs lay a crescent inside a circle. He followed the decorated bag until he lost sight of it behind a fold of Yutrenta's robe. When she crossed between them and disappeared behind the black curtain, he looked back at the man and noticed creased brows that weren't there before.

"I'm not a thief," he told the man, but his surety floundered. What had he been? "This is ridiculous!" He started to rub his forehead but caught himself in time. His hands could tolerate very little pressure and right now the pain was bearable.

Yutrenta returned with blankets and Shurna helped shake free their folds. Between them, they began making a bed in the juncture between the curtain and the tent's back wall.

He was suddenly struck by the absence of goods on this side of the curtain; by the realization that one of the women always happened to be nearby. "You know me," he said, staring at Yutrenta's profile while she worked. "You call me Ka'rra."

At the mention of his name, attention snapped toward him and he wondered whether Ka'rra was a name or a command. "You know that name," he told them. "So why don't you understand me?" He released the pole and took a step toward the man. Instantly, Shurna stepped between them and Yutrenta froze.

Did their reactions indicate knowledge of him before his injuries?

The man asked something.

Yutrenta's single-word answer was one he recognized: "No."

He looked at Yutrenta. "Who am I to you?"

A hand gripped his bicep and he startled. They rarely touched him anymore. Only when they had to, when they treated his wounds. He looked back and into Shurna's dark eyes. He felt her tension in the grip she maintained on his arm and looked back at the man. By all outward appearances, he remained calm, unintimidated, self-assured.

Shurna tugged, urging him back toward the red and blue blankets that comprised his bed.

"Who are you?" he asked the man, not expecting an answer, but unable to contain his frustration. "I don't hate you," he told him. "I don't know you."

He let Shurna lead him back to his blankets then, and accepted her assistance in lying down. He dropped back upon an elbow before resisting, not wanting to lower his head to the pillow while the man remained standing inside the doorway. By even that much compliance he hoped to demonstrate his harmlessness, although if he had killed someone in the fight that nearly took his life, docilely laying down wasn't likely to win their trust.

Was this man his judge? His torturer? His executioner?

He looked back into Shurna's face, so close he could distinguish the browns in her eyes. "I don't want to die," he told her, for whatever good it did. "I will talk to you," his conviction firmed. He was a child in his dependence upon them and that scared him. He looked at Yutrenta, who had nearly completed the making of a new bed, and told her back, "I will talk with you. You're going to know I'm not who you think I am."

But what was that? For the first time since gaining consciousness, he was relieved they couldn't understand him. Pain, frustration and imagination confounded his reasoning. Surely his real past was not worse than his imagined one . . . not worse than his ignorance-generated fear.

* * * * *

Manerra woke a second time to fire and darkness, and the scents of smoke and food. He tugged the blankets close, shivering with a chill the blankets did not ward. Finally, he struggled onto an elbow, convinced that if he could warm his feet he'd be able to sleep.

A cool hand touched his forehead, startling him.

"How do you feel?"

He looked over his shoulder at Yutrenta.

"Cold."

"You will be until you eat."

He rolled onto his back and closed his eyes. "I want sleep."

"The longer you wait, the sicker you'll be. Open your mouth."

He did, felt a spoon's bowl press his lower lip, and choked on broth he failed to control with his tongue.

Yutrenta lifted his shoulders off the ground and supported him until he stopped coughing.

"Easy," she said.

"Warn me," he begged.

"Sit up."

She helped him sit, and wrapped the blankets around him as snug as a cocoon.

"Where's Aya?" he asked during one of the long pauses between spoonfuls of broth.

"Asleep, I hope."

"Is he angry with me?"

"He's worried. He asked me to look at the wound on your hip."

"It's healing."

"I know. You both did well."

That she had touched him and he'd not awakened shocked him.

She lifted a fragment of flatcake to his mouth but he shook his head, shifted forward, and groaned.

"Do you want to lay down?"

"Please."

She helped him lay down without loosening the blankets, and stayed with him through the chills and cramps that wracked him.

"Did you think we had died?" he asked during a reprieve.

She didn't answer immediately. "I would not believe it."

"You could have died waiting for us."

"That's why we moved camp."

His abdomen rumbled. He winced and drew his knees closer to his chest. "I'm glad you did."

Eventually, Yutrenta made him sip an herbal tea, then more broth, and finally insisted that he leave the night wind and fireside to sleep in the tent. She helped him stand, and gripped his arm until he lay down again, this time on his pallet.

How long had they been gone? Not even a fortnight, and the ordeal continued.

Manerra rolled onto his uninjured hip, pulled a cushion under his head, and stared at the back of the blanketed figure snoring across from him. Sand-colored hair was all he could see of the cor-anda.

It hadn't had the decency to die. Instead, it had defiled their living quarters.

Yutrenta took the lantern with her through the curtain, but enough light penetrated the fabric to distinguish the cor-anda's blanket-covered mound.

Manerra pivoted, head to feet, unable to tolerate the sight of it.

Whatever else he might accomplish in life, he would be remembered foremost for that one, impulsive moment when he reached down and dragged the cor-anda to safety, knowing even as he did so that what he saved wasn't Yatren. Nothing else he could accomplish would ever matter as much.

He begged Acrahh for a sign that his visions of violent bloodshed were only horrific imaginings.

# CHAPTER 15

"

. . . severe headaches."

That murmur was not part of Manerra's dream.

"Maybe from the trepanation, maybe from the delay treating him." The whisper came from the direction of Aya's pallet. "I can't know for sure, or whether it's caused by something altogether different."

"Is he a man?" came Aya's whispered question.

Manerra held his breath, anxious to hear Yutrenta's answer.

"Inside . . . his organs . . . are Yatren, or enough alike that I know what I feel when I examine him. And my infusions haven't harmed him. I worried the dayflower might."

Aya chuckled softly. "You justify my suffering by fearing its use on anyone."

"I do not," Yutrenta protested. "Divine law does not—"

"Shh," Aya hushed her. "I know. I'm teasing."

"I can't joke right now. I'm sorry."

"We're safe."

Yutrenta gasped, and her erratic breaths made Manerra realize she cried.

"Dear, sweet Trenta."

Through her quiet sobs, Manerra imagined Aya pressing her knuckles to his forehead.

"How is Manerra?" Aya asked at last.

"I'll not let you take him from us again."

Aya chuckled. "I thought you couldn't tease."

"I don't." She paused for the length of a ragged breath. "I ask that we camp tomorrow. Manerra and Kayarra cannot handle more travel, and Shurna and Dee will appreciate the rest when they return."

"It was my intention to do so. And to sleep tonight."

Yutrenta expelled a breath. "You needed the tea as much as Manerra did."

"Bless the gods, they kept him safe," Aya said with such emotion that Manerra lifted his head before he remembered he was eavesdropping and lowered it to the pillow. He waited for an indication that Yutrenta or Aya had seen him move but none came.

"Gods bless, they kept you both safe," Yutrenta whispered. Then, raggedly, "Sleep." Fabric rustled as she stood. A softer rustle as Aya stood, and in the faint light that filtered through the curtain, Manerra saw them embrace.

"I love you," each whispered simultaneously, which brought a half laugh, half sob from Yutrenta. She turned and hurried through the curtain. Light from the other side illuminated Aya, naked and aroused, for the brief moment before the curtain fell back and plunged them into darkness.

It was awhile before Manerra heard Aya lay down.

* * * * *

Mia bleated.

The sound brought Manerra toward wakefulness. He listened for a repetition, heard none, and began to doze.

Sand crunched outside the tent flap.

Manerra reared up, heart pounding, and grabbed for his belt knife. It was gone. He groped in a wider circle while struggling free of the blankets that tangled his legs. "Aya!" he shouted and leapt aside, away from the spot his voice placed him.

The footsteps halted.

"We're janquer!" Manerra recognized Denassa's alarmed cry.

"Forgive us," Shurna called. "We're tired. We weren't thinking."

"Not thinking can get you killed," Aya yelled. "Come in here."

"No!" Manerra shouted. "My knife's missing."

"I moved your belt." That was Yutrenta's confession. The tent flap gaped and a woman hurried through, disappearing into the women's quarters.

"Someone light a lantern," Aya ordered and Manerra heard him dressing.

Shurna and Denassa entered the tent: dark silhouettes hardly distinguishable from the night.

"Shon regis. Shecaren," Shurna acknowledged them.

"It's a bit late for formalities," Aya stated.

"Tahh?"

Manerra froze.

"Dee. Tahh?" the strange voice persisted.

"You will address her as janquer lady Denassa," Manerra shouted at the cor-anda.

"He doesn't understand," Denassa intervened.

"Why not?"

As if in answer, Kayarra spoke again, meaningless sounds that shocked Manerra with their bizarre inflections.

"Where's a lantern?" Aya bellowed.

"Patience," Yutrenta pleaded, returning from the women's quarters.

"Not on the brief sleep I've had," Aya retorted.

"Here," Yutrenta said.

"Thank you," Denassa replied and hurried from the tent.

"Shon regis," Yutrenta said, "no one has had much sleep." She approached, went to one knee in front of Manerra, located him by touch, and pressed his belt into his hand. "Please forgive me, shecaren. We have been storing all weapons beyond Kayarra's reach. *Not* because he has shown himself to be dangerous, but because we have not seen him frightened."

"Stop it, Yutrenta," Aya snapped, although his order lacked the anger of his earlier commands.

"Shon regis?"

"Speak *to* me, not around me."

"Shon regis."

The tent wall streamed light and Manerra raised an arm to shade his eyes before Denassa pushed through the flap carrying a lantern. She crossed to the central support pole, suspended the lantern on a hook, then bowed her head.

"Denassa," Aya acknowledged her while Manerra's attention fixed on the cor-anda. The creature was sitting, its face averted from the light. Its arms were browner than Manerra remembered, its chest whiter, and the stubble of its beard, more pronounced. Then it looked up and Manerra gasped.

"Shecaren?" Yutrenta inquired.

"What is it?" Manerra demanded. Fear alone did not account for the amount of white in the cor-anda's eyes. He'd seen an animal carcass in Kita once—a nocturnal tree-dweller—with bluish-gray eyes like that.

"His eyes?" Yutrenta asked. "They are his, nothing more."

Manerra looked into her eyes: glistening brown, their pupils contracting and expanding in the flickering lamplight. Only when she glanced at Aya did the whites of her eyes show—thin crescents in the corners.

"Lady Shurna, bring me a bowl of water," Aya said.

Manerra's attention snapped to Aya's face. "You don't intend to share water with it," he said.

"I do," Aya answered.

"He's not . . ." Manerra floundered in horror. The ritual Aya intended imposed responsibilities Manerra rejected. Safekeeping escorts was one thing. Protecting a demon was altogether different. He took a step toward the tent flap but stopped before Aya said, "This problem comes to both of us. We would do well to face it together."

"The decisions are yours. I learn about them when everyone else does."

"Blame for consequences is also mine. So explain your fear."

Manerra whirled. "You know nothing about him. How can you

charge us with his safekeeping?"

"The alternative is to abandon him. Is that your counsel?"

"No." *Yes!* "But he can travel as far as the Shangren without our formal protection."

"If he is in this company, he will have my protection."

If they weren't so far from any civilized place, Manerra would have walked out. But he could not reach either Ringgal or the Shangren Oasis alone.

"Sit, Manerra. Please."

He had no choice. He sat. But when Aya finished the proclamation of protection, sipped the water, and passed the bowl, Manerra stated his name, his title, his last five generations of lineage, tilted the bowl against his lips, and could not drink. His throat would not contract, even to swallow his own saliva in deception. He passed the bowl to Yutrenta, wiped his mouth on his sleeve, and glared at the edge of the mat upon which he sat.

When Yutrenta named herself, Manerra flushed with guilt and fear, followed by overwhelming anger. He leaned forward over clenched fists until he could control his emotions.

The farce ended when Kayarra took the bowl Shurna passed and gulped down the last of the water, driven by thirst rather than understanding of what his actions meant to those around him.

"Name yourself." Aya stopped him from returning the empty bowl.

"Tahh," he said.

Denassa patted her chest. "Denassa," she said. "Dee. You." She pointed at Kayarra.

"Ka'arra," he answered.

"That's not his name!" Manerra shouted.

Everyone startled.

"It's all he knows," Denassa protested.

Yutrenta gasped and clutched Denassa's wrist.

"Trenta?" Aya demanded.

She shook her head. It was a moment before she spoke. "Shurna, where is the dysie you gathered? I need one. Please."

The Kitarin rose and hurried into the women's quarters. Moments later, she returned carrying a small, green, lumpy fruit that she placed in Yutrenta's outstretched hand.

"Who has a knife?"

Manerra did not trust himself to touch the carved ivory hilt protruding from the belt sheath in his lap. Yutrenta sliced the hard fruit using Denassa's knife. Green rind parted to expose pink flesh replete with seeds the size of fly droppings. She cut a slice in half and offered a piece to Kayarra. "Taste it," she urged. When he took it, she brought the half she held to her open mouth but did not touch it to her tongue. Ripe, the fruit was bitter; unripe, it was even more so. Dysie's appeal was its juice's sweet aftertaste. Its flesh was a purgative.

Kayarra put the fruit in his mouth and chewed.

"Aya!" Yutrenta rose to her knees in alarm, but Aya had already snatched the bowl from Kayarra's hand, forced a finger into his mouth, and got him to spit the chewed pulp into the bowl.

Manerra began laughing.

"Stop, Manerra."

Manerra tried to control his laughter and failed. "There's his use," he gasped, grinding the heel of a hand into a tearing eye. "Entertainment for the masses."

"Enough!"

"Kayarra does not know his name, or his tribe, or anything that happened to him," Yutrenta said.

"What?" Denassa and Shurna demanded.

"A child once fell from my father's garden wall and hit her head on stone. She slept for two days. When she woke, she didn't recognize her mother. It happened so many years ago, I'd forgotten. But until Kayarra ate the dysie, I couldn't be sure. He cannot taste it."

Manerra watched Kayarra's eyes dart from one speaker to the next.

"Has he forgotten how to speak?" Manerra demanded, incredulity replacing mirth.

Yutrenta frowned. "The child I treated could speak."

"Then he understands us?"

Yutrenta met his eyes. "I think he does not."

"You mean, we've pledged protection to an animal?"

"Manerra!" Aya stood abruptly. "Come with me. Now."

# CHAPTER 16

Manerra returned to camp alone after morning abbah. Without acknowledging any of the women, he flopped down on his pallet and pulled the blankets over his head. Aya's parting suggestion was that he sleep, but sleep was impossible.

In the years he'd been away, he'd grown accustomed to his preferences and opinions mattering. Only Aya called his fears immature. Only Aya upbraided him for "upsetting the janquer" while discounting his own fears and concerns. "Oppose me privately," he'd yelled, "not in front of the janquer. They see you flaunting my decisions and despair."

"You won't take my counsel!"

"It's not that I won't take your counsel. It's that I don't agree with it. I hear what you say. I consider what you say. But the final decision is mine. You don't have to like my decisions, but by the gods, you will obey them."

Had Tackta been right, that his behavior and his backtalk were what had gotten him beaten?

He pressed his temples, feeling the pain intensify.

He refused to ask one of the physicians for a headache remedy and would not fix one for himself. He did not want to answer any more questions. He did not want to face explanations or apologies or small talk. He wanted to forget. But like everything else he wanted, it wasn't likely to happen.

# CHAPTER 17

Footsteps back and forth between curtain and door flap, far more than usual, along with rustlings and whispers, finally decided the tug between curiosity and sleep. He raised his head and blinked in the light that streamed through a gap in the curtain. The first thing he noticed was the empty pallet across from him.

Relief that the boy was gone lasted until he realized that the boy had been awake while he slept. He couldn't shake the memory of the hatred in his stare. He now knew how an animal felt upon spotting the carnivore that had selected it for kill.

He strained to see past the curtain—an impossibility at this angle. Then the door flap bulged and he recognized Dee. He struggled onto an elbow. Her eyes crinkled at the corners and he realized with a start that she smiled at him behind her veil.

Dee had taken two steps toward the curtain when Yutrenta stepped through it carrying a sack. Dee accepted the sack, then each turned back the way she'd come.

"What are you doing?" He lurch-crawled toward the central pole, the robe he wore hampering movement and speed.

Yutrenta said something through the curtain, probably, "I can't understand you."

He used the pole to gain his feet and was standing by the time Shurna came through the curtain gripping a drawstring bag in each hand.

"No!" he shouted and startled her into halting.

She stared at him.

"Stop." He waved a damaged hand at the bags she carried, needing her to understand. He'd been sick to the point of death after their last move. He couldn't face another move so soon. "I can't," he told her. "I won't. You don't know what you're asking." He kicked the nearest bag from her hand.

She gave a startled cry, but a scream from the doorway so jarred him, he lost his tenuous hold on the pole. Dee stood inside the doorway, a hand clamped over her mouth. His cheeks burned. He started to apologize when the door flap exploded inward. He locked eyes with the man who leapt at him.

Instinctively, he raised an arm to block the lunge. The collision knocked him off his feet. He lost consciousness when he hit the ground.

*****

Aya felt Kayarra go limp when they hit the mats, but did not loosen his grip until his breathing and sense of time began to return to normal.

"Aya, please!" Denassa cried. "He scared us. That's all. I swear it."

Aya shifted weight onto Kayarra's arms as he pushed up, then released the man's wrists and sat back, straddling a leg. Scabs had torn lose under his grip. Blood smeared his hands. He made fists to keep the blood off his robe.

"What happened?" he demanded.

"He kicked a bag from my hand," Shurna answered. "It startled me. Nothing more."

"Who screamed?"

"I did," Denassa answered.

He looked at her. "Who else has he hit?"

Denassa flushed but did not flinch, much to her credit.

"He hit Shurna once when he woke from a faint," Yutrenta answered. "It was a reaction, not malice."

Aya's anger exploded. "So when he strikes again, it will be frustration rather than malice? Tell me. Does he maim in anger?"

"Aya—"

"No! You listen to me. All of you. Actions show nature. I want him taught to speak. I want no more excuses for violence." He stood.

Yutrenta stepped forward, crouched beside Kayarra, and touched his head, his throat.

Aya turned and glimpsed Manerra in the doorway, holding aside the flap. "Denassa, you will teach him. Everyone will assist her. Everyone will learn his words before we reach Ayahn Rahh."

"We need answers before we enter the Shangren," Manerra said.

"We need nothing more than our own decisions," Aya replied and strode for the door. Denassa and Manerra stepped aside. "You will ride with Kayarra until he can ride alone," he told Manerra as he passed.

*****

He regained consciousness with a start, at once disoriented and alarmed. The ground moved and the world spun. Part of the movement was real—he sat on animal-back. Arms encircled his waist and hands clasped leather straps in front of him. He gagged, shut his eyes, and gagged again, this time bringing up bile. The third retch filled his mouth with his stomach's contents and exploded against the cloth someone had wrapped around his face. He tore the fabric away, but not before slime slid down the neck of his robe.

Again, he gagged—a deep, gut-wrenching spasm that burned his throat. He tried to vomit over the shoulder of the animal but filth hit his cloth-covered knee and streamed down his leg. Moisture soaked through the fabric.

A cry of disgust beside his ear made him wince. The hands in front of him dropped the reins and a shoulder struck his back as his co-rider leapt to the ground. He clamped both hands over the animal's shoulders and gripped its sides with his legs even as he retched again, a painful gag that brought up nothing. He coughed and swallowed, tried to clear his throat, then swallowed again, desperate to prevent another gag. He failed.

Hands grabbed his leg as his eyesight dimmed. He slumped against the animal's neck, fearful of falling. Pain pounded through his temples with the intensity of thunder.

Voices jabbered around him, but the speakers might as well have been a flock of birds. Then the animal ducked and he cried out, certain that even the grip on his leg wouldn't prevent his fall. But the animal's hindquarters dropped down and the blood pressure in his head lessened. He risked opening his eyes although he couldn't lift his head from the animal's neck. He saw a whirling blur of gray. He shut his eyes and didn't open them again even when hands pulled him off the animal's back. They lay him on his side on the ground, where sand stuck to the slime caught in his beard.

All he cared about was the ground: the only solid thing in his world. That they loosened the ties of his robe, pressed handfuls of sand down his neck, and rubbed sand into his beard where his face wasn't already pressed against the ground, he vaguely knew and didn't care. He was far too keenly aware of the earth's spin, of how his pinpoint of ground spun through the planet's thin atmosphere.

He would have thrown up again if there had been anything left in his stomach to evict, if he had had the strength such an effort required.

# CHAPTER 18

Heat waves shimmered off rocks and sand beyond his canopy's small patch of shade. To his right, Manerra's canopy cast a second shadow, but he avoided looking in that direction, not wanting to meet, even accidenttally, Manerra's hostile glare.

He didn't have to close his eyes to envision the slash scar on the boy's hip. The first time he'd seen it—when Yutrenta applied a salve—shock had tingled the length of his body.

He was injured. Manerra was injured. No one else was.

Why were both men gone when he gained consciousness? Where, in this godforsaken place, was there to go?

He rubbed the heel of a hand over the back of the other and winced at the resulting pain; welcomed the temporary reprieve from the maddening itch.

"Kayarra."

His canopy partner had noticed his rubbing and held her hand out in expectation. He placed his hand on Denassa's palm. She dribbled oil from a vial onto the back of his hand, and her too-light touch when she smeared the oil across the discolored skin caused his arm to jerk convulsively. He bore the irritation until she finished, then clenched a fist and grit his teeth over the resulting pain. The skin felt like a newborn's glove stretched over his fist. That it didn't tear each time he flexed his hand amazed him anew.

"When will the goddamn itching stop?" he asked, desperate to know. It was his fantasy that he'd wake one morning, they would answer him, and he'd learn this horror had been a nightmare. But that hadn't happened, and now he spoke in order to hear a voice he understood. He feared forgetting how to talk, or forgetting how to understand any language.

"Your hand."

He gave her his other hand and suffered through the same ticklish, itching treatment. Again, he used pain to counteract the irritation, trying to avoid the use of fingernails on new skin.

The burn of pain passed and the itching returned.

"I'm going fucking insane." He slumped back onto the mat and stared at the roof of the canopy. Its red stripes glowed in the sun. He rubbed the heel of his left hand over the back of his right, the oil decreasing the effectiveness of friction.

Denassa caught his wrist. He jerked out of her grip and rolled onto his side. "You try not scratching," he said.

Knuckles brushed his bare ankle. He jerked and peered past his shoulder. She tugged the hem of his robe down to keep the sun off his feet. He lowered his head.

She wasn't a danger. She was doing her best to aid his recovery. But that was the damn problem. Misery frayed his nerves. He was losing control. If he'd died, he wouldn't be suffering.

Fingers pressed a spot between his shoulder blades, their pressure tentative.

"You're goddamn right to be afraid of me," he said, then swallowed hard, glad his back was turned.

She pressed harder and moved her thumb in a circular motion.

Pain answered her pressure—the pain of clenched muscles—but that pain was not as intense as his desolation. He turned his face into the crook of his arm.

Denassa began talking and he lay still because she continued the massage while she spoke. Although he couldn't understand the tales she told, her voice often lulled him to sleep, and sleep was his sole escape.

"Why do you care?" he asked through the jumble of her words. She stopped talking. "You know, sometimes I think you understand me. How stupid is that?"

"Sahnd," she said.

He squeezed his eyes shut when rising laughter carried him to the verge of tears. "Sand," she had said, not "sad," as he'd first thought. It was their latest word.

When he stopped laughing, she resumed her story, and this time he listened. Eventually, he slept, and dreamed the quiet music of her words into a song of the wind.

# CHAPTER 19

Days later, he waited, balanced atop a rock, one hand pressing his temple, while Manerra brought the shuren around. Neither headache nor resistance was sufficient reason to forfeit a day's travel. He'd learned that lesson the day he refused to mount a shuren and they started away without him. Lacking survival skills, his choices came down to cooperation or death.

Manerra passed. He looked down upon Manerra's cloth-covered head, then up, across the clay-colored back of the shuren Manerra halted in front of him. Kayarra assessed the gap between his body and the shuren's side—greater than he liked—but a strong spring would get his chest across the animal's back. Lying facedown, he could throw a leg over the animal's rump and sit up.

He positioned both hands on the shuren's shoulder and crouched for a spring. The animal sidestepped. He lost his balance, grabbed for Manerra's neck, and caught it. Manerra ducked and turned.

He cried out as his head and shoulder struck the shuren's flank. He slammed into clay and slid across pebbles while massive, three-toed feet shuffled inches from his face. He lay stunned, catching his breath, while the shuren shied.

Manerra said something, the tone derogatory.

Kayarra rolled onto his side and kicked at the boy with all his strength. Cloth tangled his foot and sapped the force of the blow, but he was rewarded by Manerra's cry of pain.

Kayarra jerked upright, palms stinging, arm raised defensively. "Fuck you!" he shouted.

Manerra kicked, a sideways sweep that raked his sandal across Kayarra's thigh. Pain sent Kayarra scrambling to his feet, seeking an opportunity for attack.

A body hurled between them, a knife blade leveled at Kayarra's chest.

Kayarra froze, panting, his attention focused on the oily black blade. Sunlight glinted off the facets that fluted its glassy edges. As slow as melting ice, he released his fists and lowered his hands.

Aya's knife hand didn't waver. His left arm remained outstretched.

". . . back," Aya said.

Manerra took a step back, then another.

"Kayarra, . . . back." Aya's eyes conveyed his readiness to enforce compliance.

Kayarra stepped backward.

"You . . . " Aya began a declaration that ended in "Manerra." At the end, Aya added an expletive that Kayarra interpreted as "Never!"

Kayarra nodded.

"Kayarra!" Aya shouted, and Kayarra understood his mistake in using an affirmation his companions didn't understand.

"Yes," he said.

Only then did Aya lower his knife hand and the arm that protected Manerra. Without glancing aside, Aya asked questions that only Manerra understood, and Kayarra wondered what lies the boy told to make himself appear innocent.

Kayarra glanced past Aya and Manerra and spotted the women. Yutrenta and Denassa stood so close together their sleeves touched; Shurna remained with the horned goats—*mia*, his burgeoning vocabulary supplied . . . all watching them . . . all tense . . . all grave.

"Do you care about my side of the story?" Kayarra blurted.

Aya and Manerra looked at him, and Kayarra was struck by a similarity of stance that linked them into a single unit.

"You son of a bitch," Kayarra told Manerra.

Aya stepped in front of the boy.

Kayarra defiantly held Aya's eyes, but in the end, broke that glare. Maybe his reaction to the fall hadn't been completely justified, but Manerra wasn't blameless either. If he hadn't shrugged him off, he wouldn't have fallen.

Kayarra sat down, closed his eyes, and gripped his aching head in his hands.

"Yutrenta!" Aya shouted, but Kayarra didn't care why. Neither did he try to understand the conversation Manerra resumed. Adrenalin had begun to dissipate and his temples throbbed.

He didn't regret the altercation. It began to answer an ongoing wonder: whether Manerra could have bested him in a fight.

Whatever punishment Aya ordered could hardly isolate him more than he was. Besides, the greater punishment was his rising illness.

A hand gripped his forearm and he blinked into Yutrenta's worry-creased eyes before he noticed the wooden cup she waved under his nose. He took the cup and gulped its contents before he wondered whether she would poison him.

Too late to worry about that now.

Beyond her shoulder, Aya handed Manerra his knife belt, then passed the elaborately tooled pouch that Aya alone carried when they traveled.

Kayarra stiffened.

Yutrenta stood. Kayarra started to rise before Aya said "Kayarra" and motioned for him to follow. Kayarra noticed that Manerra headed toward the shuren they had intended to ride.

Yutrenta accompanied Kayarra, and for that, he was grateful. They passed the rock from which he'd fallen and stopped two feet from Aya. When Aya's attention did not shift from something happening behind Yutrenta, Kayarra glanced over his shoulder.

Manerra led the shuren back to the mounting rock.

Kayarra closed his eyes and wondered whether Aya guessed the severity of the punishment he inflicted by his unwavering intention to travel.

Kayarra pressed his throbbing temples and futilely wished away the pain.

When the shuren stood beside the rock, Aya gripped Kayarra's arm and didn't let go until Kayarra had safely mounted. Throughout, Aya kept himself positioned in front of Manerra. Once Kayarra straddled the shuren, Aya mounted behind him.

Manerra approached to hand Aya the reins and Kayarra resisted an urge to kick him in the face. The experience in the tent, when he'd knocked the sack from Shurna's hand, restrained his impulse. Even unarmed, Aya was dangerous.

# CHAPTER 20

An oily bulge formed on the rim of the wooden spoon and swelled as liquid accumulated at the lowest point of the utensil's curve. Before the drop elongated, Kayarra rotated the spoon so the shimmering substance flowed across the bowl's back and began a new formation on the opposite rim.

A robe's skirt appeared in his peripheral vision. He glanced up, expecting Denassa, but met Manerra's disdain. He looked back at the bowl of the spoon, hoping Manerra would go away, but the drop he had preserved through a dozen rotations had fallen to the ground, cementing and darkening grains of sand into a single flattened ball of . . . not sand, not broth, but something new, something nameless.

Cloth rustled, objects clanked, and Manerra grunted as he sat. Kayarra tensed. Manerra stayed—beside him—when the whole desert stretched around them. If Manerra was cold, he could have chosen the opposite side of the fire.

Kayarra stared at the pot he had been assigned to stir. When Manerra said nothing, Kayarra glanced back. The jerk searched through a cloth sack cradled in the circle of his legs.

Kayarra reached for a folded cloth pad, rose to his knees, removed the pot lid, and stirred the beans and rice.

Surely, supper was almost ready. Kayarra scanned the desert; Shurna hadn't returned with the flock. But Yutrenta bent over a shuren's leg, inspecting its footpad. Her proximity reassured him.

He looked back at Manerra, uncomfortable ignoring his enemy even though he suspected his scrutiny annoyed the boy. He noticed anew the almost feminine curve of Manerra's eyebrows, well spaced above the bridge of his nose. Was Manerra's hateful disposition rooted in conceit or the expectation that he could eventually get his way? He was the youngest, and favored by Aya. Kayarra assumed he was Aya's son and Denassa's brother. Yutrenta was close enough to Aya's age to be his wife. Who Shurna was, he didn't know. Yutrenta's sister? A second wife? A servant? One family group wasn't enough to answer all his cultural questions.

A shudder of dread rattled him. He wasn't ready to encounter more of them, but suspected he couldn't avoid encounters unless he left—and maybe not even then. Until they reached a hospitable region, escape wasn't an option.

Unless they knew him—or others like him—and were taking him home.

"It's that damn language thing," he said aloud without thinking.

Manerra looked up, held his eyes, then returned attention to his activity. Kayarra followed Manerra's gaze and experienced a jolt of shock.

Manerra pushed the short blade of a bronze dagger across a flat stone cupped in his palm. Kayarra started to reach for the knife before he caught himself and redirected his hand to his knee. Manerra gave no indication he'd noticed movement, but Kayarra didn't depend on that. He didn't understand why the susurration of metal against stone hadn't penetrated his rumination.

Kayarra watched the angled blade circle the oiled stone. He now understood why stone knives generated a vague impression of quaintness. He knew metal knives. Stone knives were "wrong."

He wondered whether the knife Manerra sharpened had been his. Did Manerra taunt him with it?

Pain shot across his hand, and Kayarra relaxed the fist he'd unconsciously made. He could put that pain to better use. He shifted weight and stirred the pot in order to keep attention off Manerra.

Nothing the boy did ended up benign.

When he resettled and looked back, the bronze knife lay on the mat between them. Manerra again searched for something in his sack.

He reached for the knife. Its hilt retained the warmth of Manerra's hand.

A black stone blade flashed through his field of vision and halted below his chin.

Kayarra dropped the knife.

He recognized that obsidian blade. For the second time, Aya had drawn it on him. He looked up from the hand that gripped the hilt, jolted to discover that Manerra held the obsidian knife.

The boy balanced on one knee, his free hand braced against the mat. The sack that had occupied his attention lay on the ground.

"Manerra!"

That shout jarred them both. If the knife tip had pressed his throat, it would have cut him.

* * * * *

After that one horrified shout, Aya stood frozen in place by what he'd seen upon leaving the tent. Not until Manerra drew back and Kayarra turned his head was Aya certain Kayarra lived. He knew Manerra's reflexes. Thank gods the shecaren hadn't intended to kill Kayarra.

Anger broke against that wave of relief. "My god, our father, what were you thinking?" Aya shouted.

Manerra stood, turned, and started toward the desert.

"Don't you leave!"

The shecaren stopped.

"Explain yourself. Now."

"He had a knife."

"He's unarmed!"

"He took the one I sharpened."

"Where is this knife?"

"Beside him. On the ground."

"Yutrenta," Aya said, grateful when she started toward Kayarra without need for instruction. She'd come running at his second shout. He heard Denassa's panting breaths behind him.

Yutrenta reached Kayarra and bent to the ground. He saw a flash of gold in her hand. When she approached, he held out his hand. He glanced at the weapon when she placed it on his palm, reached for its tip, and flung it hilt-deep into the ground. The force of that throw wasn't nearly enough to satisfy his need for violence.

"If you so fear him, what were you doing beside him?" Aya shouted. "Carelessness isn't your habit, Manerra. Were you looking for an excuse to kill him?"

"No!" came Manerra's shocked reaction.

"Then why?"

"I wanted to make peace."

"By threatening him?"

"That wasn't supposed to happen."

He took a step toward Manerra, saw him flinch, and stopped. It was better they remain apart. He wasn't certain he could control his need to slap his successor.

"Is your guilt so great you believe Kayarra has reason to harm you?"

Manerra did not answer for so long, Aya thought he intended to defy him.

"Yes, shon regis," Manerra answered as Aya opened his mouth to demand again. The shecaren's whispered reply stunned him into silence.

"Is that why you didn't drink in oath to his protection?" Aya asked when he could speak.

Denassa gasped.

Manerra appeared thunderstruck, but did not deny the accusation, much to Aya's relief.

"I couldn't," Manerra finally said, which wiped out the fragments of Aya's relief and threatened his control.

"It was a choice, Manerra!"

"I intended to drink," Manerra shouted back. "I thought I could. I swear it."

"So when were you going to tell me?"

"When I understood why."

Control teetered on the verge of annihilation.

"*Why* doesn't matter. I would rather you passed the bowl than fake acceptance. Who did you think to fool? Me? Shurna? There are no escorts to impress this trip."

Manerra's head had lowered during the tirade, but at mention of escorts, his head snapped up.

"Aya," Yutrenta whispered.

"I will drink with him, if that's what you want," Manerra cried, voice heavy with anguish.

"I trust no pledge made under duress. I will make decisions based upon your hostility toward Kayarra."

"I saved his life!"

"Because you thought him Thurrang."

"I could have left him in the desert. I didn't."

The breath caught in Aya's throat. "There's more here than an unfair fight," he said. "Remove your belt."

Manerra startled; made no move to comply.

Aya did not shift his attention from Manerra's eyes.

Slowly, Manerra reached for his belt clasp. The shaking of his hands hindered his compliance.

When the belt hung from Manerra's hand, Aya ordered, "Remove your knife sheath."

Another delay while Manerra complied.

Dread reared its head. Aya denied those fears in order to maintain focus.

"Give the sheathed knife to Kayarra," Aya told him at last, prepared for the shecaren's protest but resolute in his decision. The gods help him—help them all—if he misjudged Kayarra's temperament.

Manerra turned, walked woodenly to the firepit, and dropped the sheathed knife on the mat in front of Kayarra.

Kayarra didn't move.

Manerra turned his back on Kayarra, lowered his head, and stood awaiting acknowledgement or dismissal.

"That knife is Kayarra's from this day forth," Aya said, his voice as clenched and cold as his stomach. "If you carry another, it will be one you've made. In the future, know that you insult an armed man. If you draw against him, know that he has the ability to defend himself. And by both gods, in the name of kinship, I pray Acrahh teaches you self-control."

Manerra did not move. His hands, which had betrayed him during compliance, indented his thighs with the force of applied pressure.

"Forget this hatred, Manerra. It will grow and come back upon you. Upon Yatra's nation. You are shecaren. Nothing you do affects only yourself."

"I ask for leave," Manerra said.

"Given," Aya replied, lacking a reason other than anxiety to hold him.

Aya's heart pounded when Manerra's head came up and the shecaren's attention slewed sideways. If Manerra did not cast fear and hatred from him then he would divide the nation, its loyalties split behind two different children of the same god. Aya dared not close his eyes, to see behind those lids a nation driven by civil war.

He watched his brother walk out into the desert, weaponless and angry, understanding the choices that only Manerra could make . . . choices he must decide now if they were to go on. Without so much as a stone to throw, not yet sworn to the Oath of Yatra, Manerra was tremendously powerful; moreso than perhaps even Manerra understood.

*Step back and see what he does to us even when he cannot speak*, Manerra once demanded. *Will you still take him to Ayahn Rahh?*

"He goes to Ayahn Rahh with or without us," Aya whispered to that stiff, departing back. "It's safer if he goes with us. Safer if we go together."

"Aya?" Yutrenta pressed his arm between her hands. He cupped her hand, grateful for her presence but not so easily comforted. "The sun sets," she murmured, drawing him back to duty: an obligation to his father and the nation he could not forsake, even as national unity crumbled with every angry step Manerra took.

He looked back but couldn't hold her gaze. He stepped from her clasp and circled the tent, choosing a direction opposite that taken by Manerra. The shecaren needed time to make up his mind. Any other way and Manerra's resolve would doom them. Aya would rather fight his brother, seeing him strong in what he believed, than stand side-by-side with him under the scrutiny of four tribes, uncertain over the course they took. One way led to disaster as surely as the other.

Aya performed abbah—the reverence of their ancestors—with hands that shook and a voice hoarse with emotion. Rather than shroud the stone at the conclusion of the rite, he fell to his knees and prayed, an old man hunched over a dangerously brilliant stone. He begged Acrahh for guidance in preserving and sustaining Yatra's nation. For Manerra, he asked protection and a long life, and for both of them, he asked the ability to recognize and embrace the right decisions.

When, at last, Aya cloaked the temple stone, his hands burned from the stone's heat, even through the protective chamois that covered his hands. He pressed the cloaked stone between his knees but did not rise. Around him, the desert dimmed and chilled while Ryna and Trys walked the sky, shedding kinder light over shrubs, cacti and deep-rooted grasses than the sun or temple stone afforded. In the stillness, a rodent gnawed a seed and the settling mia bleated. Aya thought that if he spoke Manerra would hear him, but resisted the temptation, even to tell him he loved him. He did not want his desires to confuse Manerra's decision, and certainly did not want the burden of his love laid on him at this time. That, most of all.

At camp, a robed figure crossed in front of the cook fire and Aya suffered an image of Kayarra huddled beside the fire with Manerra's knife in his hands. He hoped that decision was wise. Not for Manerra's sake did he worry as much as for Kayarra's. An armed man was considered able to defend himself, whether or not he could handle the weapon he carried.

When he returned to the tent in the early morning hours, Yutrenta pushed up from his pallet where she'd fallen asleep.

"Manerra has not returned," came her worried whisper.

Aya set aside the temple stone with hands that still smarted and settled cross-legged on the mat beside her. He drew her hand to his knee. "He will not come to harm." Of that, he was certain. He knew Manerra's skills. Danger might come upon him if he slept, but Aya doubted Manerra slept.

"He's unarmed."

"It's one night. He knows the desert. Hush, Trenta. Rest." He pressed her shoulder.

"What about you?"

"I will take my rest in other ways." His thoughts no longer spun a frenetic whirl, but what remained denied comfort. He might lie down upon a mat, but he'd find no relaxation in that action.

Hearing Manerra's decision might permit rest, or eliminate it forever.

"Rest, Trenta," he urged again and stroked her hand.

She settled back upon his pallet and he straightened the blankets over her shoulder, then covered her warm hand with his cold one and watched her close her eyes. After awhile, he thought she slept.

At his back, Kayarra tossed in a haunted sleep. An occasional moan broke through his arrhythmic breaths.

Aya wished for the ability to walk beside him in those dreams, to see what he saw, to learn what he feared. Perhaps such seeing would make wiser his decisions. Did he fight legends, history, and his own brother to secure acceptance for the Kayarran, or let bloodshed decide the outcome? There were no certainties either way.

How could he risk Manerra's love and national unity for the life of a stranger?

He tried to extract assurance from years of instruction but remembered Tackta's viciousness and was left with uneasiness. More influences than his must be tallied in any outcome.

"Consider all things," he'd advised Manerra when they spoke of decision-making. "At its purest, problems involve objects. There are as many solutions as there are sides of an object. Find a third, and a fourth.

Your options are limited only by your angles of viewing. When you understand your options, you will understand your choice." And a warning: "Remember the lesson of the mirage. Deception is part of nature, part of man. But trust that truth can be discovered, even if not immediately."

Despite his distress, he was thankful for the hours Manerra spent away, thankful that the shecaren allowed himself time on a problem of such gravity.

Denassa entered the tent and Aya waved her to wait. "I'll watch the flock," he told her.

"Manerra?" She searched his face.

His movement woke Yutrenta. "He hasn't returned," he told both women at once. Yutrenta's head lowered and her eyelids closed. The worry lines, however, did not smooth, and had not, even in sleep.

Aya accepted the bow, quiver, and staff Denassa offered and stepped into the cold night breeze. Leaning on the staff, he passed through the twin moons' light to where the animals dozed. Once there, he remained as vigilant for the one who did not come home as he did for the stalking carbic.

# CHAPTER 21

Aya stepped through the black curtain and paused, both to allow his eyesight to adjust to the dim shadows and his sensibilities to adjust to a feeling of violated trust. As shon regis, he was not bound by conventions that governed demotic behavior, while being bound by divine laws that governed only he and Manerra. Nevertheless, he did not violate social conventions needlessly, and the curtain that afforded the women privacy was, to him, a symbol of mutual trust.

At last able to discern the locations of sleepers, he shuffled toward the larger of the two shapes. Crouching between their pallets, he whispered Shurna's name.

She reared up with a jerk.

"No danger," he assured her.

"Is Manerra back?" A knife hilt clicked softly against a sheath's wooden rim.

"No. But I request your presence. Attend me when you're ready. Let Denassa sleep." He stood.

"What if Denassa is awake?" a voice near his heels asked.

"Then join us, if you wish." He retreated through the curtain, pausing to blink in the lantern's dim light.

Yutrenta, claiming to have slept as much as exhaustion permitted, stood watch over the mia, while Kayarra slept the sleep of the sick. It was Kayarra's acceptance of the necessity of travel that had decided Aya's decision to give Kayarra the knife—a knife dangerous for anyone not-shecaren to carry, a twin of the one he wore, both engraved with the shecarens' double crescents. As long as Kayarra traveled with the temple ruler's company he remained safe, but that might not always be the case.

Shurna and Denassa pressed through the curtain and stopped, awaiting his instruction.

"Dee, wake him. Please."

Denassa crossed to Kayarra's pallet, knelt, and stroked stray hair from Kayarra's forehead. Aya held his breath. Had she forgotten he was armed?

Kayarra slept through her initial touch and first two strokes. Finally, he flinched, blinked and squinted up at her.

Aya stepped forward, crossed his legs, and sat down beside her.

Shurna joined him. Denassa scuttled aside.

"Peace, Kayarra," Aya said, raising a hand to show his empty palm. "Events have grown serious. I need any information you can share about your tribe."

Kayarra pushed to a sitting position and reached for his robe, donning it while seated.

"I've used the silent speech with him," Denassa said. "It seems easier for him than speech."

"Kayarra," Aya signed as he spoke, "where are your people? Where is your tribe?"

Kayarra frowned.

Aya tried again. "Where is your home?"

"No . . . oh-stand . . . you," Kayarra spoke haltingly.

It took Aya a moment to understood what he'd said. "What does your tribe want?" Aya asked. When Kayarra made no reply: "What does your tribe seek?" Then, in frustration, "Denassa, what words does he know?"

Kayarra burst into speech, the only Yatren word used being "you." Aya studied Kayarra's face as he spoke but saw little more than intense frustration and a yearning to be understood.

"He knows the names of things we can point to and say," Denassa said when Kayarra ran out of words, "and simple actions like 'drink' and 'come.' I don't know how to make him understand 'tribe' or 'family.'"

Aya saw the truth of that in Kayarra's reaction to the words he understood.

Suddenly, Kayarra threw back his blanket, searched the mats between them, then twisted and patted the blanket-covered mat behind him. His hand shot under the cover and withdrew Manerra's sheathed knife. He thrust it toward Aya. When Aya didn't take it, Kayarra tried to shove the sheath under Aya's hand.

Aya caught Kayarra's wrist and gently pushed it back. "Yours," he said.

Kayarra dropped the weapon on the blanket between them. "What?" Kayarra demanded, and then, "You," he pointed at Aya. "You," that finger stabbed at Denassa and Shurna in turn while Kayarra repeated, "What?" Finally, "You?" he pointed to himself.

"Shurna." Aya touched her knee. "Denassa." He pointed to his Ringgangley representative. "Aya." He touched his chest. "You?" he invited Kayarra.

Kayarra repeated his earlier pantomime but used names instead of 'you,' ending with "Ka'arra?"

"Yes," Denassa said.

"No," Aya answered at the same time.

Kayarra emitted a frustrated cry and covered his face with his hands.

"I think he asks whether Kayarra is his name," Aya said, "not whether he is lost." Aya sighed. "We get nowhere here."

"Maybe someone else should teach him," Denassa said.

"No," Aya answered without hesitation. "He learns. In time, he will speak."

"You drink water."

A chill prickled Aya's spine at the clarity and strangeness of that voice. He looked back at Kayarra, who watched him intently.

"D'assa drink water," Kayarra said. "You drink. You, you," he stabbed a finger at each of them, ending with a finger stab in his own chest.

"Yes," Aya said, understanding Kayarra's words but not his question.

Kayarra's eyes brightened with tears and Aya finally understood Kayarra's wish simply to be understood. For the first time in nearly a moon, one of them had spoken and the other had understood more than a single word. Aya returned the stranger's painful smile. "Lady Denassa, you've done well. Shurna . . . ."

"I cannot add to your understanding of him, shon regis," Shurna said in the pause he took to gather his thoughts.

"That wasn't what I intended to ask. I want Kayarra taught Ofrann manners and forms of address. I know the burden I place upon you, but Kayarra's safety requires his acceptance, which will not be an easy thing to win. I will tell Yutrenta." He rose and paused for his legs to stop tingling. Tonight, age weighed heavily, while the lives he safeguarded grew more precious.

He left the tent and halted outside the door flap while his eyes adjusted to the gloom. The eastern horizon bore a faint gray blush. He listened to the chup-chup-twee of cacti-dwelling barra birds and welcomed the chill breeze that fanned his hot cheeks.

One ill-fated decision fifteen years ago had changed the lives of innumerable people, continued to impact his decisions, and would affect the nation long after his death. He had trusted a man and wife to honor a promise they broke. At the time he made that decision, permission to leave Ayahn Rahh had seemed a small thing—an easy decision—beside Hyran's violent attempts to secure an appointment to the janquer. Two years later, that permission turned out to be the worst decision of his life.

In his darkest days, Aya trusted no one, had faith in no decision he or anyone else made. And in the ascension of his successor—the great prize of Tackta's greed and jealousy—he saw the failure of everything he had striven to accomplish. Luckily, those bouts of depression were few, but their legacy left self-doubt.

Even if his veins held not a drop of mortal blood, he reminded himself, he could not control the actions of every man alive. And, thank the gods, Tackta's influence was not alone in Manerra.

This unescorted journey to Ayahn Rahh was, historically, a weaning of the shecaren away from janquer maternity and toward recognition of janquer strengths and equality. But Manerra's early deprivations were confounding that lesson and Aya was losing confidence in his options. Manerra, having fulfilled the obligations of his training, could not be denied the Oath of Yatra if he reached Ayahn Rahh. The janquer were obliged to administer the oath if the shon regis could not, no matter the reason. That law prevented sibling jealousy from interrupting the succession.

"I cannot take your life," Aya whispered across the desert after the fast-fleeing Night. "Whatever else I've failed, I will not fail my sacred obligation to protect you." His eyes burned in the wind. He turned his head aside. After a few breaths, he went to speak with Yutrenta before dawn began anew the daily rites.

# CHAPTER 22

The tent still stood when Aya returned from abbah, and few bags lay on the ground outside the tent. The only notable difference was Kayarra seated beside the firepit, eating.

Aya threw aside the tent flap so hard, the women startled.

"Do not fail me today," he said before they had time to recover.

"We're packing." Yutrenta, as usual, was first to defy him.

"The mia can do so quicker."

"Please, Aya," Denassa pleaded, "let us search for him."

"He went north when he left camp. He's waiting at the Shangren for us even now."

Shurna, carrying a sack from the women's quarters, halted in the juncture between curtain and communal area.

Yutrenta's face reddened. "The blood of a god doesn't flow in our veins," she answered his retort. "Allow us our weaknesses. Allow us our grief."

"He hasn't so much as a water skin," Denassa said.

"He knows our route and our obligations," Aya answered.

"Will you have us pledge fealty before you agree?"

Yutrenta's question chilled his bones. The last thing he wanted was a declaration of loyalties from the janquer.

Shurna spoke before he recovered. "I think it best we not commit ourselves to a single action."

"What if he doesn't return?" Denassa asked.

"Then we know his decision," Aya said with more fortitude than he felt. He crossed to the place his pallet had been and reached for the pack he intended to carry. "I wish to leave before midday," he said.

"Kayarra, stop!" Manerra's shout, heard through the fabric wall, caused Aya to drop the pack. He whirled as Kayarra burst into the tent, eyes wide. Aya brushed past Kayarra's shoulder on his way out.

Halfway to the firepit, Aya stopped and waited while Manerra approached. The shecaren was pale and his brow deeply creased, but he held himself erect and his step did not falter. Manerra passed the firepit before he stopped. "Shon regis." He bowed his head and awaited acknowledgment.

"Shecaren," Aya said.

Manerra lifted his head. In his eyes, Aya saw resignation. "Shon regis," Manerra said and drew a half-circle in the air with two fingers, a sign of reverence, "I wish you to hear my vows before the janquer."

Aya glanced over his shoulder, not surprised that the women flanked him at a distance. He signaled them closer, then faced Manerra. "Speak."

"I recognize that I am shecaren only, unsworn to the Oath of Yatra. Until I am sworn, know that you have my pledge of service. I wish you to hear my counsel, but I know the decisions affecting the nation and every individual in it are yours alone. I pledge not to dispute your decisions with violence." Manerra swallowed. "I swear, Aya, as long as I live, I will not knowingly divide the nation of Yatra. These are all promises I have within my power to give. I ask that you accept them as my solemn vows."

"I accept them," Aya said.

"I ask the janquer to acknowledge them."

Behind Aya, the janquer murmured agreement.

"Shon regis," Manerra said, "Please forgive me for my mistreatment of one in your protection. I would have asked forgiveness from Kayarra but he will not stand before me. I only ask that you not request my love of Kayarra. That, I cannot give."

"I ask that you afford him the same opportunity to prove himself trustworthy that you offer a Yatren in your care."

"I will try. I can't promise more."

"As for forgiveness, you have the same chance any man has. If your actions prove your sincerity, I shall forgive your thoughtless behavior." He drew a breath. "At dawn tomorrow, by rite, I am affirming Kayarra and his people as a tribe of Yatra."

His announcement was met with silence so complete, he heard sand crunch under the weight of a shifting shuren.

"There is no precedence for that," Denassa whispered behind him. "Nothing that explains their existence."

Aya did not shift his attention from Manerra's face. The shecaren's stun had transformed into horror.

"The only one you protect him from is me," Manerra said, at last, in a gusty breath, as though his mouth had gone dry. "There are less drastic ways to assure his protection."

"None I choose to pursue," Aya answered.

With a badly shaking hand, Manerra sketched acceptance. He stood paler than he'd been upon arrival.

"We were packing," Aya said. "That task needs to be finished." He turned and strode toward the tent, past the statues that were his janquer, whose robes fluttered in the wind and whose eyes followed his departure. No one moved. No one spoke.

Kayarra stood in the tent's doorway.

An irrational dread stole Aya's breath, as if Kayarra were death instead of flesh and bone. In that instant, he feared touching him.

He reached the tent, gripped Kayarra's shoulder, and urged him back inside. This stranger was not the challenge he wished to face in his final years.

Aya was packing when the janquer entered.

"Janquer lady Denassa," he said. Dread flooded her eyes, "place your sewing supplies where you can reach them. You'll have need of them at midday."

"Yes, shon regis."

He had already packed the item he needed.

*****

During packing, Kayarra's spirits soared despite the ominous silence. Aya had confronted his idiot son. That miracle relieved a burden of anxiety. That they expected him to walk rather than ride seemed of little consequence. He could have flown had they asked that of him.

Yutrenta, gripping a shuren's lead rope, touched his arm and walked beside him. She passed the time teaching him a phrase, then had him repeat it until his pronunciation satisfied her. What the words meant, he had no idea, but he linked the syllables to the rhythm of their steps until he'd created a song of sorts. The trick worked so well, the rhythmic sounds sang in his head long after she'd outpaced him.

More and more, their nouns replaced his words in his thinking. He looked at a rock and identified it with their word, not his, bypassing the translation process he'd used in the beginning. He'd recently startled awake from a dream in which he spoke bilingually. That remained a peculiar memory. He supposed the dream meant he no longer feared forgetting how to talk in a language only he spoke.

When they rested that afternoon, Manerra and Shurna shared a canopy near the animals and Aya and Denassa shared another, which left Kayarra sharing shade with Yutrenta. He watched Denassa, curious whether she'd recite stories to her father, but she passed the time decorating a robe. He returned his attention to Yutrenta, who had withdrawn packets from a leather bag and now sprinkled dried leaf fragments over a handful of crumbled flatcake. When she finished, she closed her fist around the bits of bread, crushing them into a finger-indented mass that she carried to Manerra and Shurna's canopy.

Kayarra stopped watching Yutrenta as soon as he realized that her activities benefited Manerra. The boy didn't need coddling, he needed a slug; preferably from Aya, who seemed least likely to do it.

Kayarra reached for the sheath that now hung from a belt Denassa had given him. He withdrew the knife, held the blade by its central ridge, and studied the hilt, amazed anew by the skill required to shape such a piece of art. A rearing doe formed the hilt, the same circle and crescent symbol seen on Aya's pouch, carved between the tightly bend forelimbs of the doe. The deer's tucked head formed the butt of the weapon, the fur between her ears, rubbed smooth from years of handling. Kayarra dug grime from an incised line with a thumbnail, then stroked the circular symbol and an eye.

Manerra could not be happy about losing such a treasure. Kayarra wondered what promise he could barter in exchange for the knife. Although, for beauty alone, he would regret returning it.

He replaced the blade in its sheath, careful to secure the tip inside the wooden rim before pressing it home. A shallow cut on his thumb attested to last night's curiosity about its edge. The black blade was volcanic glass. Obsidian. If there existed a sharper rock when broken, he didn't know it.

He glanced back at Denassa, watched her take a few stitches in the blue fabric that filled her lap, then settled onto his side, kicking the hem of his robe until it covered his feet. Seeing her sew during their noon stop felt odd. She'd only ever sewn during his convalescence. Maybe she mended Aya's robe; or sewing was her way of passing time when she wasn't telling stories. Before he fell asleep, Yutrenta returned to their canopy. He remembered nothing else until she woke him to begin their afternoon trek.

By the time they'd established camp, Kayarra doubted his ability to cross from the firepit to his pallet. He fell asleep in the fire's warmth before supper. Denassa roused him to eat. He chewed dutifully, then stumbled to bed, vaguely aware that Denassa had resumed sewing by the light of the campfire.

Snores sounded from the section of tent floor Manerra's pallet typically occupied. Kayarra wondered with resentment why the boy had been allowed to sleep through supper when he hadn't. Manerra starving to death was probably more than he could hope for.

Kayarra avoided the area near Manerra's pallet, undressed, and fell asleep soon after his head indented the pillow.

*****

A hand stroke down his arm was Denassa's method of waking him, so he wasn't alarmed until he opened his eyes and saw everyone—Manerra included—standing behind her. He'd seen before the under-robes they wore—"tribal robes," the term surfaced—but never worn by everyone at the same time, as they did now. Unlike the gray outer robes, tribal robes were brightly colored, ornately pleated, and embellished across the chest with beads, shells, and embroidery. The women wore pale blue robes; the men wore white. Aya's and Manerra's robes were decorated with the crescent-inside-the-circle symbol he recognized from the knife and Aya's pouch. Smaller versions of the same symbol decorated the right shoulders of the women's robes. Similarities ended there. A triangle intersecting a circle decorated the breast of Shurna's robe, a palm tree superimposed upon a circle decorated Yutrenta's, and a fish leaping a wave embellished Denassa's.

He stared until Denassa tugged his arm. "Come," she urged.

He reached for clothes that were not where he'd left them. He widened his search.

"Come." Denassa tugged harder, wanting him to stand.

"Robe," he said.

"No. Come."

His heart pounded.

Denassa tossed off his blankets. He grabbed to snatch them back, but she caught his wrist in a surprisingly strong grip and yanked, insisting upon obedience.

He obeyed, with all eyes watching. Manerra's revulsion caused his cheeks to burn. He looked toward Aya, who turned and started toward the door flap. "What's going on?" he demanded in his language.

"Come." Denassa tugged him toward the door.

"No!" he shouted.

Aya spun, passed Shurna and Denassa, and gripped the arm Denassa wasn't holding. "Come, Kayarra," he ordered. The narrowing of his eyes warned of his intention to enforce cooperation.

Kayarra took a hesitant step toward the door, then another.

If Aya intended to end through violence the fighting, threats, and tension, would he have given him Manerra's knife?

Manerra's knife had disappeared along with his clothes.

Denassa released his arm, but Aya propelled him through the door, and didn't release him until they stopped walking, well away from camp. Kayarra shivered with cold in the predawn breeze. Surely, Aya would not have been so mindful of his bare feet around rocks and low-growing cacti if he intended to kill him.

Aya gripped Kayarra's shoulders and turned him until he faced the rising sun.

* * * * *

When Aya stopped walking, Manerra circled to Kayarra's elbow and the janquer formed a semi-circle behind them. Manerra squinted into the translucent band of gray-white clouds that separated earth and sky. A barra bird, perched on a nearby cactus, screeched before darting away, its body a silhouette against the breaking dawn.

Out of the corner of his eye, Manerra saw Kayarra open his mouth. Aya touched Kayarra's lips.

"Close your eyes." Aya covered Kayarra's eyes.

Aya removed his hand, again commanded, and again touched the cor-anda's eyes. On the third command, Aya smiled, and Manerra assumed the man-thing had voluntarily closed its eyes.

*Good pet.* Manerra looked away across the desert. *One blinding by the temple stone would have taught the same lesson.*

Aya's trust was dangerously rash. By teaching the cor-anda to talk, the creature could learn about their tribes while sharing nothing about his own.

Manerra removed his veil and head covering and shook free his braids. Much of the day's dust remained locked in frost and dew, but it still felt dangerous to breathe the raw air.

Manerra tossed his head cloths beside Yutrenta's foot and she stepped on them so they wouldn't blow away. On the other side of Kayarra, Aya removed his head coverings and handed them to Denassa.

Did Vantrann's absence mean the Thurrang didn't have to recognize the Kayarran as a tribe of Yatra?

Foolish wishing.

Manerra rested a hand on the water skin at his belt and stared at his brother, willing Aya to stop this sham with a simple signal for abbah. Then their eyes locked and anger choked him. Aya did this to protect the cor-anda from him—as a test of his vow of compliance.

"Close your eyes," Aya ordered.

Aya lifted the flap on the temple stone's pouch and Manerra knew the order was no longer a game of instruction. With every nerve and fiber rebelling against the rite, Manerra closed his eyes and freed the water skin from his belt hook.

The temple stone flared.

"Acrahh, father and most powerful god," Aya's voice matched the power of the burning stone, "your children welcome the return of your sun. Let its light guide the way for all Yatren who seek your wisdom, even as its light nurtures the bounty of your harvest.

"At this new beginning, your living son Aya . . ."

"Your living son Manerra," Manerra said.

" . . . bring before you a child of an unknown tribe. We ask that you judge him, and if he is worthy, accept him into the haven of your safekeeping."

Manerra raised the mouth of the water skin to the place he'd last seen Kayarra's shoulder. His knuckles struck bare skin. He lifted the bottom of the water skin. Kayarra jerked, but Manerra kept his knuckles pressed against Kayarra's flesh while he circled. Water streamed across Manerra's fingers . . . water they had risked their lives to acquire.

*I clung to the shuren's cheek strap to keep from falling that final day of travel.*

"The child who comes to us without a name," Aya said, "I name Kayarra after the manner of his founding."

*Even after reaching camp, our suffering did not end.*

"His tribe shall be called the Kayarran, in honor of their lost son."

*Nothing the cor-anda—or any man—sacrifices forgives blasphemy.*

"To the Kayarran, I bequeath the sun, symbol of the spirits of the faithful. May Kayarran service in our gods' names nurture strength and unity throughout Yatra's nation."

Manerra finished the anointment and fumbled to hook the nearly empty water skin to his belt. Even overlooking the life-threatening waste of water, this rite was wrong.

"Let no harm befall those who cleave to Acrahh's law."

*Where does that leave us?*

Manerra joined Aya in the refrain, "Blessed is Acrahh, our father, above all gods, and blessed are Yatra's children who honor his word." Then the janquer joined them in the vow of their covenant, "Peace to all the nation through eternity."

At last, the light dimmed and Manerra blinked against the glare of sunlight. He reached back to take a folded blue robe from Yutrenta. Their hands collided. His clumsiness disturbed him.

"Stay," Aya said, and Manerra startled, hoping his brother intended to forego the remainder of the ceremony.

Aya held Kayarra's arm, and released it to reach for the robe Manerra gripped.

With hands gone numb, Manerra helped Aya gather the robe's skirt.

When each could hold no more cloth, Aya said, "Kayarra, name the tribes that have come before you."

"Ofrann," Yutrenta prompted.

Kayarra looked over his shoulder.

"Kayarra!" Aya demanded his attention and got it. "Name the tribes that have come before you."

"Ofrann, Ringgang—" Yutrenta whispered.

"Ofrann-Ringgangley-Kitarin-Thurrang-Manteen," Kayarra named them as if they were a sentence rather than separate tribes, repeating something memorized and meaningless.

Aya lifted the robe and Manerra moved with him, stepping close enough to position the robe's open neck above Kayarra's head. Kayarra raised his hands as if to stop them and Manerra hissed, "No!" Together, he and Aya lowered the robe over Kayarra's head. They waited while he fumbled for the sleeve openings, then Manerra stepped away. Aya released the robe, waited while Kayarra straightened it, then embraced the cor-anda. "Welcome, Kayarra, son of the Kayarran, lost child of Yatra."

When Aya stepped aside, Manerra stepped forward, keenly aware of his brother's scrutiny. Manerra's flesh crawled where it contacted Kayarra in embrace. "Welcome, Kayarra," he forced the words, "son of the Kayarran, lost—" His throat shut down on the lie. He jerked free of the embrace, so horrified by the farce that he couldn't watch the janquer repeat the welcome. He started toward camp before he stopped himself, then stared at the ground until the fog that obscured his eyesight cleared. Only then did he look back. Shurna withdrew from her embrace and looked down at the sun that adorned Kayarra's breast. The radiance of her smile chilled him.

How could she approve of what they had done? Did she think the man-thing would be accepted by anyone with eyesight?

*Aya ordered it*, memory placed blame.

*But the consequences are my inheritance. If the Kayarran are like the Manteen . . .*

# CHAPTER 23

Kayarra slid his fingers along the valleys and ridges of the scallop shell sun that adorned his robe, amazement battling denial. Manerra started back to camp, but it was Denassa's approach that finally shifted his attention away from the sun. Her brow had creased, and her eyes searched his as if seeking answers to troubling questions.

"Kayarra, come." Aya gestured toward camp.

Kayarra hastened after Aya, his attention on the ground and the placement of his bare feet. He clung to the memory of Shurna's eyes, to her pleasure welcoming him into their family group, an approval he hadn't realized he'd wanted so desperately.

When he glanced up, he watched Aya's and Yutrenta's white and blue backs as they walked side-by-side. They had donned tribal robes for his dressing ceremony. All of them, including Manerra. He stroked the finely woven wool on his right, front shoulder. The circle and crescent, absent from his robe, must be a family symbol. He wondered what the designs on the women's robes meant.

They reached camp and one-by-one, passed into the tent. Inside, Kayarra discovered his gray robe, belt, sandals, and loincloth lying atop his disheveled pallet. Denassa touched his forearm when he reached for his belt and made him understand through gestures and words that he was to wear only his new robe and sandals. She gave him a drawstring sack for his belongings and indicated that he should pack his bedding, as well.

When they began the day's travel, Kayarra carried all his possessions—everything his caretakers had given him, including the sack that contained them. By day's end, the drawstring's cord had abraded each shoulder, and his back muscles cramped. Kayarra sat beside the cook fire trying to reach and massage the aching muscles, dreading tomorrow's trek.

A metallic clunk drew Kayarra's attention to Denassa, who had replaced the lid on the cook pot. She circled him, pushed aside his groping fingers, and pressed her thumbs against the fist-tight muscle in the center of his back. He jerked in pain.

Denassa massaged his back until Yutrenta arrived carrying an assortment of cloth and leather-covered bundles and arranged the bundles in a semi-circle upwind of the fire. Then the men arrived for supper, and Shurna left the flock to join them.

While seats were chosen and supper bowls passed, Kayarra stared at the full moon. The smaller moon, a sliver of a crescent, hung barely visible above the cloudless horizon. He reached for his robe's sun and looked across the flames at the symbol glittering on the shoulder of Aya's robe. The moons and sun sat on opposite sides of the fire. He wondered at the irony of that, then wondered where the symbolism placed him in a hierarchy he didn't understand.

When Aya signaled the end of meal, Denassa caught Kayarra's arm and signaled him to stay, while their companions reached for the bundles Yutrenta had placed about the fire. The bundles held ornately painted and inlaid tubes; a small, bulbous gourd with wooden tubes protruding from either end; and in Aya's lap, an hourglass-shaped drum intricately laced with white rope. Aya held the hollow base of the drum above the fire, while Denassa slipped a polished, hollow log from its suede cover.

* * * * *

When instruments were taken up at meal's end and Yutrenta began playing, Denassa discovered that she wasn't alone in her search for balance. The tune Yutrenta played evoked images of sand grains blowing off the eaves of dunes, their settling creating new forms from the old structures.

When Yutrenta concluded her song, Shurna tried to lighten the mood with a bird song, but Manerra, who normally bested all musical challengers, unexpectedly quit playing, leaving Shurna and Yutrenta competing for the title of Songbird. Shurna finally conceded to Yutrenta with a gasp and a laugh.

The first to quit a bird song was next to play, and within three notes, Denassa recognized Manerra's choice: an ancient tune attributed to Yatra. She matched her drum's voice to Aya's beat, but one by one, their companions' instruments fell silent, until her own tears threatened and she stopped playing, leaving Aya's drum and Manerra's flute to conclude the song. Music had always been the voice of Manerra's soul, and this evening his flute spoke with exquisite pain of a lost homeland and the search for hope.

Denassa watched Kayarra as the musicians played, his expression full of wonder and awe. She smiled in sorrowful pride at Manerra's ability to touch even a stranger's heart—while his music stirred the well of grief buried in her own chest.

Silence followed the conclusion of Manerra's song. His flute, a decorative length of hollow wood, once again lay in his lap. Of his face, only the top of his head and a curtain of braids were visible.

Someone sniffled and a scattering of laughter broke the tension.

Yutrenta lifted her veil and wiped her nose. "Tell me you were not moved," she blustered in response to the laughter.

"I cannot," Shurna confessed.

"Shon regis, I ask for leave," Manerra spoke, his voice hoarse.

Aya hesitated, obviously wanting to deny Manerra's request. "Go," he finally said.

Denassa caught a fleeting glimpse of Manerra's face as he rose. It was flushed with grief. Her desire to go with him was strong, to be with him even if words found no useful place between them, but she remained seated, bound by covenant to his brother. Despite the tears, this celebration honored and welcomed a new tribe into the nation of Yatra, which had not happened since the Manteen were recognized as a separate tribe, an event described in stories handed down from one historian to the next. Besides, she was least among the janquer—only Vantrann had served the shecarens fewer years—and Manerra had paid dearly for his privacy.

# CHAPTER 24

Kayarra wiped his hands down his thighs before accepting the reins from Manerra. Controlling the shuren was frighteningly different from clinging to the animal with the hope of not falling. Adrenalin sharpened his senses, made him keenly aware of the size and strength of the animal he straddled; the distance to the ground; the pressure of Manerra's knees against the backs of his thighs.

Kayarra flicked the end of the reins against the shuren's neck the way Manerra had shown him. A shiver ran down the animal's neck. Kayarra struck harder. This time, she took a step forward, shook her head, and stopped.

" . . . your leg." Manerra leaned into his back and slapped Kayarra's knee.

Kayarra rammed his elbow into Manerra's ribs and Manerra pulled back. "Talk—" he said before Manerra's knuckles slammed into a kidney.

Kayarra gasped, frozen by pain. By the time he could draw breath, Manerra's shoulder had jostled his back and the boy had dropped to the ground. The shuren sidestepped. Kayarra dropped the reins and grabbed the animal's shoulder fur for balance.

"Shit on you!" Kayarra shouted, sure that Manerra understood the menace if not the words. "You just wait." Manerra didn't look back, which only increased Kayarra's anger. He looked from the fallen reins to Manerra's retreating back and fought an impulse to kick the shuren hard and drive her against Manerra's back.

Kayarra leaned forward, swung his leg over the shuren's croup, lost his flimsy grip in the animal's fur, and fell. He scrambled to regain his feet, dignity and bruises forgotten in the fear of being trampled.

Safely away from the shuren, he whispered, "Fuck you," turned, and started walking, not caring where he went as long as it wasn't back to camp. Let Manerra take the blame for the shuren's escape. Let Aya know there were consequences for forcing Manerra on him. If Aya wanted to yell, fine. He couldn't understand most of what Aya said, anyway.

* * * * *

The ghost of a moon, one day away from full, hung in the afternoon sky above the cactus Kayarra used as a target. It was odd to see Ryna, the larger of the two moons, in daylight, but not until this moment did he remember the last time he'd seen the moon full: the first time he'd heard Manerra play a flute, the night of his dressing ceremony.

How ironic that Manerra's flute playing was the thing he remembered most poignantly from that night. Maybe it was the contradiction between the boy's viciousness and the beauty of the song that gave the memory such lingering clarity.

Kayarra pulled on the bow cord, sighted along the arrow's shaft, and raised the point higher than his imaginary bull's-eye in an effort to compensate for the weight of the tip and the distance. Wind had something to do with accuracy, but what, and how it factored in, escaped his fledgling skill. For now, he hoped the wind blowing against his back would propel the arrow toward the cactus without sending it too far off mark.

A movement in the corner of his eye startled him just as he released the bowcord, and when cord friction-burned the inside of his arm, he didn't have to see the arrow miss its mark to know he'd overshot the cactus.

"You lack . . . ." Manerra started.

Kayarra dropped the bow and whirled, his fist rising as he turned. Swifter still, Manerra's arm deflected the blow and his "No!" held unfeigned fear.

Shocked by Manerra's reaction, Kayarra aborted his attack.

Manerra lowered his arm, turned, and walked away as if nothing had happened.

Kayarra watched Manerra leave, too stunned to move, while the boy's "No!" played and replayed in memory. Manerra's fear was not of him. He was sure of that.

When Manerra reached camp, Kayarra picked up the bow, felt for damage to the wood, then went to retrieve arrows. The two he pulled from the cactus he cleaned of sap, then went in search of the third. He found it embedded in the ground and pulled it free. Anger returned when he saw the broken point. Denassa had been reluctant to lend him her bow. A broken arrowhead was likely to end future generosity.

Kayarra grimly returned to camp, stopped beside the cold firepit, and waited until Denassa finished counting out handfuls of dried seed. She looked up from her bowl and reached for the bow when he extended it. "Arrow break," he told her.

"Manerra told me," she said. "You have the shaft?"

He gave her the broken arrow, puzzled by her statement. She looked at the point, then set the shaft aside.

"Who hit Manerra?" he blurted.

Her attention returned, her surprise obvious. "No one," she said.

"I hit Manerra," he told her. "I—" He drew back a fist. "Manerra—"

He demonstrated Manerra's reaction; saw her frown.

Denassa looked away, pulled a stick from the pile of fuel beside the fire pit, then began smoothing a patch of sand.

Kayarra set aside the quiver and crouched beside her. She drew a stick figure with breasts, another with a penis. Below those, she drew a single line; above them, a circle. "Manerra," she named the single line. The circle, she called "Acrahh." It was a name from the stories she told. The words she used for the man and woman were not ones he recognized.

"Aya?" he pointed to the man, "Yutrenta?" he pointed to the woman.

An odd expression he couldn't interpret transformed Denassa's face. She waved him to silence.

"Name, Tackta," she indicated the man. "Name, Matera," she indicated the woman. "Tackta hit Manerra," she said.

Kayarra stared at the primitive drawings.

She pointed to the circle. "Acrahh," she named it, "Matera," the woman, "Manerra," the line.

"Aya?" Kayarra asked.

Denassa drew another female figure beside the first and a second line beside the line representing Manerra. "Acrahh," she indicated the circle, "Inja," she named the new woman, "Aya," she named the new line.

Understanding came with stunning force. Aya and Manerra were stepbrothers. Manerra's stepfather hit him. That's why Aya protected Manerra.

Were all his assumptions wrong?

"Who is Yutrenta?" he demanded.

"Aya's Ofrann janquer."

"Who is you?"

"Aya's Ringgangley janquer."

He recognized the words from his dressing ceremony. "Who is Ofrann-Ringgangley-Kitarin-Thurrang-Manteen?" he recited the phrase the way he'd learned it.

Denassa smoothed the sand and drew six semicircles, their curves facing inward, so the resulting image looked a bit like his sun. "Ofrann batok." She pointed to one of the semicircles.

"Yutrenta batok?" he asked.

"Yes," she answered and named each of the semicircles, using his name's variation on the last one.

"Kayarra." He stabbed the last bowl shape. "Who is batok?"

"*What* is batok," she corrected and spread her fingers in a gesture of helplessness.

After a momentary silence, she drew a male and female figure under the sun, naming each as she finished it, then drew a single line underneath them. She stabbed the single line. "Denassa." She spread her hand over the three-figure diagram and said a word while watching him.

"Family?" he asked in his language.

She repeated her word, then drew numerous hash marks surrounding the family diagram. When she finished, she waved her hand over the hash marks and the family. "Ringgangley batok," she said.

Something larger than a family. Maybe an extended family.

Kayarra stared at the depressed curve in the sand that represented his batok. "You, Aya, Yutrenta, Shurna walk to Kayarra batok?" he enunciated each word with care.

"Yes," she said, and that affirmation brought a rush of emotion that threatened his composure. He looked away, toward the shuren.

She pressed his arm.

He looked back. "How I wake? How I no talk Denassa talk? How you no talk Kayarra talk?" he demanded.

He saw the frown that frequently appeared when he attempted more than two-word sentences.

"I don't know," she said, and he didn't know whether she was confused by his questions or could not account for their differences.

"How I come—" He stabbed the ground between them.

"Manerra . . . you."

His heartbeat accelerated before he realized she misunderstood. He didn't mean the days spent on shuren back traveling to this exact location. He tried again. "I wake. I hurt." He didn't know words for time, for "before." He touched the soft spot on his head but jerked his hand away, still disturbed by that violation.

Denassa reached for his head but he jerked back. He didn't want her touching the spot either, as irrational as that was.

He realized that he'd confused his initial question, and now distress interfered with his ability to assemble his vocabulary into coherent sentences. He started to stand, but Denassa caught his sleeve.

"Stay," she said and started talking.

He watched her while she spoke; watched her hands, her eyes, her face. He heard Manerra's name, and Yutrenta's . . . and slowly realized that she told him what he most wanted to know: how he'd been injured; why he lived with them . . . and he understood nothing more than that vague realization.

He stopped himself from rubbing the back of his left hand with the heel of his right.

That Manerra was involved with his injuries wasn't a surprise. That Yutrenta was somehow involved, was. Or, maybe it wasn't surprising. Yutrenta and Denassa had alternated care of him during those early days of pain, fever and hallucination. The memories were fragmentary and vague, but there.

"Say to me . . . ." He sketched a circle in the air because he didn't know their word for "later."

Denassa started talking again. "No," he stopped her. "I no—" He tapped his temple.

"Understand?" Denassa supplied.

"Understand," he repeated, and again to himself, to set the word into memory. "Say to me a day. When I understand. Yes?"

"Yes," she said the word he was desperate to hear.

He rubbed his forehead. She touched his arm. He held up a hand to indicate he was all right and forced a smile. "Thank you." He stood up, headed toward the tent, passed it, and kept walking.

When he finally stopped, he stood beside a whorl cactus. He knew its name only because Denassa had told him. He squatted and reached toward a spike. The needle pricked his finger. He jerked back.

Gratitude for the predictability of that pain dissolved into anger. He brought his fist up, intending to crush the cactus, but brought it down upon sand. He drew his hand back and watched beads of blood ooze from abraded knuckles.

Two months he'd been with them. At least two. If anyone searched for him, they would have found him by now.

He stood and pivoted. The tent was the only man-made structure as far as he could see.

Why did that fact frighten him now? Because Denassa had destroyed the neat order he'd assigned to his companions when he had wanted something—anything—to make sense? Did it really matter that Aya wasn't Manerra's father? Far more disturbing was having strangers tell him his name because he didn't know it.

He paced, but his consternation wouldn't ease. If he was wrong about their relationships, what else had he gotten wrong?

# CHAPTER 25

Denassa topped a rise, spotted a verdant splash of color on the northern horizon, and stopped walking. Had Manerra, Yutrenta, or Kayarra, who walked ahead of her, seen that green? If they had, they gave no indication.

Denassa looked west, seeking comfort from the jagged peaks of the Rahhe Mountains still visible on the horizon. The Rahhe . . . home. North of the Shangren, the peaks would disappear from view, but for now, their northern-most reaches provided an emotional link to family and tribe. She imagined walking sunblind into the west, going home.

"Are you well?"

Denassa started, looked back. "The Shangren." She pointed north, watching Aya's eyes as he approached. Abreast of her, he stopped, his attention on that distant green, his eyes unreadable.

"I've never been afraid to approach the Shangren before," she said.

Aya's attention returned to her. "You will have an escort for the duration of our stay. All commensal companions will."

"Commensal," not "janquer," he'd said, revealing his concern for Kayarra's safety.

"Walk with me," Aya invited and angled across the hill, avoiding the mia as they streamed over the hilltop. Shurna trailed the animals, wind billowing her robe, her crook serving as a walking stick.

"A pleasure!" Shurna called and offered veneration.

"Not now, Shurna," Aya pleaded. "There will be enough formality in the days ahead. I want friends, not counselors, today."

"Sometimes it's not easy separating the two," Shurna said.

"Gods forebear!"

Denassa's head snapped around. Aya's exclamation was as close to a curse as she'd ever heard him come.

"Aya, I'm sorry," Shurna said.

"I'm sorry, Shurna, Denassa. I'm not fit company today." Aya turned aside, leaving them.

"Aya!" Shurna cried.

He lifted a hand without turning, did not stop walking.

Denassa watched him leave until she stumbled, then returned her attention to her feet. "He's not been this tense since Thurra," she said.

"That was upset," Shurna said. "This is different."

Denassa glanced into Shurna's troubled eyes. "Has he confided in you?"

"No. I'd have been surprised if he did."

"May I?"

Shurna's attention rounded on her. "I don't have any answers, Dee."

"I need camaraderie more than answers."

"I can't talk about Manerra." Shurna tapped the rump of a lagging mia with the worn end of her crook.

"It's Kayarra I'm worried about."

Shurna smiled. "Two moons ago, you feared him."

"I know. And that's what scares me. I'm not a village girl, Shurna. If he so frightened me, how much worse will be provincial reactions?"

"The Shangren Oasis is hardly provincial. Its traders accept differences as readily as the Ringgangley."

"I'm Ringgangley," Denassa whispered through a tightening throat.

Shurna sighed. "It's not you or Aya, Denassa. It's me. I'm fated to offend anyone I speak to."

"I'm not offended, Shurna, I'm scared. I can't reconcile Aya's vision of Kayarra with Manerra's. How can one shecaren be right, the other, wrong?"

"They don't have to be right or wrong. Two brothers can represent different sides of the same leaf."

"If you see them that way, please explain, because I can't. Our explanations must influence Ofrann acceptance of the Kayarran, and I don't know what to say."

Shurna lifted her hand in a gesture of helplessness. "I don't have answers, Dee. Only a suspicion that the shecarens balance each other. Which is hard on them when patience is frustrated by impatience; caution, by apparent recklessness."

"That intimates the shecarens are divided, that they have weaknesses. In a crisis—"

Shurna interrupted, "Hyran claimed the shecarens could not dress without janquer assistance, and yet their strength and positions survived the lie."

Frustration overpowered Denassa's reticence. "To kill with a bow keeps blood from your hands. But do clean hands mean you didn't kill?"

"Dee, I understand your anxiety. What I don't understand is whether you fear for Kayarra's safety or ours."

"For Kayarra. Even with escorts."

"The Shangren's citizens will see our acceptance of him."

"They will see Manerra's hatred of him." Too late, Denassa searched for Manerra, spotted him far enough ahead that she doubted he had heard her remark.

Shurna walked with her attention on the mia.

"Manerra's confided in you, hasn't he?" Denassa guessed.

"I told you earlier, I cannot speak of him."

"How do the Kitarin-trained live with knowledge they can't share?"

"Aena became a gardener. I became a herder."

Aena, Shurna's sister, whose fame as a reader spread among the Kitarin before she broke under the strain. Aena, who did not remember she had a sister.

Denassa tried to think of something to say that was neither personal nor critical, but could not think beyond the blessing of the city on the morrow.

"Tell me the legend of the founding," Shurna requested, sparing Denassa the awkwardness of a reply.

"Please, Dee," Shurna urged, and Denassa realized she'd hesitated even to do the safe thing.

Denassa fixed her attention on the Shangren's trees. "Long before men occupied Axxord, the god Acrahh shared the heavens' glittering beauty with Crysus, his consort. They lived in peace and prosperity, their union fruitful. But in their wanderings, they met a jealous god who saw in their riches an opportunity for power. He sent demons to take by force what he failed to obtain through guile. But Acrahh learned of this danger and sent Crysus to find safe haven while he faced the demons alone.

"Crysus fled across the heavens until she discovered Axxord, and settled in the valley of Ayahn Rahh. There, she and her children awaited Acrahh, who swore to join them after he slew the last demon.

"Years fled, and Acrahh's children multiplied with children of their own, and those children who were strangers to Acrahh grew restless. When Crysus could hold them no longer, she gifted the temple stone to her firstborn, Yatra. With that gift passed responsibility for the land's steward.

"Thus graced with Crysus's blessing, Yatra left the valley of Ayahn Rahh with his children and those siblings who loved him best. From the summit of Mt. Tayenya, they looked down upon the land for the first time. To the north spread an endless forest. To the west, cold and poisonous water. In the south, wind blew sand into wondrous patterns, and east lay mountains of fire.

"The youngest children begged to venture north, but Yatra's heart heard the song of the desert and yearned to climb its mountains of sand. S-so, atop Mt. Tayenya, the first division of Acrahh's children took p-place." Denassa stopped talking. This was not an auspicious tale to tell upon their approach to the Shangren. It damned Kayarra and made a farce of the rite that claimed the Kayarran as a tribe of Yatra.

"Why did you stop?" Shurna asked.

"Why did you ask for this story?"

"I wonder if the children who descended Mt. Tayenya further divided when they reached the forest. Kayarra could be the first of those lost children to return."

Kitarin history contained no tale of tribal division. Shurna, of all people, must know that. Besides, all of Yatra's siblings, being descendants of a single father, shared Acrahh's hair and skin color. "Even if an albino man is possible, is revered by the Kayarran," Denassa said, "that doesn't account for his eyes. An albino's eyes change color, they don't change . . . everything."

"We will have answers when we locate his people." The swing of Shurna's crook matched her stride.

"Meanwhile, we face the Shangren and the joining without answers. By the time we learn what he is, fear and prejudice will have set Kayarran fate. It would be kinder to hide him until we know who he is, until we know what we're doing."

"Hiding is not Aya's way."

"I know."

A mia stopped to strip leaves from a bush. Shurna commanded it to move. When it did not, she rapped it with her crook and the animal sprinted forward, jostling stragglers in its zeal to find refuge among its kind. Denassa watched it, followed its progress even after it matched gait with its companions.

"Does Kayarra understand the words of abbah?" Shurna asked.

"He recites them. How much he understands, I don't know. Sometimes, I think he understands more than he can say. Other times, I know he's only repeating something he's memorized. I do know that he's figured out cor-anda, though. He knows it's a slur."

Shurna looked at Denassa. "How do you know?"

"'Man' was easy enough to teach him. The other day, he finally understood 'thing.' He said cor-anda after he understood thing." Denassa met Shurna's gaze. "It took a shecaren to teach him disrespect. How shameful is that?"

"The Shangren's citizens will assume Kayarra knows the words of abbah if he speaks them."

"I thought about that." Denassa looked back at the wayward mia. "It's true that a demon cannot speak the words of a holy rite, but what if he doesn't understand what he's saying? While Casta can do many things, I don't think preventing his housekeepers from gossiping is one of them. The truth of Kayarra's limitations will become known."

"Are you questioning Kayarra's innocence?"

"No. Maybe. I don't know." Denassa shook her head. "Mainly, I'm spending too much time worrying about our reception."

"Worrying won't change whatever happens."

"Have you tried telling that to Yutrenta?"

Shurna flashed a wry smile. "She heeds me as often as you do."

Denassa barked a laugh. Upon impulse, she caught Shurna's hand, squeezed it, and received an answering squeeze. After that, they walked in silence; Denassa, consumed by homesickness.

# CHAPTER 26

The next day, the sun angled hours away from zenith when Aya gave the signal to halt. Kayarra, confused, looked toward his companions. Denassa was kneeling, removing the cover from a drum she'd been carrying. Everyone else watched her, which further confused him.

He looked back at the Shangren—the name of the low mountain toward which they walked—and tried to ignore the clash of curiosity and trepidation. The green of that near distant foliage—richer, brighter, more intense than the gray-greens and blue-greens of scrub and cacti—nagged at memory until he remembered other trees. Deciduous trees. Conifers. He knew that green.

Shading his eyes, he distinguished stone houses that blended into the cliffs that backed them.

A boom from Denassa's drum startled Kayarra. Denassa faced the Shangren, the drum suspended from a strap that encircled her neck. As he watched, she lifted a mallet and brought it down then up, sending another boom fleeing after the first.

Kayarra looked back at the Shangren. He felt exposed, vulnerable. That their company could be no more than a speck upon the plain, if they were visible at all, did not relieve the knot of tension in his chest. He wanted Denassa to stop striking the drum; wanted Aya to hide their presence and location and slink into the city by moonlight; he wanted to disappear into a house without the attention-attracting exposure of walking past strangers.

A boom sounded from the city, so faint, it could have been an echo. Aya looked toward the city; others' attentions remained on Denassa. She started playing then, beats without patterns, striking the drum along its length, sometimes rapidly, sometimes slowly. Each section of the drum answered with a different tone.

When Denassa stopped playing, the distant drummer answered, his beats as erratic, as discordant and peculiar as Denassa's playing had been. Denassa listened, eyes closed, mallets poised. A slow smile curled her lips.

Aya chuckled.

"The Shangren welcomes the sons of Acrahh," Denassa said when the distant drummer fell silent. She struck her drum three times, and Kayarra heard the same signal echo from the Shangren.

"'And their keepers,'" Manerra added.

"That's why Aya laughed," Denassa said without rancor while she freed her drum from its harness latch.

"We will sleep in beds tonight," Aya announced with pleasure, but his statement fell like a boulder in their midst. Kayarra saw a glance pass between Denassa and Shurna. Solemnity had aged the faces of his companions. He shifted his sack bag to his right shoulder and followed Aya when he started away.

By late afternoon, Kayarra distinguished people hoeing and harvesting gardens and children running circles around grazing mia, their playful screams audible above the crunching grate of sand. Aya called a halt and Kayarra looked around for direction. When Aya reached for the knots that secured the tent to shuren back, his confusion increased. After momentary indecision, he set his sack on the ground and assisted with the work of encampment.

When the tent was nearly erected, Aya called Shurna and tilted his head toward the mia. She quit pounding stakes and pulled canopy poles from the baggage still lashed to the shuren. With poles and rope, she begin construction of a temporary corral.

While Yutrenta, Aya, and Manerra secured the tent's final guy ropes, Denassa touched Kayarra's arm and indicated he should help her remove the remainder of the baggage from the shuren. "Wear your tribal robe," she told him while they worked. "Leave your belt in the tent." She tugged his belt and pointed to the tent as if he'd forgotten how to talk. "No knife. No veil. Do you understand?"

"Wear tribal robe. No belt. No knife. No veil," he repeated and grinned, but his pleasure disappeared when the skin around her eyes reddened. He wondered what he'd done to bring her close to tears, but she turned aside and reached for a bundle of mats, and, after that, they labored in silence. Within minutes, their supplies lay inside the tent.

Shurna corralled the shuren with the mia, strung rope to close the makeshift gate, then ducked through the ropes to hobble the shuren.

"Kayarra, get dressed!" Manerra shouted from the tent's door flap. The shecaren wore his tribal robe.

Kayarra left the corral. He had to search for his sack among the haphazard scattering of baggage inside the tent. Yutrenta and Denassa left the women's quarters while he changed clothes, and Shurna hurried through to don her robe.

When Kayarra left the tent, he was startled to see everyone except Shurna standing in a formation they'd recently practiced, their robes fluttering in the breeze. Then he realized this wasn't a practice. This was the event they'd practiced for.

Kayarra took his place beside Yutrenta. While they waited for Shurna, he studied his companions. Manerra and Denassa stood shoulder-to-shoulder in front of them, so all he saw were their backs. Aya faced them. Aya's expression, although intense, no longer contained the worry lines that had creased his forehead for days. Had Aya resolved whatever bothered him, or simply resigned himself to fate? His tooled leather case hung at his side and Denassa's drum hung from its harness, but they were the only items anyone carried.

Aya approached and Kayarra's attention snapped to his face. Their eyes locked. In Aya's midnight brown eyes, Kayarra saw Aya's desperate desire for his safety; felt a connection that went beyond obligation and sympathy.

Aya's next step broke that ephemeral connection with such abruptness that Kayarra startled when Aya's hand closed upon his wrist. Aya tugged Kayarra's hand down and Kayarra realized he'd been standing with a hand covering his sun. Contact with the emblem reassured him; touching it had become a habit. He would have worn the robe daily if tears and soiling weren't concerns. Even its color, matching the women's robes, gave him a sense of belonging, of anonymity, of safety.

He heard Shurna hurry into place behind him and Aya turned toward Yutrenta. For a moment, Aya and Yutrenta locked gazes, and Kayarra realized with startling suddenness that Aya's silent communion was deliberate. The realization made him wonder about Aya's passions, about the sheer presence of the man. Then he wondered about the unguarded glimpse he caught of Aya's yearning.

Aya stepped away and Kayarra did not turn in order to keep Aya's face in sight. He felt like a Peeping Tom at the window of the man's soul.

When Aya passed Denassa on his return, Denassa's mallets rose and descended. This time when the drum's boom sounded, they were close enough to the city that Kayarra saw people turn in their direction. He reached for his robe's sun, but lowered his hand after his fingertips brushed the shell. Then Denassa stepped forward and Yutrenta followed.

Aya matched their pace to the beat of Denassa's drum. None of Aya's misgivings were apparent in either his demeanor or his step. Beside him, even Manerra managed a dignity of bearing Kayarra had not seen before, although Manerra's present demeanor struck Kayarra like a mockery of dignity, attempted way too late.

Their shadows created a temporary road that stretched ahead of them, creeping steadily closer to the palm trees that grew on the outskirts of the oasis. People had abandoned work, forgotten destinations, to gather under the trees. As their company approached that gathering, Kayarra distinguished the edge of a paved road that began and ended at the tree line.

A scattering of people broke from the crowd and ran toward them. "Shon regis!" someone yelled, and that shout was taken up and repeated with both startle and wonder. Men, women and children reached them, flowed around them, fell into step beside them, or fell to their knees. Tears flowed down cheeks. Laughter mixed with sobs. Hands reached out to touch Aya's and Manerra's robes, Denassa's robe . . . jerked back so quickly from his robe that a woman's hand struck the man beside her. Kayarra looked into a face contorted by horror, mouth wide, and still jumped when the woman screamed. His next step carried him beyond her, but that flash-image of horror went with him.

"Janquer lady Yutrenta!" a man shouted.

Yutrenta kept her eyes on Aya's back and did not reply.

A boy at Kayarra's elbow lurched backward and collided with two men behind him. A woman gasped. Denassa's drum drowned out many of the sounds, but not the shouted words, and none of the expressions of confusion, shock, and fear; the sudden burst into tears; the hand motions that looked like signs of warding. At one point, Manerra glanced over his shoulder, but Aya gave no indication that he was aware of a disturbance in his wake.

Kayarra stumbled over the edge of the paved road and bumped Yutrenta's arm. She caught him and discreetly set him back into position behind Denassa.

People lined the road several deep, calling the shecarens by name and titles, reaching over and around those in front of them in an effort to touch their robes, women wailing when their efforts failed.

Individuals walked or ran past those who lined the road, hurrying ahead of the shecarens or keeping pace with them, while Denassa's drum proclaimed their arrival and location to anyone not yet aware.

Kayarra felt naked without his veil. He labored to breathe. He jumped when Yutrenta's knuckles brushed his fingers, then clung to her hand. Sweat trickled from his armpits and seeped through his fingers.

The road climbed the hill. Stone houses formed solid barriers on each side of the street. Those who matched Aya's pace shoved through the crowd or joined the masses who trailed them. Children on roofs shouted and waved.

The street leveled and alleys appeared between houses. The road emptied into a plaza. Waiting in the center of the plaza, in the only clearing they'd seen since their arrival, stood a man with hair as white as clouds and facial skin molded from runneled clay, his robe as snowy as his hair. On the breast of his robe, and on the chests of the men and women who flanked him, resided the palm tree and circle that adorned Yutrenta's tribal robe.

Denassa's drum fell silent on Aya's final step.

Almost as one, the white-haired man and his companions bowed their heads, which was the signal Kayarra had been told to expect. Denassa and Yutrenta stepped right at the same time Kayarra and Shurna stepped left, forming a vee behind the shecarens.

"Casta, lord of the Shangren and of the Ofrann, I greet you with joy," Aya said, his voice carrying as onlookers hushed nearby others.

The white-haired man's head lifted and his attention locked on

Kayarra. Shock flashed so quickly across Casta's face that Kayarra could almost believe it had not happened, except for the silence that followed.

"All Shangren welcomes the sons of Acrahh," Casta began a belated reply, "and welcomes the children who serve them, who are . . . Ofrann kin. Quench your thirst from our waters, which are kept sacred in accordance with the covenant sworn to Crysus at the gifting of the stone of fire. Before these witnesses, I give to you, Aya, shon regis, son of Acrahh, the city of the Shangren for as long as you stay. Honor be to Acrahh the father and Crysus, his consort."

"To you, lord Casta, and to the people of the Shangren, I share my father's greetings. For your diligence in keeping the covenant of Crysus, and for the gift of the Shangren, I give fecundity and honor to all citizens at the Gateway to the Sun. Any who can attend are invited to join me there."

Together, Aya and Manerra inclined their heads, then Aya crossed in front of Manerra, headed toward the mass of people who jammed the right side of the plaza. Individuals pressed against others in their haste to open a passage before him. Manerra followed Aya. Yutrenta signaled Kayarra to follow Denassa.

Walking side by side was impossible. So, too, was walking without brushing people on both sides. Kayarra fixed his attention on Denassa's head, fearful of losing sight of her in the crush. The faces of strangers passed inches from his, hair follicles and blemishes visible, their breaths in his face. He saw in the eyes of strangers a range of browns he'd never imagined, even while lids narrowed and pupils contracted. Their fear made him acutely aware of the knife sheaths he brushed. Sweat trickled down his temples, tickled his sides, and he breathed through his mouth in an effort to draw more air into his lungs. Yutrenta's hand pressed his back, forcing him to close the widening gap between Denassa and him. By the time he became aware of a lessening of the crowd's crush, his vision had narrowed to a dim tunnel.

Gradually, he became aware of people shuffling the same direction he walked. By that time, he'd lost track of direction and guideposts. He sucked in air, trying to counter the constriction in his chest with pressure in his lungs. Yutrenta kept a hand on his back and gripped his arm.

The road curved left and he felt the steeper incline in the effort required to walk. The crowd bunched and slowed. Kayarra noticed stone pillars looming above the crowd like man-made tree trunks. He nearly trod on Denassa's sandal heels when they passed between those pillars. He felt rocky ground beneath his sandals. Well beyond the pillars, Denassa broke through the crowd. Kayarra followed, and stumbled on the steep incline of a weed-covered slope. He hiked up the front of his robe and climbed. The mound rose sharply to the height of his chin before flattening.

Aya and Manerra stood atop the mound, watching as they cleared the edge. At Manerra's back rose a stone arch devoid of ornamentation, its keystone level with Manerra's head.

"Does a Thurrang attend this rite?" Aya shouted into the crowd.

The roar of talking quieted among those nearest the mound.

"I require a Thurrang representative," Aya shouted over the upturned faces.

"Thurrang! A Thurrang!" cries rippled outward from the mound like the ringed disturbances in a pebble-violated pool.

Minutes passed before a man was seen pushing his way forward. At the edge of the crowd, he dropped to his knees and pressed his forehead to the ground.

Manerra left Aya's side, went down the slope, and spoke to the man, while those nearby strained to touch Manerra's robe. Kayarra watched the man rise, remove his belt and travel robe, drop each on the ground, then climb the slope behind Manerra.

At the slope's summit, Manerra rejoined Aya and the man approached the janquer. Kayarra's attention fixed on the symbol on the man's robe. First impression suggested a stylized bird, but closer inspection made Kayarra doubt that impression. Before the man reached the janquer, he halted abruptly.

Kayarra looked away from the man's stare, disturbed by his expression of shock.

"Come," he barely heard Denassa's command above the steady roar of the crowd.

The man approached. "I am to say my name is Vextra," he shouted.

"Welcome, Vextra," Denassa yelled. "Your service to the sons of Acrahh blesses this rite."

"I am blessed," Vextra said, but his tone gave the impression he thought himself cursed.

Kayarra gazed across the heads of the crowd at the upright pillars that marked the entrance to this place. The road leading past the pillars remained hopelessly jammed with people attempting to enter an area that could not accommodate them. People climbed a steep hill that ringed the far side of the park. Past the mound's arch spread a dizzying view of treetops and a great, circular lake that reflected the pinks and blues of sunset. A brush of vertigo made Kayarra focus on Aya.

On the far side of Denassa, Vextra stood facing forward, and Kayarra stepped backward in order to complete the semi-circle his companions had created. He squinted against the brilliant orange sun bisected by the arch's voussoirs. The shecarens' white robes were afire in that light. Kayarra shut his eyes against the glare.

Denassa's drum roll, close and unexpected, startled Kayarra. He looked toward her, watched her play, and gradually realized that her drum was cutting through the roar of the crowd, silencing it in a slowly widening circle. When, at last, her drum's voice was the only voice heard, she stopped playing.

"The sun rose this morning upon the marvel that is the Ofrann desert," Aya shouted, his voice loud in the crowd's hush, "and lit the fire within the stone of Crysus, which is the light of Yatra's nation. That stone, in turn, lit a second sun this day, the sun upon the breast of a sixth tribe—"

A wailing roar drowned out whatever else Aya intended to say. Kayarra saw him glance at Denassa, who poised her mallets above her drumhead. Aya signaled no, and Denassa lowered her hands.

While Aya waited for the reaction to abate, Yutrenta's hand closed over Kayarra's fist. He was grateful for the contact, although escape from this crowd was the only cure for his anxiety.

In this day of revelations, Kayarra again wondered who Aya was. Before this evening, he'd had no inkling of the power Aya wielded and the respect he commanded. But Aya was one man. His traveling companions numbered five, all of them unarmed. If the thousands who surrounded them objected to Aya's proclamations, or panicked, all six of them together could not stop the crowd's intentions or escape a trampling. Who would heed an order they could not hear?

Kayarra could do nothing to control his trembling.

"That member stands—" Aya shouted, paused, shouted again into the ebbing roar, "That member stands in service to Acrahh, that the strength and prosperity of Yatra's nation shall grow alongside Kayarran prosperity."

Kayarra wasn't certain how many, if any, heard that declaration. No one along the borders of the ledge. Certainly, none cramming the road or clinging to the hill.

Finally, Aya signaled Denassa, but for a long time her drum only contributed to the noise and confusion. Men tried to overshout her drum. Meanwhile, the sun slipped below the voussoirs and hung between the arch's uprights. Without waiting for silence, not expecting to gain it, Aya covered Manerra's palm with a suede chamois and signaled Denassa to silence.

"Great Acrahh, god and father," Aya began the ritual of abbah, "see this city of the Shangren and look to its everlasting waters."

An uneasy hush began to fall among those closest to the Gateway's mound.

"Grant health and prosperity to all who dwell and pass here. Let those blessings go forth with every company who departs the Shangren, that health and well-being spread to every child of Yatra's nation."

Yutrenta lifted Kayarra's hand skyward, and he adjusted his grip so their fingers intertwined. Denassa caught his free hand, and together they lifted their clasped hands above their heads. Among the crowd, palms lifted toward their semi-circle, fingers splayed, although a frightening number of people kept their hands lowered.

"Close your eyes!" Yutrenta shouted. "Shield all eyes from the temple stone!"

Kayarra closed his eyes and, after a pause, red light poured through his eyelids.

"Spirits of our forebears whose light we honor," Manerra's voice added strength and harmony to Aya's, "behold the light of Yatra's children, which is the godlight of our sacred promise. We seek your wisdom as a guide for minds and hearts. Illuminate the path home when our birth-fates are complete.

"Peace throughout the nation for all eternity."

Kayarra remembered to join the refrain on "throughout," then repeated it with the crowd's response.

Even Kayarra's inexperienced ears heard hesitancy and uncertainty in the crowd's response. By some fluke of mixed tones and doubt, the intended statement ended on a note of question.

The temple stone's harsh light vanished, leaving the less intense fire of the setting sun. Kayarra felt Yutrenta's and Denassa's hands lower and opened his eyes.

As soon as their handholds separated, strangers swarmed up the slope and passed between and among them. Kayarra leapt toward Yutrenta in startled fright, landing so close to her foot their sandals scraped.

"They're friends," Yutrenta shouted and blocked the upsweep of his hands when he tried to knock a sack from the hands of the nearest man. The man froze while that information penetrated. Only then did Kayarra recognize the sack as a gaping robe. He lowered his hands, and the man threw the robe over Kayarra's head. When Kayarra couldn't locate the sleeve openings, the man grabbed his wrist and guided his hand through one of the holes. Kayarra located the other sleeve opening on his own.

"No talk," Yutrenta yelled while the man yanked a twisted sleeve down, concealing the blue sleeve of Kayarra's tribal robe. "Stay with him." Then someone threw a robe over Yutrenta's head and she turned away. The man tugged Kayarra's arm and Kayarra pulled back.

"Come. Hurry," the man said, urgency as strong in his voice as tension had been in Yutrenta's.

Kayarra stepped away, bumped into someone, and looked back into the face of a stranger.

"Janquer lord—"

He surged forward, past the man who was talking, and half fell, half slid down the Gateway's slope. Someone fell over him. Legs and bodies stopped his slide. Someone grabbed the neck of his robe and pulled a hood over his head, then grabbed his arm and jerked him away, into a wall of bodies.

# CHAPTER 27

"Look down," a man ordered. "Keep your head down."

Kayarra pressed a fist against his chest, trying to slow the pounding of his heart so he could breathe. Counter pressure wasn't working.

"Look down!" The voice grew more insistent, more panicky with each repetition.

To comply would compress his windpipe and further restrict airflow.

Around him, strangers wailed, tearfully clung together, flailed fists while shouting.

An opening appeared between two shoulders and Kayarra shoved through, but a head turned toward him and he looked down, into the upturned face of a child. He whirled, spotted a narrow opening between two bodies and lunged through.

Ahead, a cluster of people inched toward the pillars. He shoved forward, received a hard elbow jab in his ribs, but reached the rear of that group. He inched forward behind the group before he wondered whether his escort had made it through. He didn't know the man's name. In the confusion of his panic, he'd not gotten a good look at his escort's face. He barked a laugh of such nervousness that someone's head turned toward him. He looked down, but felt his skin prickle and crawl, and waited for a shout of discovery that didn't come.

The laugh loosened something rock tight in his chest, allowing him to take deeper breaths than he'd managed so far. Nevertheless, a long time passed before he looked up to judge his progress in the slipstream of his unaware hosts. The pillars were closer, but still impossibly far away. He ached to look back, to see whether Aya's white robe remained visible atop the mound of the arch, but that was too risky. He stared at dark shoulder skin visible through the thread-bare garment of the man he followed, until dusk stole his ability to distinguish between thread and skin.

He remembered only fragments of the route they'd taken through the city to the plaza; could remember practically nothing of the walk from the plaza to the place he'd looked up and seen the pillars. As he neared those pillars now, progress became a standstill, then resumed at inches per hour.

He needed to go downhill. If he could get off this mountain, he could find the tent and Aya.

Tent walls could be slashed with a knife. He'd not be safe there.

What he'd never feel again was a sense of safety.

His group finally passed the bottleneck at the pillars and then shifted onto the rock-embedded shoulder of the road. Someone jostled his arm, then squeezed past, heading uphill, while most headed downhill. Kayarra stayed behind the people who had guided him this far, as if the familiarity of proximity meant safety.

Another person wanting the uphill road shoved him, causing him to stomp on his own sandal edge and stumble. The pusher grabbed his arm, but not before he collided with someone's shoulder.

"Sorry," the pusher's tone was anxious. "So sorry."

Kayarra looked back, but the pusher addressed the man with whom he'd collided. Kayarra tried to shrug off the pusher's hand, but the man's grip tightened.

"Excuse us," the pusher shouted. "Excuse me." He forced Kayarra crosswise of the flow of people headed downhill. Kayarra jerked against the man's hold. The tent was his only link to Aya.

Unable to free himself, Kayarra peered into the man's hood, but Ryna's crescent shed too little light to distinguish more than a veil. People behind them began to shove and hit. Kayarra sidestepped, acquiescing to his captor's insistence, and the man used that momentum to shove him uphill through the moving crowd.

At last, they broke free of that living tide. A draft of air teased the robes of those climbing the darkened street ahead of them.

"It's not far," the man said, and Kayarra hoped this stranger was the same man who Yutrenta had called a friend.

The road curved left around the side of the mountain and climbed forever. Houses lined the left side of the street. Trees bordered the cliff edge on the right, their leaves and fronds further darkening the night-shaded street.

As exertion consumed adrenalin, the day's images returned like vicious ghosts. Most persistent remained the face of the first woman who had screamed during their approach to the city. Her teeth overlapped, her tongue had sunk against the bottom of her mouth and her lips shaped a distorted O. She had rushed to welcome them only seconds before she screamed.

Manerra's revulsion and hatred had been constant, had never dropped from the sky to shake him so thoroughly.

"Here." The man tugged his sleeve.

Kayarra realized with a start that the roar of the crowd had faded. This was the first time the man hadn't yelled to be heard. Kayarra glanced over his shoulder. People strolled behind them, scattered along the breadth and length of the road. Beyond the ledge, through the branches of trees, firelights sparkled and glimmered . . . the city at night.

The house the man approached, built from stone the color of the cliff behind it, had the same blank, windowless facade as every other house they'd passed. His escort opened the door without knocking and urged Kayarra forward by a grip on his elbow. Kayarra passed the doorframe before he froze. His guide jostled his shoulder as he pressed in behind him and the door clicked shut.

Strangers crowded the room, every face turned toward him.

"We have him," his guide announced.

"Are you sure?" a woman asked.

Kayarra felt a tug on his hood and tried to catch its front edge but missed. The fabric slumped about his shoulders. His blond hair and white skin in that room full of black-haired, red-skinned strangers provided an irrefutable answer to the woman's question.

Silence and stares halted time.

"He's blessed," a woman remarked.

Kayarra's attention flew in alarm and desperation to movement in an arched doorway barely visible behind the crowd. He stared for seconds at a woman's face before recognizing Shurna. He stepped toward her just as the door behind him opened. A hooded woman entered, followed more slowly by another hooded figure.

The newcomer swept the hood from her head. Yutrenta caught his eye and smiled before her gaze swept the assembly. "Gorrow!" she exclaimed, crossed the room, and entered a man's embrace. "I wasn't certain this was your house. It's been a long time. Years."

"Indeed." The man released her, stepped back, and offered a belated nod. "I was in Kita your last visit. Your entrances create quite a furor these days."

"Since when were the shecarens predictable?" she demanded.

Gorrow's smile appeared forced. "My house is yours while you stay. Supper is ready, if you would break fast. Please," he swept a hand toward the arched doorway. "Housekeepers will attend you."

Yutrenta frowned. "I see lord Kayarra and janquer lady Shurna but not janquer lady Denassa. Is she here?"

"She's not arrived."

"And the shecarens?"

"Lord Casta extended hospitality to them."

Yutrenta laughed. "I imagine lord Casta did."

Gorrow smiled, and turned toward Kayarra. Gorrow dipped his head. "I extend welcome to the sixth tribe from the city of the Shangren," he said. "I am Gorrow, lord Casta's nephew."

"I am called Kayarra," Kayarra answered as he'd been taught, conscious of his enunciation. The effort made his words labored.

People shifted, glanced at one another, frowned. Gorrow's expression went blank. "After meal, I hope you will share the story of your name," Gorrow invited.

Kayarra looked at Yutrenta.

"There will be no tales tonight, lord Gorrow," she said. "I beg for patience. What the shecarens have to say will be shared tomorrow. Tonight, we ask only food and rest."

"Then please, take both." He again gestured toward the archway. People shuffled aside, shuffled toward the doorway.

Kayarra caught Yutrenta's hand signal, preceded her into the room, and was greeted by Shurna, who caught his hand and drew him aside. When he looked back, Yutrenta was nowhere in sight. He'd thought she followed him.

The people who entered behind him drifted toward low, octagon tables spaced about a mosaic-work floor that combined geometric shapes with floral vines. Many of the newcomers took seats upon the tables. Others headed toward clusters of people who stood about the room. Their greetings held a note of solemnity. All about them, conversations were hushed.

A shelf arrayed with burning oil lamps encircled the room at shoulder height. Spaced among the lamps stood sculptures. Kayarra stepped toward the wall, drawn by the sinuous curves of a feline descending a rocky ledge. The cat was black stone, the ledge, light brown stone. On one forepaw, the cat's toes were the brown of the rocks it descended. The rocks below the cat's tail were tipped in black as if muddied by the animal's passage—attesting to the fact the sculpture had been carved from a single rock. He looked farther along the shelf at ivory flowers; at animals he couldn't identify; at a tall, blocky stone containing the vague vestige of a face; at the crudely carved wooden bust of a man.

"Janquer lord Kayarra," a woman spoke behind him. He whirled and she dipped her head. "You are . . . ." she repeated a word used earlier, in the outer room, and touched her head. With shock, he realized she indicated the place on his head where the bone had been removed. "I not talk"—that wasn't right—"not know," he corrected himself, "talk."

Puzzlement and skepticism clouded her face. She opened her mouth but Shurna intervened with a hand on her arm and words Kayarra couldn't understand. The woman flashed an uncertain smile, nodded to each of them in turn, then backed away a step before turning and crossing the room. Shurna tugged him toward an unoccupied table.

Two children carrying porcelain bowls approached as they reached the table and stopped. Kayarra saw Shurna dip her hands into one bowl and started to do the same with the other child's bowl, but the child jerked the bowl away. Water splashed his robe and sprayed the floor. The child wailed and burst into tears. People whirled and stared.

"Your hand," Shurna whispered urgently.

She didn't wait for his comprehension, but caught his hand and drew his fingers across her palm. She started talking then. He heard "hand" and "fire" and realized she explained the mottled discoloration and scars. The girl turned a reddened, tear-wet face to Kayarra and gravely told him something he assumed was an apology. He forced a smile. She dipped her head and he nodded back, which earned him a wide-eyed stare.

Shurna pressed his hand into the water that remained in the bowl. He rinsed both hands then, and dried them on the towel Shurna lifted from the child's arm. Afterward, Shurna helped him remove his damp outer robe, tossed it onto the table behind them, and urged him to sit, although she remained standing.

Even half concealed behind Shurna's robe, Kayarra felt the attention his appearance drew. He stared at the floor, studying the stones that formed the interlocking geometric and floral pattern. The greens appeared to be jade, the blues, turquoise. Were the reds actual rubies?

"Janquer lord."

Kayarra looked up, saw a bowl thrust toward him, and took it before noticing the meat heaped inside. Hastily, he looked away.

His first encounter with meat had been the evening Shurna returned to camp with a small animal carcass. He'd not been able to watch the women skin and clean it; later, had glimpsed the carcass on a spit over the coals—decapitated, bloody flesh, paws intact—and had vomited until he'd dry heaved. The meat in his bowl didn't retain the shape of the animal from which it had come, but his throat closed and his stomach clenched. Sweat beaded his brow and upper lip.

A shuffling at the door distracted him. Yutrenta entered. She saw him, smiled, and wove her way through people and tables toward him.

"Please, Kayarra," she said and pressed the bowl she carried into his free hand. Instinctively, he took it while Yutrenta removed her travel robe. She tossed her robe atop his wet one, then reached for and took his bowl. In surprise, he glanced into the bowl she'd left him and saw vegetables without meat.

"Thank you," he whispered as she settled beside him.

She patted his knee.

Musicians seated in the four corners of the room began playing. Talking ceased.

During the meal, children shuffled among the tables, offering platters of dried and raw fruit, bowls of pink-tinged milk, fried cakes, nutmeats, and foodstuffs of unknown origin. Kayarra tried a fried cake, was repulsed by the coating of oil it left on his tongue, and ate nothing else. Driven by thirst, he drank two bowls of the pink milk only because Yutrenta and Shurna drank it. Of more interest than food were the musicians. The one who played a stringed instrument didn't play long enough to satisfy Kayarra's craving for the soft, bell-like tones of the instrument. When the flutists seated in the four corners of the room alternated play, the effect resembled the chatter and call of birds.

Finally, children placed platters of nutmeats, honeyed cakes, and fruit about the room, then returned with bowls of water and embroidered hand towels for any diners who wished to rinse their hands.

"Janquer lady Yutrenta," Gorrow called across the space that separated them while he dried his hands, "I have been assured that janquer lady Denassa received safe passage to lord Casta's house. She will rejoin the janquer at morning abbah."

"Did lord Casta offer better fare?" Yutrenta asked.

Startled expressions and a faint scattering of uncertain laughter passed through the room.

Gorrow smiled. "I did not ask."

"I say that her host will not be half as pleasant."

Gorrow's smile broadened and he bowed from the waist. "What is the janquer's pleasure in the city?" he asked.

"The baths!" Shurna and Yutrenta answered together, which drew laughter.

"Has the shon regis a planned length of stay?"

"Our stay will be a few days, nothing longer," Yutrenta answered. "The harder trek faces us, and the winds have been unusually kind. Surely, Acrahh's attention must turn elsewhere before long."

"And your company's needs?"

"Water, food supplies, fodder. Little else."

"Lord Gorrow," Shurna said, "we left mia and shuren unattended. Have you knowledge of their care?"

"Lord Korrane arranged for their care, and for the safekeeping of your belongings. Please attend to your comfort without worry."

"Our thanks to you and your uncle." Shurna nodded and leaned back, resting an elbow upon a cushion, her attention repeatedly straying to one of the housekeepers.

"Janquer lord Kayarra—" Gorrow began before Yutrenta cut him off.

"He is not janquer, lord Gorrow."

"Lord Kayarra?" Gorrow asked, and Yutrenta signaled acceptance of that title. "Have you needs or wishes of your own?"

Kayarra had looked up in startle at being addressed, glimpsed Yutrenta's hand signal, said, "No, lord . . . Garra," he fumbled the name.

Gorrow flushed but maintained a smile. "Your ascension to the tribes of Yatra will long live in this city's memory. For once, the devout claim greater furor than the criminals."

"Is there a reason for that comparison, lord Gorrow?" Yutrenta asked.

Gorrow blushed dark maroon. "I intended no offense, janquer lady Yutrenta. I meant only that the criminals have for so long demanded our attentions, it's pleasant to contemplate matters of a less threatening nature."

Considering they had been secreted to this house because the city lay in uproar outside its walls, Yutrenta thought Gorrow was not doing so well. She decided to spare her cousin further embarrassment. "Lord Gorrow, we cannot discuss what you really wish to know. It is the shon regis's duty to announce matters of national importance, not ours to preempt or second guess his announcements. Please, if you'll have patience, your questions will be answered in time," she said, then added as an afterthought, knowing full well that the announcement would gall him, "Probably during the celebrations at Ayahn Rahh, when lord Kayarra's public ceremonies occur."

"Nothing sooner, to settle questions here?"

He was dismayed, indeed.

"That choice can be shon regis Aya's alone," she answered. Then, because she enjoyed this besting of her arrogant cousin, "Perhaps you'd have done better to have broken fast with your uncle this evening." And because she knew he was bound to them, perhaps even by Casta's order, "Do you suppose they've eaten yet?"

# CHAPTER 28

Aya noticed the cloaking of his companions and turned to touch the hands that reached out to him, keeping attention on himself in order to assure the janquer's safe retreat. He had no fear for his safety. The Ofrann was his mother's tribe. Blood bonds and god fear protected him where affection failed.

When, at last, he noticed Neetria's signal, he touched Manerra's arm and made his way to her side while the devout and the scared called his name, clutched at his robe, and shouted questions he couldn't answer even were it possible to be heard above the din.

Men forcibly encircled them, creating a barrier against the desperation of the devout. Others pressed ahead, opening a path through the cloying throng. Behind them, hundreds followed.

Once past the pillars that marked the Gateway's entrance, their party bore right, climbing the road that wound around the side of the mountain. Before they reached Casta's house, their escorts fell back and blocked the road, while Neetria alone accompanied them to the door of her father's house. There, she tapped once before she opened the door, but did not follow them inside.

The closing of the door settled a shroud of quiet over the room.

*****

Casta heard the single knock and was standing when the shecarens entered the antechamber. He stepped away from his chair, stopped, and lowered his head. "Aya, shon regis. Manerra, shecaren."

"Lord Casta," Aya answered.

Casta raised his head and Aya started forward. They met in embrace halfway across the room. "Manerra," Casta grinned at the shecaren, "this journey heralds the conclusion of your education, does it not? No more frolicking on garden walls."

Manerra did not smile. "My education never concludes, lord Casta."

Casta chuckled and clapped Manerra's shoulder. "Not for any of us," he said. "Come. Take your rest." He led the way into his audience room and gestured toward the cluster of cushioned chairs grouped about the hearth. But as Aya passed, Casta stiffened. "Aya, don't sit," Casta's tension was audible. "There's blood on your robe."

Aya halted and tugged his robe, bringing the fabric around until he, too, saw the blood. Manerra, frozen, stared at the bloodstains.

"You both shall have escort throughout your stay," Casta said.

Aya looked up from the bloodstains. "Manerra, turn around." Aya watched Manerra pivot. Manerra's robe was dirt-smudged from hundreds of hands but not bloodied.

"There are clean robes in your rooms," Casta said.

"We will change," Aya said and started for the door, holding the bloodied section of robe away from his legs. Casta motioned a housekeeper to follow.

By the time the shecarens returned, all pleasure in their reunion—real or feigned—had disappeared. Citizens had been upset enough by the city's blessing to have bared a knife at Aya's back and sliced their palms. They declared by those bloody imprints to oppose his decisions even unto death. How many had seen those marks?

Casta nodded to Aya. "Shon regis." Casta gestured to the nearby chairs. "While you changed, I ordered a search of the city. Anyone with a fresh hand wound will be held until your departure."

"I'd like to speak with anyone who is taken." Aya sat down but did not reach for the tea that rested on the tiny table beside his chair.

"Of course," Casta agreed. "Also, after we eat, the household has orders for dismissal. We can speak in confidence."

A knock on the door caused Casta to square his shoulders and tense. Surely no dissidents had been found so quickly. He heard a housekeeper open the door, and experienced a rush of dismay when Denassa and her escort entered the antechamber. When she crossed into the audience room, he stood and forced a smile.

"Ringgangley janquer lady Denassa was separated from her companions," his housekeeper announced. "Shall I arrange for her safe escort to lord Gorrow's house?"

"Only if she wishes it," Casta answered, watching Denassa. "Otherwise, she is welcome here."

"Your generosity is appreciated, lord Casta." Denassa approached their semicircle of chairs.

Casta waved away her escort, his disappointment keen. He embraced Denassa, and she removed her travel robe while housekeepers shifted furniture to accommodate her inclusion in their group. As soon as she was seated, he ordered the meal served in order to stave off further interruptions, willing to let the musicians attempt to relieve the tension that pervaded the room.

Appetites were poor, but Casta was unwilling to rush the meal's end. After he indicated the conclusion of supper, he inquired about the ease of their journey and the state of their health while the remnants of the meal were cleared away, hands rinsed, and fruit and drinks set within easy reach. The musicians gathered their instruments and departed with the housekeepers.

Casta sipped fresh tea from an incised and glazed bowl, then replaced it on the inlaid table beside his chair. "Were you able to visit your father during this trip, lady Denassa?" he asked.

"Time did not permit it, lord Casta. We came straight away from Thurra."

"Without your Thurrang representative?"

Aya answered, "I asked Vantrann to oversee the negotiations involving Hyran's death. I assume you are aware of it."

Casta let his surprise show. "We've heard so many rumors of Hyran's death, I discounted this one, as well. So it's true?"

"Hyran's latest scheme involved mian theft. When herders began marking their animals, the thefts became slaughters. Hyran and several others were caught in ambush and murdered on a field outside Varaar."

Casta felt the chair cushion mold to his back and was glad of its support. The known problems multiplied.

"Vantrann was to have led a delegation from Zarthon," Aya continued. "It concerns me that they've not arrived."

"You did not decide the matter yourself?" Casta asked, surprised again.

"I chose not to. I thought it best to remove myself from the decisions in this matter."

Casta scrapped his fingernails through his beard. "No one lives who believes you harbor love for your brother."

Manerra stiffened, which alarmed Casta.

"It was better to avoid even the appearance of bias," Aya said.

Manerra still had not inhaled.

"If Vantrann's delegation arrives while you're here, we can conclude the matter before you depart."

"Our stay will be short. A couple days, nothing longer. We were delayed nearly a moon getting here."

"Lord Casta," Denassa said, "please forgive my interruption, but have you received word of the destruction of the cistern at Rajma's Head?"

"The news came a fortnight ago. Benta is concluding arrangements for repairs even now. You saw the damage yourselves?"

"We did," Aya answered, but it was Denassa's frown that evoked misgivings. Aya's "we" must not have included all members of his company, but why that upset Denassa, Casta couldn't guess.

"I was told the destruction appeared deliberate," Casta threw out the best bait he had.

"I concur," Aya said.

"Do you suspect Hyranians? Retaliation for Hyran's murder?"

"Any company could have destroyed the cistern. If not in retaliation for Hyran's murder, then to discourage pilgrimage to Ayahn Rahh. Those are the obvious possibilities. I won't guess without knowing more."

"I assume, since you're here, that the loss of the cistern was an inconvenience, nothing more."

"Assumptions can be accurate." Aya's answer silenced the room.

Denassa leaned forward. "I wish to thank you for your assistance in our retreat from the Gateway to the Sun, lord Casta. Your arrangements were as effective and farseeing as ever."

Casta chuckled. "I merely extended the shecarens' reputation for invisibility to their companions."

Denassa's creased brow did not ease with her smile. Her face remained haggard with what could have been exhaustion if not for the wariness in her eyes. Missing was the openness, the spunk, he was accustomed to seeing in her.

"Shon regis," he said, "I assume the Shangren's citizens will survive the knowledge that even the divine employ allies."

"It can be no greater blow than that dealt the sixth tribe's reputation for flight," Manerra said.

"Shecaren?" Casta wasn't so bewildered by Manerra's comment that he missed Aya's flinch. That flinch could have been nothing more than a silent belch, but Casta didn't believe it. His heart beat a painful tempo as he realized that the real danger in the sixth tribe lay with the division of the shecarens.

"Kayarra was found at the base of a cliff," Denassa explained. "The refute of that rumor nearly cost him his life."

"Kayarra is the stranger who presented in the plaza," Casta guessed, without shifting his attention from the shecarens. "I think it time we discussed the sixth tribe. If the city does not stand through the chaos of its blessing, its governor would like to know why." He took a breath. "Rumors I've heard place a strange tribe north of the Tydonddy Mountains. Are those rumors false?"

"No," Aya answered. "Our rumors agree. Even Hyran placed them in the north. And Kitarin stories repeated by Ringgangley traders place them in a valley between Bana and Kita, very near the coast."

Casta had not expected that much candor. "Yet this member—Kayarra—joined you in the south?"

"He was taken from Manteen hunters in a canyon near the Ofrann's rim, just south of Rajma's Head."

Rajma's Head again. Injuries required water and Kayarra's had been life threatening for Yutrenta to have resorted to trepanation. Casta desperately wished Denassa had not arrived. Although her loyalty lay above question, experience had taught him the value of caution, and Aya's current reticence encouraged nothing less.

"I'd like to extend formal greeting to lord Kayarra in the morning," Casta said.

"He can tell you nothing, Casta," Aya said. "He has no memory of his tribe. Denassa and Yutrenta named him and he cannot refute that name with another."

"This . . . not knowing. How far does it extend?"

"It is complete."

Manerra had developed a sudden interest in the carpet, and by so much did Casta understand one reason for the shecarens' schism. Casta gripped both armrests. "This Kayarra . . . I saw his physical differences in the plaza. And for any who missed him there, you set him on display at the Gateway to the Sun—"

"Excuse me, shon regis, shecaren, lord." Denassa stood. "Perhaps I should have Neetria arrange an escort for me to Gorrow's house."

"No," Aya said.

Casta silently cursed him.

"Your covenant permits your presence at this and any other meeting. Stay. Please."

Denassa tilted her head and reluctantly sat.

Her interruption gave Casta a moment to regain control. His wits were badly shaken. He chose a safer approach. "Shon regis, you have reasons for sheltering this man. I can see benefits to that myself. But why are you proclaiming his people to be a lost tribe of Yatra? I beg Acrahh that you share those reasons."

Aya hesitated.

"What information you've shared hardly settles the anxieties of this city's citizens. It will not avert division of the nation at Ayahn Rahh. As Acrahh is my god and witnesses my heart, know that I wish to divert bloodshed. Please direct my influence toward that goal."

Aya held his eyes without blinking, with an intensity that made him uncomfortable.

"Damn you, Aya!" he cried.

Denassa gasped. Manerra's attention flashed to Aya's face.

"I hope not," Aya replied calmly.

For that small reprieve, he was thankful.

"You ask for my reasoning," Aya said. "I will share it in return for a favor."

"If it is within mortal power, I will do what I can," he swore, and prayed that Aya's logic held more sanity than he felt in that moment.

"Kayarra was named at abbah and the sun's orb given as his tribal symbol in order to extend his protection beyond me."

Manerra returned his attention to the rug and Casta's stomach knotted.

"My announcement of a new tribe at the Gateway to the Sun and Kayarra's participation in this evening's ceremonies were measures to insure his recognition as a member of my company. Without those precautions, I fear his tribe will become hunted for their differences as surely as the Manteen.

"You expressed exception to his public display, Casta, but that was necessary. People must see him so they recognize his tribe when others come into our lands. Eventually, more will come, and I do not want bloodshed in those meetings. I don't want a second tribe hunted and despised."

"A common enemy heals tribal wounds," Casta murmured, quoting one of Denassa's ancestors who voiced that argument in support of the Mante war.

Denassa paled and Aya's face clouded. "Wounds healed by blood are injuries festering," Aya said, voice devoid of modulation.

"He will be confused with the Manteen," Casta persisted. "The lands are wide. Most know the Manteen only as a horror explained by a bit of history. Few enough among those who travel have seen one. Few will know the man you flaunt isn't Manteen."

"The Manteen are kinsmen," Manerra murmured. "However distant."

"The Kayarran," Aya said, "have skills with fiber and weaving unknown among the five tribes. I cannot believe it their only or their greatest skill."

"Few tribesmen will care what their skills are except in weaponry," Casta replied.

"We must discuss your promise," Aya said. "As you say, the lands are broad. No one, not even Manerra yet, knows that as well as I. Nor are distances and mountains all that separate our tribes. Hyran used hatred as both weapon and shield. The Kayarran must be removed as a weapon of the Hyranians or national unity will suffer. The south will view a northern war as an opportunity for succession, and no one, not even I, can win two battlefronts. I will not be maneuvered into a position where I must chose between deserting Kita in time of strife or losing Thurra. If I can prevent it, I will not allow arrows drawn on kinsmen. It's being threatened along Thurra's border. We've seen the consequences in Ringgal. If we cannot learn from history, why tell it?"

In Aya's pause for breath, Casta watched the vein in Aya's neck jump with the pounding of his heart.

"Casta, I require use of the Shangren's position and influence. I want a company sent to Ayahn Rahh at dawn to announce the inclusion of the sixth tribe in the nation of Yatra. Before they leave, I want the members of that company to see Kayarra so they can describe him accurately, and I require that company's arrival in Ayahn Rahh before any other company that departs the Shangren on the morrow. That is crucial. I trust your judgment in deciding the company's members.

"My second demand tests your imagination. As companies arrive and leave the Shangren, I want them to carry news of the sixth tribe. I care not where their destinations lie, be it Ayahn Rahh or elsewhere, but I do care that their information not be solely the rumors started tonight by the city's blessing. I will hope for some accuracy, and discouragement of the Hyranian claims of flight, burning iron, and trapped souls. Again, I place no restriction on your method of execution. You know my requirements; I trust your judgment."

Casta was simultaneously relieved by the simplicity of Aya's demands—he could have ordered actions with far graver consequences—and dismayed by the responsibility Aya placed upon his shoulders. Everything Aya planned for the assimilation of the sixth tribe rested upon the effectiveness of Ofrann efforts.

"Your requests are reasonable." Casta signaled acceptance of the responsibility with the sign of acquiescence. There was little else he could do. He'd already promised support. However, because his personal responsibility extended far beyond the boundaries of a city thrown into confusion by this company's arrival, he dared much to ask, "Are the shecarens agreed upon this action?"

Manerra's eyes widened almost imperceptibly, which did not afford the assurance Casta wanted. "The shecarens staunchly share a desire to avoid civil bloodshed," Manerra vowed. "It is one of the reasons we solicit Ofrann counsel and aid."

Casta uneasily accepted Manerra's proclamation because the idea that Manerra could lie was not a consideration, and the consequences of any other course taken by the shecarens was far too uncomfortable to consider. However, the absence of a simple "yes" in Manerra's reply seemed to him a dire omission.

# CHAPTER 29

Late that night, Casta walked his guests to their rooms, gained assurances they wanted nothing else, then recalled the house staff in order to gain an explanation for Denassa's unplanned arrival.

Denassa's escort flinched before his anger. "She insisted the shon regis ordered her attendance. Should I have refused her claim and asked questions later?"

"No," Casta grudgingly approved the man's actions, disconcerted that Aya had anticipated his desire for privacy so accurately. He had tried to manipulate a demigod. He could blame no one but himself for the plan's failure. "I would have you broach no offense to the janquer," Casta admitted, dismissed the man, confirmed arrangements for the house's security, then left with escort to arrange for a delegation's departure to Ayahn Rahh. After that, but not least, he had a city's safety to secure.

* * * * *

The predawn chill intensified a cold Denassa had been unable to overcome by bed coverings, hot tea, or woolen robes. During the bustle to leave the house, no one had remarked upon the shaking of her hands, but she wasn't confident her distress had gone unnoticed. Standing on the edge of the cliff outside Casta's house, she tucked her hands inside her sleeves and looked down upon rooftops and gardens, orchards, and streets that were both hard packed footpaths and paved roads. She shifted attention to the weak blues and grayish-white of the near-dawn sky. With dawn in her face, the Rahhe Mountains lay at her back. The Rahhe's absence from the horizon made her feel impossibly far from home.

"Janquer lady Denassa."

She turned at that soft-spoken call and started down the hill, taking her place behind the shecarens in their subdued procession toward the Gateway to the Sun. Every dawn and sunset would find them at the Gateway for as long as they remained in the city . . . a fact their enemies, detractors, and opponents could depend upon. If a strike against them occurred, it was likeliest to occur at the Gateway to the Sun or on their walk to or from that place. At any other time, they remained cloaked, armed, sequestered, and heavily guarded.

She glanced at the bundled robe carried by one of her escorts, then back at Aya's heels. This was her second trip down the mountain this morning. The first had been with armed escorts on horseback to retrieve Aya's spare tribal robe from their tent's supplies.

The threats were no longer imaginary. With luck, the threats were impulsive, and the fear driving those impulses, short-lived. An unorganized threat might not have time to coalesce into violence before they left the city. Although a coalition was easier discovered, rage and impulse were deadly because of their unpredictability.

She looked up, around, anywhere in an effort to escape her thoughts. She remembered a time not long ago when the position and honor of being janquer felt sacred, felt invincible. How naive she'd been.

Seeing the blood on Aya's robe this morning brought back memories she'd hoped she'd buried. But the similarities between Aya and her father had collided this morning, shaking her so thoroughly that she felt herself withdraw from Aya, afraid to love him, to stand close to him, because she feared seeing him drenched in blood as she'd seen her father that day.

She started counting steps to avoid remembering. It worked better as the numbers got higher and she had to concentrate so as not to miscount. The past retreated to a red mist that vibrated with her mother's screams.

She bumped into someone and jumped backward with a strangled cry.

Both shecarens whirled, although it was Manerra she'd bumped. Aya paused, assessing her cognizance before reaching for her arm. She looked past him and recognized Gorrow's house by the approach of their companions, then blushed hotter than she had in years. "I'm sorry," she mumbled, unable to say more because she couldn't think of a way to explain her inattention.

"Citizens are watching," Manerra hissed, completing her humiliation.

She bowed her head, more to hide her face than in veneration, although both were necessary.

Aya squeezed her arm then let go, and she was grateful for his restraint. Grateful, too, that he did not delay in front of Gorrow's house. Shurna, Kayarra, and Yutrenta fell in step with them as they passed, and their escorts merged with theirs as they walked. Above, the sky had lightened toward the clarion of morning. Birdcalls and the lowing of livestock drowned out the scuffling grate of leather sandals on sandy stone. Dawn was near. The scent of wood smoke reminded her of the scant meal supper had been.

The drone of thousands of voices warned of the nearness of their destination long before they rounded the last curve and Denassa saw the crowd. Shouts deafened her. Individuals on the fringe of the crowd rushed forward, hands outstretched. Their escorts threw up arms to ward off the zealous devout.

A pathway through the crowd, opened by peacekeepers sent ahead, forced them to walk single file in order to accommodate escorts on either side. People straining to reach past their escorts slowed progress to a crawl.

“Demon!” someone shouted above the din behind Denassa, where Kayarra walked.

Relief upon reaching the Gateway’s mound lasted only until Denassa cleared the edge and saw tufts of wild grass scattered about, roots shriveled, blades yellowing. Where the janquer stood at sundown, the soil had been torn up and imperfectly tamped down.

After that first glimpse, Denassa focused on the shecarens and did not look down, although she knew her face must show her stun.

Vextra surprised her by again volunteering his service as Thurrang representative, but by that time, gratitude lay beyond the capability of her rent emotions. Abbah was a blur of strangers’ faces and excruciating length. At the conclusion of the rite, in impulsive need, janquer and tribal representatives kept their hands clasped long after the final refrain. Denassa drew from that physical union a steadiness she desperately needed. Their handclasps silently defied anyone to threaten janquer and tribal solidarity.

"Peace throughout the nation!" someone shouted, and that cry was repeated, spread, became a roar of approval and support, drowning out those who shouted that Acrahh was dead and the shecarens were controlled by a demon.

Aya signaled everyone to hold their positions and descended the mound alone. Denassa saw Manerra stiffen, which was a greater emotional reaction than he'd ever displayed in public. Aya touched the hands that strained to reach him, circled the mound, then signaled his companions to follow and entered the still-open pathway alone.

Aya's escorts ran after him, followed with amazing restraint and dignity by Manerra and his escorts. Denassa turned and followed Yutrenta down the slope, fists tight-clenched to counteract tremors, careful to keep her fists hidden by her sleeves.

Kayarra, paler than a dead man, trembled uncontrollably. Denassa was thankful he did not understand the shouts, although demotic expressions and gestures could not be mistaken for anything other than hostility, anger and fear.

They passed the Gateway's narrow entrance and gained the uphill road before they were able to walk side-by-side.

"Where's the shon regis?" an escort asked.

"He'll join us later," Manerra answered, and Denassa’s head turned at the strain in Manerra’s voice.

Nothing was certain anymore.

Someone pressed her shoulder. "We need to talk," Shurna shouted in her ear.

"Come to my room after breakfast," Denassa shouted, keeping her attention on the road.

Shurna slowed, letting space open between them.

Before they reached Gorrow's house, their escorts fell away and blocked the road, stopping those who followed. Only Manerra's escorts remained at his sides.

In front of Gorrow's house, Manerra called to Kayarra and gestured, but Kayarra backed away from the shecaren and Denassa thrust out a hand to prevent him from bumping her. He jumped at her touch.

"Go with Manerra," Denassa told him and looked into his face as he looked back and down. His pupils were contracted, his breath shallow and fast. If he wasn't suffering panic, he hung on the verge of it. "Aya will be there," she told him, "and others. You won't be alone. You'll be safer there than here."

How much he understood beyond the assurance of Aya's name, she couldn't tell, but he turned and approached Manerra, and Manerra—whether from callousness or an awareness that Kayarra obeyed her rather than him—turned before Kayarra reached him and started up the hill toward Casta's house. Denassa wished she could go with Kayarra for assurance, but turned and entered Gorrow's house behind her companions.

* * * * *

Shurna and Yutrenta waited in Denassa's bedroom when she arrived well after breakfast. Their escorts obstructed the hall outside her door, but parted to allow her entrance. Her escorts added congestion to the dim and narrow confines of the hall. She paused in the doorway and turned. "Wait at the top of the stairs," she told the entire group, and watched them shuffle away from the door before she closed it.

Shurna and Yutrenta watched her enter, Shurna seated on the edge of the bed, Yutrenta occupying the end of a bench opposite her. Denassa crossed to the bench, sank down, slumped against the wall, and shut her eyes.

"Are you well?" Shurna asked.

"I no longer know," Denassa said and opened her eyes, meeting Shurna's concern before lowering her gaze to the folded bundle on the bed. "Have you looked at the robe?" Denassa indicated the bundle.

"No," Shurna's surprise was audible. "I would not pry into your belongings."

"It's not mine. Open it." Denassa straightened from the wall but did not stand, and regretted the loss of the wall's support. Her body felt leaden. She had forced herself to eat, but the food became rocks in her stomach. She had been concerned about getting sick by not eating, now she worried about getting sick after eating.

Shurna broke the string that bound the cloth and began spreading the robe across the bed. Yutrenta spotted the abalone moons on the robe the same time Denassa did and stood. In a step, she reached the bedside. Her gasp told Denassa she'd seen the bloodstains. She pulled the fabric wider, straightening the remaining folds.

"This is Aya's robe?" Yutrenta asked.

"Yes," Denassa said. "I've made arrangements with Gorrow for escort to the baths. I'm cleaning the robe myself. No one knows how many saw the blood before Casta did."

"Where were the shecarens' escorts when this happened?" Yutrenta demanded, alarm audible amid her growing anger.

"It had to have happened while he stood on the mound, or descended it."

"He knew this when he ordered his escorts back this morning!"

Denassa leapt from her seat in time to catch Yutrenta's wrist as her hand rose to her mouth. "And proved he wasn't cowered by their threats. You know he hates escorts, hates the fear they imply, hates the isolation. He would have ordered them back without the threats, been more vulnerable without that knowledge. Trust him, Trenta."

Shurna stood up, touched Yutrenta's other arm.

"He's unarmed, Dee! I don't care his training! Your father survived attack, but not everyone does. He's half mortal. He can die." She jerked from their hands, crossed the room, stood facing the wall, both hands covering her face.

Denassa watched Yutrenta's back, said nothing, didn't know what to say. For all her upset, Yutrenta wasn't crying. Denassa looked into Shurna's eyes.

"Did Gorrow offer housekeepers to accompany you?" Shurna asked, and it took Denassa a moment to understand Shurna's reference.

"Yes. Two."

"Which ones?"

Denassa hesitated, trying to remember their names, although the arrangements had concluded only moments ago. "Tayna is one. Ressa or Resha is the other."

"Rasha?" Shurna asked.

"Yes," Denassa answered, and in the corner of her eye, saw Yutrenta whirl.

"Oh gods!" Yutrenta cried.

"What's wrong?" Denassa demanded.

"I think Rasha's a Kitarin witch," Shurna said.

That blasphemous term, coming from Shurna, was alarming. "She wore the palm and sun," Denassa said.

"We know," Yutrenta said.

Denassa's heart pounded and her eyesight dimmed with yet another emotional blow.

". . . Gorrow's deceit," Denassa heard Yutrenta say when awareness returned.

"Are you sure?" Denassa demanded.

"I'm accompanying you to the baths," Shurna said. "I should know for certain by the time we return."

Denassa sank onto the edge of the bed, lifted a sleeve of Aya's robe, dropped it. "Why would Gorrow risk such a thing?"

"I suspect Casta and Aya will ask him," Shurna said.

Denassa rubbed her face, stood, and began refolding Aya's robe so the bloodstains were hidden inside the folds.

"What decisions were made last night?" Yutrenta asked.

While she worked, Denassa shared Aya's and Casta's plans for the assimilation of the sixth tribe at Ayahn Rahh and nationwide. By the time she finished talking, she had donned a travel robe, replaced her veil, and armed herself. "I'd intended to order my escorts to the baths ahead of us," she told Shurna. "My preference is to walk the city anonymously. If you wish yours to accompany you, then—"

"No," Shurna interrupted. "It will take me but a moment to change." She hurried toward the door.

# CHAPTER 30

Beyond Gorrow's house, the road curved around the side of the mountain then looped back upon itself and rose steeply. No houses loomed beyond the hairpin turn, which increased Kayarra's misgivings. Only the presence of Manerra's escorts kept him trailing the shecaren.

Another sharp turn in the road, this one right, and sky greeted him: the pale blue of early morning broken by a feathery brush of white clouds. He halted. A palm tree's uppermost fronds swayed beyond the ledge upon which he stood. Beyond the fronds, desert stretched to the horizon. Kayarra started toward the rim, heard his name called, and turned.

Manerra stood on paving stones before a house three times the size of Gorrow's. Palm trees rooted in stone piles shaded a patio. Vines draped the sides of large glazed pottery. Upright plants bloomed above the vines' tendrils, yellow and red flowers competing for his attention.

Manerra turned and entered the cavernous doors that stood open to the breeze. The men who had accompanied Manerra waited in the shade of a palm.

Kayarra approached the house warily, stepped through the doors, then sidestepped along the interior wall and paused for eyesight to adjust to the gloom.

Across the room, Manerra stood motionless, his profile to Kayarra. Within minutes, Yutrenta hurried into the room through an arched doorway. After formal greetings, Manerra asked about Aya and Casta.

Kayarra took a step toward Yutrenta before she turned and he realized the woman wasn't Yutrenta. Although her height and voice were amazingly similar, her face was rounder, more youthful, and some trick of braiding caused her hair to fall about her shoulders in a way Yutrenta's did not.

She dipped her head. "I am called Neetria," the woman told him.

"I am called Kayarra," he gave the memorized response, then added, "You are janquer lady Yutrenta."

Neetria appeared stunned, then laughed. Genuine delight underlay her laughter, something he had never generated in any of his companions. "Janquer lady Yutrenta is my . . . ." The term she used sounded familiar. He suspected it meant sister. Neetria turned toward Manerra. "Please."

She gestured toward an ornately carved door, crossed the room, and held the door open while they passed through.

Low tables lined the walls of the room they entered. Cushioned chairs and tall, thin tables formed a semicircle that faced a shoulder-high mantel. Manerra headed for the chairs, but Kayarra hesitated, uncertain of protocol. "Come." Neetria brushed the back of his arm in passing, urging him toward the chairs. Kayarra sat as far away from Manerra as possible.

Polished stone, carved and inlaid woods, and intricately patterned fabrics vied for attention. The refined richness made Gorrow's house appear garish by comparison.

Neetria asked Manerra something, and while he answered, musicians entered and slipped along the walls to the four corners of the room. A woman entered bearing a bowl of water, and Kayarra recognized the pre-meal preparations.

As soon as food arrived, talk halted and the musicians began playing. Kayarra sampled the prepared dishes, but settled upon nutmeats and raw foods, preferring their crunch and snap to the oily coating left on his tongue by the fried foods. The housekeepers kept his drink bowls full, so finally, the thirst that had persisted from the night before was slacked.

"Lord Kayarra," Manerra said at meal's end and Kayarra's distrust reared full-blown, "go . . . ." Manerra signaled to a woman standing beside the door, spoke to her, and she turned toward Kayarra with trepidation.

Kayarra remained seated—pretended not to understand even the words he knew. If the woman was disturbed by Manerra's order, he sure as hell didn't want anything to do with it.

"*Go with her*," Manerra said.

Kayarra's head snapped around, stunned. Manerra had spoken his language.

Manerra had hovered about the edges of his evening language lessons. Sometimes, his and Aya's canopy had been close enough to Denassa's that he could have eavesdropped, but never had Manerra exhibited interest in learning his language. A chill traveled Kayarra's arms. He stood, willing to go with the woman if only to get away from Manerra. The woman turned and Kayarra followed her from the room.

The woman led him through the entrance hall, through the arched doorway, and along a gallery that glittered with lamplight. They passed stairs, closed doors, and doors that stood open upon small, intimate rooms warmed by rugs, tapestries, and simple, carved furniture. At the end of the gallery, beside closed, double doors, stood a copper pot large enough to conceal a crouching man. When the woman paused to open the doors, Kayarra peered into the pot. It held water. His attention left the pot and traveled the length of the right-hand hall, which ended at a kitchen. Idle workers stared back at him.

"Lord," his guide said.

He pulled his attention from the kitchen workers and followed her into a walled garden. Gnarled and twisted trees shaded stone paths that divided beds of creeping vines and groundcover from clusters of round-leafed plants. Other beds held plants with broadsword and saw-toothed leaves; one even held short, round cacti covered like ticks with the hard, green fruit Denassa called dysie. Plants bore an array of blossoms, stalks bent under the weight of fleshy pods, and throughout the garden, insects hummed, birds chirruped or squawked.

The path his guide took veered left toward a shaded bench. Beyond the bench, a stone-lined pool nestled in the el of the outer wall. Ferns crowded the shady corner behind the pool, and a fleshy vine hugged the wall, reaching chartreuse tendrils skyward. The same tree that shaded the bench thrust glossy leaves over an edge of the pool, creating a welcoming grotto of shade, water, and life.

The woman stopped beside the bench and turned, able to go no farther. Kayarra stopped before he reached her, wondering why she'd led him here. She stood, hands layered at her waist and head bowed. He stood in awkward silence. Was he supposed to remark upon the beauty of the secluded pool? Acknowledge her? Wait for enlightenment?

Gradually, he realized she would stand there forever before violating whatever protocol he failed to grasp. He stepped closer and touched her arm.

She started, then gestured toward bowls set at the pool's edge, one full of sand, another full of leaf fragments, and spoke in a rush. She indicated a robe lying across the bench, lifted an edge of the robe to show him a length of gray cloth underneath, and the realization struck that he was expected to bathe in the pool.

He looked at her then, wondering whether custom required her presence, and what services she was expected to perform during that bath. He felt the pulsing pressure of arousal.

"Go!" he shouted in reaction to the clash of embarrassment and need.

She jumped away as if stabbed; did not wait for another command. He listened to her running footsteps dwindle toward the house, and sat down hard on the bench. He started to reach under the hem of his robe, stopped, and dropped his face into his hands. When he stirred, it was to look back at the house. Tree branches obscured some of the view, but what he saw was a flat wall of interlocked stones towering above the garden walls.

He was thankful for the absence of windows. He felt small, naked, and exposed. After further hesitation, he undressed and stepped into the pool. At its deepest, the water rose to his knees. He sat down, gasping at the chill. Ripples spilled over the edge of the pool and splash the ferns. He cupped water and splashed his face, scratched fingers through his beard, then plunged his head underwater and scratched sand from his scalp.

Rubbing leaves from the bowl over an arm produced a mild lather. He used a handful on his hair, rinsed, and lathered again. He scrubbed foot calluses with sand. Finally, he lay back and soaked.

For the first time in memory, hair and skin were free of sand and dust. The dribble of water at his dressing ceremony paled in comparison to this extravagance.

As he reached for the new robe, he realized the absolute wealth of the Shangren; the power this much water gave the people who controlled it.

When, at last, he reentered the house clutching his tribal robe, the woman who had guided him leapt from a bench against the wall, bowed her head, and spoke.

"I talk no," he said.

She looked up, frowning. "Please." She indicated the bench she'd occupied and waved him to sit. When he approached, she reached for his tribal robe but he pulled back. "Please," she entreated.

He sat down, but jerked away when she lifted a comb toward his hair. She emitted an exasperated cry and words spilled out too fast to follow.

"Please," he told her, "please," and held out a hand. She gave him the comb, then turned her back as if ashamed or afraid to watch. He placed the robe in his lap and combed his hair by touch, tearing tangles from the longest strands.

"Lady," he said when he finished.

The woman whirled, an expression of shock on her face that changed to confusion until he held out the comb and she realized he addressed her. She blushed, took the comb, then led him toward the room with the chairs.

As they approached the door, Kayarra heard Aya's voice. The woman stepped aside and Kayarra entered, then hesitated when he saw Aya standing beside the white-haired man who had greeted them in the plaza. He started to withdraw, but Aya spotted him and motioned him forward.

"Casta, lord of the Shangren and of the Ofrann, I show you Kayarra of the sixth tribe," Aya said.

Casta stared until Kayarra remembered to nod; and was still staring when Kayarra lifted his head. "Lord Kayarra, I welcome you to the city of the Shangren," Casta said.

Kayarra looked toward Aya for guidance.

"He understands very little of what you say, Casta," Aya said.

"Did the trepanation fail?"

"No. He speaks, but only words Denassa has taught him."

"Great gods, Aya! You, more than anyone, know what one man will dare. How many problems do you think you can solve?"

"I will handle whatever happens."

"What about Manerra? The janquer?"

"I will have answers before Manerra's assumption."

"I meant that your love targets them. They are your vulnerability."

Aya stood silent. He spoke quietly when, at last, he said, "None of the janquer accepted their responsibilities blindly. They knew the risks."

"And Manerra? You?"

Aya signaled Kayarra. "I would show Kayarra the city."

Casta caught Aya's arm. "I know you had no choice. Just know you're not alone in this."

Aya tilted his head, motioned again to Kayarra, and started for the door. Casta went with them up the stairs, then from the second floor, up a narrow flight of stairs that opened onto a roof. Aya strode to the edge and leaned against the low wall that encircled the roof. Kayarra stopped well away from the wall and stared at the view.

The mountainside descended in a series of terraces. At its foot lay the pool that sustained this hive of life amid the desert's sands.

The Shangren's aquifer was a glittering, flanged cone pressed point-deep into the desert floor. The point grew darker toward the center until it vanished into shadow, giving the fearsome impression of bottomless depth. "The Shangren's pool is called The Eye of the Ofrann," Aya said into the breeze blowing up from the desert's floor.

Kayarra pulled his gaze from the liquid vortex and followed its run-off through stone-lined ditches to cultivated fields that ended with the slice of a knife at sand. Beyond those fields, desert stretched as far as he could see.

"The Shangren's source waters may be withdrawn for drinking and cooking," Casta said. "Water for other uses is drawn from its overflow." He pointed down slope of the pool, at the bustle of activity along the ditches.

Kayarra's attention returned to the mountain. He spotted the park that contained the Gateway to the Sun on a ledge above the pool. From the Gateway, he traced the turns of the road along the terrace, but the mountain's shoulder blocked the plaza from view.

"How does your tribe handle water, lord Kayarra?" Casta asked.

Kayarra looked back at him. "I know water," he said. "You water. Not sand water."

"What else do you know?" Casta asked before Kayarra's attention strayed back to the city. Aya turned around.

Kayarra pointed to the roof. "House," he said, although that wasn't quite right. He knew houses with windows, constructed of wood and brick. He'd never seen houses like Casta's and Gorrow's. He knew, too, the bronze knife, but memories of that incident with Manerra kept him silent. He looked back at the panoramic view, and Casta's and Aya's voices drifted past him. He dared another two steps toward the edge, far enough to see the road that climbed the mountain from the Gateway to the Sun. One of the many houses that faced that road was Gorrow's, but which one, he couldn't tell. He watched three heavily laden horses climb the road until they and their handlers disappeared behind trees and houses. Then his attention swung left and he glimpsed movement on a nearby road. Two of the eight travelers' unbraided hair brushed their waists. Sunlight sparked iridescent highlights in hair as black as raven feathers and he watched them because he'd not seen anyone with unbound hair. Vextra wore his unbraided hair tied at the nape so it hung down his back.

Movement in his peripheral vision caused him to look up into Aya's eyes. Aya touched the bundle he clutched, and Kayarra let Aya take the robe. Aya then followed the line of Kayarra's earlier stare to the approaching newcomers.

"Ladies Shurna and Denassa come," Aya said, and Kayarra looked back at the group, wondering how Aya could tell from this distance, but most of the group had passed the hairpin turn and disappeared from sight. Only the last three travelers were visible, and they vanished around the curve as he watched.

"Is lady Yutrenta with them?" Casta asked.

"No," Aya answered, turned, and started toward the stairs.

Kayarra left the roof with reluctance, following the men down both flights of stairs into the dim confines of the house. They entered the room with the chairs well before Denassa and Shurna burst into the adjacent entrance hall.

The women's sandals and voices rose echoes in the cavernous room, bringing with them a liveliness that rang like cricket song. They spotted Aya and Casta. Their heads bowed, loose hair falling forward over their faces. Their murmurs of "Shon regis. Lord," reverberated in the entrance hall.

"Lady Shurna, lady Denassa," Aya acknowledged them.

Shurna entered the audience room and offered veneration a second time, speaking rapidly in murmurs Kayarra could not distinguish, while Denassa searched through the folded bundles of clothing held by an escort.

"Rasha!" Aya's shout caused everyone except Shurna to jump. His attention was fixed on Denassa's group. "Which one of you is Rasha?" Aya demanded.

One of the women hastily pressed her bundles into her companion's arms and stepped forward. "I am, shon regis."

"Disarm her," Aya ordered.

Rasha stepped back in alarm as escorts sprang forward and caught her arms. One removed the knife at her belt while others ran their hands down her body and up her legs. She gasped and flinched from their search, but grips on her arms held her firm. No more weapons were found and they released her.

"Approach," Aya ordered.

The escorts advanced beside her, pulled her to a halt a body's length away.

"What is this?" Rasha demanded.

"Remove your travel robe," Aya ordered.

Kayarra looked at Shurna, whose attention didn't waver from Rasha, then at Denassa, who was grim but unsurprised by Aya's sudden anger.

"If I've given offense—" Rasha said.

"Remove your travel robe."

Rasha hesitated, then reached for the ties at her throat. The trembling of her hands slowed her compliance, but eventually she stood within the circle of the crumpled robe. The palm tree and circle on the breast of her tribal robe was a simple embroidery in colored threads.

"Name your employer," Aya said when her travel robe lay on the floor.

"I serve the household of Lord Gorrow, shon regis."

"Name your tribe."

Rasha sent Shurna a glance of searing hatred.

"Name your tribe," Aya repeated.

"The Kitarin, shon regis."

"Witch!" Shurna hissed.

"Quiet," Aya snapped, then to Rasha: "Have you received Kitarin training?"

"Yes, shon regis."

Aya's expression went grim. "Why does a Kitarin talent wear an Ofrann symbol?"

"I was employed to discover traders who attempted deceptions against the Shangren government."

"You wear a symbol you weren't born to amid members of the janquer. Does Gorrow doubt their honesty?"

"I don't know what lord Gorrow believes, shon regis."

"He has forfeited that title," Aya said. "I will hear what Gorrow thinks soon enough. But you. You shame the Kitarin by blaspheming their greatest skill. You accepted an honor and broke that covenant." Aya paused, but Rasha stared straight ahead, her face rigid, her attention unswerving from the wall. "You will leave for Kaytron before dawn. Lady Toma shall decide Kitarin fate. Now remove the false robe."

Rasha flinched and the rest of the color drained from her face.

"You cannot shame yourself more than you have," Aya said. And when she did not move, "You will remove the robe or your escorts will remove it."

Rasha reached behind her neck for the ties and eventually dropped the cord on the floor. Then she pulled the fabric off both shoulders at the same time, freed her arms, and let the material fall to the floor. As she stood naked before them, only her companion's crying was heard.

"Take her to Gorrow's house. Tell Gorrow the shon regis orders her escort to Kaytron. The expense is his."

A scream of fury caused Kayarra to jump backward, even before sight registered Rasha's leap. Shurna whirled away from her attacker, caught by Rasha's hold on a sleeve, which broke when Rasha fell beneath the weight of the men who tackled her. Escorts leapt in front of Aya and Casta and rushed to Shurna's side, while Shurna clutched the arm Rasha had gripped.

"You set your brothers against each other rather than face Hyran," Rasha screamed at Aya from the floor.

A guard's slap silenced her.

"Enough violence!" Aya shouted. "Take her to Gorrow's. Be certain she stays there until she leaves the city."

Rasha's guards dragged her to her feet kicking. One side of her face flamed an angry red. Spittle and blood smeared her lip and chin. "Acrahh's line is tainted," Rasha yelled, fighting her guards' holds. "The demon is proof Acrahh's dead. Fear for your souls," she screamed as her guards forced her from the room.

Aya sidestepped his escorts, caught Shurna's elbow, lifted her bloodied sleeve, and stared at the scratch marks that welled with blood.

"Bring my physician!" Casta shouted.

"Ride to Gorrow's house," Aya yelled. "Get Yutrenta out of there before Rasha's guard arrives."

# CHAPTER 31

"Assemble enough peacekeepers to bring Gorrow here," Aya ordered. "He alone is to be brought."

The man Aya stared at flashed the sign of acquiescence and hurried from the room.

"Casta, I'd like you present during Gorrow's questioning. You, too, Shurna. After your arm's treated."

A woman carrying a physician's bag burst into the room. "Lord Casta—?" She spotted Aya and hastily dipped her head.

Shurna started across the room toward her.

"I will not embarrass the Shangren government by withdrawing from the city," Aya said, "but my companions will require new accommodations."

"They are invited to rest here while new accommodations are readied," Casta offered.

"You have my gratitude," Aya said, but his voice held anger rather than gratitude. "Denassa, keep Kayarra beside you today."

"Yes, shon regis." Denassa reached toward Kayarra, who saw her signal and went to her.

Two escorts preceded them from the room, then fell into step beside Denassa when she passed through the door. Two others followed.

Denassa entered one of the gallery's side rooms and motioned Kayarra toward a cushioned bench. Their escorts took up positions on either side of the door.

Kayarra spent the rest of the day in the room off the gallery while three housekeepers braided Denassa's hair and armed escorts stood outside the closed door. When he had to relieve himself, two escorts accompanied him to the chamber room, inspected the room before he was allowed to enter, waited outside the door until he finished, then escorted him back to Denassa. Their extreme caution increased his anxiety. If armed men broke into their room, they had no exit, and only Denassa wore a knife.

Kayarra moved a bench to the wall behind the door and sat with his back against the wall, straining to hear sounds in the gallery. He tensed each time voices spoke outside the door and shut his eyes in an effort to improve hearing. At some point, his eyes remained closed and his head slumped sideways onto his shoulder.

The closing of the door woke Kayarra with a start. He squinted at the newcomers, disturbed that they had entered without waking him. That the newcomers were Shurna and Yutrenta did not comfort him. They could as easily have been attackers.

Housekeepers shifted chairs from the walls to the center of the room to accommodate the newly arrived janquer and Kayarra slumped against the wall.

"The inquiry's ended?" anxiety was strong in Denassa's voice.

"Yes," Shurna answered. "A little while ago."

"What explanation did Gorrow give for his orders?"

"He claimed the deception prevented traders from cheating the Shangren government and assured fair exchanges for its citizens."

Yutrenta snorted. "Gorrow is not known for his generosity. If anyone benefited, he alone did."

"Gorrow believed what he said," Shurna said.

"What was his reason for using Rasha among the janquer?"

"He claimed if she'd revealed her tribal affiliation, safety concerns would have compelled her return to Kaytron."

"It wasn't Rasha's safety Gorrow worried about," Yutrenta remarked.

Denassa said, "Gorrow did not appear so short of help that he needed to use Rasha among us."

"Aya asked that," Shurna replied. "Why, when Gorrow sent only two assistants with us to the baths, why Rasha was one of them."

"What did he answer?" Yutrenta demanded.

"That she was one of his most trusted assistants and he would not have sent anyone less skilled, out of regard for our safety."

Yutrenta gave a bark of scorn. "Gorrow wanted information. He wanted it so badly, he risked Rasha's disclosure to gain it. That she was discovered should not have surprised him once he learned Shurna accompanied you to the baths, Dee."

"By the time he learned that," Shurna said, settling her head against the back of the chair, "he could not substitute another without raising questions."

"What is Aya's decision?" Denassa asked.

"Gorrow has until mid-morning to leave the Shangren. He can take only those housekeepers who ask to go with him, and he can take only what goods three shuren can carry."

"And he lost his title," Denassa added.

"Yes, he lost his title," Shurna agreed. "And lord Casta declared a severance of kinship. That announcement will be made public. Gorrow's life is now in danger from those he's dealt with."

In the silence, Shurna rubbed the wrist of her injured arm. "Yutrenta, you should know that your father was innocent of Gorrow's deception."

"I never thought him an accomplice."

"I know. But Aya had to be sure."

*****

Manerra recited morning abbah's final refrain with anticipation and dread. Relief over leaving the Shangren collided with the realization that his oath taking was less than two moon cycles away. Trys had risen from the horizon to become a dominant presence in the nighttime sky, and his ghost shape hung visible at dawn. The night he kissed Ryna, Manerra's future was sealed.

After the janquer broke handholds, Manerra turned away to accept his travel robe from a housekeeper who had accompanied them to the Gateway. He watched Shurna and Kayarra, surrounded by armed men, don travel robes, then fasten belts. Yutrenta and Denassa, fully cloaked, slipped into the crowd. Their abandoned escorts joined those encircling Casta.

Casta massaged his arm as though kneading a cramped muscle. Lack of sleep made dark caves of his eyes and sweat beaded his forehead. Manerra suspected that Casta's offer of a temporary travel escort was based as much upon a wish to hasten their departure and ward against their immediate return as for protection against followers.

At last, Aya signaled and Manerra followed his brother down the slope of the mound while escorts fell in around them. This time, instead of turning right at the pillars, they turned left, joining the flow of people down the mountainside. At the entrance to the plaza and market, they passed a water merchant attempting to drive horses against the flow of people streaming downhill, his curses revealing his ignorance of the shon regis's presence.

Where the road to the aquifer split from the plaza road, a runner caught Manerra's attention. Manerra thought the man intended to pass them, but at the last moment, he veered toward Aya and Casta. Knives hissed from sheathes all around. The man threw up his hands and danced backwards, his panting making it impossible for him to speak for those first, frightening moments.

The standoff drew attention from passers-by, who veered clear of the threat then stopped and stared.

"L-lord," the runner finally gasped, "Casta. We drew a body . . . from the pool. Stabbed. Come. Somebody. Hurry." At that moment, the runner suffered a fit of coughing so severe, one of their escorts grabbed his arm to steady him.

"Who?" Casta demanded, but had to wait through the coughing bout until the man could draw a full breath. "Who?"

"A woman. Someone said . . . Lord Gorrow's housekeeper. But I don't know."

"Rasha?" Shurna gasped at Manerra's side.

Casta started toward the branching road with Aya close behind. Their escorts moved with them, pulling the messenger along.

From Manerra's position, Casta appeared to swerve to miss something lying in the street and failed to recover his balance. Aya lunged for him and caught fistfuls of robe.

A woman cried out. Strangers surged forward.

An escort caught Casta's shoulders before Casta's head struck stone, but fell with his arm under Casta's neck. The escort's shout of pain was drowned out by screams.

Escorts leapt into a circle surrounding them, knives drawn against the fear and chaos of the Shangren's citizens.

Manerra helped Shurna pull the injured guard away from Casta while Aya kept a hand on Casta's throat.

"Give me a knife," Aya yelled, and grabbed the first one offered.

"Get a physician!" Shurna screamed.

Beads showered paving stones as Aya sliced through the front of Casta's robes to the waist.

Manerra dropped to the ground beside Casta's shoulder.

"Cover your eyes," Aya shouted as he reached for the temple stone. "Don't just close them. Cover them. Or turn away." He didn't wait for compliance. The temple stone flared with blinding light even as Manerra threw an arm over his eyes. Against Manerra's knee, Casta's body jerked.

When Manerra dared open his eyes, Aya's mouth covered Casta's. With rising panic, Manerra feared that Aya's robes merely blanketed the uncloaked temple stone.

"Keep your faces covered!" Manerra shouted, wanting a signal from Aya that he was wrong.

Aya gasped breath, and Manerra watched Aya force air into Casta's lungs again and again. When Aya finally stopped, he supported his weight on his arms above Casta while he recovered his own breath. Manerra slipped a hand through Aya's braids to locate the vein in Casta's neck. He felt a pulse and a faint, moist draft across his wrist.

"Where's the temple stone?" Manerra asked while his mouth hovered close to Aya's ear.

Aya lifted Manerra's hand and pressed it down amid the bunched cloth between Aya's knees and Casta's arm. "It's covered," Aya gasped.

Manerra reached down with both hands, started to lift the stone, felt it slip within its cover, and caught the heavy stone before it slipped from its casing.

"We need a litter," Aya gasped and then straightened.

Manerra searched Aya's face, saw his eyes closed, and Manerra's heart pounded against his breastbone.

"Bring a litter," Manerra shouted without glancing aside. "Or make one."

With the temple stone cradled in his lap, Manerra reached for its tooled pouch. He secured the stone inside that protection, and only then breathed easier.

"Shurna," Aya called, "go to the aquifer."

"Yes, shon regis." Shurna pressed through their circle of guards. Two left formation to follow her.

"Get back!" Manerra shouted as bystanders risked the threat of knives to snatch a glimpse of their fallen lord. Manerra flipped the edges of Casta's robe over the darkening mark on his chest. Casta still breathed on his own. But for how long?

Someone bumped Manerra's arm. "Get back!" He channeled all his anger and fear into that shout; had to have been heard above the fearful speculations, the pleas for information, the wails of women and children. Almost as one, their escorts took a step forward, forcing spectators back.

Where were the physicians? Any physician?

"Kayarra!" Manerra shouted. "Get Yutrenta. That way." He pointed in the direction of the market. "Hurry."

Kayarra leapt as though stung, dashed through a gap in their escorts, and forced his way through the pressing crowd . . . alone. Too late, Manerra realized his mistake and looked toward Aya. Aya's eyes remained closed. He hadn't seen Kayarra's unescorted bolt.

Kayarra was untitled. In an emergency, their escorts' first duty demanded protection of all titled members of a company.

Aya's lips moved in silent prayer and Manerra turned away, searching the faces beyond their escorts for more immediate help.

Nothing.

He hadn't seen any stranger turn and follow Kayarra. Maybe Kayarra would pass unnoticed.

An agonizingly long time later, Manerra heard shouts of "Let us through! Let us through!" and saw the end of a ladder above the heads of the crowd.

"Open a path!" Manerra shouted and pushed an escort until the man stepped aside. The ladder carrier broke through the crowd and Manerra recognized the carrier as one of Casta's personal escorts. Manerra caught the end of the ladder before it struck Aya's head and guided it to the ground beside Casta. The man lifted his elbow and a blanket tucked under his arm hit the ground.

Manerra grabbed the man's forearm. "What's the nearest house we can take him to?" he demanded.

"Lord Patran's house faces the plaza. But by your order—"

"Patran's is fine. You—" Manerra grabbed another escort's arm. "Go to Patran's. Tell him we're coming. And for Acrahh's sake, have a physician there!"

The man took off running.

"Lift him on my command," Aya said and Manerra turned. Aya was standing. Manerra watched the men secure a grip in Casta's robe, preparing to lift him onto the blanket-covered ladder. Aya's eyes were open. Tears streamed down his cheeks.

Manerra was the only one there who knew Aya's tears were a consequence of the temple stone's use, not grief over Casta's collapse.

Aya was blind.

Manerra whirled and ran, as much to escape that reality as fear of his own action's consequences. In memory, he wasn't certain whether he'd shouted he was going to find Yutrenta or not, but by now, it didn't matter. He had to find Kayarra before the cor-anda's body was the next one pulled from the Shangren's pool.

# CHAPTER 32

Kayarra rushed along the road Manerra had indicated, dodging people, colliding with others, running in short bursts where he could—ignorant of his destination, but driven by the urgency to find Yutrenta. When the road ended at a plaza, he didn't, at first, recognize the place, then wondered how he could find Yutrenta within that crowd.

"Yutrenta!" he shouted, saw strangers turn and stare, then pressed ahead, toward the far side of the plaza. People strolled in every direction. Few loitered. This couldn't be Yutrenta's destination. He didn't know why she would be here. He ran the direction most people headed. He reached a distant road out of breath but didn't pause before plunging into the crowded street.

"Yutrenta!" he shouted. People nearby looked back, then jerked away. During his entrance into the city, their reactions had been hurtful, but now his appearance opened a path before him.

"Yutrenta!"

The street ended at a plaza larger than the first, jammed with people, with animals, with crates. Arranged atop blankets spread over paving stones were birds in bentwood cages; stacks of wood, horn, bone and metal utensils; glass jars; produce of every kind; sandals; fly-attracting animal carcasses suspended from metal and wood tripods.

Kayarra veered aside. This place had become a nightmare of blood and raw flesh. He was afraid to look anywhere for fear of seeing more.

"Yutrenta!" Kayarra yelled, praying for her to hear him, to find him so he could leave this place. Buildings loomed ahead so he pressed left, treading across blankets in order to get past barterers, browsers, vendors.

"Yutrenta!"

"Kayarra!"

At first, he doubted his hearing. She wasn't anywhere in sight. Then he saw her dodge a man laden with hides and he staggered toward her, hyperventilating from a panic that threatened to overwhelm him.

"Casta," he gasped when she reached him. She grabbed his arm and pulled too hard. He stumbled. "Aya."

She caught him. "What about Aya? Kayarra, tell me. What's wrong?"

"Casta hurt."

Her nails dug into his arm. She pulled, obviously wanting to run, but he couldn't. Not yet. Not so soon. "Go," he told her. "I come."

She looked back at him . . . uncertain, torn.

"Go fast to Aya," he shouted.

She released his arm then and ran, back the way he'd come, disappearing through the crowd with a crash, clatter, and bang of pans that went skittering in her wake. A man yelled at her. She didn't stop.

Kayarra bent, gripped his knees, and took gasping breaths until the awful constriction in his chest eased. Yutrenta knew. She knew. Casta would be all right. They would still leave the Shangren.

He straightened and started back, giving wide berth to the pot vendor.

When he reached the return road, two roads left the market where he'd only remembered one. He scanned the buildings, the vendors, trying to figure out which road he'd taken from the plaza, but his arrival was a blur of impressions wiped from memory by discovery of the meat sellers. The remembered imagery set him walking again, wanting to escape the possibility of encountering the skinned animals a second time. The tent stood on the plain. He would find it if he went down the mountain. There weren't too many ways to get lost on a mountain.

Halfway down the road, sight of a low branching tree with multi-fingered leaves stopped him. He hadn't passed a tree on the way to the market. He turned and saw a knot of men on the street behind him fan out across the road. He froze. One held a bare knife, and as he watched, others drew knives. He stepped backward.

"He's armed," someone shouted.

"Even a demon can't take us all," the nearest man growled.

With supreme effort, Kayarra lifted his arms away from his sides, showed empty palms, and backed away. He stopped retreating when he stumbled in the rut of a missing paving stone and the men following crouched, ready to spring.

"Manteen spawn," one spat.

"No," Kayarra said, recognizing the family name but ignorant of its connotations.

Men passed him, keeping out of striking distance, and he could do nothing to prevent them from surrounding him. Sweat trickled down his side and he jumped as though its runnel were the stroke of a blade.

All around him, knees bent, nostrils flared, eyes narrowed.

"Demon bastard."

Spittle struck a stone in front of his sandal.

"Let him go," came a high-pitched plea somewhere behind the men.

"Hand him your children now, then, Maytel," a man answered without turning. "Save him the trouble of stalking them."

"He came with the shon regis," she said.

"He possesses the shecarens."

"You don't know that."

"Go away, Maytel."

"Help me!" Kayarra shouted at the woman, at anyone.

"Kill him!" a man shouted back.

"No!" the woman screamed.

"Pull your knife, cor-anda," the nearest man ordered. "You might see our blood before you die."

"Coward!" another man shouted.

Kayarra felt a tug on his belt sheath and jumped, certain the attack had begun.

"*I* have his knife."

It took Kayarra several painful heartbeats to recognize Manerra, who had ducked under his arm and come up in front of him. The shecaren held his knife, its tip pressed against his chest. "He can't attack you unarmed," Manerra said, "but if you fall against my hand, the shon regis will kill him. My brother will recognize his knife in my chest. The demon's blood need never defile your hands."

No man moved. A woman began sobbing.

"Come." Manerra stepped forward. "Just a stumble. Anyone who objects to bearing witness can leave."

Offered an escape, knives vanished into sheathes and most men retreated, two of them, at a run. The man Manerra had challenged remained, his knife unwavering.

Kayarra lowered his hands but made no other move. He was afraid to look behind him, to take his eyes off the stalemate before him. The man's slit eyes planted the knife blade deep in Manerra's heart.

But the crowd was dispersing and the man finally flung his knife to the pavement. The blade broke upon impact. "Acrahh is all that protects you," he hissed in Manerra's face.

"As he does you," Manerra replied evenly and lowered his knife hand.

"That Manteen spawn will be your undoing," the man said. "Take his blood before he takes yours." The man whirled. No one in the vicinity hindered his retreat.

Manerra watched, then turned around and yanked Kayarra in the direction of the tree, away from the market.

Kayarra's extremities were numb, his steps clumsy, stilted. Only Manerra's grip on his arm kept him walking.

A path remained clear before them, although Kayarra, when he could think beyond the numbing image of drawn knives, could not believe the rumor of the attack had spread so rapidly beyond that one narrow street. Heads turned, following their passage. This occurred all the way to the plaza, where Manerra stopped and finally broke the silence between them. "Do not tell Aya this story." He thrust the hilt of the knife into Kayarra's hand. "Go." The shecaren shoved him toward the door of a house. "The janquer are inside." Manerra whirled and hurried away, headed back the direction they had come.

*Manerra!* Kayarra wanted to shout but lacked the nerve to do so.

Manerra quickly vanished among the throng in the street, leaving Kayarra alone among strangers. He bolted the final steps to the door and burst inside, scaring a housekeeper and startling two guards. He slammed the door, slumped against the wall, and did not move.

Neetria rushed into the room to investigate the disturbance and hurried over to clutch his arm between her hands. "Are you hurt?" her voice was remarkably controlled, although she appeared extremely pale. Her eyes were dry but red rimmed.

"No," Kayarra answered.

She slid her hands down his arm to his fist and, by gentle hand pressure, got him to sheathe his knife. Afterward, she stayed with him, holding his arm. He pushed away from the wall when he thought he could walk without assistance, when he thought he could tolerate the presence of other people without breaking down. She accompanied him into the adjacent room, where strangers with grave faces—standing, sitting—stared at them. Only a few looked away.

Later, he found himself seated without a clear recollection of how he got there. Neetria wasn't beside him, and he couldn't remember her leaving. He released his death grip on the edge of the table and clutched his hands between his knees. His fingers were numb.

"Kayarra."

He started and looked up into Denassa's face.

She offered him a bowl. "I made you a tea."

"No," he said.

"Please drink." She lowered it toward his hands.

He looked down into the bowl but did not take it. "No." He couldn't hold the bowl without spilling the greenish liquid it held and he couldn't tell her that.

She sat down and slid an arm around his waist.

"Where have you been? What happened?"

"Manerra said not tell Aya."

Two heads turned in their direction.

Denassa slid a hand up his side and hooked his elbow. "Come," she whispered, drawing him up with her. She led him into a hall.

*Cor-anda*, the man shouted. Before today, only Manerra had ever called him that.

Light from the room behind and from an open door ahead was all that illuminated the corridor. Kayarra ran his hand along the wall while Denassa pulled him forward. When she opened a door halfway down the hall, he blinked in a glare of lamplight before following her inside.

Kayarra drew back when he saw a man lying on a cushioned bench in the middle of the room. A woman knelt on each side of the bench. The woman with her back to him was either Neetria or Yutrenta. A folded cloth covered the man's hair and eyes.

"Shon regis," Denassa said, and Kayarra's assumption that the man was Casta shattered, "I bring Kayarra."

"What bad to Aya?" Kayarra blurted. Casta had collapsed, not Aya.

"He will be blind for a time," Denassa said.

"What blind?"

"His eyes." She touched hers. "He will not see." She turned back toward Aya in obvious distress. "Tareen, please leave us. I will assist lady Yutrenta until you're needed."

"Yes, lady." The woman on the far side of the bench left the room.

The thump of the closing door made Kayarra jump.

Aya reached to the bandages covering his eyes. "You have news of Casta?" there was urgency in Aya's question.

"No, shon regis. Other news. Manerra asked Kayarra not to tell you something. Unfortunately, lord Fayna and one other overheard Kayarra tell me."

Aya pressed the cloth against his eyes and rose onto an elbow.

"Aya, please," Yutrenta protested.

"Nothing you do will prevent my blinding, Trenta. Stop." He removed the cloth and handed it to her, then swung his feet to the floor but kept his eyes shut.

"What happened, Kayarra?"

Kayarra hesitated.

"Tell me, Kayarra. Now," Aya ordered, and Kayarra did. When Kayarra drew his knife to pantomime Manerra's actions, Denassa and Yutrenta tensed and did not relax until he sheathed the blade. Aya opened his eyes and ordered him to repeat the pantomime, then questioned him on who he portrayed as he did so.

Why did Manerra intervene? Kayarra wondered. When he saw the threat, he could have turned around and left . . . pretended he'd arrived too late.

"Is Manerra in the house?" Aya asked.

"No, shon regis," Denassa answered.

"Denassa."

"Yes, shon regis?"

"Find him. Discretely. I don't want the Shangren's citizens aware of his disappearance. If you can't find him, don't feel you've failed me. If he lives, he will return before abbah."

"Yes, shon regis."

"Go."

Denassa dipped her head and left.

"Kayarra," Aya said, "go nowhere without another company member. Do not separate from that member. I will speak with Manerra so he knows not to order you to any task that will separate you from an escort."

"Do you hurt?" Kayarra asked when Aya stopped talking.

"Not yet," Aya said, then added, "Do not grieve for me, Kayarra. Lord Casta lives. For many reasons, his life is as precious as mine. Pray for his recovery."

Yutrenta brought both hands to her mouth but failed to stifle a sob.

Aya pressed her shoulder. "Yutrenta," Aya said, "attend Casta. Tareen and Denassa—"

Yutrenta recoiled. "No."

"We will leave tomorrow. Go to him," Aya said.

"My father has the resources of the Shangren and the Ofrann. He has other children. You have—"

"I want to know that my sacrifice was not given in vain," Aya interrupted. "If you attend him, I will know everything possible was done to save him."

"His physicians will not welcome my interference," she said, but stood, bowed her head, and left, leaving the door open behind her.

# CHAPTER 33

The infusion that quieted Aya's headache allowed thoughts he'd rather not have. His increasing infirmity combined with Casta's teetering health and Manerra's disappearance left him battling depression. As his pain increased, memory and reasoning abilities would lessen, which were consequences he could least afford in the current crisis. If he had to take dayflower for pain, he would be unable to perform the rituals required of his position. Making decisions would be impossible.

"Shon regis." Shurna's quiet call penetrated the lethargic haze of the drug.

"Come in, Shurna."

"You wanted to know when lord Casta woke. He has."

Aya sat up, keeping a hand on the cushioned bench until his equilibrium adjusted. Then he reached behind his head to remove the cloth that bound his eyes.

"Shon regis—"

The unfamiliar voice startled him. He forgot that Tareen served as his present guardian.

"—you should not risk light."

"I will risk it, Tareen," he told her. "Some things are more important than my comfort." He set the bandages aside, stood, and held out a hand. "Shurna, take me to him."

Casta's sick room lay at the end of the hall. Shurna brought Aya as far as the doorframe, then stepped away so he stood alone. "I would speak with lord Casta privately," Aya told the room's occupants. "Janquer lady Yutrenta, attend your father. Everyone else, please wait in the audience room." He wanted no possibility of eavesdroppers. Shurna, in the hall behind him, would assure his orders were fulfilled. He ducked his head as they filed past, a ploy of courtesy—an acknowledgement of the nods accorded his position—that partially concealed his face. A touch on his back let him know when the room was empty of unwanted occupants.

"So, it's true," Casta said when Shurna led Aya into the room. Casta's voice came low and breathy, a man speaking through shallow breaths.

"What's true, Casta?" Aya asked.

"Your sight. You lost it to save me."

"I was not ready to lose your counsel."

"Aya—" Casta paused, his breaths audible. "You will suffer a lifetime to spare me a day. Your sacrifice—"

"Is not as great as it seems. This blindness passes."

He heard a woman's intake of breath. Yutrenta's.

"I cannot repay you," Casta said. "No words, no wealth—"

"There is a way," Aya said.

Casta's chuckle was cut short by a gasp of pain. A moment passed before he spoke. "Only a godling would make such a claim. After all these years, you still astound me. Tell me. If it is within my failing power, it shall be done."

"Advise your successor of our agreements."

"Korrane handles part of the task already. But I will discuss our plans with him in what detail I've devised."

"Thank you. I wish to gain acceptance of the Kayarran before the matter is passed to Manerra."

"There will be no acceptance of the Kayarran. Tolerance, maybe, but only out of god fear."

"I need more than that, Casta. They're here, already among us."

"Then warn them away. There is no outcome but massacre in welcoming them." Casta paused, his breath rasping. "The gods witness, Aya, I have nothing left to lose or gain. I don't want all we've accomplished to unravel in Korrane's lifetime—not from Hyran's mad prophecies or even your own ideals. Forgive me, Aya, but I haven't time for diplomacy. This is my final counsel."

"Yatren futures can't ignore this development, Casta. Acrahh's hand is in it, and Crysus remains at Ayahn Rahh for a reason still unknown."

"Then deal fairly with them, but do not make them a tribe of Yatra. You're giving the Hyranians the weapon of your downfall."

"I will deal with the Hyranians," Aya said. "But what benefits them or us if we hold the Kayarran outside our laws? I have no ward to keep them from Yatren soil."

"Laws only restrain honest men. My dear Aya—" Casta groaned. "I'm wanting assurance that my tribesmen will not be forced to kill cousins or strangers. Death has a way of turning on murderers, even righteous ones. I do not consider myself faint hearted, but your decisions scare me."

In the ensuing silence, Casta's labored breathing sounded loud.

"I was born to make the decisions no one else wants to make," Aya said.

"Aya, speak to Korrane yourself about our agreements."

"Korrane has greater love for you. What you cannot accomplish may not be possible."

"No flattery. Please."

"I speak the truth, Casta."

"Trenta, stop!" Casta exclaimed.

"She is merciless," Aya said.

"I have perfectly competent physicians who are not my offspring."

"You mean," Yutrenta said, "physicians you can intimidate."

"Can't she be ordered away?" Casta asked.

"I am here by the shon regis's order," Yutrenta said.

"To spare himself," Casta retorted.

Aya chuckled. "She is your child, Casta, but also one of the best physicians in the nation. Give her a chance and she may spare your life."

Casta did not answer for a moment. "I do not lay that burden upon her, Aya. Your use of the temple stone gave me a day more than I would have had otherwise. I know my age. I have prepared for my death. Korrane has. Only you have seen death as something that can be postponed, and Acrahh gives you that power. But don't mistake. My passage is imminent. I am at peace with that."

Aya felt Casta's groping hand and caught it; returned his squeeze; held it.

"Dayla was proud of you," Casta said. "Much of what I admired in her I see in you. Thank you for this chance to conclude my affairs. I have no concern for Yutrenta's future."

"She has honored the Ofrann throughout the nation."

"Korrane will serve you as well. My position is confidently passed. I am honored to have known the children of Acrahh."

"As we have you." Aya squeezed Casta's hand a final time then signaled Shurna his readiness to leave.

Conversations in the audience room fell silent when Aya entered at Shurna's side. "Korrane," Aya called, certain that Casta's eldest son waited with the others.

"Shon regis," Korrane answered.

"Do you know a woman who answers to Maytel?"

"Maytel? No, shon regis."

"I want her found."

"Yes, shon regis."

"But first, attend your father. Alone," Aya added when he heard a widespread rustle of clothing.

"Yes, shon regis."

Those who had stood, sat down.

Aya felt a brush of air on his hand as Korrane passed. He reached for Shurna's arm and followed her back to his room.

"Tareen, leave us," Aya ordered when they entered the room.

"Yes, shon regis."

Aya heard the door click behind her and felt for the chairs he knew fronted his sleeping bench.

"Was it Rasha's body in the aquifer?" Aya asked as he located a chair and sat down.

"Yes, shon regis."

Aya rested his head against the chair's carved backboard. Either the headache was upsetting his stomach or the willow bark was.

"I questioned the man who found her body."

Shurna's robe brushed his knuckles as she turned to sit in an adjacent chair. "Rasha wasn't bleeding when he pulled her from the water."

"Her body was taken from the Shangren's Eye," he guessed, because that location assured the greatest outrage, the greatest blow to Shangren morale. Hands rinsed in bloody water were unclean. To drink such water was akin to cannibalism. People would refuse the water until their current stores were depleted. A purification rite would only accomplish so much.

"It was," Shurna confirmed his guess.

Was Manerra the next complication he faced?

He would have been notified immediately had Manerra's body been discovered anywhere. For now, he blessed the silence.

"Was she clothed?" Aya tried to focus on the information he needed to know.

"No. A bloody Kitarin robe was found on the pier."

"What about Gorrow?"

"A groundskeeper at the baths claims to have seen him depart the Shangren before dawn." Shurna hesitated. "Three peacekeepers were found dead inside his house."

Aya groaned, "No more, Shurna," and covered his face with his hands.

Shurna remained silent, waiting for him to free her from the order, and he could not.

"Should I recall Tareen?" she asked, a long time later.

"No."

"Aya, I'm sorry."

"You can't be sorry for the truth. It simply is."

"I'm sorry for the pain I can't lift from you."

That flustered him. "Have you spoken to Kayarra since your arrival?"

"I looked in on him. I was told he was given a sleeping draught."

"He was caught alone and threatened in the market. Manerra—" Aya stopped talking. He took a breath. "When Kayarra wakes, question him about the attack. Tell me what you understand. For now, please recall Tareen, then send Lord Fayna to me."

"I will."

He heard her stand, but it was a moment before she turned away. He listened to her footsteps cross the room, wishing it was as easy for him to leave.

# CHAPTER 34

Aya pressed a palm hard against his forehead then brought that hand down, looking for blood. If there had been blood, it would have been Manerra's.

That realization so jarred him, he startled awake, then flinched from a hand on his forehead. He went for his knife and heard a woman gasp. The hand on his forehead jerked away.

Thank Acrahh he slept unarmed.

"Aya?" Denassa's voice, full of concern, came from the far side of the room. Her footsteps approached.

He clutched the cushion upon which he lay. The pain in his head kept beat with the pounding of his heart. He swallowed against a flux of vomit.

"Aya—" Denassa stopped at the foot of the bench.

"Who's here?" he gasped.

"Lady Tareen, janquer lady Shurna, myself, you."

It must have been Tareen who had touched him. "Tareen, give us privacy."

"Yes, shon regis."

He heard the rustle of her robe beside the bench, her footsteps, then the opening and closing of the door. He levered himself to a sitting position and braced himself against the bench until dizziness passed.

"Only janquer are present," Shurna said.

"Did you find Manerra?" Aya demanded.

"I searched everywhere I knew to look for him," Denassa answered. "If I could enlist help—"

"No," Aya said. "If he's moving, there is little hope of finding him. Stay. He will return, or meet us at the Gateway to the Sun."

"I'm sorry, shon regis."

"You have not failed me." He heard a step, as though she turned to go.

"Stay," he said.

"Yes, shon regis."

"Shurna."

"Yes, shon regis?"

"Have you heard Kayarra's description of the threat?"

"All he told me."

Always the skeptic. "What are your thoughts?"

"Kayarra told the truth as he saw it. That a threat came in the manner he describes is not a surprise to any of us, I believe. He is badly shaken by it, which again, is expected. But what concerns me is the form of Manerra's intervention. It was a dangerous risk."

An understatement. "I want you to intervene with Kayarra. Ayahn Rahh will be a harder test of his courage. I wish him to understand he is neither isolated nor alone."

Aya questioned the wisdom of discussing Manerra with Denassa present, as slow witted as he was, but this new problem affected the janquer . . . affected far more than his counselors if Manerra's actions remained public.

"I approach the end of my imagination with Manerra," he said, "and I believe he fails patience with me. Are there signals you read that I cannot? Was he serious in his offer to die in order to obtain Kayarra's death?"

"I have not seen him since Casta's collapse," Shurna said. "I don't know his state of mind."

"Did Kayarra believe him serious?"

"Manerra would not have appeared otherwise in so dangerous a situation. He is Kitarin-trained. He would have done what he deemed necessary. It is true that he has little love for Kayarra, but until today, he has kept their feud away from demotic witnesses."

"Do you spare my emotions?"

Shurna exhaled, an exasperated sound. "I don't know Kayarra's skill in reading others. I certainly would not trust him to read accurately someone with Manerra's skill. Manerra is complex even for me, when he means to be. I would trust your reading, blind, to Kayarra's."

That verbal slap jarred him. Aya rubbed his forehead.

"If you send Manerra to me when he returns," Shurna continued, "I will question him. I will be able to tell you more then. But I'm unwilling—"

Aya heard the door open.

"—to conjecture based upon what, right now, is rumor."

"What rumor?" Manerra asked and Aya started.

"The one that involves you and Kayarra," Aya answered.

"I will answer whatever questions you have," Manerra said, "unless they require lengthy explanations. The sun sets. I came for the temple stone."

Aya rose and stretched a hand in the direction Shurna's voice placed her. "We will perform abbah together," he told Manerra. "After Casta's collapse, it's imperative that I perform abbah."

"Your eyes, Aya," Denassa was full of distress, "Yutrenta should—"

"Yutrenta is not given the power of choice in this. Denassa, summon her. And Kayarra."

"Immediately, shon regis."

Footsteps hurried from the room.

Aya reached behind his head to remove the cloth covering his eyes.

"That may be unwise," Shurna objected.

"This, too, is not debatable. Manerra, the temple stone lies at the foot of the bench. Reach it for me."

Yutrenta delayed their departure with anxious protests, but Aya did not recant. Finally, Yutrenta begged him to keep his eyes tightly shut, worried that precaution alone would not prevent exacerbation of his injuries when the sun's rays lit the fire within the temple stone.

* * * * *

After abbah, their escorts attempted to open a pathway through the crowd that jammed the downhill street, but with houses a solid barrier lining the road, citizens had nowhere to shift but forward. Their escorts, forced shoulder-to-shoulder, chest-to-back, walked with hands grasping sheathed knife hilts to the door of Patran's house.

Kayarra made it through the front door, sidestepped, and slammed his back against the wall with his knees on the verge of collapse. He clung to the wall, sweating and panting, while members of Aya's party filed past.

"Kayarra."

He jumped at Shurna's touch. She clutched his wrist. "I'll ask Denassa to prepare a tea for you," she said.

"Thank you," he choked.

"Talk with me after supper."

"I not eat."

"Join us, even if you don't."

He avoided her eyes. He should be handling his fear better than this.

Shurna tightened her hold. He wished she'd go away. The others had already passed.

"You're . . ." Shurna said. Her arms encircled him.

He jerked back but the wall blocked him. He had no place to go. He opened his mouth to speak but a sob came out.

Suddenly, her arms were the only lifelines in a sinking world and he grabbed hold of her as he drowned. His back scrapped along stone as his knees buckled and she sank with him, never letting go. Her arms were all that held the pieces of him together.

* * * * *

Two lords arrived before supper to inquire about Casta's health, leaving Manerra, as the highest ranked individual present, to host the meal. Aya, Yutrenta, and Kayarra were noticeably absent. Forced to make light conversation to the background accompaniment of flutes, Manerra's stomach had knotted by the time the lords departed.

Finally free of social obligations, Manerra withdrew to Aya's room, knowing full well what awaited him.

Tareen knelt before Aya's bench. She turned at his entrance and bowed low over her hands. "Shecaren," she murmured.

Behind her, Aya rose upon an elbow, then shoved upright. "Leave us, Tareen. Please," Aya said. "See that we are not disturbed."

"Yes, shon regis." She rose and headed for the door.

As Tareen passed Manerra, their eyes locked for a moment.

Was Tareen's expression one of curiosity, or had she an inkling of the trouble awaiting him? It would be unlike Aya to confide in a stranger; however, she might have overheard comments not intended for her ears.

"Manerra, thank you for coming," Aya said.

A bad beginning, when Aya chose courtesy over bluntness. "I would have come sooner but I needed to be present at supper."

"I heard. Thank you for handling that responsibility."

Manerra shifted weight. "I assume you heard Kayarra's version of what happened in the market."

"Have you a different version?"

"I trust he told the truth."

"Would you mind Shurna's presence?"

The question caught him off guard—and should not have. He was surprised by how much it hurt. *Do you believe her skills are needed?* he wanted to ask. A noticeable lag passed before he said, "She helped raise me. I cannot resent her presence."

"I will bear that in mind." Aya pushed to his feet and extended a hand toward him.

Manerra dutifully stepped forward and offered his arm to Aya's hand. Aya's fingers closed around his wrist.

Manerra's heart thudded, while Aya held that grip on the pulse at his wrist.

"I'm frustrated that you won't speak plainly with me," Manerra said, before Aya could attach a different interpretation to the rapid heartbeat.

"For once, I find it difficult to broach a subject with you. My emotions are interfering with my need to know. Perhaps, for now, ignorance is the less painful course, but I cannot tolerate the thought of waking one day and hearing that my brother's spirit must join Acrahh's sun."

"I stopped their menacing of Kayarra," Manerra began his prepared defense, "in a way that allowed them to leave with dignity. Surely, Shurna said as much."

"Shurna would not judge you based upon another man's words."

That wasn't what Manerra expected, and yet it was very like her—

painfully fair. He felt guilty for his earlier hesitation even while he knew what he hid. "I had no time to devise a more elaborate plan. They were demanding that Kayarra draw his knife. They were prepared to strike him if he did not."

"Perhaps I will hear this tale from you," Aya replied.

Manerra told what he had seen of the threat to Kayarra.

"A shout to stop, from the shecaren, was not enough?" Aya asked.

Manerra used Kitarin relaxation to slow his heartbeat. "I did not consider anything except the need to remove Kayarra's knife. Unarmed, they could not justify his murder."

"Even if his blade was found lodged in your chest?"

"I did not think they would dare." Too close to a lie. *Acrahh is all that protects you!* and a look that had him dead already.

"But you hoped."

*Not* what he expected. "Aya!" *Damn* his heart!

Aya removed his hand—too late—and stepped away, turned his head.

"Aya—"

"Is that—" Aya's voice broke. "Is that your answer to the problem of the sixth tribe or your final defiance of me?"

"Aya!"

"Which, Manerra?" Aya turned his face toward him, but there was that withdrawal: the small distance between them that felt unbreachable. Even with the cloth binding Aya's eyes there were pain lines visible on his brow, around his mouth.

"Neither." Manerra wondered what to say, how to lie, but discarded those thoughts as they formed. Honesty would achieve the same result as dying, although the pain would never end. "Nothing is as easy as one or the other." He thought he might have to sit down, even if it was on the floor.

"I'm listening."

"There was a child—" Manerra's throat collapsed, remembering that child's hopeless desperation. For a few moments, Manerra could only breathe shallow, gasping pants. "Tackta was angry. Matera told me to hide. I hid in the darkest corner of the tent, curled into the smallest bundle I could make. I willed myself invisible. I heard their argument . . . ."

*Out of my way, you divine whore.*

*What can he tell, Tackta? He's a baby.*

*He* threatened, *damn it. Move!*

*No.*

Curses and screams that would not end. Then silence. His mother! Tackta had killed her!

"I begged, if Acrahh was my father, that he save me from Tackta. That he make me invisible." He knew how pathetic that sounded, but the terror had been real. The fracture of his faith began that night. "I thought he had killed Matera. I thought he would kill me." Manerra flinched and came out of those visions; returned to the room with Aya. *Father, forgive me!* Words became choked, "Acrahh didn't save me."

Aya crossed the intervening space and threw his arms around him. The cloth binding his eyes dampened Manerra's temple.

*'There can be nothing of failure between us.'*

*You said that, not knowing my memories, not knowing my doubt. I can't be what you need, Aya. Tackta saw to that. Before you ever found me, Tackta made me his son.*

Manerra wept then, both the child who had had no defenses, and the man who lacked the faith vital to his position.

"I did wish to die, Aya," he choked. "I'm not what you need me to be. My thoughts are shaped by Tackta's hand. I feel his urges. It's Acrahh's line he's defiled. I can't let him reach Ayahn Rahh."

"As long as you are self-aware, Tackta's influence cannot rule."

"All the same, I pray . . . every day . . . for the birth of a shecaren."

Aya's strength crushed him, and yet Manerra was afraid of losing that embrace.

"I require no other shecaren," Aya's voice was husky, firm.

"I can't become shon regis."

Aya pushed him away by a painful grip on his shoulders. "You can. You will."

"A son who doubts his father?"

"A son with compassion for those who suffer."

"I haven't your faith."

"You have your own, which is neither blind nor weak. Acrahh has use for your doubt. The years ahead will include changes that will not be easy for me. You aren't shackled by my conventions."

Manerra wept.

Aya's arms encircled him and Manerra clung to him, even as he wondered how Aya could still care for him.

*****

Wailing screams shattered the household's silence. Aya jerked awake with a heart- and head-pounding start, his first thought of Manerra. Then footsteps pounded past his door headed toward the end of the hall and he knew that Casta was dead.

# CHAPTER 35

At dawn, Yutrenta stood with the janquer at the Gateway to the Sun, grief-stricken but dry-eyed, insistent upon this honor to her brother. After abbah, Aya and Manerra stood upon the Gateway's mound and flanked Korrane while he announced his father's passing to the assembled multitude.

Wails, sobs, and shouts of denial were so loud and long, the janquer could not hear Korrane swear fealty to the sons of Acrahh and pledge his life in service to the Ofrann tribe. The shecarens publicly acknowledged him as high lord of the Shangren and the Ofrann, then accompanied him to Casta's house, where matters of government waited.

Aya made it almost to the hairpin turn before he lurched sideways and stumbled into Manerra, whose quick grab kept him from falling. Other hands grabbed him then, held him upright, while Yutrenta rushed forward and wiped a hand through the sweat on his brow.

"Korrane!" Yutrenta shouted. "I need a horse litter or a cart or even a shuren. Let him down," she told the men who held him upright, and they did, laying him in the street, where sand stuck in the sweat of his hands and face and he remembered little besides the pain.

* * * * *

"Lay still," Yutrenta ordered, but Aya could not. He turned, trying to find a position that quieted the ferocious pain behind his eyes. The sheet that covered him, the robe he wore, were twisted. They restricted movement. He found the mattress edge, gripped it hard, pulled on it, trying to pour the pain into the fabric, or exhaust the pain by exertion.

"The dayflower's cooling," Yutrenta said.

"I need it now." He rolled onto his side and pulled at the sheet, trying to free his legs from its restriction. He couldn't do it. He tried to lift his hip off the bed, could not raise high enough to free the sheet, then tried to bend a knee. "Trenta!" he shouted and then wished he hadn't. He arched and pressed the heel of a hand into each temple, attempting to crush the pain.

"Help me!" Yutrenta shouted.

He didn't understand the desperation in her voice. He was the one who wasn't dying and wanted to.

Hands caught his wrists, his shoulders, his legs. They forced his hands away from his head. He fought their intentions and shouted, but they were too many.

* * * * *

"Aya."

He resisted that call, afraid if he acknowledged it, the pain would return with sanity-robbing intensity. He clung to the colors of the dream, both fascinated and appalled by the vividness of the images. He lifted his wrist toward the bird that hovered, that wanted to alight, but the bird was being plucked by the wind. Its feathers cascaded around him like iridescent snow.

"Aya, I need you to hear me."

He opened his mouth and gasped a breath of air.

"Someone saw you fall, saw you carried here, and told others. Citizens have panicked. Korrane's on the roof, so is Manerra, but they aren't being heard. The mob thinks you're dead. They want Kayarra."

Aya turned his head but could not open his eyes. Something prevented him from doing so. "House," he whispered, although it was hard to talk. Even harder to think.

"If we carry you to the roof, can you stand, just until you're seen?"

"Yes," he said, although Shurna didn't answer his question about the house, about its security. How many peacekeepers were there to hold the doors? The garden entrance was the weakest barrier.

Hands dug behind his shoulders, brought him to sitting; shifted to his armpits and started to lift him before he gasped, "Slowly." They let him sit then, just for a moment, before they lifted him. When his feet touched the floor, he tried to support his weight and could not. His muscles had the strength of water. He couldn't lock his knees. His arms were brought around necks, across shoulders, and held against chests with bruising grips on his forearms. Arms crossed beneath his buttocks and he was lifted off his feet. They carried him across the room, shuffled sideways through the door, hitting his knee on the doorframe before they made it into the hall.

A sound like the distant roar of a river grew louder as he was carried along the hall, and louder still as they started up the stairs to the roof.

"Hide Kayarra," he said, not certain the men who carried him up the stairs could hear him over the sound of their own panting breaths. It was crucial that Kayarra not be on the roof when he arrived and he wasn't certain they understood that. Shurna would understand, but he couldn't figure a way to tell her.

His carriers stopped and one stepped closer, squeezing him between them while the heaving expansion and contraction of their chests constricted his own breathing. A hand left his arm and the door that held back the river of sound swung wide. The sweaty hand hastily caught his wrist again and his carriers stepped through onto the roof.

"Demon," "Acrahh," "kill," "free," were some of the flotsam that bobbed to the surface of the aggrieved river of hatred and fear.

Hands at the back of his head fumbled with bandage ties while his carriers still held him. The bandage fell away. They lowered his feet to the roof, keeping his weight on their shoulders. The shouts from below made it impossible to talk and be heard. He freed a forearm, groped with that hand until he hit someone's shoulder, caught the fabric of their robe and made a fist. A hand patted his fist and he let go; felt someone catch his robe at his back, over his shoulder, and grip it tight. His need had been understood. Someone else did the same over his other shoulder blade before his carriers released him. The fabric constricted his chest, but he could walk, and did, with their support, with their guidance. He knew they neared the roof's edge when the volume of shouts faltered and diminished; when his title became one phrase amid the few words understood among conflicting shouts. He felt like the bird in his dream: hovering, starting to falter, starting to scatter colored feathers as the breeze blew through him before it blew him away. He raised a hand toward the low wall before him, splayed his fingers, and imagined his arm extending until he could touch away the fear of these people who had come here wanting to kill because they didn't know another way to handle their grief and fear.

A wail seeped through the shouts.

His handlers pulled him back and he almost fell. They felt him lose his balance and jerked upward on his robe to catch his weight. He hoped he kept the fright of falling from his face, and caught his balance with his own grip on someone's arm.

Out of sight of the mob, arms encircled him, held him, supported him until two men again lifted him and carried him to his room.

"Manerra must stay," he told them on the stairs going down, when he thought they could hear him. "Manerra must stay," he told them again in the hall in case they'd not understood him on the stairs, because the janquer held decision-making powers now and he was certain they intended to leave the city as soon as they could smuggle him from the house and down the mountain. He asked for Shurna, and then for Yutrenta, and told each of them in turn, in case they doubted his carriers' words.

# CHAPTER 36

Manerra performed evening abbah on the roof of what had been Casta's house and was now Korrane's. It was not the first time he had handled the temple stone alone during abbah, but the first time he had done so in necessity. At the conclusion of abbah, Manerra cloaked the temple stone but did not turn to leave.

Very close to where he stood, he and Korrane had gripped Aya's robe so the shon regis appeared to stand on his own. They had intended that Aya should merely be seen, but Aya had reached out to the mob as if he expected them to join him in the communion of abbah.

Aya's raised hand had broken through the mob's anger. The mob did not immediately disperse, but the tone of the shouting changed. A few fires were abandoned. The angriest lost their rapt audiences, and, although they worked hard to rekindle the flames of passion they hoped would consume the mountaintop, they failed.

Under similar circumstances, Manerra would not have thought to do what Aya did by instinct. How did one learn such things?

"Shecaren, will you perform morning abbah here or at the Gateway to the Sun?"

Manerra looked back and into Korrane's grief-rimmed eyes, glazed with fatigue. Casta still breathed the last time any of them had slept, which seemed like a seven-night ago. Manerra glanced past Korrane, past the janquer, at the archers who flanked them, before returning his attention to Korrane. "I will risk the Gateway for the release of your father's soul. Not sooner," Manerra said.

Korrane gave veneration, turned, and started toward the stairs.

"Lord Korrane," Manerra called.

The Ofrann leader turned, and Manerra was shaken by the stark contrast between father and son. Korrane appeared altogether too young to lead the nation's largest tribe. Casta had been the eldest of the four tribal leaders. His successor was the youngest.

"Shecaren?" Korrane asked.

"I'd like to know the destinations of the companies leaving the Shangren. I want warning if the Hyranians develop an unusual religious fervor."

"They can lie about their destinations, shecaren."

"Then they'll have the inconvenience of heading south and looping back around, out of sight of the Shangren, in order to head north."

"I'll have the reports to you after supper each day."

"You won't be inconvenienced for long," Manerra said.

"How long will you stay?"

*Manerra must stay.* Had Aya decided it was too dangerous to allow his shecaren to complete the journey to Ayahn Rahh? Aya could not refuse him the Oath of Yatra if he completed this journey, but that was a right accorded him by birth. He had never wanted it.

"There's been no time to discuss a new departure. Certainly, we won't leave before the shon regis can travel."

"Know that you have the Shangren's resources and my hospitality for as long as you or the janquer remain."

Manerra wondered how much of Korrane's offer was formality, how much was generosity. Even in Manerra's earliest memories, Korrane had been reserved, withdrawn, aloof. Their age differences accounted for some of the lack of familiarity—Korrane was more than twice his age—but a greater part was the man himself. Manerra lacked personal knowledge of Korrane's passions, desires and heart. All he knew for sure was that Korrane was well respected and had yet to sire a child.

"Thank you, lord Korrane. I've nothing else."

Korrane bowed his head again and left, followed by his escorts.

Manerra turned aside and looked down into the yard. The ground was littered with debris, soot-blackened where fires had burned. Paving stones were missing, or bloodied where injuries had occurred during the violence. Damage to the garden had been as severe.

What he did not want, ever again, was to experience the gut-wrenching fear he'd felt when facing that mob and realizing his inability to influence them.

"Will you join us in counsel?" Shurna asked and he turned his back on the yard and its damage.

"Yes." He was grateful that she included him. Despite his birthright, his age did not require them to.

He followed Shurna to a second floor sitting room and had to quash his resentment when Kayarra followed them into the room. He said nothing, but doubted Aya's order for Kayarra to remain in janquer company extended to a private counsel inside a heavily guarded residence.

Kayarra crossed the room, sat down on a bench, and leaned against the wall. Manerra remained standing, as did Shurna. Yutrenta slumped into a chair in the center of the room, her eyes closed before she fully seated. Denassa settled in the chair beside her and slipped one hand beneath Yutrenta's, then reached toward Manerra even as Shurna extended a hand.

With hands clasped, Shurna murmured, "May our wisdom recognize the value of compromise, and our love for one another and the nation prevail."

"Pray Acrahh," Manerra said as they released hands, then asked, "Has Aya explained his order that I stay?"

Yutrenta's brow furrowed and she opened her eyes. "He's not yet coherent. As long as I'm administering dayflower, there will be no pressing him for information."

"You're still administering it," Manerra said.

"I'm watering what I give him. When I left, he was sleeping, so the pain is still manageable."

"You need sleep," Manerra said and saw her tear up. "Please, Trenta. Sleep while he does."

"The woman Maytel was found," Shurna said, and Manerra wondered why Shurna intervened, "and is being held in a house near the Gateway. Korrane asks whether we will question her there or here."

"Here," Yutrenta's vehemence erupted. "I want citizens to see what damage the Hyranians did."

"We don't know the rioters were Hyranians," Denassa said.

"Rasha accused Aya of hiding behind his brothers," Yutrenta said. "Who but Hyranians would dare such a claim? Gorrow had to have known what Rasha was, which makes me question his sympathies, as well."

"He may have killed her only after he found out, because he knew her affiliation would cast doubt on his claims," Denassa said. "Rasha was using Gorrow as surely as he was using her."

"Someone Gorrow dealt with could have killed Rasha," Shurna said.

"I don't doubt that," Yutrenta said, "but you will not convince me the Hyranians aren't using demotic fear against us at every opportunity. Aya's injury isn't being told in conjunction with the miracle he performed. His collapse and my father's death, along with Rasha's murder and Gorrow's escape, are behind that riot."

"Speculation isn't terribly useful," Manerra interrupted.

"Casta offered us an escort from the Shangren," Denassa said. "Maybe we should consider it."

"No escorts," Shurna said.

"Aya insists upon fulfilling the precise stipulations of this journey," Yutrenta said. "I must agree with him."

"Tradition can get us killed," Manerra said, and found himself the focus of attention.

"It can," Shurna agreed, "but we knew that before we accepted the unification prayer."

"Adherence to covenant doesn't mean we must be careless with our lives," Yutrenta said. "There are safeguards Aya will not protest if he doesn't know about them."

Manerra reached for the back of a chair and looked away.

"That's a promise we can't make, Trenta," Shurna said.

"I'm not asking for complicity. I'm asking for permission to arrange the details of our departure with Korrane."

"No escorts," Shurna insisted.

"I promise, there will be no escorts."

"Make the arrangements," Denassa's reply was a near whisper.

"Do," Shurna said.

"Shecaren?" Yutrenta asked.

Manerra raised both hands. "I'm unsworn and underage. I'm sorry I heard any of this."

Yutrenta leaned her head against the back of the chair and closed her eyes.

"Must we decide anything else?" Shurna asked.

"If there is anything else, I can't remember it," Yutrenta said.

"Trenta, promise me you'll sleep," Denassa pleaded.

"I must. But after I speak with Korrane."

Denassa stood. "If that chair was a bed, I'd leave you in it." She reached for Yutrenta's hand and assisted her rise. Across the room, Kayarra stood up.

Manerra watched Kayarra trail Yutrenta and Denassa from the room and wondered how safe the unguarded women were in his presence.

"What do you see when you look at him?" Shurna whispered at Manerra's side.

"A man/child," Manerra replied, uncomfortable that she'd noticed his attention.

"I would have guessed a cor-anda."

"Witch," he snapped.

She laughed. "Tell me about this man-child of yours," she urged.

"He's not mine!" he protested.

"Your father insists upon linking your lives," she said.

Manerra shuddered. "There will be blood in Kayarran meetings," he said. "There would have been in Shangren streets if I'd been a moment later finding him. Shurna, what do we face in Ayahn Rahh, where we've so few peacekeepers?"

"Aya's taken measures to remove the shock from our arrival."

"I don't have Aya's—" *faith*, he almost said. ". . . optimism," he said instead. "His warning gives our enemies time to prepare for our arrival."

*****

Lord Casta's body lay atop an unlit pyre in front of the Gateway's arch when the janquer and both shecarens arrived for evening abbah. Shurna spotted the pyre before they reached the mound, but returned her attention to the shecarens, keeping watch on Aya, who was guided by an unobtrusive grip on Manerra's sleeve. Atop the mound, she left the shecarens and took her place beside Kayarra, facing the pyre. Casta's white hair and white robe glowed in the light of the orange sun as if his soul strained to escape its cold confines.

Casta's relatives lined the foot and head of the pyre. Encircling the mound were the lords of the Shangren and their escorts, who created a buffer between those atop the Gateway and the multitude who jammed the park and its surrounding slopes. Except for weeping, the Shangren's citizens stood silent, as if the violence of yesterday's riot had exhausted the city's anger.

Shurna was mildly surprised that Yutrenta did not join her family at the conclusion of abbah. Yutrenta's steadfastness was a silent renewal of her pledge of service to Acrahh and the shecarens. She'd already forsaken the Ofrann leadership position that was her birthright as Casta's eldest child.

When the temple stone was cloaked, Casta's escorts stepped forward and lit the pyre.

Sobbing increased.

For a time, the sun's rays paled the fire's flames, but as the sun sank lower, the flames cast flickering shadows among the mourners.

While the pyre burned, Aya commended Casta's soul to the spirits of the sun, henceforth to be honored with all other ancestral souls at the morning and evening passages of that life-giving and life-taking orb.

Then the flames ignited Casta's robe and Yutrenta turned aside, hugged Denassa, and sobbed in earnest. Kayarra whirled and slammed into Shurna, knocking her into the escorts behind her. She caught only a fleeting glimpse of his face—mouth open, eyes terror-stricken—before he lunged down the slope. Shurna jerked free of the hands that caught and supported her and leapt after him.

She followed his progress by the jerky motions of the people he collided with and shoved in his panic. She was elbowed and hit during her efforts to reach him, but succeeded in overtaking him when he tripped and fell. He had gained his knees when she reached him. She dropped to his side, her gasping breaths joining his as she threw an arm around his shoulders . . . like hugging a rock, his muscles were so tense. "Kayarra!" she shouted, needing him to recognize her. "Kayarra."

"Man in fire," he cried, twisted, and almost escaped her hold.

She moved then, afraid of where his mind dwelt, not strong enough to handle his reaction if he confused hallucination and reality. She knew the pressure point from Yutrenta's teaching. He screamed and flinched away, but his eyes focused, the pain bringing him back.

"Kayarra." She caught his face in both hands. "Kayarra."

He grabbed her then, pressed his face into her shoulder, and sobbed like a child, her strength hardly enough to hold him.

"Kayarra."

His scream had drawn attention; his appearance held it. Perhaps even her own face, which could hardly be anonymous.

"Kayarra, we must leave. Now."

Their escorts reached and surrounded them, but their presence did little to ease Shurna's tension. She grabbed an escort's robe. "Help me lift him," she ordered.

Together, they got Kayarra on his feet, got him walking toward the pillars, then along the uphill road.

Kayarra wiped his face and nose on his sleeve when his tears finally abated.

"I'm taking him to Neetria's," she told their escort once they were free of the crowd.

"If I may advise, it's safer at the top of the hill, janquer lady Shurna."

"I want him isolated."

There was danger in what she did, not only to Kayarra, but through the separation of his and her escorts from those protecting the shecarens and remaining janquer. "When we reach Neetria's, I want you to return to the shecarens," she said, hoping she wasn't compounding one mistake with another.

"Our orders for your protection came from Lord Casta, janquer lady Shurna."

"The shecarens' lives are more—" She abandoned that argument. "When we get to Neetria's, assign replacement peacekeepers to guard us. As many as you like. But I want you to return to the shecarens. I trust their lives with you, as I don't with untested men. I take responsibility for Kayarra's and my lives."

Her escort still hesitated. She was relieved to hear, "If I have permission to choose those who remain with you."

"Yes," she agreed before the man could change his mind, and hoped his scruples were more honorable than Gorrow's.

Kayarra pulled his arm free of her hold. His increased pace demonstrated better than words his desire to flee the cremation and the crowds. The distance he kept from her, she interpreted as his effort to deal with the embarrassment of his breakdown.

Shurna was not at all reassured by her arrangements once they reached Neetria's house. Her escort knocked on the door once, and opened it to a deserted room. They were inside before a housekeeper came running from the kitchen, pale-faced at finding strangers in her employer's house.

"Janquer lady Shurna is here," Shurna's grim-faced escort told the woman. "Where are your lady's security staff?" he demanded.

"I need a sleeping draught," Shurna interrupted her escort to tell the housekeeper. "Bring it to my room when it's prepared."

"Yes, janquer lady Shurna," the woman acknowledged her order.

She hooked Kayarra's arm and led him from the room. Behind them, the woman told the guard that the house staff had accompanied lady Neetria to the Gateway.

The hall was dark, but a lantern burned low on the small table in her bedroom. She released Kayarra's arm, and he began a circle of the room: from door to left-hand wall, past the bed, to the far wall and back. Shurna watched his face when he made the loop back, aware immediately that he wasn't inspecting the room. His eyes remained wide with fear.

"Do you remember?" Shurna asked, her own fear rising.

"Remember what?" he asked without stopping.

"The Manteen."

"I not know Mante."

"The tribe you were with. Before Manerra found you."

He whirled and grabbed her injured arm before she could evade him. Her cry of pain mingled with his exclamation of "*What?*"

He released her.

"What Manerra found me?" he demanded.

"Manerra found you," she gasped, cradling her injured arm against her midriff.

"Tell me," he demanded, but jerked away and turned his back as if afraid of what she might say. He paced to the end of the room, returned, circled, while she described the day Manerra returned to camp with his body slumped across shurenback.

"Manerra found . . . ." He shook his head. His face was flushed again. "Denassa said. I not know. Ask . . . ." He rubbed his face with both hands. He looped toward her and stopped, stared into her face. "Why Manerra hit me?"

"You came to him. He's afraid of you."

"What 'afraid'?"

She demonstrated fear.

"No. No." He walked away, starting the loop of the room again. "Manerra not afraid me." He came back. "What is?" He caught her head in both hands and touched his forehead to hers then released her.

"Love," she told him.

"What not love?" he asked.

"Hatred."

"Manerra hatred me." He started pacing again.

"Because he's afraid of you."

"No," Kayarra said.

"He's afraid of your tribe."

Kayarra whirled. "Where my tribe?"

"We think it's north-west of Ayahn Rahh."

"We go Aya Rahh?"

"Yes. After the ceremonies of the joining, Aya intends to search for your tribe."

"'Search for'?"

She tried to remember which words he knew. "Find. Found."

"Found Kayarra tribe?" he asked.

"Yes. After Ayahn Rahh. After the joining."

Suddenly, he looked over her shoulder and she turned, seeing the housekeeper standing in the doorway.

Shurna hurried to the woman and took the bowl from her hands. "Thank you," she said and closed the door. She carried the bowl to the room's bench but did not sit. Instead, she blew on the liquid and sipped it. It was not too hot, but stronger than Yutrenta made. Under the circumstances, that was probably good.

"Come," she invited Kayarra. "You know this tea. Yutrenta makes it for you." She sipped it again while he watched to demonstrate its safety.

He came then, took the bowl, and downed half its contents before he handed it back. Then he paced, with a nervousness he couldn't seem to exhaust.

"Kayarra, I am not alone in understanding your pain," she tried to divert his attention from whatever drove him. "You've lost more than any of us would wish to lose. Perhaps your tribe can return to you what we cannot."

"What is Aya Rahh?" he asked.

She wasn't certain he'd understood her. "The place Crysus arrived upon our world. The place of the gods. The shecarens' home."

"Acrahh is gods."

She smiled at his comprehension. "Yes."

"Aya Rahh is Shangren?" he asked.

It took her a moment to understand his question. "No. Ayahn Rahh is a valley north of the Ofrann."

"Man in fire." He shuddered, jerking in his turn-around.

"Casta's spirit must be freed," she told him. "It would be cruel to bind his spirit to his bones."

"I love Denassa," he said while his back was turned.

She gasped.

He pivoted. "Love is bad?"

"Have you told Denassa?" she demanded.

"I not know word."

She tried to gather her wits. "You see love"—she brought her wrist up, touched her forehead to it in imitation of their head touch—"where?"

"Aya, Yutrenta."

Shurna blushed. "Aya loves Yutrenta. Aya loves Manerra. Manerra loves Denassa." She saw the clench of his jaw and her alarm increased. "Manerra loves Yutrenta. This love is good. This love . . . ." She brought a loose fist up and inserted a finger into its center, "—is sex. Denassa must not have sex. Not with you, not with Manerra, not with any man. Do you understand?"

Kayarra nodded.

"Do you understand me, Kayarra?"

"Yes." He crossed the room and touched the edge of the table that held the lamp.

"As long as Denassa is janquer, she is forbidden sex with any man. This is a law she agreed to before she accepted the unification prayer."

He turned and started back across the room. "Denassa not sex man?" he asked. "Denassa not sex me?"

"Denassa not sex man."

"Denassa not love man?"

"Denassa loves Aya. Denassa loves Manerra. She loves Yutrenta. She loves me."

Kayarra reached the wall, turned, started back across the room, and swayed. He caught his balance with a grab at the bedpost. He paused there, then left the bed, crossed to the bench, sat down, and reached for the bowl Shurna held. He finished the draught, misjudged the surface of the bench, and set the bowl down too forcefully. "I lay down," he mumbled.

Shurna steadied him to her bed, helped him remove his sandals, then covered him with the half of the blankets he wasn't laying on.

"Acrahh, protect this one," she pleaded. "Ease his pain. If you cannot return his past, at least return his family."

She crossed the room to the bench, sat down, and waited until Kayarra's breaths came evenly and shallowly. When she brushed stray hair from his cheek and he didn't flinch, she trimmed the lamp wick then left the room, closing the door behind her.

A man stood at the end of the hall. She told him not to allow anyone who was not janquer or shecaren into Kayarra's room. Then, as tired as she was, she left Neetria's house for Korrane's. The shecarens might be there by now, along with Denassa and Yutrenta and a great many others she would not be as grateful to see.

# CHAPTER 37

Denassa gripped a male shuren's reins in the moonlit yard of Korrane's house. Around her, groundskeepers completed departure preparations without benefit of torch or lantern.

Ryna, the constant moon, the one by which they counted days, flew in wane, so smaller Trys, in full, cast the darker shadows. It was Trys who governed the religious rituals of the joining; his cycle that dictated the timing of their journey.

Denassa reached skyward and spread her fingers, her thumbnail touching Ryna's arch, the tip of her little finger not quite reaching Trys's curve.

"We will reach Ayahn Rahh in time," Shurna spoke behind her.

Denassa jerked her hand back and turned.

"I didn't mean to startle you," Shurna said.

"It doesn't take much these days," Denassa confessed.

"I know." Shurna yawned. "How is it we get more rest traveling than we do in residence?"

"You're the one who fell asleep during last night's vows."

"I'll live with that shame till I'm divested."

"We won't let you forget it even afterward. Let me test the sleeping draught next time."

Shurna chuckled. "You are shameless."

"I'm Ringgangley."

"That's not amusing, Dee."

"You call yourself a witch. It's only derogatory if another tribesman so names us?"

Shurna sighed. "Did Aya sleep last night?"

"He was awake when I went to bed. He and—" Denassa stopped talking when a man approached. She watched him throw a pack over her shuren's back and tie the cords under the animal's belly. He tugged on the cords before he left.

When they were alone, Denassa said, "Aya and Manerra were talking privately when I left. I doubt either of them slept."

"Are you concerned about Manerra staying?" Shurna asked.

"I'm confused. Aya wouldn't risk leaving Manerra in Thurra where there were no riots, but will leave him here, when we've little leeway for delay. Do you understand his reasons?"

"Only instinctually."

Denassa laughed. "Spoken like a Kitarin."

Voices from the doorway drew her attention. A group of people emerged from the house followed by Aya and Manerra. Korrane accompanied the shecarens, as did Yutrenta and Kayarra. A groundskeeper hurriedly placed a stool beside Denassa's shuren, then circled to the beast's flank while a second groundskeeper reached for the shuren's cheek strap.

Aya walked between Manerra and Korrane, a hand on each arm. They brought him to a halt beside the stool.

"The mounting stool is directly in front of you, shon regis," Korrane said.

Aya tilted his head. "Don't accompany us to the plain," he said. "It's an unnecessary risk."

"I'm coming with you," Manerra said.

"No," Aya's swift reply ended the possibility of argument. "I'll send your supplies back with our escorts. It's safer if we separate here."

Manerra dipped his head and did not look up until after Aya mounted.

When the shecaren lifted his head, it was to give a perfunctory hug to Yutrenta and the two female decoys who accompanied her. Denassa was distressed that Manerra's embrace of Yutrenta was as lackluster as his embrace of the decoys.

"I return the city of the Shangren to its rightful guardian," Aya said from shurenback. "Protect its citizens well, Korrane. Acrahh guide you in prosperity."

Korrane gave veneration. "Walk safely in Acrahh's care, shon regis."

The groundskeepers stepped away from the shuren, taking the stool with them.

Shurna touched Manerra's sleeve as she joined their escorts in a protective formation around Yutrenta and the decoys.

"Have care, Manerra, shecaren," Aya said. "I ask Acrahh's watchcare until our reunion."

Denassa saw Aya's signal and pulled on his mount's lead, but the beast resisted until someone slapped its hind leg.

"Shon regis, shecaren." Manerra stepped forward as if to follow them.

Denassa focused her attention on the road and the armed men who preceded her, distressed by the anguish in Manerra's voice.

Once past the road's hairpin turn, Denassa's adrenalin and heart rate surged, sharpening her awareness of the shadows cast by houses, walls, trees, and cobbled wagons. She glanced back at Aya and saw him lying along the shuren's neck, a position that safeguarded vital organs in the event of an attack.

Although no one spoke, their footfalls grated on sandy paving, a sound amplified by the houses and cliffs they passed. Penned mia bleated queries answered by shuren snorts. At the Gateway's park, a tethered shuren bellowed a challenge to Aya's male, whose head swung toward the challenger before an escort sprang to Denassa's aid. His grip on the reins, then on the cheek strap, helped guide Aya's male safely past the Gateway. Denassa sucked a leather burn on her hand and silently cursed their borrowed mount.

In a palm grove that shaded the end of the road, an escort in front of Denassa stopped so abruptly she collided with his back. Before she could recover and sidestep, his arm jerked and a shush of knives drawn sounded all around. Then a body struck Denassa's back so hard, air whoosed from her lungs, cutting short her cry of alarm. The man behind her grabbed the waist of the one in front, smothering her in a cocoon of clothing and flesh.

"Don't hurt us!" a man cried somewhere ahead of them. "I've not drawn. I swear."

"What's your business?" an escort demanded.

"We were sleeping. We done no harm. In Acrahh's name, I swear. Don't hurt us."

"Surrender your weapons."

"Swear you'll not hurt us."

"Cooperate and you won't get hurt. Now clear the road."

In response to Denassa's struggles, her guards relaxed their crushing grip but did not step away.

"Dee?" Kayarra's cry came from the shadows behind the shuren.

"Silence!" a man ordered.

"Dee!"

"I'm all right," she answered Kayarra's rising fear, risking establishment of her location to any hostile listener.

"Silence!" the man in front of her hissed and stepped right while the man behind her stepped left. They linked arms across her back and hurried her away.

Denassa looked over her shoulder as additional escorts closed in ahead and behind her. Assured by the protective formation encircling Aya, she let herself be directed past the standoff. She tried to catch a glimpse of the men who had alarmed their escorts, but saw only the backs of the guards lining the road.

A drop-off marked the end of the paved road, that single, jarring step carrying Denassa from oasis to desert as if a knife had hewn away not only the road's surface but the city's lifeblood.

If only that drop-off marked the end of their worries.

Where their tent once stood waited a line of strangers: the members of their advance party. Only their animals were recognizable from this distance: the mia, low, ghost-like apparitions; their shuren, miniature buttes laden with goods and supplies.

As their company approached that line of men, Denassa's guards reached for knife hilts.

"Ho, Bachra, all is well," one of the waiting strangers called. Denassa's guards brought her to a standstill and kept closed ranks while their fellows advanced. Not until someone in the advancing party signaled that all was well did Denassa's guards urge her forward.

"Trenta," Aya called, "locate Manerra's pack."

"Yes, shon regis," Yutrenta's answer sounded somewhere behind him.

Denassa's guards brought her to a halt near the waiting shuren, remained in formation until the reins of Aya's shuren were pressed into her hand, then stepped back, gave veneration, and joined a new line forming, facing their advance guard, leaving her standing between the lines of men.

"We've reached camp," Denassa said for Aya's benefit. When Aya did not reply, Denassa stepped closer, placed a hand on the shuren's shoulder, and peered up at him. "Aya?" she asked.

"I heard," he answered.

"Do you need dayflower?"

There was a delay before he answered, "No."

Denassa resisted an impulse to summon Yutrenta, believing Aya might be more candid with her. Instead, she returned attention to their escorts, understanding her obligations in this formal departure, and trusting Aya to tell her if he needed a physician's assistance.

"All escorts stand in protective formation," Denassa whispered.

"Can Bachra hear my voice?"

Denassa bent forward and scratched the shuren's brisket while she searched for the man. She spotted him and straightened. "He can."

"Has Yutrenta located Manerra's pack?"

"Not yet."

Denassa lost sight of Yutrenta behind one of the pack shuren. When the Ofrann reappeared, "She's found it," Denassa announced.

Aya pushed up and braced himself against the shuren's neck.

"Goodman Bachra," Aya called, "please approach."

Yutrenta reached them before Bachra did.

Bachra stopped and bowed his head. "Shon regis."

Aya signaled. "Bachra," he said, "please deliver this pack into shecaren Manerra's hands."

Bachra looked up as Yutrenta extended the pack. He took the leather bag. "By Acrahh's witness, I will, shon regis."

"Thank you." Aya raised his voice, "My gratitude and wish for prosperity to each of you for the services you've rendered. I grieve for every life lost. Know that I honor your kinsmen's lives every time I lift the temple stone in abbah. Acrahh protect every one of you."

Denassa slapped the shuren's neck. This time, the animal stepped forward without prodding. She brought the animal to the southern end of the lines, circled, then walked the center of the formation headed north, her throat clenched at sight of their escorts' veneration. The tribulations of these men did not end with the shon regis's departure.

Neither did her grief end with their leave-taking. Exertion could not overcome the image of Manerra's perfunctory farewell embrace. Did the shecaren intend to rejoin them, or was that embrace his final farewell?

Fear prevented tears. Fear not only of Manerra's unknown decision, but of what awaited them in Ayahn Rahh. High dunes, The Divide, and a mountain pass separated them from the House of Moons, and the entire nation knew where they had to be and by what time.

# CHAPTER 38

When the sun's rim appeared above the eastern horizon, Denassa halted. She turned in time to watch Aya's leg clear the shuren's croup and his feet strike the ground. Behind him, her companions brought the three pack shuren to a halt.

Her attention shifted past them to the glow of sunlit rock on the mountain's eastern face. The walls of houses touched by sunlight burned white.

Movement on the plain caught Denassa's attention. She squinted, gasped, and took a step toward Aya before stopping.

"Dee," Aya said, "what is it?"

"We're being followed."

"How many? How close?"

Yutrenta answered, "They look like a family group."

*There are safeguards Aya will not protest if he doesn't know about them*, Yutrenta had said. Was this one of her safeguards?

"There's time for abbah," Denassa said. "They're still well behind us."

"Come then." Aya motioned, and Yutrenta approached and offered her arm.

Denassa hobbled the male shuren, tied its reins to scrub, then hurried after her companions. She joined the end of the formation, caught Kayarra's hand, and shut her eyes against the dawning sun.

"Acrahh, god and father," Aya began the prayer. "As a son's fear is lessened by his father's strength, so do I draw strength from those who have pledged their lives in service to me. By their love is my fear shattered; through their knowledge does my wisdom grow. I beseech your protection for each of them in ways I cannot provide, that they will know how dearly their lives are held."

Tears welled behind Denassa's closed lids.

The temple stone flared and a shuren shrieked. Denassa's flesh prickled even as Kayarra's startle transmitted through their handclasp. He jerked his hand back. She gripped tighter, but lost her hold.

Aya continued, his voice strong, confident, "As the light of our ancestors is greeted by the earthly light of Yatra's children, know that we keep the promises sworn before Crysus at the gifting of the stone of fire.

"Peace to all . . ."

Denassa picked up the refrain with, "nation through eternity."

The temple stone's light vanished. Denassa started to whirl, but froze when she caught sight of Yutrenta. She wasn't alone in believing that their broken tribal link was ominous.

"Is the shuren gone?" Aya's demand shifted Denassa's attention back to him.

"He's hobbled." Denassa's distress was audible.

Yutrenta's hand flashed in frantic motion, *Silence.* "He's not gone far," Yutrenta answered.

Denassa pivoted. Kayarra stood in a self-hug, shoulders tense, an arm's length away. Well beyond him stood the male shuren. The beast's reins dragged the torn bush to which it had been tied. Yutrenta was right. It had not gone far.

"Denassa's retrieving him," Yutrenta said.

Denassa grimaced, but started after the beast. The animal avoided her initial approach with a three-legged lurch-jump. It allowed a second approach when she told it over and over in a soothing tone how much she hated it.

As she reached for its reins, the beast flicked its ears. Denassa slapped its nose as the head shot forward, teeth bared, and barely caught the dangling reins as the shuren tensed for another leap. She threw her weight onto the reins and yanked the animal's head around. "You evil beast!" she shouted. "Thank the sands, we get to return you."

She watched the animal's head and shoulder for warnings of additional nips while she freed the brush from its reins, then removed the hobble and walked him in circles, as much to calm herself as to pace away his skittishness and reassert her control. She saw Shurna leave with the flock and glanced back at the approaching strangers. They were noticeably closer. She headed back to her waiting companions.

"I'm sorry I took so—"

Aya lifted a hand. "Trenta told me the shuren ran from you."

At Aya's side, Yutrenta signed, *He took dayflower.* "I'll take the male, if you wish," Yutrenta offered.

"Please," Denassa said, her hand and nerves raw from the animal's willfulness. *Do you know followers?* she signed before their transfer concluded.

*No*, Yutrenta flashed.

Aya mounted and Denassa retreated to Yutrenta's pack shuren. "God Acrahh, please spare us," she whispered, her attention on the company that gained on them.

* * * * *

They constructed camp well before abbah. Raising the tent took twice as long as usual, exhaustion defining the limits of their endurance. Afterward, Denassa sat cross-legged in the sand, too tired to kneel, her attention divided between supper making and the approaching strangers. Throughout the day, she'd caught herself touching her knife hilt, a reassurance she resisted now only because her hands were occupied. *Stop that*, she ordered herself. During a hail, such an action would convey hostility. As slow-witted as she was, it was a mistake she feared making.

Shurna approached carrying a bowl. "Milk," she said as she circled the fire. "For you. Drink it." She held out the bowl.

Denassa dropped another handful of rice into the cook pot and accepted the milk. "Thank you."

Shurna stared along their back trail. "They've a child," she remarked.

"Tackta once traveled with a child." Denassa held out the empty bowl.

Shurna looked down as she took it. "Tackta fled the shon regis, too."

The approaching company stopped. Denassa stood.

"I'll summon Aya." Shurna hurried toward the tent.

A man approached alone.

Denassa loosened her veil, let it fall around her neck, and waited. The approaching man lowered his veil. His long, narrow face appeared harsh in its solemnity.

Sand grated behind Denassa, but she didn't turn as Shurna, with Aya, approached. Their arrival steadied her faltering courage.

The stranger stopped walking and bobbed his head. "Coltra cum Tebbe of the Ofrann requests permission to approach," he called across the distance.

"Does Coltra of the Ofrann know the company he approaches?" Aya demanded.

"I did not before this moment, shon regis, although I'd heard that your company departed the Shangren during the night. I will understand if you ask us to leave."

Denassa glanced over her shoulder. Aya stood bareheaded, the unobstructed moons on his shoulder glistening darkly.

"Approach, Coltra cum Tebbe," Aya ordered.

Denassa's attention flashed to the tent before she looked back. Kayarra had fallen asleep while spreading pallets. She hoped he slept through this encounter.

Coltra halted a respectful distance away and bowed his head in formal greeting.

"Shon regis Aya acknowledges Coltra of the Ofrann," Aya said, no longer shouting. "What is the purpose of your hail?"

"To ask permission to camp nearby. But that was before I knew the company I approached."

"Name your companions," Aya said.

"I travel with my daughter's family: Uhle and her husband Mentan, their daughter Teeka, and infant Alton."

"Was your company the only one to leave the Shangren this morning?"

"I saw two other companies preparing to leave."

"Heading north?"

"We left while they were assembling."

"Camp where you will," Aya offered, "but share our fire this evening."

Denassa hoped that her sleeves hid both clenched fists.

# CHAPTER 39

Kayarra opened his eyes and jerked his head back as something black swept toward his face. *The tent curtain.* He dropped his head back upon his arm while his heart pounded. For the first time in memory, he was safe. Aya left Manerra at the Shangren.

Pin stabs of returning circulation shifted his attention to his hand. He sat up, flexed his fingers, then rubbed his wrist. And noticed the quality of light that filtered through the tent walls: the peculiar dimming toward dusk that meant abbah was imminent.

Kayarra shoved upright, stumbled across the tent, pushed aside the door flap, and froze at sight of a second tent and too many people clustered around the cookfire. He shook his head in increasing denial, released the door flap, and stepped back. The fabric shushed across the opening.

He returned to his partially made pallet and began finishing the task he'd been performing when he fell asleep.

The other tent must belong to the people who had been following them. But why were they here, in their camp, when an entire desert stretched out around them?

Resentment made his hands tremble.

They left all those people behind! What were they doing here?

He threw a pillow at the back wall. It hit and fell with dull plops.

Light flooded the tent from the doorway. Kayarra started but didn't turn.

"It's time for abbah," Denassa said.

He rolled from knees to buttocks to face her. "What is them?" He jabbed a finger toward the strangers.

"Coltra, Uhle, Mentan, and Teeka."

"Why here?" he demanded, not caring whether his complaint carried to those seated beside the fire.

"They travel to Ayahn Rahh."

"To see me die?" He startled himself with that demand; was at first confused by it, then recognized the dread that had filled him since the marketplace threat. He would die at Ayahn Rahh. He knew that with certainty.

"You will not die." Denassa's tone was the dismissive retort one used with a child. "Come," she ordered. "Abbah won't wait." When he made no move to stand: "Kayarra!"

He straightened his veil, then reached behind his neck and raised the hood of his robe. Only then did he follow her, keeping his face averted from the strangers who rose from the cookfire and trailed them.

He took his place at the end of the janquer's crescent; his punishment for breaking the tribal link when the shuren screamed. "You are expected to stand," Yutrenta had scolded, "no matter the disturbance nearby."

"Stand and die?" he'd snapped.

Yutrenta's sharp "Yes" had made his skin crawl.

At the conclusion of abbah, Kayarra attempted to escape back to the tent, but Yutrenta caught his elbow and began formal introductions: a blur of words from which he mentally fled. The strangers' responses appeared rote; his responses were recited from memory. The silence of mealtime provided relief from the strained formality.

"Lady Denassa," Aya ended the meal, "I would hear the legend of Yatra's tears."

Denassa dropped the bowl she was about to add to a stack. Its rim struck and clattered off the stacked bowls, and her face blushed maroon.

The child sitting beside Kayarra giggled . . . and was silenced by her mother's frown and raised finger.

Denassa retrieved the bowl, added it to the stack of used bowls, then stared at her clutched hands. "Yatra, the father of our tribes," she began, voice strained, "grew restless awaiting his father's return to Ayahn Rahh and begged Crysus to allow him to explore the world that had become haven and home. At first, Crysus refused, fearful for her son's safety, but Yatra's passion ignited the dreams of his children, so they, too, begged Crysus to let them go." Denassa lifted her head, her eyes distant, as though she watched the events she described. "Finally, Crysus could deny her children no longer.

"Yatra left Ayahn Rahh with his many children and climbed the Tydonddy's greatest peak. Looking west, he saw the restless ocean with its dark waters and wild storms. To the north spread an endless forest with clear-running rivers. East lay mountains that spewed deadly fire over black rocks. South, he beheld the desert, a great, dry land of strange beauty.

"It was the desert that whispered to Yatra, that urged him to walk its sands and learn its wonders. His children begged him not to go, but their pleas fell upon silence. Yatra descended Mount Tayenya and entered the desert.

"A few of his children followed him, but there was much weeping at their departure. Those who begged their father to go north, entered the endless forest, and their siblings called them Kitarin, for their knowledge of soil and plants.

"Those who heard the song of the waves traveled west. At the ocean's edge, they shaped bright boats from great trees, and a powerful current swept them south. Their siblings named them Ringgangley for their love of the wild waters and its fish.

"Yatra himself, and the children who followed him, learned the desert's secrets and prospered, but some of his children grew weary of endless travel. When they saw the vast savannaland south of the desert, they left their father, entered the grass-filled plain, and learned to shape tools of great beauty from the land's riches. Seeing their skill with hands and clay, their father named them Thurrang.

"Then all the tribes who were named, called the faithful of Yatra the Ofrann, and gave that name to the desert, so there was no distinction between tribe and land.

"Thus was the world divided, but also joined by kinship. And while Yatra was glad to see his children prosper, he grieved for those who left him. His tears of pride and sorrow are the stones that litter the desert floor, covered with sand, but containing the bright glitter of water." Denassa ended the tale with her head bowed and hands clenched in her lap.

Shurna squeezed Denassa's arm, then rose and hurried toward the tent.

Aya dug into his belt pouch and handed something to Yutrenta, who glanced at the object, smiled, and passed it to the eldest of the strangers.

The object passed hand-to-hand around the fire. When it reached Kayarra, he discovered a stone little larger than his thumb. Grains of sand clung to its cluster of leaf-shaped crystals, which sparkled like glass where they'd broken, were white-edged where they'd abraded.

The child flung herself across his thigh, grabbed his wrist, and yanked his hand down. "Yatra's tear!" she exclaimed.

"*Gypsum*," he said. His heart lurched and pounded. He looked at Denassa, but she remained unaware of his fright. Which made him wonder why the naming of a rock caused such a strong physical reaction . . . except that it was a desert rock, and everything he knew about the desert had been taught by his present companions.

"Teeka!" That shocked scold came from the woman.

The child jerked upright and clutched her elbows.

"I'm sorry, janquer lord," the woman apologized. "Teeka forgets herself."

It took a moment to absorb what she'd said. "I not janquer," Kayarra spoke slowly to assure understanding.

"I promise, she'll not be a bother."

Kayarra handed Teeka the crystalline tear. "Teeka is good."

The child beamed as she clutched the tear.

At that moment, Shurna emerged from the tent carrying musical instruments, and Teeka's mother rose and hurried toward her own tent.

*I lay down*, Kayarra signaled Denassa.

Her forehead wrinkled. A moment passed before she signaled *come*. She stood even as he did and bowed her head toward Aya. Kayarra halted, nodded to Aya, then followed her to the tent.

"Why are you leaving?" Denassa demanded before they reached the tent.

"I sick," he said.

"What hurts?"

"Head."

Denassa held the door flap aside and waved him to enter.

Kayarra entered the dark tent and heard Denassa pass into the women's quarters. Moments later, she crossed to the door flap. Light from the campfire illuminated her silhouette as she left.

Kayarra located his pallet by touch, sat down, and removed his sandals. He was lifting the blankets aside when light fell upon the tent fabric. He closed his eyes before Denassa entered, then blinked in the lantern's glare. She hung the lantern on the ceiling hook before returning to the women's quarters. This time, she returned with her physician's bag and knelt by his side.

He watched her withdraw a vial, uncap it, and sniff the contents. Satisfied, she poured a measure of liquid into the small cup used for dispensing infusions. He'd witnessed the same ritual countless times; could perform it himself if she'd teach him how to interpret the knotted cords on her bottles.

He drank the portion she gave him then held the cup out so she could refill it with water.

"You not like story you say tonight?" he asked while she freed her water skin.

The whites of her eyes appeared for no more than a second. "That story . . . ." her voice trailed off. "The tale of Yatra's tears describes the division of the tribes."

"Ringgangley, Ofrann, Kitarin—" he recited.

"Yes," she interrupted. "But it doesn't tell . . . . I don't understand why Aya wished it told tonight, in this company."

Kayarra downed the water in a gulp and returned the cup. He understood her seriousness but wasn't sure he understood the tale. "Yatra travel. Yatra children go away. Who Yatra children?"

"Ringgangley, Thurrang, Ofrann, Kitarin, and Manteen."

He absorbed what she'd said. "Kayarran?" he asked.

Her brow creased, her eyes full of distress. "The founding stories do not name the Kayarran. Your tribe bears your name because we know no other name to call them."

His hand went to his temple, pressed, returned to his lap. "I here," he said, speaking slowly, as though clarity could give that fact a history, even the personal one he'd somehow lost.

Her bowed head and silence frighten him.

"I here," he repeated and grabbed her hand. "Aya give me sun at abbah. You say Kayarra. You know Kayarra."

"No." She finally looked at him, her eyes full of pain.

"No, me? No, Kayarra tribe?" he demanded. They had called him by name when he had no name. The bedrock of his existence sprang from that fact. He released her hand and drew back, suddenly aware of the fireside music. He wanted to laugh even as his eyes burned. "Shurna say Kayarra tribe—" He couldn't remember the word she'd used. His frustration peaked. ". . . at . . . soon . . . Aya Rahh."

Her brow furrowed. "We do not know your tribe," she said.

"Shurna know!"

"She doesn't. We've heard only rumors."

"What is 'rumors'?"

"Stories. Told by men who hate Aya. Who would see him dead."

Gooseflesh prickled Kayarra's arms. His clenched fists went numb.

Denassa closed the flap of her bag and slipped the strap over her shoulder. "I must return to Aya." She stood.

As she reached for the door flap, he blurted, "Kayarra tribe bad?"

Denassa paused, looked back, met his eyes. "We don't know," she said. "Aya refuses to believe they are." She turned then and ducked through the door flap.

# CHAPTER 40

The fireside music failed to distract Kayarra. The Shangren had destroyed everything he thought he'd figured out. Everything.

Maybe Aya's pick of him over Manerra wasn't flattering. Maybe Aya needed him as a hostage, as a pawn in negotiations with a foreign tribe, and had ordered Manerra to remain at the Shangren for his safety.

Memories of the physical fights and name-calling returned. The knife Manerra had leveled at his throat. Manerra holding that same knife tip over his heart in the marketplace.

Some of their fights he'd started, but not all. He'd done nothing to provoke Manerra that day the arrow tip broke. And Manerra had called him by a derogatory name long before he understood the insult.

Manerra, who hated him but had saved his life. Twice, if he'd understood Shurna's explanation.

Fuck it all! What he didn't know could fill a desert.

* * * * *

In the morning, the strangers broke camp the same time they did, joined them as onlookers during abbah, and paralleled their route, matched their pace.

Had he misunderstood Aya's decree that there must be no escorts?

He'd fallen asleep over an unmade pallet and awakened into a world that made no sense. A world where he feared their destination as much as he feared the city they'd fled.

At midday, Kayarra settled beneath the canopy he'd erected, his back to the Shangren's mountain, even though his view was the canopy's windbreak backcloth. When he noticed Denassa approach, he turned his head away and stared at a distant mesa. He listened to her final approach, heard her pause, then felt cloth brush his sleeve as she settled. For minutes afterward, he listened to the murmur of indistinct voices from other canopies, the lazy bleating of mia, a shuren's snort, the flap of cloth in a gust of wind that blew sand grains against the windbreak.

Finally, he looked back and down at Denassa, who sat gazing at the Shangren, her arms hugging bent knees. Her dark eyes were alight with reflected sunlight, and he longed to know her thoughts, to understand what she knew.

"You teach me talk?" he broke the silence between them.

Those eyes met his but shifted away. "Rest," she said. "You didn't sleep well last night."

He grabbed a handful of sand and threw it. "Goddamnit!" came out in his language. "Why the hell did you save me?" He dropped his forehead onto his knuckles, eyes shut, breath coming hard and fast.

He heard Denassa leave but did not open his eyes. He deserved to be alone. He hated Manerra for finding him; hated Denassa and Yutrenta for saving his life; hated the world for not making sense.

Later, when footfalls approached, he cringed but opened his eyes, expecting a lecture. He wasn't completely surprised to see Shurna crouch beside the canopy. He supposed Denassa had had enough of his temper. Shurna clutched a bundle of filthy rags pressed against her midriff.

"May I sit?" she asked.

He scooted to the edge of the shade so she didn't have to sit close to him.

She entered, settled cross-legged facing him, and thrust the rags into his lap. He looked down at them.

"Denassa says you've been asking about your tribe," Shurna said. "These are the clothes you wore when Manerra found you. Maybe they can tell you more than they tell us."

Kayarra lifted the top rag. Once, it had been a long-sleeved, white shirt. Now, it was ripped, heavily soiled and brown-stained. The blackened sleeve hems crumbled into powder between his fingers. Beneath the shirt were brown- and yellow-stained briefs. The final item was so tattered and dirty that it took a minute to realize they'd been trousers. One leg had been sliced to the crotch, the cloth so heavily stained it remained stiff to the touch.

"Blood," he said, suddenly understanding the significance of the stains. "My blood." In a rush of blinding anger, he wadded the clothes and thrust them at Shurna. When she didn't reach for them, he threw them into her lap.

The pounding of blood in his temples renewed his headache.

Shurna gathered up the scattered clothing and held them out. "They're yours."

"No." He reached for the ground, turned his back on her, and lay down. "I sleep. I sick." He cradled his head in the crook of an arm and brought the other arm across his face to shade his eyes.

* * * * *

Bare feet and knobby knees protruded from a skirt breeze-molded to shapeless hips. Kayarra squinted, blinked at the sight, frowned, then pushed to a sitting position, groggy with sleep. He rubbed temple and forehead under Teeka's watchful stare.

"What's wrong with your eyes?" Teeka asked.

"My eyes good." He reached for the water skin he'd hung on a nearby canopy pole and drank.

"Why can't you talk right?" Teeka stepped closer and lifted a fist from which protruded a hollow wooden rod. "I brought my flute. Do you want to play?"

Kayarra lowered the water skin, inserted its stopper, and twisted in order to latch it onto his belt hook. "I not know flute," he said as he fumbled for the hook.

Teeka knelt and thrust the flute under his chin. "This is a flute."

"I know flute," he said, annoyed. "I not know flute talk." He located the belt hook and fastened the loop.

"I can teach you." She turned the flute and rapidly covered each hole with a stick-thin fingertip. "You cover the holes, like this."

"Teeka!"

That shout brought Kayarra's attention around. The child's mother hurried toward them. Behind her, Yutrenta dropped the canopy she had been folding and hurried after Uhle.

Teeka clutched the flute to her chest. "I have to go." She leapt to her feet and started toward her mother.

"Teeka, stop right there," Uhle ordered, halted, then bowed her head. "Lord Kayarra, please forgive my daughter. I should have kept better watch on her. I'll be more careful in the future."

"Teeka good," Kayarra said. "Teeka can come."

"Can I ride his shuren?" Teeka blurted.

"Silence!" her mother snapped. "The shon regis's company prepares for travel. So should you. Bid lord Kayarra well and go back to your canopy."

Shoulders drooping, Teeka faced Kayarra, bowed her head, and mumbled something he couldn't understand.

"Walk well, lady Teeka," he said when she stopped talking.

Teeka's head snapped up and she grinned. She stared for a moment, then whirled and ran toward her campsite.

"You are kind." Uhle dipped her head, turned, then froze and immediately bowed her head again. "Janquer lady Yutrenta."

"Goodwoman Uhle," Yutrenta acknowledged.

Kayarra's attention shot toward Yutrenta's eyes, which crinkled at the corners as she stepped past Uhle.

# CHAPTER 41

The sun hung low in the western sky, blinding reminder of another laborious day trek nearing an end. Scrub and cacti, grasses and rocks had grown increasingly rare, replaced by mounds of sand that bowed in veneration at the feet of the Tydonddy Mountains.

"Lord Kayarra! Lord Kayarra!" Teeka's close, excited cries jerked Kayarra's attention from the dunes. She rode her father's shuren, clinging to the pinnacle of their supplies. "Riders!" She pointed southwest, toward the Shangren.

Kayarra halted his pack shuren and searched the direction of Teeka's outstretched arm even as Mentan halted his shuren and looked back.

The gray of approaching shuren and riders so blended with the sand and rocks that Kayarra distinguished them by movement alone. Two riders.

He turned around. "Dee!" he shouted, forgetting the formality he was supposed to use among strangers.

Denassa whirled and other heads turned. Kayarra pointed along their back trail, then tugged on his shuren's lead. Yutrenta, farthest ahead, turned Aya's shuren and started back.

Kayarra angled toward Denassa, whose attention remained fixed on the approaching riders.

Yutrenta halted well away from Denassa's shuren and shouted, "Two riders could be Manerra with an escort. Or word from him."

At mention of Manerra, Kayarra squinted back at the riders in an effort to distinguish features. Impossible at this distance.

"Should we wait for them?" Denassa asked.

"No," Aya answered. "We need to travel while daylight holds. They'll overtake us soon enough."

"I pray we've no need to go back." Denassa's murmur alarmed Kayarra. Yutrenta turned Aya's mount and Denassa followed. This time, Kayarra kept pace with his companions, leaving Coltra's company to bring up the rear.

The sun hung low enough to dazzle the eyes of anyone looking west when Denassa glanced back and announced, "They've stopped."

Kayarra shaded his eyes.

"It's Manerra!" Denassa waved her arm over her head.

"Why he not come?" Kayarra voiced his skepticism. Both riders were hooded and veiled.

"The size of our company confuses them. His escort won't let him approach."

Denassa thrust her shuren's reins into Kayarra's hand and walked briskly toward the riders. "Dee!" he called, fearful for her safety.

She ignored him. When she passed Mentan, one of the distant watchers slapped his shuren forward and rode to intercept her.

The rider passed Denassa, circled back, then halted his shuren beside her. Kayarra didn't realize he'd been holding his breath until the rider reached down, caught Denassa's upraised arm, and aided her spring onto shuren back. Only then did the second rider approach.

Coltra's company halted abreast of Kayarra and watched the riders approach. Denassa's arms encircled the rider's waist. The crown of her head barely topped his shoulder. The stranger reined his mount to a halt in front of Kayarra, nodded, then caught Denassa's arm and steadied her dismount. Instead of returning to Kayarra, Denassa ran to greet the second rider, who slid from his shuren and opened his arms to her.

Manerra swept Denassa from her feet and whirled her around before setting her down. Denassa's relief was evident in the tight press of her brows, her parted lips, her gasps of half-laughter, half cries.

Kayarra turned his back on the reunion, spotted Aya a body length away, and experienced a tingle of shock. Aya stood alone, his eyes uncovered.

"Shon regis," the stranger's voice hailed behind Kayarra. Manerra's escort had discovered Aya's presence.

"Aya, shon regis, shecaren," Manerra's sobered greeting followed his companion's.

Kayarra glanced over his shoulder and saw Manerra and his escort standing with heads bowed. Denassa lifted a hand and wiped her cheek.

"Manerra, shecaren," Aya answered, "and he who has seen my brother home." Aya stepped forward and Manerra closed the gap between them. Their embrace was formal, brief.

"I present to you Farra, shon regis," Manerra made a belated introduction.

The escort dipped his head again.

"You will stay the night," Aya invited. "Share our fire and tent. For now, I'd like to travel a bit longer before we camp."

Mentan and Coltra slapped their shuren and started away. Denassa joined Kayarra and reached for her shuren's reins.

"Your sight . . ." Manerra murmured.

"Better," Aya answered. "But time for news is later. Let's use the remaining daylight." Aya started toward Yutrenta, who kept the male shuren well away from the females.

Manerra locked eyes with Kayarra.

Kayarra dipped his head. "Shecaren."

"Attend me," Manerra said, and passed him, headed toward his shuren. Manerra reached up and began untying a sack that hung from his supply bag.

Kayarra's knuckles whitened on the reins. Was Manerra's order a demonstration of power for his escort's amusement? He wondered what Manerra would do if he walked away.

Manerra freed the sack and motioned for Kayarra to follow. With great reluctance, Kayarra trailed Manerra away from the escort, halting his shuren the moment Manerra stopped walking.

Annoyance was apparent when Manerra turned. Manerra shortened the distance between them by three steps. "You've nothing to gain by defying me," Manerra said, his expression grim. "I concluded your business at the Shangren. Maytel identified two men who threatened you, and they named three others. They claimed the rest were opportunists—strangers who saw an opportunity and took it. I do not believe they lied. Desora, the man who remained when the others left, has paid the heaviest price for his crimes."

*For not killing you—or me?* Kayarra wondered.

Manerra held out the sack. When Kayarra remained motionless, Manerra dropped it. A muffled thunk-clank sounded when it hit the ground.

"More was demanded than this," Manerra continued, "but not all could pay. I gave Korrane their public work days and the remainder of their forfeited property." Manerra stepped around the sack and started back the way they'd come, angling away from Kayarra.

Kayarra stared at the sack before approaching, then prodded it with a sandal toe. When nothing moved, he crouched, loosened the drawstring, and lowered the fabric like a nest around its contents. The sack held assorted knives in sheaths. His face burned. He leapt to his feet and whirled. "What is this?" he shouted at Manerra's retreating back, certain the shecaren used him as the butt of some sick joke.

Manerra halted and pivoted, irritation apparent in the hard press of his brows. "What do you question?" Manerra shouted back.

"Knives," Kayarra accused.

"You had no objection when Aya ordered it," Manerra's anger rose. He started forward.

Kayarra dropped the shuren's reins and clenched his fists, but Manerra halted beyond striking range.

"A crime was committed," Manerra's tone ground out anger. "The penalty is the same no matter who commits the crime. Additional payments were demanded because the threat was made against a member of the temple ruler's company. Those who threatened you were not wealthy men. If you want full payment, take what you like from my belongings. It's a price I gladly pay to rejoin my brother. I go to join him now." He pivoted and started away.

Only Manerra's escort waited, mounted, holding the reins of Manerra's shuren, and Kayarra realized that he, walking, would bring up a distant rear. He stepped forward before reconsidering abandoning the knives. Full of resentment, he turned to retrieve them.

* * * * *

That evening, Coltra's company kept a separate meal, but joined the shecarens afterward for storytelling and music. Early on, Manerra was urged to solo. The aching beauty of the shecaren's tune contradicted the callousness of the one who played.

At Kayarra's side, Teeka, who rested her weight atop his leg, squirmed. "That's my shon regis," she whispered in awe.

"Aya is shon regis!" The force of Kayarra's denial surprised even him.

The child jerked back, eyes wide. "H-he is," she flushed, "but when I grow up, shon regis Aya won't be here. That's what Marmar says."

"Teeka, apologize," Uhle snapped.

"I-I'm sorry," the child whispered, eyes downcast.

"Now go to the tent."

Teeka's head snapped upright and she gripped Kayarra's robe. "Will you come with me? You can play my flute."

"No," Uhle overruled her. "Get going. Now."

Teeka's face clouded with disappointment and anger.

"I sleep," Kayarra told the child as she used his leg for leverage while rising.

"Will you play with me tomorrow?"

"Teeka!" Uhle warned.

"Yes," Kayarra promised.

# CHAPTER 42

Manerra rolled onto his back and opened his eyes to a shadowed tent, then closed them, reassurance secured. The tent could hang in tatters from its support poles and he'd still prefer it to the down mattresses and softly gleaming woods of Shangren houses. He stroked the pallet's thin padding, comforted by that confirmation of home.

"You're awake," Aya said from the shadows.

Manerra looked up then around and spotted Aya dressed, sitting cross-legged atop his pallet. "You never sleep," Manerra's accusation came heavy with languor.

"Get dressed."

Manerra frowned. "What's wrong?" He wedged an elbow under his side and raised himself, heart pounding. If danger existed, Aya would not be so calm.

"Yutrenta's been instructed to keep pace with Coltra's company. If he ends travel early, the janquer are to go on alone."

"Aya!" Manerra sat upright, self-assurances gone.

Kayarra moaned and shifted in his sleep.

"Don't wake the others." Aya reached for the strap of the temple stone, stood, and started for the tent flap. "Bring a full water skin. If you delay too long, you'll need to track me."

Manerra's mouth opened then shut. He threw off the blanket, reached for a sandal, rammed his foot in, and got a lace caught between two toes. He tugged his foot free as Aya opened the door flap and passed from the tent.

Manerra's hand shook with the effort of not slamming the sandal onto a mat and shouting his frustration. He was still being treated like a child. What did he have to do to earn his brother's respect?

He got his sandals on and laced, then yanked a travel robe atop his unlaced dress robe, grabbed his belt and a water skin, and bolted for the door, leaping the blanket-covered mound of Farra's legs.

The desert lay ablush with the diffused light of approaching dawn. Manerra spotted Aya west of camp and hurried after him, fumbling with the fastening of his belt as he jogged.

"What have I done to rouse your anger?" Manerra called ahead as he neared. "I've been gone for days."

Aya stopped, waited until Manerra drew abreast, then began walking. Manerra matched his brother's stride, taking a single, deep breath in an effort to slow his panting.

"Maybe I only seek a day alone with my successor," Aya said. "It's our first opportunity for privacy since leaving the Shangren."

"I explained the market attack," Manerra said. "I told you everything I ordered after you left."

"That's not all I need to hear. The shecaren was heard to utter unintelligible sounds."

"When?" Manerra demanded before he remembered the wait in Casta's audience room, when he'd ordered Kayarra to accompany the housekeeper. "Kayarra was pretending ignorance. I had to repeat an order in his language before he obeyed."

"Who overheard the exchange?"

Manerra hesitated, searching memories of that precise moment. Sand under their feet shifted backward as they climbed a second dune. "A housekeeper. Neetria might have heard, but I'm not sure. No one else."

Aya rubbed his forehead.

"What did you hear?" Manerra demanded.

"That the shecaren is possessed by a demon."

Manerra barked a laugh. "If the lords feared that, they didn't show it. They begged me to stay."

"Who begged you?"

"Lord Rayda. Some of his friends."

"Including Korrane?"

"No. Korrane extended me formal accommodations, nothing more."

The light of dawn struck Aya's face as he cleared the sandy crest. He stopped walking and reached to unfasten his belt. "We'll perform abbah here."

The summit afforded a panoramic view of dune crests transformed into islands of light amid seas of shadow. Manerra removed his weapons belt, shifted to face the dawn, and held his hand out to receive the temple stone.

Aya said nothing upon the conclusion of abbah; stood without moving for so long after securing the temple stone and refastening his belt that Manerra shifted, wondering whether beauty or dread held his brother silent. "Aya?" he inquired, at last.

Aya turned. "You rejoined us," he said. "Does that mean you accept the Oath of Yatra?"

"I don't have a choice," Manerra answered, alarmed by the topic.

"A shecaren can refuse to take the oath of his position."

Manerra's mouth went dry. His tongue stuck to his palate and made a clicking sound when he said, "And is killed."

Aya's eyes could have been carved from wood his thoughts were so veiled, his face, so rigid. Manerra's attention darted to Aya's hands, but they hung with deceptive ease at his sides.

"You sought your death at the Shangren," Aya said. "You confessed it."

"Aya—"

"Have you," Aya shouted, hands curling into fists, "made a decision about the Oath of Yatra?"

Manerra's heart thudded so hard he was sure Aya could see the fabric covering his chest jump with each pounding stroke. "I . . ." Manerra fought for focus against a fog of blackness stealing his sight, "I accept the Oath of Yatra."

"Why? Why now?"

He couldn't think! While Aya watched his every struggled breath, his every tremor.

Anger contorted Aya's face. "I'll not accept silence in private when your actions and comments are public. I will reach an understanding with you, a compromise, if necessary, or we will stand in open opposition, but we will not fence words behind a façade of agreement. You are an example to those I rule. When you lie—"

"I haven't lied!"

"Lies of omission," Aya overshouted him. "I want your honesty, Manerra—"

"You have it!"

"—and an end to the verbal sidestepping and snipes. Did you believe your subterfuge too clever for Shangren lords?"

"What? No."

"Then it was your intention to mock my decisions?"

"No!"

"Then what?" Aya was panting, his face flushed. "Why do you oppose me despite your claims of support?"

"He scares me!"

"Who?"

"Kayarra."

"He's a man."

"He's not a man!" Manerra's panting matched Aya's.

"Convince me," Aya demanded.

"I've seen how men react to him."

"As I have. They confuse him with the Manteen."

"He's not even as Yatren as the Manteen."

"Then you advise me to announce to the combined tribes that Kayarra is a demon?"

Manerra shrank back, silent, scared, haunted.

"Is that the claim you want made public?" Aya demanded.

"No." Manerra's agony consumed him. "No. But as we argue who and what he is, others do, too, and I have no factual counter. Kayarra can't explain himself. How do we?"

"By logic. By reason."

"Demons attack our father. Why would they not destroy his sons? Look at us, Aya!" Manerra's throat and eyes burned. "Is he not destroying us?"

Aya answered in a near whisper, "We are doing this to ourselves. To each other. Kayarra is a complication. He is not the problem."

Manerra shook his head side-to-side in an effort to clear it, felt sand shift as if he stood atop flesh and staggered forward, seeking firmer ground. A hand closed around his arm with bruising strength. With an outcry, he threw his weight against that hold.

"Manerra!" Aya's shout brought the desert into focus, separated ground and sky, then sand grain from sand grain.

"Let go." Urgency and panic rose with equal speed. "Please let go."

Aya's grip released.

Manerra stumbled, fell, landed with jarring force on hands and knees.

"Manerra."

"You're saying I'm flawed," he said, the words resounding through a fog of distance. "Because of Tackta. Because of something I had no control over." The tremors wouldn't stop. Even with elbows locked, he wasn't sure his arms would continue to support his weight. "So you choose . . . Kayarra. Or me."

"I choose national unity," Aya's voice gave no sympathy, no apology. "You chose that pledge when you made the decision to return. You chose it again when you agreed to the Oath of Yatra."

*I chose you* was Manerra's only coherent thought, the shameful truth that Aya interpreted as altruistic.

Manerra forced himself to his feet, arms braced should his knees collapse. He stumbled past Aya and down the side of the dune, heading north, when self-preservation demanded a southern route. The suffocation that gripped him was the same he experienced the night he thought Tackta had killed his mother.

He walked until his knees and hands steadied, until the daze began to lift, until he felt pain again. Only then did he turn.

The sand behind him was empty.

It took a moment for that shock to register, for his face to burn. Aya was right; he was wrong. The shon regis did not trail the shecaren.

Manerra retraced his steps and climbed the last dune. Aya sat in the trough between hills. Manerra descended the dune, unable to feel his feet's contact with the sand, and halted before his shadow fell across his brother.

Manerra bowed his head. "Shon regis," he said, and waited for acknowledgement.

"Sit," Aya said, his voice cold, distant.

Manerra crossed his ankles and sat. He felt lightheaded and insulated from sand and sun. "I've been presumptuous," he said. "Forgive me."

Aya said nothing.

"Shon regis—"

"Who are you?"

The force of Aya's demand stunned Manerra into momentary silence. "Your brother," he answered. "Your successor."

"What does that mean?"

"I was born to be the nation's steward."

"What are you without the nation?"

Manerra flushed. "Nothing."

"Then it's wise to preserve the nation."

"I've done nothing to—" that protest died when Aya looked away.

"Name the powers greater than yourself." Aya's growing anger was apparent in the new demand.

"You, Aya," Manerra whispered. "And Acrahh. And nature, which some men believe is the manifestation of Crysus."

"Any others?"

"No."

"Then why do you fear Kayarra?"

"I . . . I found him." Speech felt disembodied. "I will be judged by the ill that enters the nation through him."

"He and his tribe will be judged by their own actions."

"The Ofrann reacted to his appearance alone."

"Kayarra's intentions are not malicious. Despite your provocation and ample opportunity, he's not harmed you."

"It's not his intentions anyone cares about. Aya, please, hear me."

Aya straightened, shouted, "You hear me!" The veins in his temples throbbed visibly. "He recognized your bronze knife. His clothing bears witness to a skill we lack. I cannot afford to believe that metalwork and weaving are his tribe's greatest skills. Unity is crucial if our nation is to survive this tribe's discovery."

"My commitment," Manerra guessed, the words a bitter recognition of Aya's distrust.

"Yours, mine, the janquers', the tribal leaders'."

Manerra averted his face and dug fingers into the sand, flashing upon a memory of Hyran's guarded grave in Thurra. Guarded, to prevent Hyranians from exhuming the body and cremating it. Aya had ordered that, done that to his maternal stepbrother. By so doing, he had solidified Hyranian hatred of shecaren rule by giving credence to Hyran's claims of a selfish ruler who defied divine directives.

"What if I can't do it?" Manerra asked while he stared at his buried fingers. "Can't . . ." *lie* ". . . convince anyone that he's mortal born and Yatren?" He looked up then, his agony searing. "We will stand upon the Altar of Acrahh and they will kill us."

Aya's expression remained grim, resolute.

*He's not afraid to die*, struck Manerra with numbing force.

"You are shon regis," Aya said, setting Manerra's heart pounding.

"Instruction?" Manerra blurted out of fear, as if Aya had heard his thoughts.

"Instruction," Aya confirmed.

Relief was eclipsed by anger. He was still being treated like a child. He considered leaving. A knife and waterskin were enough to see him safely to the Shangren.

And he'd do what there? Korrane wasn't obliged, even by formality, to hand him the city's rule. Not until he swore the Oath of Yatra.

Manerra became aware of the fistful of sand he gripped, relaxed his fingers, and dragged his palm across his thigh. Instruction could take the guise of counsel. Manerra reached up, loosened his veil, and tugged it down around his neck. Across from him, Aya did the same.

"Does the shecaren live?" Manerra tested the boundaries of this instruction and was relieved to hear, "Yes. There is position reversal only. Nothing else changes."

"What is Korrane's position?"

"He committed men to your peace efforts."

"That leaves the remaining tribal leaders and the shecaren's positions in doubt," he said ruefully.

"You have the means to gauge the shecaren's position."

"By a test of his intentions, disguised as instruction?"

"Are his intentions questioned?"

Lack of sleep and food, combined with tension, had made him careless. He'd forgotten instruction's traps. With bitterness, Manerra admitted, "They are."

"How will that insecurity affect your decisions?"

"It won't," Manerra declared and watched Aya's brows draw together. "He's a child. I have the janquer's counsel."

"A fatal mistake," Aya answered. "Your enemies would welcome such a tool."

"Do you mean 'such a fool'?"

Aya's eyes locked on his and narrowed. The muscles in his jaw clenched.

Manerra broke eye contact and stared at the sand between his knees.

"What are your plans for handling the problem of the sixth tribe?" Aya finally broke the strained silence.

"Make a law to protect them," Manerra answered, remembering Aya's protection ceremony the night they returned home and found Kayarra awake.

"Such a law would divide the nation. Would target the Kayarran for resentment. Would challenge men to test its limits. So long as the Kayarran are a tribe of Yatra, Yatra's laws protect them."

"Claiming the Kayarran as a tribe of Yatra only protects them from the shecaren," Manerra blurted. "The Manteen are Ringgangley descendants and their lives are targets for Yatren arrows."

"Then tell me how to safeguard them."

"Warn them away. Give them ships and Ringgangley navigators and the land beyond the sea."

"What if they came from there?"

"Then order them back. If they refuse to leave, kill them. If their scouts don't return, maybe more won't follow."

"If we don't win that war?"

"What war? I'm not suggesting—"

Aya held up a hand and Manerra clamped his jaw shut, returned his attention to the sand.

"Imagine the power the shon regis hands the Hyranians by marking a tribe for annihilation," Aya said.

Manerra said nothing; awaited a lecture.

"What aspect of a shecaren's training binds the shecaren to the tribes?" Aya asked.

Manerra looked up, confused by Aya's question.

"Think beyond your fears," Aya advised.

Comprehension and alarm arrived together. "No!" Manerra denied Aya's implied suggestion that Kayarra live a year among each tribe.

"It's easier hating the idea of a man than to hate an individual," Aya said.

"If he's a man!"

"We've had this discussion," Aya said.

"He claims to have no memory of his tribe or why they're here. Can he have forgotten how many men he's killed? Forgotten his tribe's aggression?"

"A man can forget facts, but he can't conceal his nature. Let go of your fears, Manerra."

"I can't! I paid with broken bones for what I learned from Tackta. I won't pay that price again. My suffering can warn someone else. I need to know that my pain wasn't solely for Tackta's pleasure."

In the ensuing silence, Manerra became aware that he was panting. He drew deeper breaths.

"The nation can't make right what I lost because of my birthright," Manerra broke the heavy silence. "I know that. The nation takes. It does not give back."

"Return comes from a child teaching another something you taught her," Aya said. "It comes from the generosity of people who have nothing more than their faltering strength, laboring for days—" Grief brought Aya back to silence.

"Learn from Tackta," Aya urged when he spoke again, "but don't look for Tackta in all men."

Manerra said the only thing he knew with certainty, learned not only from Tackta, but from the Thurrang, and confirmed again during their Shangren sojourn. "Acceptance of the Kayarran is impossible."

"Then plan for failure," was Aya's only instruction.

Manerra went lightheaded before instinct overrode shock and he sucked the heated air of late morning. He was shaking again. He'd stumbled upon the conclusion Aya had intended he reach. He was sure of it. "The Kayarran tribe must be located," Manerra said, again the only thing he was sure of. "Their numbers, their weapons, their location and nature are things we must know."

"Your oath won't allow weapons drawn against a tribe of Yatra," Aya reminded him.

"Divine law required Tackta to surrender—" Manerra bit his lip to silence that bitter outburst, to halt a tirade that had no resolution.

"Your oath doesn't allow weapons drawn against a tribe of Yatra," Aya repeated.

"If Hyranians attack the Kayarran," Manerra stated, "I need to understand what the nation faces. The Kayarran do not know our laws. They will not distinguish law breakers from devout, will not distinguish peacekeepers from criminals." Manerra paused, searching threads of fact and logic and possibility. He felt Aya's attention on him; hated the truth he was seeing in his search for answers.

"My task is to establish the Kayarran as a legitimate tribe," Manerra said. He waited for a reaction that didn't come, then remarked from a wellspring of certainty: "Success or failure will come at Ayahn Rahh."

Aya neither confirmed nor denied that likelihood, and his eyes gave away nothing. "Plan your strategy for success," Aya instructed.

A burst of bitter laughter escaped Manerra's control. In the subsequent silence, falling sand grains whispered against his robe. "Contact with the Kayarran to learn what can be known," Manerra said to free his thoughts from obvious obstructions. "Assertion of their tribal status . . . ."

When he added nothing else, Aya prompted, "Manerra?"

Manerra rubbed his face. "If the shecarens are united in purpose," he began again, "men would risk Acrahh's anger to oppose them. It would take an attack upon the temple ruler's company to remove Kayarra, a breech of law to make war." But nothing was so simple. Murder of shecarens and janquer left tribal rule . . . and Vantrann as sole leader, who knew nothing about Kayarra. Longstanding Ofrann-Thurrang animosities would interfere with Vantrann's willingness to accept Korrane's counsel.

"Are the shecarens united?" Aya asked with an intensity rarely heard in instruction.

Manerra met Aya's eyes when he said, "They must be."

# CHAPTER 43

The setting sun edged blue-gray clouds in brilliant white . . . a display of transient beauty that held Kayarra enthralled.

"Lord Kayarra!" Teeka's laughing cry snapped his attention back to his surroundings. He barely had time to brace before she broke a running charge against the immobility of his leg. "Can you play flute with me?" she panted.

He shifted the bundle in his arms—the task forgotten by the beauty of the sky. "I put in tent, then play."

"Can I come with you?"

"Yes," he said before wondering whether he violated etiquette by inviting her into their tent.

Teeka dashed toward the tent flap and Kayarra hurried after her, but she stopped and awaited his arrival.

"Pretty!" she exclaimed as she followed him inside.

He crossed the narrow communal area, placed the bundle on the ground beside the tent wall, then turned to find Teeka crushing the center of Manerra's pillow. "We don't have pillows," she announced, stood, and advanced upon the dividing curtain. "What's behind here?" She reached a hand to the curtain.

"Women's quarters," Kayarra said, reaching for Teeka's wrist. "Not go there," he said. "We play by cookfire."

"I don't want to go there." Teeka's bottom lip protruded. "Everybody's there. They'll tell me to be quiet." She grabbed his robe. "But I know a good place we can play." She tugged him toward the door.

He followed her from the tent, aware of stares as she pulled him toward her tent. Before he could tell her that he didn't want to go inside her tent, she veered around it and he spotted a folded brown blanket on the ground behind the tent.

Teeka released Kayarra's hand, ran to the blanket, dropped to her knees, and fell forward, arms outstretched. When he reached her, she rolled over, sat up, and giggled, "Isn't this perfect?" She patted the blanket. "Sit here."

Kayarra knelt on the edge of the blanket, glancing over his shoulder as he did so. Coltra's tent blocked his view of the communal cookfire.

On hands and knees, Teeka scurried to a corner of the blanket, reached under it, and produced her flute with a flourish. "You play first." She thrust the instrument toward him.

"I not know flute talk," Kayarra reminded her.

Teeka covered the holes of the flute with her fingertips and played a fragment of tune. "Now, you do it." She thrust the flute at him.

He took the instrument, covered each hole with a fingertip and blew.

"Lift this finger." Teeka tapped his index finger. He did so and heard the tone change. "Now, this one." She tapped another finger. "No!" She pushed on his raised index finger. "Put that finger down."

He followed her instructions, amused by her confident authority, while the notes changed and then changed again. He felt Teeka stroke his hair—a single, hasty brush—but ignored the gesture as an act of curiosity.

Finally, the child took the flute back and demonstrated the song she'd been teaching. While she played, Kayarra glanced toward the tent and saw someone standing there. Uhle? He couldn't be sure. The eyes were shadowed in the deepening gloom of dusk.

The woman turned away and passed from sight around the curve of the tent as silently as she'd arrived.

How long had she been watching?

Teeka finished the demonstration. "That's how you play it," she announced and pressed the flute against his hand.

"I go," he said, and shifted forward in preparation to rise.

"Don't go!" Teeka grabbed his shoulder and flung her weight onto her hands.

"I go," he insisted and broke her hold. When he looked down, she sat with head bowed. The flute lay on the blanket beside her foot. "You show me flute talk again?"

Her head snapped up. "I can sit with you at midday!" She leapt to her feet and skipped after him when he started toward Aya's tent.

"If Uhle say yes, you come." But as Kayarra rounded the side of Coltra's tent, he wasn't certain the event would occur. Aya and Manerra had not returned. If they didn't return tonight, he doubted the janquer would move camp. He'd understood enough of the women's conversations after Farra left with the borrowed shuren to know that Yutrenta had expected the shecarens' departure this morning, but even she was disturbed that they'd left without waking anyone.

* * * * *

Voices outside the tent roused Kayarra before he'd passed into sleep. He recognized Aya's voice and lifted his head, but could not distinguish words.

The tent flap opened and Kayarra dropped his head upon the pillow, wondering whether his movement had been seen in the faint flash of moonlight through the open door. He listened to the shuffle of footsteps cross the tent and stop beside Manerra's pallet. A rustle of fabric was followed by a grunt at ground level.

Kayarra thought he should say something—at least acknowledge Manerra's presence—but fear that Manerra was poisoning Aya against him kept him silent.

A blanket struck a mat. Mats and sand grated against each other as Manerra settled.

The individuals outside the tent drifted toward the campfire, leaving Manerra's rhythmic breaths as a foreboding lullaby.

*****

The Gateway rose above a darkness that roiled with entwined snakes. Aya stood on the mound above the snakes, framed by the stone arch and setting sun, the sky ablaze around him.

Laying on his back at Aya's feet, Kayarra watched Aya's robe billow in the back draft of that celestial fire. The updraft sucked dust through the mass of seething snakes.

As if created by vortex and dust, Manerra appeared at Aya's side, leaning close, whispering, "I can put out the fire. I can smother the flames."

Aya's hand rose and his fingers started to signal *yes*.

"He's lying!" Kayarra shouted, desperate to stop Aya from giving Manerra that power. "He'll never help me!"

Both shecarens looked down. Kayarra followed their gazes and saw flames curling around his legs, burning away his robe, blackening his skin. He kicked and cried out.

His eyes flew open upon darkness. In the silent tent, his gasps were loud. He shifted his head from the pillow onto an arm that he curled around his head.

"Peace, Kayarra," Aya's sleep-heavy voice mumbled in the dark. "You're safe."

*I'm not*, that truth hit him in the gut.

*****

Nightmare woke Kayarra the next night, a dream so disturbing that he sat bolt upright, drew his knees to his chest, and pressed his face into the cross of his arms lying atop those knees.

"Are you all right?" Shurna's murmur came from the break in the curtained partition behind him.

"I—" He lacked the vocabulary to describe the dread that had followed him into consciousness.

A hand touched his shoulder and he shuddered. "Kayarra?" Shurna's concern was audible.

"Kayarra should stand watch over the mia until he can sleep," Aya suggested from the direction of his pallet.

Kayarra reached for his robe, losing the warmth of Shurna's hand in the process. He didn't regret the loss. He wanted to be alone, to pace away his anxiety without having to explain his actions.

The moons illuminated the chill desert in clear light. Even the tent's guy ropes stood out against the pale backdrop of sand. The shuren rested belly-down on the ground, while the mia slept curled. The few standing mia bleated and shuffled away from Kayarra's approach, snapping their watcher's attention around.

Too late, Kayarra recognized Manerra.

"Kayarra," Manerra's voice held disdain.

"I watch," Kayarra said and held a hand out for the crook Manerra held.

"Mentan said he'd take my watch. Go back to sleep."

"Aya tell me watch."

Manerra averted his face.

In frustration, Kayarra turned to leave. He'd walk out his anxiety on the far side of a dune rather than argue with Manerra.

"Kayarra, wait."

That call struck like a plunge into ice water. Kayarra halted but did not turn.

"I'll tell Mentan that you took his watch."

Kayarra turned then, and Manerra extended the crook. Keenly uncomfortable, Kayarra approached the shecaren and reached for the staff, but Manerra kept a firm grip on it.

"I'll never believe you're Yatren born," Manerra said, "no matter how Aya explains you. But he's given you protections I will not dispute. If you want to leave, and the decision is yours, he won't stop you."

Alarmed, Kayarra released the crook. He thought he should maintain dignity and silence and leave, but found himself unable to move. "You trap," he said.

Manerra shifted the crook. "Broken trust is not easily restored." Manerra released the staff and Kayarra caught it as it fell, before it struck him. "But you understand pain," Manerra said and walked away.

* * * * *

Kayarra ducked under Denassa's midday canopy and came to rest sitting shoulder-to-shoulder beside her.

"Where's your escort?" Denassa inquired.

He laughed. "Uhle keep Teeka. Say, 'Give lord Kayarra rest.'"

Denassa smiled, but her gaze returned to the sun-heated dunes.

Kayarra twitched a smile, asked, "Sand different there," he pointed west, the direction she gazed, "from sand there?" He swung his arm south.

She chuckled.

"Give lady Denassa rest," Kayarra said and her attention shot toward him then away. "Lady Denassa love sand, not Kayarra."

His silliness evoked a hoarse laugh. But his pleasure vanished when she swiped at a cheek. "Dee?" he inquired.

"The Rahhe is gone," she said.

He looked west, then southwest, and saw only dunes. The saw-toothed peaks that had shaped the western horizon for as long as he could remember were no longer visible. He wondered how he had missed their disappearance before realizing that the Rahhe had been at their backs for days now.

"'Rahhe is gone' is bad?" he asked, confused by Denassa's distress.

"The Rahhe is my home, my tribe."

Kayarra glanced back at the western dunes, curious anew. "What lady Denassa see in Rahhe?"

She looked at him then, brow furrowed, but chuckled. Her attention strayed back to the west before she said, "In Ringgal, I see tides rising, and ships like colored petals bobbing upon waves. The sun glints upon the water, sometimes so bright, my eyes tear." Denassa ducked her head and dragged a fingertip through the sand. "The mountains split at the water's edge, one finger forming a peninsula and Tes-Raly's harbor, where I was born."

Kayarra looked down and realized that Denassa drew an outline of the area she described.

"Tes-Raly is here," she touched a point on the curve of a backwards C, "atop the cliffs of the Rahhe." She drew her hand back, encircled her knee with an arm. "A narrow stretch of beach separates the city's cliff wall from high tide. The poor build stick houses on that strand and ply the waters and beaches for food. The site is safe until Ryna and Trys enter the same sky, then high tides cover the sands. When the moons touch, the waves break against the cliff wall." Denassa drew her hand into her lap. "Every year of the Ingathering, my father deals with resentments caused by the retreat of the poor. Many would as soon have the ocean sweep them away as share ground with them."

"Is me 'poor'?" Kayarra asked.

Denassa gave a startled laugh, but grew serious when she pressed his wrist. "Your health and weight were not those of a poor man. The clothes you wore . . . ." Her hand left his wrist and plucked at a sandal lace. "White is not a color the poor wear."

"Tell me Tes-Raly story," he urged, shying from the uncomfortable speculation about his status and tribe.

Denassa glanced toward the canopies of Coltra's company, erected on the far side of their flock.

"On the day of shecaren Urna's birth, a great storm struck Tes-Raly. Winds sent swollen tides over the cliff wall and flooded the lower terraces. In those days, many of Tes-Raly's citizens built houses of wood. Three hundred and eighteen died the day of the storm, and many more in the days that followed, some from injuries, most from illness.

"High lord Bayda asked citizens to house as many of the homeless as they could accommodate. He gave shelter to as many homeless as he had beds, and fed many more.

"During the years that followed, the lower city was rebuilt in stone taken from the high cliffs. And in the year after the storm, lord Bayda's wife—"

Kayarra waved frantically for silence.

"What's wrong?" Denassa caught his sleeve. "Kayarra?"

"I not want hear," he said, knowing that made no sense but floundering for an explanation. "You talk Tes-Raly, Aya Rahh, Ofrann, Acrahh, Crysus story. I know tent, hand, leg, you." He rocked forward, backward.

"You know arm," she said.

He stopped rocking, stared into her eyes, then burst out laughing.

She grinned.

Still breathing hard, he said, "I love you, lady Denassa."

Her smile faltered then vanished, and the warmth of camaraderie disappeared. "I would rest," she said, rolled away, and lay down, cradling her head on an arm.

Kayarra watched her tuck her feet beneath the hem of her robe then snug her elbow into the curve of her side. The desire to lay along her back and slip an arm around her waist was strong, but he turned his back on her and lowered himself to the ground.

Despite his broken sleep from the night before, rest was not what he wanted.

*****

"Wake and move," Manerra's order jarred Kayarra awake. "I need to pack this canopy."

Kayarra shoved onto both hands before pausing for breath. Beside him, the sand remained indented where Denassa had lain. Squinting at Manerra, Kayarra saw him reach for a stake and pull.

He lunged for Manerra's robe, caught a fistful of fabric, and jerked. "You can damn well wait until I'm awake!" he shouted.

Manerra's fist struck Kayarra's wrist, breaking his grip on the robe. Manerra spun and lunged. Their impact drove Kayarra backward. He hit the ground with Manerra's knee in his side, Manerra's hands clamped around his throat.

A woman shouted; a child screamed.

Kayarra grabbed Manerra's wrists and strained to jerk his hands apart; brought a knee up and around and hit something, but not hard enough to loosen Manerra's grip. Then hands appeared on Manerra's shoulders and yanked Manerra off.

Kayarra rolled onto his side, gasping for breath, hands covering his bruised throat.

Aya's "You . . .!" was the only word Kayarra understood of Aya's too-rapid yell, while Manerra shouted back, "He attacked me!"

A hand falling onto Kayarra's shoulder made him flinch before he saw the whites of Denassa's eyes in a face gone pale. She tugged his hands from his neck and removed his crumpled veil.

"Kayarra, what happened?" Aya's angry demand made Denassa pull back.

Kayarra rolled onto his back in order to see Aya's face. "I—" It hurt to talk. He reached for Denassa's robe, gripped it, and pantomimed a yank.

"Never touch Manerra again!" Aya shouted. "Stay away from him. Manerra, stay away from Kayarra! Kayarra, fold the canopy. Manerra, go help Shurna."

Manerra shot to his feet and started away as if slapped. Aya stalked after him, but veered toward the shuren.

Kayarra sat up, looked beyond the retreating shecarens, and was shaken to discover an audience. Uhle stood with a restraining hand on Teeka's shoulder. Teeka faced Kayarra, her cheeks flushed and tear streaked. Coltra and Mentan had stopped work to stare, but it was Teeka's upset from which Kayarra turned.

Denassa rested a hand on his back, but he jerked away from her. If he was to lose the brief pleasure he'd found in Teeka's company, he wanted his isolation to be complete.

# CHAPTER 44

In the rapidly rising heat of morning, breakfast remained an undigested mass in Kayarra's stomach. Walking only compounded his discomfort. Strength oozed from his pores along with perspiration, and drinking sun-heated water neither cooled him nor aided digestion.

By mid-morning, he lagged behind his traveling companions. He watched Teeka, clinging to the baggage atop her father's shuren, pull farther and farther ahead. The distance separating them made him ache for the loss of her companionship.

Kayarra shambled, eyes closed, through a trough between dunes when his intestines rumbled and abdominal muscles cramped. He clutched his stomach, stopped walking, and looked up as Denassa's shuren disappeared over the crown of the dune. For the first time that morning, he was grateful to be alone. He hastily dropped his loincloth and squatted. Gas bubbled through his gut again and he strained to relieve the cramping pressure.

The first foul gush of diarrhea sent a sickening pain through his wrists and triggered a gag. He yanked off his veil and gagged again, vomiting breakfast. Another gagging heave dropped him to his knees, the gush of vomit drowning a cry of pain. He fought to remain conscious, was aware of moisture soaking through his robe before and after he lost balance and fell.

He tried to shove to his knees, stuck a hand in slime, and moaned, aware that help drew farther away with each passing second. "Dee!" he shouted with half a breath between a dry heave and a cramp that left him curled into a ball.

A wave of cold rose gooseflesh on his arms. He rolled over, oblivious to the filth he rolled through, trying to reach dry sand. He'd feel better if he could get warm.

He dug fingers and toes into sand and inched toward the slope of the dune. If he could reach the crest, he had a chance of being seen.

A quarter of the way up the dune, a woman shouted his name.

"Dee," he croaked, his throat acid raw and parched. He lay still for a moment, absorbing warmth from the sand, drawing strength to rise onto hands and knees.

"Kayarra!" her shout sounded closer. "Kayar—"

He opened his eyes when her hand gripped his shoulder. "What happened?" she demanded.

"Sick," he whispered.

"Can you stand?"

"No."

She leapt to her feet and dash away before he cried, "Stay!"

Seconds later, she shouted, "Yutrenta!"

He shook with unshed tears. How had he gotten so sick so fast?

Denassa returned and rubbed sand on his arms, then shifted his soiled robes and heaped sand on his legs.

Manerra arrived before Yutrenta did, completing Kayarra's humiliation. Yutrenta arrived, dropped to her knees and pressed Kayarra's temple, then his neck.

"What happened?" Aya demanded.

"I found him like this," Denassa answered.

Yutrenta looked around, spotted the place where Kayarra had fallen sick, and descended the slope, angling left of the site, breathing shallowly against the stench.

"Manerra, fetch a shuren," Aya ordered as she returned. "Ask Coltra and Mentan if they will help set camp."

Denassa had removed one of Kayarra's sandals and struggled with a matted knot in the other lace.

Yutrenta squatted beside Kayarra and brushed sand- and sweat-matted hair from his temple. "I need to roll you onto your back," she told him. She tucked his left arm against his side, then rolled him over that arm. He groaned, drew up his knees, and clutched his stomach. She allowed him a momentary rest before tugging at one arm. He shook his head, groaned, and clutched tighter.

"Aya," she entreated.

Aya broke Kayarra's grip and pinned his arms while Yutrenta probed Kayarra's abdomen. He writhed and cried out during her examination. Finally, she nodded to Aya and reached for clean sand to scrub her hands. "It's tramplyn," she said.

"But his age—" Denassa protested.

"We're a fortnight from the Shangren. He spent time with Gorrow's children, and Neetria's. Even Teeka."

"We're still a day from the nearest well," Denassa said.

Yutrenta settled back upon her heels. "Kayarra will not reach it."

"The Ingathering . . . . Aya?"

"The shecarens' arrival without the janquer is a gesture that will not be made," Aya said. "We've no choice but to camp."

"Cold." Kayarra moaned.

Denassa lowered the filthy robes over Kayarra's legs but continued to clean his feet.

"If the moons join without the shecarens?" Yutrenta asked.

"It will not happen," Aya said.

Yutrenta raised an eyebrow.

"We'll only travel soon if Kayarra doesn't survive," Denassa said.

Kayarra rolled onto his side, clutching his stomach. "Help me," he begged.

Yutrenta struggled to free Kayarra's waterskin from his belt. The loop had twisted and would not release. "Have you a cloth?" she asked Denassa. Finally, the cord slipped. The skin's light weight supported her diagnosis. He'd had fever before his collapse.

Yutrenta took the rag Denassa passed and, with the last of the water, cleaned Kayarra's face. Much of the filth on his robes had dried, but perspiration kept moist the coating on his skin. The stench made her nauseous.

"I sick," he said.

"I know," she answered.

"Help me."

She stroked his cheek and wondered how much she could.

"Trenta." He moaned and rocked.

"I will," she told him, "as much as I can." Guilt over that vague promise assaulted her. Tramplyn, a childhood disease, was rare but often fatal in adults. Dehydration was the killer—a greater threat in adults because the symptoms lingered days longer.

Manerra finally arrived on shurenback. Together, they lifted Kayarra into the shecaren's embrace. Kayarra gagged, begged them to stop, begged them to help him, and was hardly conscious when they reached the hastily erected tent.

When midday heat passed, Manerra loaded a shuren with canopy, supplies, and empty water skins, then—accompanied by Coltra's family—set out for the well that had been their destination.

# CHAPTER 45

A draft puffed across a sweat-slick shoulder. Kayarra, half aware, tugged the edge of a blanket close about his neck, blocking that draft.

"How are you feeling?"

He struggled awake; opened his eyes. Denassa sat cross-legged less than an arm's length away, the inevitable sewing project lying in her lap. "Cold," he answered.

She pressed a warm hand against his forehead. "Your fever's broken." She stroked his cheek. "But the sickness remains. Drink slowly. Eat slowly. Rest. Gain what strength you can. If the fever returns, the shecarens will be forced to leave us."

Too many words to follow. "Where is Teeka?" The child's tear-streaked face had haunted him through the days of his illness. Her misery had become symbolic of his suffering.

"Coltra's family accompanied Manerra to the well. From there, they departed for Ayahn Rahh. Do you remember her farewell?"

He experienced a flash image of Teeka's worried eyes, brows knit, but whether that memory had occurred before or after his collapse, he couldn't remember. "No," he said.

Denassa reached beyond his head and brought back a slender drawstring bag. "She gave you this."

For a moment, he stared at the gift, his throat tightening. Finally, he reached from the covers, took the bag, and drew it under the blanket, where he clutched it atop his chest.

"She wished you well to play at the Ingathering. She promised to await you there."

"What day she go?"

Denassa lifted a hand, thumb tucked. "Four days ago."

Kayarra rolled onto his side.

After four days abed, Kayarra didn't think he would sleep, but did—a deeper, more restful sleep than he'd experienced since his collapse. He woke during the night still clutching Teeka's flute.

The broth Yutrenta urged upon him knotted his stomach after three swallows. He refused more, although he defied hunger not to down the bowl's contents.

Yutrenta tugged his shoulder. "You should take more."

He tried to straighten his legs. A mistake. He gripped his stomach, its gurgling audible. "I leave." He struggled to rise.

Yutrenta gripped his bicep, aided his rise, slipped a shoulder under his arm and steadied his drunkard's steps. Somehow, he avoided treading on bedding and baggage as they left the tent, more a credit to Yutrenta's guidance than his own efforts.

He was embarrassed by his need for her assistance, and embarrassed by her presence during the diarrhea that followed. But without her grip on his shoulders, he could not have maintained his balance. Certainly, he wouldn't have made it back to his pallet with his knees as wobbly as a newborn's.

"You'll become stronger," Yutrenta said.

"No drink," he begged.

"You need the liquid and the strength it gives."

"No strength," he told her. "Hurt."

"The diarrhea will pass."

"No drink."

"Sleep, Kayarra. Wake me if you need me."

She rose, and surprised him when she settled upon Manerra's pallet. He'd never known one of the women to sleep on the men's side of the tent.

His sojourn into the night had chilled him, and chilled his sweat-soaked blankets. He groped, located what he thought was a robe, pulled it under the blankets, and spread it as a buffer between himself and the wet blanket. Still, he couldn't warm enough to sleep.

Morbid images from the Shangren played and replayed a reel of endless torture. Rolling over and changing positions did not halt the memories.

# CHAPTER 46

"Dee, we need your help."

Denassa dropped the dirty clothing she'd gathered and rushed through the tent's doorway. Her attention flew to the canopy where Kayarra slept. A mia stood with head lowered just beyond the canopy's shade. Denassa startled when a hand hooked her arm and yanked her to a halt.

"When did you get back?" she demanded of Shurna, then, "What's a mia doing there?"

"Just now. I don't know. That's why we need your help."

Denassa's attention shot to Yutrenta, who stood on the far side of the mia as if frozen in her approach. "Why don't you chase her off?"

Shurna pulled Denassa sideways. "Look next to Kayarra."

She did and spotted the female's offspring curled against Kayarra's back.

"Great Acrahh," she breathed.

"Yutrenta and I will capture the mother if you'll go for the kid. Just don't get between the baby and mother."

"I know. I grew up with mia." Denassa separated from Shurna, angling in a loop that took her around and behind Kayarra's canopy while Shurna approached the female. Yutrenta began a slow approach from her direction, while Shurna cooed, her right hand outstretched. The female watched Shurna. When Shurna signaled, Yutrenta lunged, catching hold of a horn and a fistful of back fur. The female bellowed and bucked.

With Yutrenta's rush, Denassa sprinted forward, ducked under the canopy roof, and lunged across Kayarra's body. With the female's bellow, Kayarra reared up, but Denassa flattened him with her fall. The frightened kid bolted past its mother. Shurna and Yutrenta released the female and leapt away, and the mother rushed after her fleeing, bleating offspring.

Denassa buried her face against Kayarra's back and laughed so hard the strength drained from her limbs. Someone tugged her forearm, then gave up and shoved her off Kayarra's body. She slid across his arm and dropped onto her back on the sand beside him.

"Were we that funny?" Yutrenta demanded.

"The . . . whole . . . thing . . . was." Denassa turned her head.

Kayarra's nose almost touched hers. She noticed the fine blood vessels that patterned the whites of his eyes. "Are you . . . all right?" she asked, snorted, writhed and then groaned.

Yutrenta helped him sit.

"I think canopy fall," he said.

"The canopy would have been lighter," Yutrenta retorted.

Denassa laughed, hiccupped, rolled onto her side, and struggled to sit.

"It's a shame the nation didn't see this," Shurna said.

Denassa snorted a laugh.

"Or, at least, Manerra," Shurna continued. "I could live to hear the last of his cor-anda, demon arguments."

A tingle of shock caused Denassa to whip her head around. "How so?" she demanded.

"A demon may blind men to his nature, but animals aren't so deceived."

Denassa's heart pounded.

"Surely, you've heard that," Shurna said.

"I . . . I'd forgotten." Denassa wiped her eyes with the back of a hand.

"Speaking of gods and demons, where are the shecarens?" Shurna asked.

"Walking. Talking," Yutrenta said. "They've been doing a lot of that lately."

Shurna smiled. "Acrahh's miracles continue."

* * * * *

Blue-gray light stained the eastern sky when Kayarra left the tent. He was finally strong enough, at last, to walk unassisted. The predawn sky offered light but no warmth. Like a moth, the flames in the firepit drew him. He reached out to catch the warmth with hands that appeared delicate after the severity of his weight loss.

Most of their baggage lay beside the tent, ready to be lashed onto shuren back. The tent itself, internally lit by lamplight, glowed in the gloom.

A flash of light drew Kayarra's attention to the door flap. Manerra left the tent, a bag slung over one shoulder. Loathing returned Kayarra's attention to the flames. With luck, Manerra had no business at the fireside.

Luck abandoned him.

Manerra poured water into the cookpot, then set the pot over the flames.

"Kayarra," Manerra murmured as he settled on the far side of the fire.

"Manerra."

Manerra opened his travel bag, groped inside, and withdrew a flute and rag.

From the corner of his eye, Kayarra watched Manerra clean the flute.

Kayarra's back grew cold. He wanted to warm it, but Manerra would interpret a turn-around as a snub. He wished he'd brought a blanket.

"Yutrenta will ride with you today," Manerra said. "If you relapse, Aya, Yutrenta, and I will travel ahead. Denassa and Shurna will follow with you as they can."

"Aya say not divide my company," Kayarra said.

Manerra's head snapped up. "Our obligation is to arrive in Ayahn Rahh before the joining. If you believe nothing I say, ask Aya." Manerra returned his attention to the flute, twisting and jamming a strip of cloth into one hollow end.

"Denassa say shecarens have . . . know . . . ." Kayarra closed his eyes and fought to recall the word she'd used. "Have a-gee-ment."

"She insists, too, that you're not a demon," Manerra retorted.

Kayarra clenched his jaw. "What a-gee-ment about Kayarra tribe?"

Manerra lifted the flute and blew a short rill. He lowered the flute to his lap. "Aya's decree of tribe protects you. That has not changed, nor can it. Does my pledge of protection mean so much to you?"

Kayarra gambled on comprehension. "Yes," he said.

Manerra frowned. "At Ayahn Rahh, the sixth tribe will receive sanctuary and protection. Aya will instruct you in the forms to follow. If you're asking whether I'll block a knife through your ribs, the future isn't mine to see. But murder is not tolerated, nor shall it be by me. You already have my pledge of protection. If you want, I give it again." Manerra pushed to his feet, hefted his pack, and headed toward the tent just as the central pole came down and the roof collapsed.

# CHAPTER 47

At midday halt, Kayarra's legs collapsed upon dismount. He broke his fall on his hands, and rested in the sand until his companions erected a canopy. Yutrenta insisted that he eat a flatcake stuffed with herbs. Only after the final crumbs were swallowed with water did she cover him with a blanket and leave him to sleep.

When Kayarra woke, the canopy's shadow stretched to the edge of the dune. He reared up and looked west, his view blocked by a hanging blanket, its weight sagging the roof fabric. Someone had hung it to keep the sun off him while he slept. He sat for a moment, struggling past the grogginess of sleep.

During that pause, he realized the bleating, grunts, and mewling of the mia were missing. He threw aside the blanket covering his legs and reached for a canopy pole to aid his rise.

Denassa looked up from the firepit at his approach and hurried forward to steady his steps. He reached for the ground as he sank beside the flames. "Shurna graze flock?" he asked.

Denassa circled back toward the cookpot. "Shurna and Manerra took the flock ahead. We'll join them at the Divide."

"Aya go?" he asked, alarmed that Manerra's threat had happened.

"No."

Relief swept him. For awhile, there'd be no more day- and evening-long disappearances while Manerra poisoned Aya against him.

Denassa used a slotted spoon to fish a steaming rock from a bowl of dark liquid, then passed him the bowl. "Be careful," she said. "It's hot."

He blew on the greenish-brown tea before sipping.

"We need to travel tomorrow, if you can manage it," she said, "even for half a day."

The morning's journey returned in strobes of misery, weakness, and, at the end, dizziness.

When Denassa reached for his wrist, he assumed she'd seen his dismay. "I want you well," she said. "I love you."

His attention snapped to her face, and for a moment he forgot to breathe. *I love you* echoed and reechoed until he doubted his understanding. Did she offer him intimacy, or an affirmation of friendship? Were there other words he didn't know that described a relationship between a man and a woman?

He broke eye contact and struggled to rise. Denassa hurriedly stood and reached for his arm but he flinched away. "I urinate," he said, wanting distance and isolation, however contrived.

"Do you need help?"

He groaned. "No," he said, and stumbled away, making it over the nearest dune and halfway down its far side before he had to rest. He relieved himself, then followed the curve of the dune to a patch of clean, heated sand, sank down, and began untying laces. For an hour, he scrubbed with sand, from scalp to toes. Clean at last, he dressed, lay back, and watched the sky's evening blush deepen, darken, then set fire to the clouds.

Before the sun disappeared from the horizon, light flared behind a neighboring dune. Aya performed abbah.

Kayarra shoved upright. Shangren citizens knew that Aya performed abbah at that moment, and knew his general location. And everyone knew Aya would be in Ayahn Rahh when the moons joined, and that where Aya went, he went.

Night fell before he could wrest his thoughts away from the implications of that realization. Even then, a sense of fatalism carried over into thoughts of Denassa. Beautiful Denassa. How did her confessed attraction mesh with Shurna's warnings? If she wasn't frightened of consequences, must he fear them?

If he'd stayed by the fire, he could, so easily, have culminated—or destroyed—their friendship. Was he as harmless as he thought? Was his real nature emerging in fragments?

He rocked his head in denial. His impulses to protect, to pair, to mate held no underlying brutality.

Hell, even the moons were mated!

But Manerra wasn't, and never would be.

A sense of justice swept him. For all of Manerra's faultfinding, put-downs, and snubs, he was permitted something the shecaren was not.

The night's chill penetrated Kayarra's robes and drove him from his bed of sand back to camp, his double shadows rippling across the dune beside him. Where the cookfire had burned now glowed a handful of coals. Beside the embers sat Yutrenta, her head bowed over clasped hands. She looked around at the grate of his footfalls.

"Our companions sleep," she said, "and I wondered if I'd labored over your recovery for nothing. " She reached for a folded rag and poured the cookpot's steaming contents into a bowl. "Sit." She held out the bowl. "Eat. You should be asleep, too."

"I not walk far." He settled in the sand beside the coals, took the bowl, and blew on the soupy beans.

"Whether you went far is not the point. When you didn't return, Denassa followed you. You could have fallen again. And you know we travel tomorrow. Without rest, you won't last half a day." She paused. Humphed. "Drink no milk tonight or tomorrow. Now, eat."

"I drink water," he said.

She watched him eat.

"You sleep," he violated protocol, uncomfortable under her scrutiny.

"Explain your bad temper."

Her demand took him by surprise. "Eat silent?" he asked.

"Don't remind me of courtesy!" she snapped. "If this mood of yours reaches Ayahn Rahh, you will undo in a day everything Aya's achieved since your founding."

His temper flared. "What good?" he demanded. "Shangren want kill me."

"That was handled."

Kayarra set aside his unfinished supper and started to rise.

"Don't you leave!" Yutrenta commanded.

"Manerra leave!" Kayarra shot back. "In talk, in work, Manerra leave! Manerra leave, me not leave?"

"It's your actions, not Manerra's, that will be judged. Your actions will determine whether Yatra's tribes accept the Kayarran. If you remember nothing else, remember that."

"I not mad?" he demanded. "I not hurt? I man like Manerra."

"Then release your anger privately. Don't make our lives miserable for days with your upset."

His sarcasm flared, "I sorry."

Her expression darkened and her voice went cold. "I don't ask for your pardon, I demand your compliance. You are the tribal representative for a people who bear your name. At Ayahn Rahh, you will do well to remember that." She stood and strode briskly toward the tent.

Kayarra watched her leave, but his attention froze on a silhouette standing beside the tent. He turned away, snatched up his supper bowl and flung it, angry at the lack of privacy, embarrassed that their argument had awakened Denassa. Then, because he knew Aya must have heard, he struggled to remember what he'd accused Manerra.

* * * * *

The next morning, Denassa rather than Yutrenta mounted the shuren behind Kayarra, and Kayarra regretted the depth of Yutrenta's anger that she wouldn't speak to him, wouldn't get close enough to touch him. How ironic that the woman from whom he'd fled, the one he wanted to be closest to, was the one forced upon him because of an argument. But Denassa was silent the entire morning, so he supposed neither woman wanted to be near him.

Soon after mid-morning, the swath of tracks they followed became a jumble of trampled sand surrounding a well. Kayarra assumed that

Manerra and Shurna had stopped there on their way north.

Kayarra halted the shuren across from the well, and Denassa jostled his back as she dismounted. She waited and caught his arm when he landed, but his knees supported his weight.

Although midday was hours away, Aya and Yutrenta reached for canopies while Denassa located empty water skins. Kayarra approached, intending to assist, only to have Yutrenta order him to sit somewhere out of the way. Kayarra tugged a mat from his shuren's packs, turned his back on his companions, and walked along the dune's ridge, selecting a depression that faced north.

The wall of stone that Denassa called The Divide, where Shurna and Manerra would rejoin them, rose in the distance. The cliff face wasn't as sheer as first impression suggested. Ridges scored the cliff face like miniature terraces, some supporting stunted trees.

Ground level movement several dunes away snapped Kayarra's attention from The Divide. White mia climbed the side of a dune, trailed by two robed figures and a lone shuren.

"Come sit under a canopy," Yutrenta called. When he didn't respond, "Kayarra."

He picked up his mat and returned to the well, disconcerted that they'd constructed canopies side-by-side, thus eliminating even quasi-privacy.

Yutrenta stood beside the canopies and thrust a flatcake into his hand. "Sleep after you've eaten," she ordered.

"Yes," he said. "Thank you."

Yutrenta returned to the well, leaving Kayarra alone with frustration. He ducked under a canopy, dropped onto the sand, and wondered whether anyone from his tribe had searched for him.

Watching Denassa stretch a rag over the mouths of water skins while Yutrenta poured water through the makeshift filter, Kayarra wondered whether he would welcome the discovery that he had a wife. He didn't feel married, but he didn't trust feelings. His earliest memories of waking in the tent were such vague impressions, they could as easily be memories of dreams.

He bit into the flatcake, chewed, swallowed.

Denassa hung a filled waterskin on a tripod of tent poles and reached for an empty bag while Aya, kneeling at the edge of the gapping well, pulled a knotted rope hand-over-hand, raising another full bucket. The well's wooden cover lay in the sand beside him, scarred and chipped, its weathered edges rounded and gray. The rocks used to weight the cover lay in a cluster in the sand beyond.

How many men had it taken to dig that hole? How many shuren had it taken to carry enough stones to line the well and weigh its cover? How much wealth or power did a man have who could order a well built in the middle of nowhere and have others build it?

Kayarra watched Aya with renewed curiosity.

Denassa finished filling the empty waterskins, brought a bowl of water to the canopy, and traded it for the waterskin attached to Kayarra's belt. He sipped from the bowl and swished the water in his mouth, enjoying its rare coolness.

When she returned with his filled water skin, she settled in the sand by his side.

"What is 'tribal representative'?" he asked.

"A person who speaks for their tribe in abbah and council."

"I not understand."

Denassa sighed, reached for a handful of sand, and let the grains run through her fingers. "You are tribal representative of the Kayarran. You are all we know of the Kayarran tribe. To many people, I am the first Ringgangley they've seen. I am the Ringgangley tribe, as you are the Kayarran tribe."

"I janquer?" he asked, stunned.

"No."

Aya and Yutrenta approached, and Denassa looked up as if she longed to trade places with them.

"What is janquer?" Kayarra asked, drawing her attention back.

"A tribal representative who has accepted the unification prayer. A man or woman recognized by all tribal leaders as a speaker for their tribe."

"No Mante? No Kayarran?"

"I represent the Manteen," Denassa's reply came so faint, Kayarra barely heard it above the grate of sand and rustle of clothing as Aya and Yutrenta settled beneath the adjacent canopy.

"You Ringgangley, not Mante," Kayarra objected, certain Denassa misunderstood his question.

She blushed. "The Manteen are Ringgangley."

Kayarra sat in stunned confusion. The Manteen had tried to kill him.

"I think Kayarra should hear the history of the Manteen," Aya said.

"Not from me," Denassa pleaded, eyes wide.

Denassa's reaction increased Kayarra's anxiety. He looked at Aya.

"It's my suspicion," Aya said, "that the history of the Manteen explains the existence of the Kayarran, although I expect few will agree." He bowed his head through a moment of silence. "The Manteen are Ringgangley descendants," Aya said, bringing his head up and meeting Kayarra's eyes. "I suspect there are as many reasons given for the division of the Ringgangley as there are historians telling the tale, but all stories tell of a tribal leader dying, leaving an infant daughter as his successor, and a hated wife as leader-surrogate.

"At the time of lord Bendala's death, Ringgal had entered its fourth year of drought. Mia were dying in large numbers, and demotic deaths were nearly as great.

"Lord Bendala's brother, a man called Mante, urged any Ringgangley strong enough to leave the unhealthy cities and dry fields to take their dying flocks into virgin forest. He promised them health and prosperity if they followed him.

"Lord Bendala's wife saw Mante's promises as threatening her rule and ordered him brought before her for judgment. But Mante's followers learned of the order for his capture and met the surrogate's bows and long knives with axes, clubs and stones. Before the day was through, the city of Tes-Raly burned, and it is said that the blood in the streets boiled from the heat of the fires." Aya paused, and Kayarra glanced at Denassa, who leaned so far forward, her braids touched the ground.

"Mante died in the fighting," Aya continued, "and only his followers who fled Ringgal survived the slaughter. Driven by fear, they went north, searching for the valley that Mante promised. But the land grew drier and drier until, at last, they came upon the desert's rim.

"Without strength enough to reenter the mountains and cross to the ocean they knew how to harvest, they claimed the land they stood on. Many died there, and the rest survived by consuming the flesh of their fallen siblings. In that reprieve, they located water enough to sustain them, and learned to hunt and eat of the fruits of their new home.

"By the time Ofrann nomads found them, the Manteen had multiplied, but they had not lost their frugality, or their taste for strange meat. Maybe it was their need that the young not condemn the old that they perpetuated the eating of man-flesh. No one alive can say."

"More delicately told than I could," Yutrenta murmured when Aya stopped talking.

Denassa raised a hand and wiped her cheek.

*Eating of man* echoed and re-echoed in Kayarra's head until his senses reeled. "How Kayarra . . . ." he started, but the horror of new realizations stunned him into silence.

"The discovery of the Manteen is a story preserved in Ofrann histories," Aya said. "The nomads who found them described speech that contained few understandable words."

"Shangren call—" Kayarra swallowed through a throat gone dry. "Shangren call me Mante."

"They spoke in ignorance," Aya said, "name calling from rumors of evil rather than fact. You are not Manteen. You were fleeing the Manteen when Manerra found you."

Kayarra rocked, arms hugging his knees, one thumb restlessly stroking the discolored skin on the back of his hand.

# CHAPTER 48

They left the well after midday and traveled until the necessity of abbah halted them. They left the shuren standing, weighed with baggage, heads hung low, through completion of the rite.

Afterward, Kayarra joined his companions in unburdening the shuren, but fell while helping to lower the tent.

"Kayarra, go rest," Aya ordered.

"I urinate," he said, dusted his robe, and hobbled away in search of privacy.

On the far side of a dune, rooted in massive sandstone, a stunted titi tree cast delicate shadows across exposed rock. One twisted branch—the entire top half of the tree—was dead. Bark had curled away from sapwood, endowing the nonliving portion with lacy beauty. The lower branches bore the tough green spikes Denassa said the trees shed during the summer to conserve moisture.

Kayarra descended the dune, crossed the trough, and climbed to the base of the tree to gather fallen deadwood. He paused in the tree's mottled shade and stared across the dunes at the wall of stone they'd reach tomorrow or the day after. Climbing it would demand more strength and stamina than he had, and the prospect of riding a climbing shuren was frightening.

Beyond that massive fault towered the Tydonddy Mountains, its slopes cloaked in green, its tallest peaks, snowcapped. "I know why you loved this land," Kayarra told Yatra, surprising himself by using a language he rarely spoke anymore. He sat down where he stood and watched the sky pass through the colors of sunset, watched the contrast of sunlight and shadow on the dunes fade into reflected light, then soften and brighten as the moons emerged.

Hunger urged a return to camp. He picked up the two pieces of wood he'd come for, the bark prickly in hand, and cautiously descended the sandstone. The tent glowed like a cloth lantern set on the sand. Only a few embers pulsed among the ash of Denassa's cookfire. Kayarra dropped the wood beside the fire pit and bent over the cookpot. The remains of a soup had scorched on the bottom of the pot.

"Kayarra."

He startled. It was Denassa, bow over shoulder, who approached from the dune's crest.

"I'll rest easier tonight knowing you're safe." She reached the firepit, set aside the bow, and reached for something on the ground. "Yutrenta made me promise to feed you when you returned." She added water to the pot, swished its contents, and poured the result into a waiting bowl. "Make certain I don't lie." Her eyes crinkled as she offered the bowl.

"Sit with me," he said.

She looked toward the tent.

For a moment, he thought she'd make an excuse to leave, but she crossed her legs and sat. He sat down where he stood, half on, half off a fireside mat.

Denassa tilted the empty cookpot and began dropping handfuls of sand inside.

"What you talk, me eat?" he asked.

She laughed. "*Will* you talk while I eat?" she corrected. "It's rude to do so," she reminded him.

"I not Aya," he said.

She looked at him. "You're an enigma," she said, then agreed, "You are not Aya. If you wish, I'll talk while you eat. But if you don't eat, I'll leave and clean the pot later."

He sipped from his bowl.

She laughed again, thrust a hand inside the cookpot, and began scrubbing. "We spoke while you were gone. In council," she added as though he knew what that meant.

"You talk Kayarra?" he asked.

"The council was about you, yes," she said. "Aya means to offer you the unification prayer."

"Is good or bad?" he asked, forgetting the requirement that he eat.

"It's never happened beyond the known tribes." He thought he detected nervousness in her brief laugh. "We hope it's good. Eat," she urged.

He sipped the thin soup before asking, "What is . . . prayer?"

"The unification prayer is the janquer's covenant."

"Aya give me janquer?" he asked, certain he misunderstood.

"If you agree, the unification prayer will be administered," Denassa said. "But Aya will speak with Manerra and Shurna before he speaks with you."

Considering his near-abduction on the day of his dressing ceremony, Kayarra wondered what greater ignominy required his agreement. "I wear robe in prayer?" he asked.

Denassa laughed, bending forward over the pot in her mirth. "You will wear clothes," she assured him, "for the entire ceremony." She tugged her veil free and used its corner to blot an eye. She was beautiful in daylight; the softer light of the moons gave her an achingly sensuous allure.

"I see Shangren women," he told her. "I see lady Denassa. I want lady Denassa."

Her smile wavered.

In the time it took him to set aside his unfinished supper, she was on her feet and hurrying toward the tent. He ran after her, desperate to reach her before she ducked through the tent flap.

"Dee," he called, "I say bad?"

She stopped but didn't turn, and he was confused by the tears he heard in her distressed laughter. "You said—"

He reached for her shoulder. She turned, pressing a hand to his chest. He thought she intended to push him away, but her finger brushed a nipple, igniting nerves in his groin.

"You said what I've wanted to hear."

He reached for her face, felt tears as he brushed a thumb across her cheekbone. He pressed his forehead to hers. Her hand slid around his waist and pulled him closer.

"Janquer lady Denassa!" startled them both. Kayarra jerked back. Denassa whirled.

Kayarra stared over Denassa's bowed head at Aya, whose face was bare and grim.

"When I return," Aya said, "I want to find Kayarra in the tent and you waiting here."

"I see Aya and Yutrenta," Kayarra protested, reckless in his daze. "No hurt lady Denassa, me, for Aya-Yutrenta love."

"Go in the tent, Kayarra," Aya ordered.

Kayarra looked toward Denassa, saw her head still bowed and her fists clenched, and suspected he should have given veneration rather than challenge. Denassa's tension and silence told him more than he wanted to know. He faced Aya, dipped his head, then walked past Denassa, past Aya, and pushed through the tent flap. He immediately stepped clear of the doorway and stood listening by the tent wall.

An unnatural silence held inside the tent and out. He suspected that Yutrenta listened, too, and closed his eyes in order to sharpen his senses. As he strained to hear, he saw Aya again in that second after his shout, lips compressed, brow creased. The tent flap had not been swaying behind him, Kayarra realized. How long had Aya been standing there? Why had neither of them seen him before he spoke?

Kayarra peered through a gap between the door flap and tent wall. Denassa stood in the same place he'd left her. Her head was raised but turned away so he couldn't see her face. He hesitated a moment before pushing aside the tent flap and stepping through the opening.

Denassa heard him approach, looked back, then turned her face away. He assumed she stared in the direction Aya had taken. "Return to the tent, Kayarra. Please."

"I touch you. You touch me." He stopped an arm's length away and willed her to look at him. "Aya not hatred you. Aya hatred you, me."

"You're not sworn to covenant," Denassa said. "I am."

"I sworn love you."

She made a hiccupping sound and hastily covered her mouth.

At that moment, Aya's head and shoulders appeared above an adjacent dune.

They stood without speaking, watching Aya approach, Kayarra trying to gauge Aya's anger by gait, by expression. Denassa lowered her head again.

Aya stopped a body length away. "Kayarra, leave us," he said.

Kayarra glanced at Denassa, saw her shaking, then met Aya's stare eye-to-eye. "Denassa bad," he stated, "Kayarra bad."

"Janquer lady Denassa," Aya said, "you may wish to hear what I say in private."

"He has a right to know what covenant means," she said.

"Then come with me. Both of you."

Misgivings struck. What was so terrible that Yutrenta couldn't overhear?

Aya angled away from the tent, opposite the direction he'd taken earlier. He stopped and turned at the base of the sandstone ridge. Kayarra stopped walking when Denassa did, and was acutely aware of the distance separating them—as though their earlier intimacy had not happened.

"Lady Denassa, I must know if your covenant was broken," Aya stated.

"It was not," Denassa answered.

"Then I need an affirmation of vows, or a request for divestment."

Denassa gasped.

"I know of your father's illness," Aya said. "I know there was no news of his condition at the Shangren. My request for choice has less to do with what I saw tonight than with my understanding of your situation. I ask only that you serve me through the joining."

When Denassa finally spoke, her voice was strained. "It has always been my intention to honor my vows until I am divested."

"We will take ship from Bana to Tes-Raly after we conclude our northern business. Ladies Sheron or Toma may have discovered Kayarran presence or location before we reach Ayahn Rahh, but I cannot depend on that. I ask that you assess the situation in Tes-Raly when we arrive and give me your decision there."

Denassa brought both hands to her face and Kayarra heard her short, gasping breaths.

"Meanwhile, both of you bear in mind the state of demotic sensitivities and superstitions. Rumor spread that Manerra was possessed by a demon because he spoke three words of Kayarra's language within a housekeeper's hearing. Nothing you do will appear innocent. Anything that sparks fear for shecaren or janquer safety will have severe consequences, and Ayahn Rahh hasn't the number of peacekeepers the Shangren does."

Denassa lowered her hands.

"Is love bad?" Kayarra demanded.

"It can be," Aya answered without hesitation. "Intertribal unions are not welcomed by either tribe; is considered a declaration of abdication if such an alliance is made by a tribal leader."

"Hold hand bad?"

"Kayarra—" Aya sighed. "Nothing is as easy as good or bad. We are watched by every man, woman and child we encounter. Each is our judge, our emulator, our ambassador or enemy. We must guard against even the suggestion of possible crimes committed."

"If we cannot hold hands except in rite, what sign of trust do we demonstrate?" Denassa asked.

"The tribal union shows our lack of fear and our respect for Kayarran lives," Aya said. "But our actions alone won't achieve acceptance. The devout will look at siblings' reactions. I've done what I can to remove the surprise from our arrival, but we're fighting superstition and ignorance, which will take lifetimes to overcome. If Kayarra has made vows to a wife, has sired children, then he's not free to commit to you. Until we find his tribe and learn more than we know, I remind you—I beg you—do nothing that will take you from me. Not when I desperately need you both."

Denassa bowed her head again.

"Lady Denassa?" Aya asked.

She lifted her head, and moonlight glinted on tears. "You'll have my decision at Tes-Raly," her voice was so low, so strained, Kayarra almost missed her reply.

"You love Yutrenta," Kayarra accused.

Aya met his eyes. "And I wish I could take from her the pain she suffers because of that. She gave up her birthright, knowing I'll never be more than a confidant. If I could spare you both our pain, I would. But that's not possible, is it? Sending you away would be my kindest action, but there's nowhere the Hyranians won't find you. Besides, I need you both. So I risk a decree of death—"

Denassa's head snapped up.

"—if my janquer's sanctity is violated."

Denassa started trembling.

Aya turned aside and gazed across the moonlit dunes. "Return to camp," he said without turning from that view.

Denassa stumbled as she turned. Kayarra caught the hand she threw out for balance, but she jerked it back as if burned. In the shadowy glimpse he caught of her face, she appeared dazed.

# CHAPTER 49

Breakfast did not sit well in Kayarra's stomach. Yutrenta checked him for fever, detected none, and had him chew a bit of dried root, which made him gag. He spit out the pulp, gulped water, thought for a moment he'd lose even that, but after several hard swallows, the nausea subsided.

Even when he gagged, Denassa did not look his way. Her silence, her distance, tore at his gut, while memory of her hand on his waist, pulling him toward her, kept alive the torment of possibilities lost.

Denassa avoided him while they packed, then approached his shuren after he'd mounted. He expected her to check the lashing of the supplies and then leave, and was unprepared when she reached up, gripped his shuren's back, and leapt. His skin jumped when she grabbed the fabric of his robe while pulling herself up. Once she was seated, he sat dumbly unmoving before his brain instructed his hands to slap the shuren with the end of the reins.

"I no think you ride," he said when the shuren began walking.

"Aya ordered it."

That revelation angered him and ended any direction he knew to take the conversation. It didn't make sense that Aya ordered him not to touch her and then forced them together. If this was a test, he resented it.

Later, Kayarra startled when Denassa pressed her forehead between his shoulder blades and a change in her breathing indicated she wept. He bore without comment the discomfort of her tightened grip across his tender stomach.

"Denassa?" he inquired when her tremors stopped and her breath came in small gasps.

She didn't answer, and after awhile, he thought she would not.

"I sorry, janquer lady Denassa."

"Stop," she cried, and he brought the shuren to a halt, regretting her intention to dismount. "I meant," she said, "stop talking that way. You've no reason to apologize."

He slapped the shuren into motion.

"I'm remaining in Acrahh's service," she said.

After that, there was nothing to say. She understood better than he what that choice meant, but he knew enough to understand that he was one of the things she sacrificed with that decision. Even suspecting that

that would be her choice, hearing it made his chest ache.

*****

The next day, soon after midday, they reached the base of The Divide. Kayarra sat astride the shuren and watched hugs of reunion. His companions' pleasure only increased his sense of isolation.

Shurna approached, reached up, and gripped his ankle. "Kayarra, you look better," she said, the furrow in her brow belying the pleasure in her voice.

"Well seen," he answered with a phrase he'd learned at the Shangren.

She burst out laughing. "Well seen, indeed!" She patted his leg. "I hope Yutrenta acknowledges your Ofrann upbringing."

Yutrenta turned at the mention of her name. "She does." A smile made crescents of her eyes.

"Kayarra!"

He jerked at Aya's call, looked in Aya's direction.

"You must walk from here."

Without thinking, Kayarra sketched an arch with two extended fingers—the sign of acquiescence—before dismay struck. He looked at the rim of the cliff they were to climb. Not that he harbored any desire to ride that slope—he questioned whether the animals could make the ascent—but he trusted neither his strength nor his equilibrium.

He slid off the shuren and sat on a rock while his companions redistributed supplies among the shuren. He accepted the waterskin, pole, and small bag Yutrenta handed him, then watched Shurna, Manerra, and Denassa drive the shuren toward the slope. To his surprise, the beasts hardly hesitated before attempting the climb, their horny toenails and rough footpads finding traction in crevices along the steep ridge. Manerra followed the shuren up the slope while Denassa and Shurna circled back, regrouping behind the mia. Aya and Yutrenta closed in on either side of the flock. On a signal Kayarra missed, they shouted in unison and the animals bolted toward the cliff, tried to veer aside, but were turned back by swings of Yutrenta's crook. The lead animals bunched at the base of the trail, were jostled by others fleeing shouts from behind, attempted a second bolt, and were driven back. Finally, one discovered the ridge trail, lunged up it, and others followed.

Only Yutrenta turned back from the trail. "Come!" she shouted breathlessly and waved Kayarra forward. "I'm walking behind you."

He hurried to join her, felt her encouraging push toward the trail, and heard her panting breaths close behind.

From the beginning, the trail was steep, the rock slippery, the climbing slow. Kayarra wondered how effective Yutrenta could be in preventing a fall if he slipped. Most likely, he'd take her down with him.

His panting increased with the strain of the climb, while the gap between he and his companions widened.

"I stop," he gasped, laboring to breathe. He shifted weight onto the staff and braced his right hand against the stone at his shoulder. Yutrenta's hand rested on his back.

"Dee!" Yutrenta shouted, and Denassa stopped, looked back. "Hold up!"

Kayarra turned his face toward the rock wall, unable to look down the drop-off.

"Be careful crossing!" Denassa shouted back. "It's slippery. I'll wait."

Denassa's warning brought his attention back to the trail. Between them lay an expanse of stone that sloped like a slide toward the drop-off.

"Rest. Catch your breath," Yutrenta urged.

Kayarra glanced left, then leaned into the rock face. He would die if he fell. The realization made him lightheaded.

After awhile, Yutrenta shifted impatiently. "Can you walk?"

In reply, he inched forward, keeping one hand on the rock face, not daring to look farther than the stretch of stone immediately ahead. He wanted to release the pole, to free both hands to grip the rock, but clung to the wood and crept forward, testing each sandal placement before trusting his weight to that foot.

He had to stop again when he reached the far side of the slide, to catch his breath and calm his trembling. He knelt on gravel cemented in place by rock-hard clay, but shifted aside when Yutrenta crowded beside him. "Go past?" he asked without looking back at her.

"I'm staying with you," she answered and jostled him.

He glanced back and saw her pull at the fastening of her water skin. He reached for his own, worked it free, and drank; paused with the open water skin resting between his knees as he looked upslope. He and Yutrenta couldn't be more than halfway to the top. He glimpsed shuren through the stunted trees. They were left of his position and halfway closer to the top. The trail must loop back upon itself. Not a heartening realization.

Kayarra plugged the water skin, hooked it to his belt, then used the staff to aid his rise.

The trail ahead broadened. A few stunted, wind-twisted conifers grew in sand and clay-filled cracks. Their sharply angled branches, green spikes, and speckled shade lured him onward.

Overhead, a shuren bellowed, a man cried out, and a woman screamed.

Kayarra jerked in startle, looked upslope, and saw a large pack hurling toward him. The pack had legs. And arms curled around a head.

He stepped forward and thrust his staff into the path of that tumbling body, then cried out when impact broke the staff and tore it from his grasp. He spun, lost balance, and fell. Yutrenta's scream drove home the horror. He lifted his head from the ground, stomach wrenching at the thought of seeing an empty trail, but unable to stop himself.

# CHAPTER 50

"Manerra!" Aya's shout held panic. "Manerra!"

Yutrenta's robe struck Kayarra's face as she bolted toward the ledge. He grabbed for her robe, missed, shouted "No!" as he shoved up, horrified that she would leap after Manerra.

Yutrenta fell and Kayarra shut his eyes, unable to watch her disappear over the ledge. When he opened his eyes, he stared at her hunched back for a long moment, unable to believe she crouched at the base of a conifer, balanced on the razor edge between death and sky.

"Manerra!" Aya shouted.

"He's alive!" Yutrenta yelled. Protruding beyond her robe, Kayarra saw bloody legs and part of a crumpled gray robe shaded by the tree under which Manerra lay.

A clattering shower of pebbles preceded Aya's arrival. He dropped to the ground beside Yutrenta, blocking Kayarra's view of Manerra's legs. Kayarra drew back, wanting them to move away from the edge.

A woman was crying, an odd sound in shock.

"Do you need me?" Shurna shouted down.

Aya twisted around. "Take the animals up," he yelled. "Be careful."

"Manerra, stay with me!" Yutrenta shrilled.

Aya's attention reverted. "Manerra!" he ordered, panic rising.

Kayarra stood, swayed, thrust a hand out for balance, then slumped back to his knees.

"Just numb," Manerra rasped.

"You're not all right," Yutrenta snapped. "My medical bag is lashed to a shuren. Your life depends upon candor."

"Shock," Manerra answered. "Sickness. No breaks, I think."

"I found none. We'd better move you while we can. Aya—"

They started to lift him.

"Slowly," Manerra begged.

"Slowly," Yutrenta agreed, and let him sit before she and Aya brought him to his feet.

Manerra, his veil gone, his face bloody and swelling, locked eyes with Kayarra, but that link broke when Yutrenta shifted between them.

Keeping a hand on the rock beside him, Kayarra attempted to stand a second time and succeeded. He glanced at his left palm and curled a fist over the torn flesh, then trailed Manerra's group as they inched their way up the narrowing trail. Partway up, Manerra's "Wait!" was the only delay he requested, his only concession to his injuries.

When they reached the end of the trail, Denassa came running, leaving Shurna supporting the partially raised tent.

"What happened?" she demanded, reaching for Yutrenta's arm.

"Shuren slipped," Manerra answered between shallow gasps. "Knocked me."

"Thank Acrahh you're alive!"

"And Kayarra," Manerra said.

*****

Kayarra searched for deadwood while Aya and Shurna erected the tent and the physicians huddled over Manerra. The one stick Kayarra found, he carried back to camp and dropped beside the carelessly heaped baggage. He was reaching for one of the bags when Shurna emerged from the tent.

"Leave it!"

He jerked his hand back, confused by the force of her order.

"Rest," her tone was tense. "Aya and I will take care of this." She yanked a rolled mat from the pile and thrust it into his arms, pointed toward the shade cast by the tent, then reached for the bag he'd started to pick up.

He left with the mat, spread it in the shade, then lay down, keeping his left fist clenched against dirt and pressure. He expected tension and upset to delay sleep, but underestimated his exhaustion.

In his dream, he clung to a barren shrub as its roots slowly tore from the ground. He kicked, desperate for purchase, but struck only air. In panic, he released one handhold and grappled at the rock that anchored the shrub, but broken obsidian cut flesh to the bone.

He woke shoving upright before pain collapsed one arm. He fell onto his left shoulder and rolled onto his back, clutching his injured fist to his chest. A flashback of Manerra's hurtling body made the breath catch in his throat.

Night sky glittered overhead, the two moons dimming adjacent stars.

"Kayarra?"

He looked toward the caller. "Shurna," he panted.

She approached. "I heard your cry. At first, I thought it was Manerra."

Kayarra sat up, cradling his hand in his lap. "Bad dream," he said.

"Can you take watch?"

He hesitated. "Yes." He tugged at the blankets someone had thrown over him.

Shurna held out bow and crook. He freed his legs, stood, then took the bow and hooked it over his left shoulder before reaching for the crook. Shurna pulled it back.

"What's wrong with your hand?" She caught his left wrist and turned his palm toward the moonlight.

"Pole break, hurt hand."

"It's not been treated." Then, as if the thought had just occurred to her, "You've not eaten, either." She released his wrist. "There's food beside the fire. One of the physicians is sitting with Manerra. Come to me after your needs are met." She reached for her bow, freed it from his arm. "I'll be watching the mia."

He followed her as far as the door flap, ducked past the fabric, and halted. Denassa sat beside Manerra, her head drooped far forward, eyes closed. He started to back out when Manerra moaned and Denassa's head jerked upright. Kayarra stopped.

Denassa reached toward Manerra but didn't touch him.

"Dee," Kayarra whispered and saw her jump.

"Kay! You scared—"

Manerra moaned louder, and his head shifted against the brace of baggage and clothing that held him partially seated. With the blood rinsed from his face, the wounds were visible: cuts on chin and cheek showing haloes of bruises and a gashed, swollen lip.

"Manerra all right?" Kayarra asked on impulse. It was one thing to wish Manerra ill, another to watch that wish come true. He shuddered, remembering his certainty that Manerra had gone over the cliff.

"He will suffer, but he broke no bones in the fall," Denassa murmured. "Did you find the food we left you?"

"Shurna said food at fire. She said you see hand." He lifted his fist.

Denassa straightened her back, patted the mat beside her. "What happened to your hand?"

"Pole hurt hand," he said as he sat.

Her eyes widened. "Why didn't you tell me?" She reached for his hand.

He winced when she straightened his fingers.

"Manerra hurt bad. I all right."

"There are splinters in the wound," she said, reached for a bowl, and placed it on the mat between them. A wadded rag lay in the bowl's puddle of brown liquid. Denassa lifted the dripping rag, centered his hand over the bowl, then pressed the saturated cloth against the wound.

Kayarra yelled and jerked his hand away, flinging brown liquid across mats and bedding. Aya's head jerked upright from his pillow, and Manerra startled awake with a cry of pain.

"Shhhh!" Denassa lunged for Kayarra's wrist, but he avoided her grab while flailing his hand, nerves aflame.

"Hurt!" he cried.

Manerra squinted at them, the furrows on his brow deepening.

"Argue after dawn." Aya lowered his head to the pillow. "Or treat him outside."

"My apologies, shon regis, shecaren," Denassa replied and thrust a hand out expectantly. "It burns only once," she hissed.

"No more—" Kayarra jabbed a finger at the bowl.

Denassa gave an exasperated sigh, stood, crossed to the baggage lying next to the tent wall, and eventually returned with a vial. "This will only hurt after Yutrenta discovers what I've used." She held a hand out expectantly.

"What is?"

"An herbal oil made by a handful of Thurrangy artisans. Yutrenta could purchase a shuren for what this vial cost in trade goods."

Kayarra wondered whether Denassa bullied him, although she'd never done so before. With great reluctance, he said, "Use water," and extended his injured hand.

"You are maddening." Denassa set aside the vial and gripped his wrist.

She'd told the truth. The second and third applications stung, but weren't the searing burn of the liquid's first application. After the wounds were clean, Denassa raised the lamp's wick and extracted the splinters. In the end, she used the oil on his hand anyway, a few drops smeared across the torn flesh before she wrapped his hand.

"I not hatred you," Kayarra told her while she tucked the bandage's loose ends.

She glanced at Manerra, who appeared to sleep. "We're all upset," she said. "And you're not the worse patient I've ever treated."

"Tell me one day."

She chuckled. "You want an historian, not a physician."

The smile she flashed made his heart ache. Suddenly, he didn't want to leave. "I watch mia," he said and stood.

"Acrahh watch with you, Kayarra."

"Acrahh watch you, Dee."

* * * * *

Kayarra spent the morning holding mia while Shurna inspected udders and hooves. He was still helping when Yutrenta approached near midday.

"Manerra is awake," Yutrenta announced. Kayarra looked up, surprised to see her staring at him. A breeze teased her robe. "He says he can participate in the unification prayer. Aya will conduct it this evening."

"Prayer?" Kayarra asked.

"The oath of janquer," Shurna supplied.

"Denassa will minister through the rite of unification," Yutrenta continued, "but you must choose another. Ask that person to sit beside you during evening meal. Make your choice based upon trust."

The mia struggled against Kayarra's hold and Shurna signaled him to release her. He did so, and she bolted toward the knot of animals milling nearby.

Shurna arched her back. "How is Manerra?"

Yutrenta's frown deepened. "He insists upon traveling tomorrow." She lifted a hand, palm out, then turned and started back toward the tent.

Puzzled, Kayarra stared after her.

Shurna reached for a handful of sand and rubbed it between her palms. "He'll ride with you tomorrow," Shurna remarked. "You're the stronger, this time."

Kayarra barked a laugh. "No, Shurna," he said, looking into her eyes. "Not ever." He dragged his uninjured hand through the sand. "Can Aya sit at meal?"

"You must chose among the janquer."

"You," he said.

She dipped her head. "You honor me."

"I not know 'honor.'"

Shurna laughed. "I don't know it, either. At least, not to explain it."

"Explain prayer."

She stood and extended a hand to him. He took it, although he didn't need her assistance to stand.

"Yutrenta will make a tea for you, and Aya will explain the responsibilities of the janquer. Do you wish to do this?"

"Aya want this?"

"He does."

"I want."

Something flickered in Shurna's eyes. Doubt? Distress? She turned away before he could tell, but not before he saw a ridge form between her brows. His misgivings increased.

"We need a canopy," she said.

He walked with her toward the tent.

"Manerra's accident reminds me that life can change in an eye blink," she remarked. "And not everything that happens can be fixed."

"I see Manerra fall. Again. Again." He wished he could stop reliving that moment. He hoped that admission would break the spell.

"I do, as well," Shurna admitted.

* * * * *

Manerra heard bleating and pushed away from the baggage that held him nearly upright until he sat without support. Shurna's return with the flock meant sundown, meant commencement of the unification prayer was fast approaching.

Dread so overwhelmed him, he sought Denassa's face, wanting eye contact, wanting to know whether her apprehension matched his. But she searched through a bag in her lap and did not look up when he shifted.

Footsteps approached the tent and Manerra looked toward the tent flap, expecting Aya.

Shurna pushed through the door flap. She paused and gave veneration. "Shecaren."

"Has Kayarra been advised of tonight's protocol?" he asked, hoping for denial.

"Acrahh be praised for his care of you, too," Shurna replied in a voice taut with anger.

Manerra's face burned. "Does a social blunder deserve your anger?" he demanded.

"This violation goes well beyond 'social blunder,'" Shurna retorted.

Denassa's attention fixed upon them, her expression revealing shock.

"What—?" Manerra checked himself. "Please explain your grievance."

"We were given a choice. You and Aya commit Kayarra to a way of life he doesn't understand. Denassa can attest to his ignorance."

Denassa blushed.

"If I explain and he refuses, how much protection does he gain?" *Great gods, I wish the situation were that simple!* His face warmed. How much more hypocritical could he get, defending a position he loathed?

"How much of the protection he has now would you withdraw?" Shurna demanded.

Manerra glared. "Hard consequences are the result of hard choices. This is one."

"Success need not have the consequences you give it."

"Enough! He already fills the position!"

"By default," Denassa said. "He doesn't understand the implications or the commitment."

Manerra protested, "You said he agreed."

"I'm not confident he understood what he agreed to."

Manerra exhaled, tried to release some of his anger. Pain complicated the effort. "Speak with Aya. This was his decision."

"Kayarra would speak with you," Shurna said.

Skepticism reared. "I haven't any answers he wants to hear," Manerra's bitterness rose. Then, "Not tonight. This is too important."

"Shecaren." Shurna dipped her head, pivoted, and left.

Heavy silence followed Shurna's departure.

"Denassa, please assist Yutrenta. When Aya returns, let him know I request a moment with him."

"Shecaren." She bowed her head and left.

Alone, Manerra shifted forward and savored the pain that movement brought. Shurna's rare protest had pinpointed a doubt that had nagged him since he'd first heard Aya's intention to offer Kayarra the unification prayer.

The door flap bulged again, this time admitting Kayarra. "Manerra," Kayarra said and dipped his head.

For a stunned moment, Manerra thought Shurna had defied his order. But Kayarra turned his back, bent, and opened one of the trade bundles stored near the door.

"Kayarra," Manerra remembered to acknowledge him.

Kayarra rummaged in the bag, pulled out a red robe, and spread it atop the bags. To Manerra's surprise, Kayarra reached to remove the robe he wore. Kayarra had stopped undressing in front of him. The cor-anda's ribs were shockingly prominent beneath his white skin—a result of his illness.

"What injury to your hand?" Manerra broke the silence that Kayarra seemed content to maintain.

"Splinters. Cut. Not bad like you."

The hem of the red robe slid down Kayarra's back, covering his emaciated frame. Manerra recognized the robe as one Vantrann had traded for in Ringgal.

"Your staff broke my fall. If not for you, I wouldn't be alive."

"I not think you live."

Manerra was surprised to detect distress in Kayarra's reply. Only dressed, did Kayarra face him. "As I wasn't certain the day I found you," Manerra admitted. "My father links our lives."

Kayarra's brow crinkled, as it did when he didn't understand something said. "I thank you found me."

During Manerra's silence, Aya came through the door. "Shecaren. Kayarra," Aya greeted.

"I leave," Kayarra said.

"No, Kayarra." Manerra reached for a staff to aid his rise. "I will leave." And to Aya's quizzical glance: "Shurna demands closer adherence to the law of unification. I agree with her."

Aya's eyes clouded, and Manerra knew Aya assumed he'd taken an active part in that objection.

"Manerra, stay," Aya said.

With reluctance, Manerra set aside the staff.

Aya regarded Kayarra. "The unification prayer is the formal conveyance of the position you perform," he said. "The law requires your agreement. Shurna said you gave it." Aya glanced at Manerra.

"She says he lacks understanding of the commitment," Manerra supplied.

Aya gestured toward Kayarra's pallet. "Sit," he invited, then crossed to his own pallet and settled there. "The prayer solidifies the unions among gods, land, and tribes," Aya began after Kayarra settled. "To perform the unification prayer is to share the oath of stewardship held by the shecarens. With agreement, you assure the sharing of knowledge and guarantee continuity of leadership beyond the shecarens."

Kayarra flushed. "I not know words."

"A janquer shares his knowledge with all tribes. The janquer rule if Manerra and I die."

"I not know Kayarra . . . *Kayarran*," he cor-rected himself. "Shurna say wait to moment I know Kayarra. Know me."

"When?" Manerra blurted.

"At Shangren."

Relief flooded him.

"Your service is yours to promise," Aya said. "If there is reason for change after the Kayarran are found, I will free you from service and order you back to them. But I think it important that the Kayarran have formal representation at Ayahn Rahh. I want your participation in those rites to be as janquer."

Manerra signed, *Denassa.*

"As janquer," Aya added, "you agree to celibacy. You must not touch a woman."

"No sex," Kayarra said.

The reply jolted Manerra. He wondered who had taught Kayarra that word and under what circumstances.

"No sex," Aya agreed, "even if Denassa requests divestment. No sex so long as you are janquer. Until your divestment, you serve Acrahh and the sons of Acrahh."

Kayarra's attention locked on Manerra, and Manerra thought Aya had finally named a condition Kayarra could not accept.

Aya continued, "You are not expected to know immediately all that is known by the janquer. They will teach you what you must know, and you will teach us Kayarran ways."

"I not know Kayarran. I not know Kayarran when Manerra find me. I not hide."

Aya lifted a hand. "I don't want an informer, Kayarra. I value willingness to learn as highly as demonstrated skill. You've proven your willingness to learn and to teach. I want no more from you than that."

Kayarra dipped his head and clutched his hands in his lap.

"Because your earlier agreement was based on lack of understanding, I ask again. Do you, Kayarra, accept the unification prayer, which will establish a place on the janquer for the Kayarran?"

A moment of silence followed before Kayarra looked up, held Aya's eyes. "Yes, Aya," he said, "shon regis."

Manerra looked away. Too late, he realized that Aya had probably seen his reaction.

Aya stood. "The janquer should not remain waiting, then. You've chosen your position in tonight's circle. Shurna will advise you through the prayer and responses."

Aya stepped forward and extended his hand. Kayarra reached up and Aya gripped his wrist, assisting his rise, but held that grip a moment longer than was necessary. Manerra wondered what his brother learned from the cor-anda's pulse. "Tell Denassa we come."

Aya released him.

# CHAPTER 51

The women sat barefaced beside the fire, their expressions revealing a gravity rarely seen during mealtime. Yutrenta stopped talking before Kayarra reached the fireside, and each of them turned to watch his approach.

Kayarra stared at Denassa, who had intertwined beads and braids around her head like a crown. In the firelight, her beauty was achingly ethereal.

"Is the prayer to be performed?" Denassa asked.

Kayarra nearly stepped on her hand before he got himself seated. "Yes," he said.

Yutrenta picked up a stick, slipped it through the looped handles of a tiny pot wedged among the coals, and shifted the pot to the ground in front of her.

"Shecarens comes," he delivered his message.

Denassa rose to her knees, reaching for an empty bowl with one hand and the lid of the supper pot with the other.

"The shecarens will break the fast," Shurna said at Kayarra's side.

Denassa filled bowls and handed each to Kayarra, who passed them to Shurna. Kayarra was handing Shurna the bowl she would keep when he glimpsed apparitions beyond her shoulder and almost dropped the bowl. His heart lurched, and he felt foolish as he watched Aya and Manerra approach, the dark moons on their white robes glinting in the combined light of moons and fire. Aya paused before a vacant mat and waited until Manerra stood beside him, then they knelt together and lifted their bowls, Manerra's mimic slower, his movements, less fluid.

"Father," Aya said, "we bless you for this gift of the land that sustains our strength. We are grateful for the animals and plants that feed and clothe us, thankful for the water that preserves all lives. We will tell again, and hear again, the tale of your sacrifice. We vow again to preserve all lands, to honor our commitments, to pass that commitment on to those who follow us. We are strong because of your sacrifices."

"Thank you, Acrahh," Manerra and the women murmured in unison.

Aya sipped from his bowl, then settled upon the mat. Manerra reached for the ground as he sat, winced, and shifted position.

The signal ending supper came when Manerra withdrew his flute and began playing. The tune was slow, controlled and solemn, unlike the airy, lively tunes he typically played.

Movement in the corner of Kayarra's eye shifted his attention to Denassa, who lowered a pottery bowl from her lips.

Shurna whispered urgently, "Take only two sips. The liquid will be hot."

Kayarra accepted the palm-sized bowl from Denassa and tipped it cautiously against his lower lip. The liquid was lukewarm. He drank, swallowed, and drank again before passing the bowl to Shurna.

Shurna tipped the bowl against her lips, then leaned far forward to hand it past Manerra. Aya accepted the bowl but passed it to Yutrenta without drinking.

Meanwhile, Manerra concluded the solemn song and began another, equally as grave. Kayarra became aware that Manerra's bruised hands and swollen lip made the notes sound choppy. His finger shifts lagged and his breaths were audible. Still, the new song captivated Kayarra's imagination, evoking memory of a fiery sunset seen from the roof of Casta's house.

"Close your eyes," Shurna whispered. Kayarra startled, unaware that Shurna had inched closer during the song. At the same moment, Denassa shifted closer.

"You'll feel our arms on your back, Denassa's and mine," Shurna told him. "Close your eyes. Good. Now, lean your head back into our hands. Keep your eyes closed. You're safe, Kayarra. We won't let you fall. If you feel drowsy, sleepy, lean against us. Just keep your eyes closed until I tell you to open them. I promise, we won't move without telling you what we're doing."

Kayarra felt the press of Denassa's breast against his arm even as Manerra began a new song whose notes jumped in a strange dance, like desert silt lifted by an unexpected wind.

"We're holding your hands," Shurna murmured, and cool fingers closed around each wrist.

As the notes of Manerra's third song faded, Kayarra's equilibrium swam in an unpleasant way. He reached for the ground. The women's handholds shifted with him, remaining firm.

"Keep your eyes closed," Shurna warned him. "You're safe."

He appreciated the arms that curled around him, supported him, supported his head. A lassitude began that precluded fear. He was safe. In the dark behind his eyelids, he imagined himself alone with Denassa. He flexed the fingers of the hand she held, felt her grip shift infinitesimally. How beautiful she was, the keeper of his soul. He could not distrust her without distrusting himself.

"We're going to lay you down," Shurna told him. "Keep your eyes closed. You're safe, Kayarra. We won't let harm befall you."

As they began to lower him, he tried to brace an elbow on the ground to catch his weight, but Shurna thwarted that reflex. "Don't try to help us," Shurna told him. "You're not too heavy."

They turned him in laying him back. He worried about dust on the exquisite red robe, but a mat and blanket were the impressions against his back. He felt the fire's warmth on his left side, his feet well away from the coals.

Cool fingers smoothed hair from his face.

"Open your eyes, Kayarra."

He did so and gasped. The stars had enlarged until their halos overlapped and pulsed with an invisible heartbeat.

"Behold the heavens in which Acrahh dwells," Aya intoned, quiet, strong, "and behold his sons, who keep his trust."

Kayarra looked toward the voice and forgot the sky. For a second, he thought Aya held the uncloaked temple stone, then realized that the light enveloping Aya emanated from him, moved with him, as if Aya had become the nucleus of a star that pulsed with the orange of firelight.

"Raise your uninjured hand," Shurna instructed.

Kayarra rolled his head toward the sound of her voice but his attention froze on the flames of the cookfire. A gasp and sob collided in his throat and he jerked away from the flames.

"Kayarra, what's wrong?" he heard her alarm.

"Fire." He tried to raise a hand to shield his face but someone held his wrist pinned to the ground. He tensed to rear up, but Shurna moved, positioning her body as a shield between him and the fire. The fire's flames burned through her though, globs of orange that turned purple and blue as if passing through a changing filter. "Fire," he whispered the word like an accusation, sought her face, and gasped to see her head consumed by that flowing, fiery light.

"You're safe, Kayarra," her lips moved. "We will allow no harm to befall you. You're safe."

He wanted to believe her, raised his hand toward her face to touch that light, saw his own flesh surrounded by an orange-gray light that melted into the sky he reached toward.

"Acrahh's light infuses this world he has chosen for his children," Aya said. "By partaking of the world's bounty, we partake of his light, the light of his spirit. So too when we touch, we join spirit light to spirit light."

Denassa's fingers slipped through his, and he watched his brownish light suffuse and dull the pinks of her own. He was too confused and spellbound to pull away, felt the reassuring pressure of her clasp, wondered if she noticed the dark red colors form where their flesh met.

While Aya spoke of the joining of man spirit to man spirit, regardless of kinship ties, in order to achieve mutual goals, Yutrenta and then Shurna gripped his hand in turn. When Aya spoke of the union between man and gods, Manerra reached for his hand.

Kayarra pulled back, frightened by the mud-colored light of Manerra's hand. Kayarra didn't want that light to touch him, to meld with his.

"Kayarra?" Shurna asked, caught his wrist and held it.

"The blood—" his brain wanted to describe imagery and emotions at once, tripped over itself.

"Remember Manerra's fall?" she asked.

He held still while Manerra gripped his hand.

"The truth of Acrahh lies in the light of the spirit."

Hands changed. Aya's grip replaced Manerra's, warm, strong, reassuring.

"Draw truth as strength from the sons of Acrahh. Pass that strength onto the children of Yatra, who are also Acrahh's children."

Aya's hand withdrew and Denassa's face appeared above Kayarra. Her braids fell forward, shrouding them in privacy.

"Open your mouth," Shurna whispered.

He did so, and Denassa's face lowered. Her lips parted, touched, molded with his.

"As representatives of Acrahh," Aya said, "you share the breath of life as you have shared food, water, and knowledge."

Denassa breathed into his mouth, filling his lungs with air. When she was done, the suction she created made him understand that he was to return the spent breath.

"Know that every life you touch gives up something of itself to you. What you return enriches and betters the lives you encounter . . . ."

Denassa pulled away and Kayarra started to lift a hand to stop her, but Shurna's intervention thwarted him. He opened his eyes and watched Denassa leave.

Aya's voice faded into a background tone as Yutrenta and then Shurna repeated Denassa's ritual. Manerra's bruised face replaced Shurna's so quickly, repugnance had no time to take shape. Kayarra's lungs filled with Manerra's breath before he had time to react, and Kayarra returned the breath on an exhale of shock.

Kayarra closed his eyes in anticipation of Aya's kiss, more uncomfortable with the shon regis than with the shecaren. Manerra had employed the element of surprise. Aya lacked it.

"Accept the gift of life from the sons of Acrahh as from Acrahh himself," Manerra intoned through Aya's ritual. "This gift, given freely, must be freely passed. Do not take that which is Acrahh's alone to take or you blind your spirit to the sun's light."

Moisture remained on Kayarra's lips when Aya pulled away.

"Open your eyes, Kayarra," Aya invited.

Kayarra complied, and saw the stars' light blend and emerge through Aya's aura in a way that distinguished neither—as though the shon regis truly enjoined earth and heaven.

"We will lift you, Kayarra," Shurna whispered.

His clumsy attempt to assist them caused Shurna to ask for his restraint. She and Denassa brought him to a seated position facing Aya and supported him while Kayarra's equilibrium settled.

"Cup your hands together," Shurna instructed, and Aya demonstrated her expectation. "Higher." Shurna raised his hands.

Manerra doubled a chamois and draped it across Kayarra's joined hands.

Kayarra recognized the leather cloth—had participated in abbah too many times to mistaken Aya's intentions—and tensed over the remembered injuries Casta and Aya had suffered from the temple stone's use.

"The temple stone is Crysus's gift to Yatra," Aya said, "carried by the shon regis as proof of Acrahh's life and promise. Never shall blood or unprotected flesh touch the surface of the stone. Its use honors Acrahh and preserves Yatren life. For no other purpose is it to be used.

"Light ignites the power within the temple stone. The stronger the light, the more dangerous the power. Its use is safe only at sunrise and sunset, or when firelight alone is the source of light."

Aya removed the cloaked temple stone from the tooled pouch at his side and lowered the shrouded stone onto Kayarra's protected hands. He released it only after Kayarra understood and supported its unexpected weight.

"Close your eyes," Aya warned.

Kayarra did so, and felt a tug on the stone's cover before light stripped away darkness.

"Acrahh and Crysus," Aya called, "your sons ask recognition of this man known as Kayarra who seeks entrance into your service. Your sons commend Kayarra as guardian of the stewardship entrusted to all shecarens, that the nation of Yatra may be strengthened and united by his service."

A hand slipped under Kayarra's hands as if that person intended to help him support the weight of the temple stone. A moment later, the stone's light vanished. Kayarra blinked against a white afterimage while Aya lifted the cloaked stone and chamois and returned them to the pouch.

Kayarra rubbed his tingling palms against his cloth-covered thighs. Never had he been so close to the uncloaked stone.

Aya secured the flap, then reached for Kayarra's hand, clasped it. "So long as you remain janquer, no man may dispute your membership in this company, nor shall you cause any man to question the justice of that claim without risk of judgment yourself. Know that even the tribal leaders must heed your counsel if no shecaren lives who is of age to be called shon regis. In return, you swear to the nation's unity, not to your tribe's interests, and your devotion to the shecarens shall exist without question. Knowing these things, Kayarra from the Kayarran, do you accept the position of tribal representative, of janquer, to serve until divested by a shon regis?"

Chill tingling ran through Kayarra. Not until that moment had the gravity of reality struck. His understanding wavered over the obligations of a tribal representative; however, Aya's presence, his intensity, assuaged uncertainties.

"Yes, shon regis." He tightened on Aya's grip: for reassurance, because of excitement, in promise.

"Then does this company witness your agreement." Aya smiled. "Acrahh bids welcome, Kayarra, janquer of the Kayarran."

# CHAPTER 52

Manerra started playing again, a strange tune overtly foreign.

With the first unfamiliar notes, Denassa whispered, "This song is said to have been played by Yatra," and, because of similarities in the next song, Kayarra credited it to the same source.

The persistent over-expansion of lights, dimmer now, still confounded, as did emotions that attached gravity to an event so astonishing, Kayarra came close to tears.

Yutrenta cut and shared dysie—the first he'd seen since their Shangren stay—and Manerra, accompanied by Shurna, played a final song, Kayarra's favorite.

"Enough," Aya said at the conclusion of the duet. "Sleep. Rest in Acrahh's watchcare. And to you, Kayarra, a warm and joyous welcome, my new janquer."

Janquer. The council of leaders. The tribal representatives who ruled in the shecarens' stead if events ever went badly awry. He found that inclusion incredible, and ached with joy over Aya's welcome.

Shurna stood and extended a hand, and Denassa kept a grip on Kayarra's arm as he gained his feet, swaying drunkenly. The unsteadiness confused him. His mind felt alert and clear.

"It will pass," Shurna said before Kayarra had a chance to question his condition.

The women helped him to the tent and onto his pallet, Denassa insisting that he drink yet another steeped tea before leaving him to sleep.

If the tea was supposed to induce sleep, it failed. He remained awake long into the night.

* * * * *

If not for the red robe he still wore, Kayarra would have delegated the unification prayer to the dream world. His memories of the ritual were shrouded in an eerie otherworldliness that leant incredibility, despite the reality of headache and thirst.

He was acutely aware of the janquer's stares as he approached the morning cookfire. Denassa extended a bowl of tea even before he sat down. "Drink it all," she urged. "It will lessen your headache."

He gingerly sipped the hot tea, hoping for relief from both thirst and pain, before he noticed he drank alone. "You not headache?" he asked.

"Oh, we suffer!" Denassa laughed. "From Shurna's strange wit."

Shurna slapped Denassa's arm.

"Ours was but a flavor of tanyan," Yutrenta answered. "We would not endanger your life by embracing its effects ourselves."

"Mealtime chatter?" Manerra demanded, startling Kayarra.

Kayarra watched Manerra's limping approach, his staff swinging forward with each step.

"No one eats yet, shecaren," Shurna answered.

Manerra forbore comeback, paused in front of a mat and, leaning heavily on the staff, sank down, wincing.

Yutrenta passed bowls of tea and milk, which Manerra accepted in silence. Kayarra stared at Manerra over the rim of his bowl, never having seen one of his companions so pale. He finished his tea and passed the empty bowl to Yutrenta for refill.

Aya joined them partway through the meal, a reunion of nods and passed bowls. At meal's end, he decreed, "Manerra and Kayarra will rest while we pack, and both will ride when we depart."

As the others stood to leave, Denassa began gathering empty bowls. The cloth-wrapped cooking stone went into a bag along with the bowls, then she hurried away to assist her companions. Kayarra guiltily watched them perform tasks he normally completed.

On the far side of the fading coals, Manerra hunched over a bowl he had not raised to his lips for a while, seemingly oblivious to the work others performed in his stead.

"You ride?" Kayarra asked out of increasing doubt.

"I must," Manerra snapped.

Kayarra abandoned conversation. His head hurt too much to puzzle out his new offense. He gulped down the dregs of his tea, scrubbed the bowl with sand, and forced it into the pack with the rest of the cookware.

When his companions were ready to leave, Kayarra mounted the shuren first, then began adjusting his robe and smoothing a twist from the reins, leaving Manerra to mount unassisted. A jostle, a groan, and a tug on his robe indicated both the shecaren's difficulty and his successful mount. Manerra's pain seemed a fitting repartition for the earlier slight Kayarra had not deserved. Despite the payback, Manerra's closeness still galled.

The shuren grew sullen as sunrise heated air and sand. She challenged Kayarra's rein commands by tossing her head, sidestepping, stopping, and nipping nearby shuren. Fortunately, her surlier tricks began after his headache eased.

"Your skills have improved," Manerra spoke for the first time since camp.

Kayarra snorted, caught unprepared for blatant peacemaking, not certain he wanted it.

"How long was the recovery from your fall—until the pain stopped?" Manerra asked.

"Not wake. Not know." Kayarra wondered if Manerra sought pity as a bridge toward peace. Before he could decide, the shuren threw her nose to the ground and leather burned his hand. "Goddamnit!" He yanked her head up.

After awhile, Kayarra decided that his reply had been needlessly callous, but before he could compose a truce, Manerra sighed and slumped against his back. Kayarra shrugged hard before alarm made him twist and grab for the arm sliding past his back.

"Trenta!" he shouted, scared by Manerra's faint.

The shuren sidestepped, further throwing Manerra off balance. Kayarra leaned in the opposite direction, but Manerra continued sliding and Kayarra had neither the grip nor the balance to prevent his fall. Still, stubbornly, he held on until he realized that he'd crush Manerra if he fell atop him and let go.

Kayarra tumbled backward. Impact with the ground drove the air from his lungs. He lay stunned, unable to breathe, while the shuren's body blocked the sun and her huge feet danced dangerously near his head.

Denassa appeared in a whirl of robes and threw herself against the shuren's flank. The beast's head jerked up and it lunged aside. Sunlight blinded Kayarra.

"Kayarra!"

Muscles finally responded to an urgent lack of oxygen and he gasped a lungful of air, then another.

"Are you hurt?" Denassa tugged loose his veil and gripped his face.

"See Manerra," he choked between gasping breaths.

"You're bleeding."

"Bite lip."

"Your hand, too."

That pain had not hit him. He shoved her hand away. "Manerra!" His alarm grew.

"Yutrenta's got Manerra," Denassa told him.

The shuren approached and Denassa leapt up to block its skittish sidestepping. Beyond its legs and Denassa's skirts, Kayarra saw the group encircling Manerra. The shecaren lay in Aya's arms while Yutrenta tried anxiously to rouse him. She glanced around desperately and caught Kayarra's eye. "What happened?" she demanded, her anxiety assaulting him like an accusation.

"He—" He didn't know the word for faint. "Sleep," he substituted. "He fall. I not hold him. I sorry. Aya, I sorry. Manerra fall."

"Shhh." Denassa knelt and pressed his shoulder.

"We should have held to camp," Yutrenta's tension was audible.

"Shurna, raise a canopy."

"I help." Kayarra shifted to rise.

"Stay!" Denassa ordered with such force, Kayarra slumped back. "You won't help with an injured hand."

Manerra suddenly jerked and his eyes flew open, unfocused. He blinked, twisted against Aya's hold, fixed on Yutrenta, then lay still.

"Thank Acrahh!" Yutrenta cried.

Manerra's brow furrowed. "I fell?"

"I drop you," Kayarra blurted.

"He fell trying to hold you," Denassa corrected.

"You need to learn another way to dismount," Manerra said.

Kayarra's barking laugh sprang from tension.

"I need draydine. Aya, I'm sorry I didn't make it farther."

"Lay still," Aya said.

"My position requires more than that."

"Not today."

Later, in the shade of a canopy, Manerra, supported between Aya and Yutrenta, fell asleep with his head on Aya's shoulder. Kayarra watched Manerra from the canopy he shared with Denassa. He looked back at Denassa in time to see her sprinkle brown powder into a bowl of water.

"You use one night," he said.

"And you survived." She set the mixture in the sun, then glanced toward the shecarens' canopy.

"Manerra good?" he asked.

"What happened today is not good." She met his eyes. "Did Manerra convulse before or after he fainted?"

"I not know word."

"Jerk. Like so." She jerked spasmodically—a grotesque sight.

"No."

"Then perhaps I'm wrong." She pressed fingertips to forehead. "Yutrenta won't talk of it."

Kayarra lost the gist of the conversation. "Tanyan make light?" he asked.

Denassa reached for his bandaged hand, turned it palm skyward, and poured oil onto the bloody cloth. "We suspect, as Aya thinks, that the lights are always there. The tanyan merely allows one to see them."

"Shurna not see blood light?"

Denassa's forehead wrinkled. "Each of us has accepted the prayer of unification. We understand what you saw." She bent over his hand and pressed the cloth, making oil bubble up through the bandage. "The tanyan allowed you to see the world in a way few do. We understand the promises we made to you and to Acrahh by our participation in the rite. You are janquer in all ways that are recognized by our tribes. I hope you understand that . . . understand your promises."

"I feel . . ." He knew no Yatren word to describe how he felt. "I learn," he promised.

She began unwrapping the bandage.

"You say I love you," he said and saw alarm in the glance she shot him. "Is love man, woman?"

"For us, it must be friendship."

Kayarra jerked when removal of the last layer of cloth yanked loose a scab.

"Aya love Yutrenta."

"They've spent more years together than any of us. Casta served shon regis Dayla, and Aya's mother was Ofrann." Denassa reached for the bowl she'd placed in the sun and pressed Kayarra's hand into the brown liquid. Instead of the burning pain he'd anticipated, he experienced a tolerable stinging that gradually lessened.

"Kayarra, Denassa touch like Aya, Yutrenta?"

Denassa kept her attention on his hand. "Kayarra, my future is not mine to decide. Our futures aren't. Until we are free to make promises, it is best we not seek ways around the vows we made."

"I want janquer. I want Denassa." Still, she did not look up. "Shurna say Kayarra act Ofrann. Kayarra know Ringgangley story. Dee," he touched her arm, "Aya want me tell Kayarran story. I not know Kayarran."

She finally looked at him. "We know you don't remember your tribe."

"Who is Kayarra?" he asked.

"We don't know," her reply held anguish.

Kayarra stared at the ground.

"You aren't from the desert," Denassa said. "But the Ofrann isn't my birthplace, either. My skills are with boats, with the ocean, with fishing. Knowledge that is useless here. I had to learn Ofrann ways. When I joined this company, I felt I burdened its members. Once, by my helplessness, and again by the responsibility every Ringgangley shares in the creation of the Manteen. But our companions are patient. They ask only that we learn."

He picked up the wooden vial of oil she'd used. "Oil?" he asked. "No oil?" He shook it. "Oil." He set it down. "Shake Kayarra, no oil. How find Kayarra oil?" He shut up suddenly because his eyes had begun to burn. Weakness had shamed him enough at the Shangren. He didn't want to be weak in front of Denassa.

Denassa lifted his injured hand from the water and kept it centered over the bowl as it dripped.

When he could speak again, he told her, anger rising, "Denassa not Kayarra oil. Kayarra find Kayarra." He jerked his hand from Denassa's hold. His legacy, he thought—or his doom: to reject what he wanted, to fear what he loved.

"You have needs I don't know how to understand, much less fill," she said and waited. For what, he didn't know. Did she think he could explain himself, that he could clear up her confusion by making sense out of the chaos of his existence? Aya, according to his actions, had a clearer idea about Kayarra's purpose in life than Kayarra did.

Kayarra stared at Aya. For reassurance? For answers? For hope? Or was he simply avoiding Denassa?

"Shake your hand dry."

Denassa demonstrated when he glanced back.

Her request gave him something to do that did not bring into question his missing past, or skills he didn't have, or raise the specter of what was or wasn't his to promise.

* * * * *

Midday passed and the janquer unburdened the shuren and constructed camp. Kayarra helped Yutrenta with supper preparations.

By the time Manerra woke and proclaimed himself fit to travel, the tent was standing. When Aya told him they were remaining at camp, Manerra hobbled in circles around the campsite until Yutrenta finally ordered him to sit. Manerra's stiff compliance was a rare concession to any order that wasn't Aya's.

"Even a godling needs time to heal," Yutrenta told Manerra, waved at Kayarra, and pointed to a bowl of tea she'd left steeping. Kayarra passed the bowl, which she handed to Manerra.

"Aya reminds me often enough that I am half man. Why should you refrain?" Manerra took the bowl and sipped, then lowered it to his lap.

Yutrenta stiffened. "Do not beg familiarity. To be a man is to have others believe their judgments are as true as yours. Hyran saw Aya as stepbrother rather than shecaren. We will deal with the consequences of Hyran's jealousy for years."

Manerra looked away. "Awareness of my position never leaves me."

"Drink the tea, Manerra."

"I don't need it."

"It's not for pain alone."

"Then make another with only draydine." He defiantly set the bowl aside.

"Are you a physician now?" Yutrenta demanded.

Manerra bowed to her, but Kayarra noticed that Manerra's hand remained pressed against his side when he straightened. "My teacher must say."

"You are not," her tone seared.

"I desire awareness of my injuries, Yutrenta. You say a physician must rely upon a patient's report. Without pain, I can't know if I harm myself more."

"In sleep, additional injury is not a concern."

"Save the tea and at sundown I will drink it."

"Shecaren." Yutrenta tilted her head, her eyes narrowed.

"If you wish to ease my worry, then explain your fears about bruised organs."

The look Yutrenta sent him was withering. She abandoned supper preparations. "It seems unnecessary to repeat common knowledge. Of greater interest would be an explanation for your faint."

"Pain, Yutrenta! I would have done better on my own two feet than on that shuren's four."

"Doubtful."

Manerra sighed in exasperation. "I have no chance, have I?"

"You may order me."

Manerra ducked as if slapped.

Yutrenta turned toward Kayarra, who flinched from the anger in her eyes. "Kayarra, the tubers." She thrust out a hand for those he'd chopped.

# CHAPTER 53

The next morning, travel brought them to a well-worn rut, visible as a shallow depression meandering up the hillside. At first, Kayarra thought the path was a play of shadow across the rough terrain, then noticed how his companions followed one another along its length as if funneled like rainwater into the depression.

The rut was Kayarra's first encounter with anything indicative of a significant Yatren population outside the Shangren Oasis. The immensity of the Ofrann Desert, their lone encounter with Coltra's company during all the months of travel, had created a cocoon of safety that unraveled with discovery of the footpath.

Shangren citizens hadn't known he wasn't janquer when they first saw him; those at Ayahn Rahh would not know that he was. They would react to his appearance only. That fact dampened his interest in the first grasses they passed, the first shrub-like trees, the first clumps of broad-leafed plants.

The next evening, camp was built on a slope at the mouth of a valley. The Tydonddy, Denassa called the mountains that flanked their camp—sacred in the stories of the world's founding. But Kayarra ignored the mountains and watched the sun set over the desert while he crouched beside the cookfire, palms extended to catch the warmth.

How far had they come? From their camp's elevation, the land—its hills, the Divide, the dunes—stretched toward sunset until land merged with advancing dusk and sight failed. Kayarra imagined Yatra standing on a mountaintop, gazing across those endless hills, excited by and afraid of the beauty he saw. *He* had walked those hills, those dunes, and still they called to him.

*****

Their company had crossed a low ridge and begun descent into the valley beyond when Kayarra tugged hard on the shuren's reins and twisted around.

"What's wrong?" Manerra demanded, his face inches away.

Kayarra turned back around. "Desert gone," he said, aware that his foreboding had roots in a fear of change.

Manerra kicked the shuren and the animal took a couple hesitant steps forward. "Slacken the reins," Manerra ordered.

Kayarra did, and Manerra kicked the shuren again. The animal resumed walking.

Remnants of the desert—its sand, its clay, its prickly flora—rapidly gave way to sandy loam, a broad array of plant life, and finally, the tinkling of falling water.

The mia surged forward and, shoving one another, strained to reach inch-deep pools at the base of a dripping grotto. Ferns cloaked the slope above the water-darkened rock face, and tiny ferns, rooted between exposed strata, flourished in a microcosm of perpetual rain.

Manerra slid off the shuren and limped a short distance before leaving the trail and entering a stand of trees. Kayarra was content to rest atop the shuren and watch the trickling water flow and drip down the low wall of stratified rock. When his companions began reaching for empty and partially full water skins, he dismounted and tugged his own water skin until it slipped free, but waited for the animals to sate their thirst.

The mia that had drunk their fill backed away from the crush surrounding the pools, giving up their places to those thrusting noses under bellies of companions in their determination to reach water.

Manerra returned, crossed the trail and, gripping a tree, lowered himself onto dry ground.

Even using bowls to catch drips off the rock face, filling water skins took well over an hour. By the end of that time, Kayarra, chilled, sought a patch of sunshine in which to stand while he ate the flatcake Yutrenta pressed upon him. When they resumed travel, the shuren's body heat helped dry and warm him.

Camp that night was pitched at the far end of the valley. The chirps, chitters, and whirs that began at dusk were joined by the base whollop and high-pitched screech of frogs. When Kayarra finally crawled into his pallet, the sheer volume of insect and animal noise kept him awake. He wondered if his companions lay awake . . . and was surprised when he woke in the morning from a sounder sleep than he'd experienced in over a month.

The trail they followed wound around one mountain's base and then started to climb. More and more free-running water appeared the deeper they penetrated the mountain pass: a trickle that bled down a rock face and muddied the trail before seeping away, a stream that paralleled the trail for half a day before veering toward unknown regions. With the prevalence of water came a biodiversity that confounded Kayarra's desert-acclimated senses. In an effort to overcome the claustrophobia that accompanied loss of the Ofrann's vistas, Kayarra searched for blue and yellow flowers hidden among the leaves of a viny groundcover. Bushes as tall as the Ofrann's tallest conifers and trees that towered overhead made him feel like an ant crawling through dune grass, except this monstrous grass stretched on and on without end.

As they approached the crest of a ridge, a break in the trees and brush afforded a view of a valley and the mountain opposite. A fault line of raw stone held his attention.

Something immoveable struck his knee and shoved his leg backward into Manerra's knee. Kayarra yelled, snapped around, and threw his weight against the tree trunk crushing his leg against the shuren's side. Manerra threw his weight against the same tree and kicked the shuren. Kayarra shouted with pain as the animal lurched forward and sideways.

"Goddamnit!" Kayarra half leapt, half fell from the shuren, staggered, recovered his balance, and limp-lurched toward the nearest tree.

"Manerra?" Aya came running.

"Shuren!" Kayarra shouted. He yanked up the hem of his robe, anxious to see how much skin he'd lost.

"She tried to brush us off," Manerra said.

Aya reached for the shuren's cheek strap. She shook her head in an effort to avoid capture.

Denassa pressed past Aya on the crowded trail. Reaching Kayarra, she lifted his hem higher, exposing his bloody knee. The wounds were superficial, but hurt like hell.

"She's done this before," Denassa remarked.

"Why ride—" Kayarra jabbed a finger at the animal, "bad shuren?"

"The others are worse," Manerra said.

Kayarra slammed his thigh with a fist.

"Wait here," Denassa said. "I don't have my bag with me." She pressed past Aya and hurried up the trail to her waiting shuren.

Aya caught Kayarra's eye. "Lead her," he said. "Keep a short lead. She'll try to walk on the opposite side of any tree you pass."

"Shon regis," Kayarra said and dipped his head, although he felt he was being punished for his injuries.

The scrapes were nothing more than skin loss and blood. Kayarra's robe had prevented bark from imbedding in the wounds. The oil Denassa applied relieved the sting, and a bandage protected his knee from his robe's abrasion during the trek down the mountainside.

Late that afternoon, Kayarra avoided a pile of feces crawling with bugs, and later, glimpsed the end of a broken staff protruding from brush. Afterward, he remained alert for signs of previous travelers. In the day and a half that followed, he spotted many: a complex, geometrical symbol carved with an artist's skill into a rock face overlooking the trail, a discarded sandal showing a hole through its sole, a heap of cloth or fur so old it fell apart when he poked it with a stick, a log bridge spanning a stream. The maggot-infested carcass of an unidentifiable animal could have been a natural death. It was the bridge, however, that made him wonder how close they were to Ayahn Rahh.

As dusk fell that night, they camped in a valley beside a boulder-strewn river. While Yutrenta and Denassa prepared supper, Kayarra stood on a partially submerged boulder and watched mist rise along the riverbanks, thickening the air and dampening the breeze. The pulsing scream of awakening insects and frogs gradually rose above the roar of the rapids, as though the battle of songs represented a battle for survival.

"Supper," Denassa called.

Kayarra jumped from the boulder onto the riverbank, climbed the slope, and joined his companions around the cookfire. After supper, he returned to the riverbank, drawn by the splash and roar of water funneling between boulders, thrust skyward by rocks obstructing its flow, then dragged down by gravity and suction. Nightfall blunted distinctions of detail, made the sedges growing in the lee of boulders little more than feathery mounds. The glint of moonlight on water held his attention until the reflection of the moons jolted him. He hurried down the riverbank and leapt onto the boulder he'd occupied earlier. His heart pounded as he made the leap, and was slow to calm once he spotted the moons. Their rippled reflections had shown them joined, but a sliver of night separated their brilliant rims.

Standing on the river boulder with the scream of insects out-shouting the water's roar, it was too easy to believe their company existed alone in the world—too easy to believe the lull of calm and belonging could last.

# CHAPTER 54

Their morning trail paralleled the river for a short distance, veered left, climbed a steep slope, then looped back and crossed above a falls, where a massive gneiss slab created a broad, natural dam. Water from the upstream pool flowed in inch-deep channels across the gneiss and plunged fifteen feet to the river below.

The first time Kayarra's foot slipped on the wet stone, he took smaller steps and kept an arm outstretched for balance. Denassa gripped Aya's hand until she reached the opposite bank.

Beyond the river crossing, the trail climbed the mountainside in an ascent so narrow and steep they climbed single file using exposed roots as stair steps and tree trunks as railings.

Shurna went first, driving the flock ahead of her. Aya followed. Denassa paused to catch her breath before starting up, and Kayarra followed, but quickly lost sight of her shuren as the steepness of the climb forced him to increasingly lengthier pauses. When he looked down the trail, between his shuren's legs, Manerra and Yutrenta were nowhere in sight. That fact heartened him, that he wasn't the only one lagging behind.

Half a mile farther, the slope leveled, rounded a cluster of brush and boulders, then descended—Kayarra's least favorite angle.

Trees and brush blocked view of the valley below, and a lone birdcall increased Kayarra's feeling of isolation. He clucked to the shuren, anxious to overtake his companions.

A flash of wings beyond thinning trees pulled his attention from the moss and fern-lined trail to the sky above the valley. A large bird glided on rising thermals, its wingspan as wide as his arms' reach. Kayarra angled toward a break in the trees in order to get a better look at the bird.

Both feet slid out from under him. He flailed and clung to the shuren's reins. For a second he dangled, then the animal lunged forward and Kayarra let go, fearful of being trampled. He hit and rolled once before the ground dropped away. He was airborne when he collided with a tree trunk. His side scrapped the trunk before he slammed against ground a second time, face down in leaves, lungs stunned. On his third attempt to gasp, he sucked leaf mold down his throat. He raised his head and coughed until he gagged, finally bringing up bile.

He was frightened by his involuntary reactions, but more frightened of the darkness dimming his sight. He forced a deeper breath than he'd managed so far and coughed hard, finally dislodging the dry obstruction strangling him. A gasp, then a second, helped clear his sight. He shook his head while shuddering, hacked and spit, finally clearing bile and mucus from throat and sinuses.

"Kayarra!" Denassa's panicked shout sounded distant.

He looked up and only then realized how far he'd fallen. Black humus scarred the leafy slope where he'd hit and rolled partway down.

"Dee!" he shouted, but his voice broke, his throat raw from stomach acid and coughing. He swallowed hard, looked down—past the tree that had broken his fall—and wished he hadn't. Twenty feet away, the slope ended abruptly in sky.

"Kayarra!" She sounded closer.

"Denassa!"

"Where are you?" she shouted. "Keep calling."

"Look down," he gave as much direction as he could, relying upon sound rather than description to guide her. "Help me. Denassa."

He glimpsed movement at the edge of the trail, well below the spot he'd gone over.

"Denassa!" He waved.

She waved, pulled back, and he lost sight of her.

He pressed a hand against his forehead.

She reappeared, closer, and remained visible as she followed the edge of the trail. She stopped directly overhead. "Are you hurt?"

He became aware that his robe had bunched and twisted around his waist, leaving both legs exposed. His side, where he'd hit the tree, was sore. "No hurt," he shouted, hoping that was true. He hadn't yet tried to stand.

Denassa reached toward a down slope tree.

"No!" Kayarra shouted. "I come up."

"We need a rope."

"I come up." His face burned at the idea of turning another fall into a spectacle of rescue. He reached for the trunk of the tree that had broken his fall and gripped it while he secured a toe purchase and drew his knees up under him.

"It's too dangerous," Denassa yelled. Then, "Be careful!" when she saw he wasn't going to wait.

Maintaining a death grip on the tree, Kayarra inched his shoulder along the trunk until he stood. His legs were steadier than he imagined they would be. He turned, keeping his back against the trunk, and searched for a way up.

"To your right." Denassa pointed. "There."

He saw the tree she indicated and reached for it, and soon discerned the vertical ladder of trees she had detected. Her sweating hands steadied him the final three feet to safer ground.

*Safer ground!* He nearly choked. It was the trail that had thrown him in the first place.

"You scared me!" Denassa started to probe his ribs. He caught her hands and stopped her, pulled her away from the steep slope.

"I all right," he told her firmly.

"When the shuren . . . ." Tears stood bright in her eyes. "I'm so sorry."

"Sorry? Dee, you not—"

"I slipped in the same place."

He looked back, saw the moss and ferns he remembered seeing before he spotted the bird, saw now the place on the trail stripped to bare clay, gleaming where sunbeams speckled the damp scars. More than one person had slipped there. Many more. He might not be the last. Manerra and Yutrenta followed.

"I thought to wait for you, to warn you, but we were so close, and I thought you would see—"

"Denassa, hush!" He shook her, then deliberately released his grip. "I see if I look at trail. I not. Not you bad, me." He reached for the waterskin at his belt. It came away too light. The plug was missing along with most of the water. He rinsed his mouth and swallowed that mouthful.

Denassa had not finished venting her anxiety. "To travel all this way only to suffer mishap on our doorstep . . . ."

"*What?*" He forgot the petty damage to his waterskin.

She appeared confused and stunned by his tone.

"What?" he repeated.

"Suffer mishap—"

"No. 'Doorstep,'" he stumbled over the word. "Dee, where are we?"

"Home, Kayarra. We've made it. This valley is Ayahn Rahh."

Surrounded by forest, himself begrimed and leaf-strewn, Denassa's words struck like the ravings of a lunatic. He denied them because too many recent nightmares were linked to that name, and too strong and irrational a fear: his personal premonition of doom.

Ayahn Rahh. Ayahn Rahh. He had been on its soil since he had topped the last ridge and started down. The red clay, its bloody ground, had slipped him up, attacked him, before he even knew where he was—even knew the danger or the nature of his enemy. He shuddered.

"Kayarra?"

"No one say," his cry was that of an aggrieved child, but he was deaf to his own plaint. Fear and anger mounted, virtually indistinguishable from each other. "Why no say? Where is Aya?" He lunged down the trail, knocking her back a step when he collided with her shoulder. That stopped him, brought him around with a grab for her. "Denassa—"

"No one thought," she told him, apparently oblivious to his collision. "Everyone's been so preoccupied. Kayarra, I'm sorry we didn't say anything, but you knew where we were going."

Yes, he'd known. But the shock of it without warning on the heels of his scare . . . .

He tried to clamp down on his out-of-control emotions but the trembling continued unabated.

"Aya is not far," Denassa told him, sounding calmer. "He will not approach the Ingathering alone."

Voices high on the trail diverted Kayarra's attention. He was thankful for the warning. It gave him time to assert control before facing Manerra.

"Yaahhh, Manerra!" Denassa shouted. "Yutrenta!"

"Dee?" Yutrenta's voice came back.

"Beware here. The ground is treacherous."

Yutrenta appeared on the trail above them, Manerra close behind. Yutrenta waved. Denassa pointed to the moss-covered slope.

"Where are the shuren?" Manerra demanded.

Kayarra felt his face heat and did not trust himself to speak.

"Tied down the trail a ways," Denassa answered. "Kayarra slipped and the shuren escaped him. We waited to warn you."

"Any injuries?" Yutrenta demanded. She trod through the ferns, steadying her descent with a hand on the rock face that formed the mountain side of the trail. She made it past the muddy slope without slipping. Manerra took the same route. Kayarra saw Yutrenta's attention sweep his robe, but was unprepared for the hug she gave him.

Manerra, in passing, eyed Denassa as if assessing the keeping or breaking of her vow of celibacy. Kayarra had to consciously relax his fist.

"Come," Yutrenta urged. "Thank you both for waiting."

* * * * *

Aya and Shurna rested in the shade of a tree partway across a large stone outcropping that interrupted the trail. The mia were strung along the trail on the upslope side of the outcrop, nosing the leaves of trailside brush.

Shurna rose as they approached, but Aya's come-here motion halted whatever Shurna might have intended to say.

Kayarra followed Denassa onto the rocks, glanced left, then halted and stared. The valley of Ayahn Rahh lay below him, the view unobstructed by trees.

Sun sparkled on blue water filling the valley's western end. Protruding from limestone cliffs that towered over the lake's northeastern shore loomed a multicolumn edifice.

"The Temple of Crysus," Aya's outstretched arm indicated that stone monument, startling Kayarra, who hadn't heard him approach, "and the House of Moons." Aya's arm swung east, indicating a white stone house nestled within a grove near the lake. The size comparison only made the columned structure more incredible. Aya lowered his arm. "We are among the last to arrive."

Kayarra had been squinting, trying to discern the nature of the multicolored carpet covering the valley floor. With Aya's comment, Kayarra's heart thudded. The colors were tents. And more people than he'd seen at the Shangren.

He stepped back, as though distance and denial could protect him.

"Cha-ka," Aya said, but it was a moment before Kayarra could remove his attention from the hordes and notice where Aya pointed. His outstretched arm indicated the valley's eastern end. Haze obscured clarity, but Kayarra saw rooftops in the distance, and a single large building centered in a green clearing. "Before we leave, you will go there," Aya promised.

"We not go—?" he pointed to the settlement, having already forgotten its name. Panic interfered with comprehension, with breathing. Could he survive alone in these mountains? He tried to remember the leaves of the plants Shurna had foraged, plants that had gone into their supper pot.

He jumped when a hand closed upon his elbow. He stared into Aya's eyes, wordless, desperate, naked in Aya's scrutiny, disbelieving what appeared to be understanding in his eyes. How could Aya imagine his fear? Aya, who was Yatren and Yatren myth combined.

"Our entry will be informal," Aya said as though that statement answered Kayarra's unasked questions. "In other cities, we ask for hospitality. In Ayahn Rahh, we return home. Rest before the evening ceremonies. Your naming will be one of the ceremonies I perform tonight." The grip on Kayarra's elbow tightened, Aya's gaze, intense. "You are janquer, Kayarra. Those awaiting us know of your presence in this company. I will have them know immediately your pledge of unity. This shall not be a repeat of the Shangren. Come." Aya tugged his elbow, released him.

Kayarra turned, staggered, lightheaded and dizzy. Aya grabbed his arm again, steadied him, led him. "Breathe, Kayarra. Deep breaths."

Kayarra nodded . . . didn't remember until later that the gesture held no meaning for them. Deep breathing helped clear his head.

Aya stopped in the shade where the shecaren and janquer waited. "Denassa, signal. Kayarra, remove your robe. Shurna, fetch him a clean one."

Kayarra's stomach knotted. He turned his back on Manerra before complying, unwilling to face Manerra's expression of loathing.

Before the robe cleared his head, fingertips pressed his ribs and he winced.

"You're bruised," Aya said. "Yutrenta."

A nearby drum stroke startled Kayarra. Denassa stood on the outcropping facing the valley, beating her drum to no song he'd ever heard. He detected no pattern or melody to the thing she beat. He remembered her communication with the Shangren drummer.

Shurna returned with folded robes and waited while Yutrenta rubbed oil on Kayarra's bruises. By the time Yutrenta signaled Kayarra to dress, Denassa had stopped playing, and Aya and Manerra had changed into tribal robes. While Kayarra dressed, Shurna, Yutrenta and Denassa sought privacy behind a fir, and Manerra and Aya led two of the shuren over the outcropping.

Kayarra reached behind his head to tie the robe's neck cords when a glint of dark blue at shoulder level caught his attention. Abalone moons occupied the shoulder of his tribal robe, identical to those worn by the janquer. He covered the moons with a palm and looked toward the fir, vaguely remembering Denassa sewing moons on a robe, but thinking, at the time, that she repaired her own or a companion's robe.

He finished dressing, then went in search of Aya, wanting information on what was expected of him.

A short distance beyond the outcrop, the trail skirted a miniature meadow. Aya and Manerra stood in the shade, their shuren tied to trailside saplings. Aya approached. "Wait here," he told Kayarra and passed him.

Kayarra entered the meadow, unwilling to stand near Manerra and the ledge overlooking the valley. Denassa arrived, dressed in tribal robe and leading a shuren. Yutrenta followed, with Shurna and the mia bringing up the rear.

The mia rushed forward, fanning out around Kayarra and snapping at the tall, weedy grass before they slowed. He weaved through the animals toward Yutrenta, who searched a shuren's pack as if rummaging for lost items. Two bags lay on the ground near her feet. One, he recognized as his.

Denassa tied her shuren's lead to a nearby sapling.

"You'll each carry a bag," Yutrenta said.

Kayarra reached for his.

Movement at the bend in the trail brought everyone's attention around. A shuren appeared, head low, knees lifted in the high-stepping gait of their run. The rider straightened from his neck-hugging stance as the shuren entered the meadow, slowed, and then halted. He leapt to the ground, fell to one knee, and bowed his head.

Aya started toward him. "Stand, Rayas."

The man did, hurried forward, and gripped Aya's outstretched hand in both of his. "A relief to see you, shon regis. We've been worried."

"A relief to see the valley from Lookout. You were followed, I assume."

"They're not far behind," Rayas confirmed.

Aya turned. "Janquer!" he called.

Denassa started forward and Kayarra hurried to follow, but Yutrenta caught his shoulder. "Leave the baggage."

Confused, he removed the strap from his shoulder and placed the bag beside the other. Yutrenta headed toward Aya and Kayarra followed. Ahead, Denassa embraced Rayas, whose attention didn't shift from Kayarra's face. Rayas's smile appeared forced.

"Kayarra, walk with Shurna, behind me," Aya ordered.

Kayarra was grateful for the distraction that shifted his attention from Rayas's scrutiny.

"Yutrenta, follow Kayarra. Quickly."

Yutrenta's physician bag hung from her shoulder; Aya carried the temple stone. No one else carried baggage. Shurna caught Rayas's hand, but hastily released the grip so Manerra could pass between them.

Aya turned and started down the trail, Manerra hastening to catch up with him. Kayarra followed, aware of Shurna's matched step, but locking his attention on Aya's heels and the cliff edge that paralleled his left foot.

Soon after passing the bend, they encountered two men climbing the trail. The strangers backed against the mountainside and bowed their heads.

Almost immediately, other climbers appeared: men, women, and children who chatted, shouted and laughed as they climbed. All fell silent. All cleared the trail, then stood wide-eyed and solemn among the trees and brush, reaching to touch their robes as they passed. One child grabbed Aya's robe, but her mother snatched her arm back, breaking that grip.

Kayarra searched children's faces for Teeka. Not spotting her, he searched for Uhle, Mentan or Coltra.

Kayarra returned the stares of those who stared at him, aware of the absence of screams. His flesh jumped when strangers reached for his robe and their fingers brushed his leg and hip. Despite the peaceful welcoming, a knot tightened in his stomach as he and Shurna were forced shoulder-to-shoulder in order to squeeze past the increasing number of spectators. When, at last, they reached the valley floor, the onlookers formed a sea of bodies and faces. Those without trailside vantage climbed trees. Murmurs of "Shon regis" became cries of "Shon regis Aya!" and shouts of "Sons of Acrahh!" Drummers beat drums, adding to the confusion of sounds and sights and touches. Kayarra abandoned his search for Teeka. He realized that he kept clenched fists when sweat trickled between his fingers. He pressed both hands flat against his thighs to blot them dry, then wondered whether he left handprints on his robe. That distraction vanished when revulsion, shock, and fear appeared more frequently among the faces they passed. He stepped on Aya's heel, then felt Yutrenta's hand press his back when he overcompensated for his haste.

Smoke was the haze covering the valley, Kayarra realized, as his breathing became labored.

Somewhere along the route, they left gravel and clay and crossed onto paved road. Ahead, diagonally left, the Temple of Crysus towered above the trees, more immense at ground level than it appeared from the overlook. Its sculptured pediment provided a directional bearing amid the sea of faces and trees.

Aya angled right onto hard-packed dirt, then crossed again onto paved road. This new direction took them through forest trees, then through an orchard, both overrun by Yatren devout. The House of Moons rose in silent vigil beyond the fruit-laden trees, the shecarens' dark moons inlaid in the white marble of the building's facade, a structure larger, more impressive than Casta's house.

The crowd ended at the edge of the orchard as though an invisible line marked the boundary between public freeway and forbidden trespass. Kayarra anticipated relief, but felt more exposed, more vulnerable in the open space between the orchard and House of Moons than he had in the crush of jostling onlookers. His flesh prickled, crawled, and then shivered.

A roar swept through the orchard as Aya's hand contacted the door of the House of Moons. What was shouted was unintelligible, and Kayarra didn't care. He came close to treading on Aya's sandal heel a second time in his desire to enter that cavern of safety.

The room was dusk to Kayarra's sun blinded eyes. He followed Aya's pale robe across the threshold toward the center of the room, blinking to hasten his eyes' adjustments. Lamps glowed ineffectually around the room, little pools of light illuminating tabletops of dark woods and a red marble mantle the height of Aya's shoulder.

"Don't leave," Aya ordered when Shurna started toward an inner door. A woman waited there, her head bowed and hands hidden inside a bunched apron. "Turn. Each of you. Shurna. You may go. Denassa."

Kayarra felt foolish when it came his turn to pivot, and when he was dismissed, didn't know whether Aya's approval meant passage of the unknown test or an order to leave. He hesitated, uncertain who to follow, unsure about his freedom within this place. Denassa had called Ayahn Rahh home, although she'd also applied that name to the Rahhe Mountains. No place was home to him and he didn't dare assumptions.

He scrutinized the room while he waited for direction, noted its polished stone floor tiles and the pine boughs lining the juncture of floor and walls; the finales on chair backs; the low, inlaid tables familiar from Shangren audience rooms; the grouping of cushioned chairs clustered beside the hearth. This room invited touch, rest, and comfort, where Gorrow's flaunted wealth had intended only to awe.

Aya rotated in front of Manerra, pulling Kayarra's attention back to that final, odd inspection.

"You're clean," Manerra announced.

Aya crossed to the heavy chairs beside the hearth, slipped the temple stone's pouch from his shoulder, and sank into the cushions, eyes closed, as if exhausted.

"They'd harm us more by bloodying our robes upon approach to abbah than upon return home," Manerra said.

"Kayarra," Aya said without opening his eyes, "have someone in the kitchen show you to your room. Please remind Denassa that your naming will take place after abbah."

Manerra pointed to the door the janquer had passed through, the only interior door in the room.

"Yes, shon regis," Kayarra adopted the formality he'd been instructed to maintain at the Shangren.

The first room Kayarra entered startled him enough that he stopped walking. He faced a mural of inlaid woods that depicted the desert, the door in that wall, a replication of a rock bridge. Left of the rock bridge lay the Shangren Oasis as he'd seen it at dawn the morning after their departure. He stepped toward the Shangren, heard his footsteps echo, and only then realized that the room stood empty except for the murals covering the walls. The wall to his right was a grassland plain bisected by a river, populated by animals he couldn't name. The trees had trunk bases as broad as their drip lines, which tapered sharply to umbrella-shaped canopies.

The room's left-hand wall displayed an ocean filled with bizarre fish, shells, and aquatic animals, and ships with wind filled sails. Waves broke against the foot of a cliff crowned by houses. *Tes-Raly!* that realization hit. It had to be. He recognized the description Denassa had given of her home.

Kayarra turned around and stepped backward in order to see the wall through which he'd passed. Trees framed the door, their overlapping branches forming the lintel. The scene depicted a jungle of plant life, with animal faces peering through leaves of countless shapes and sizes. Birds perched on tree branches, insects, on leaves. Vines girdled tree trunks, and snakes entwined roots.

"Janquer lord."

For a moment, Kayarra didn't react. Then he startled and whirled, wondering if he did something wrong by loitering in this room.

The woman's eyes went wide and she sketched a symbol in the air that Kayarra had last seen used at the Shangren.

"I not a demon," he told her.

The woman paled. "Forgive me, janquer lord. You startled me." Her neatly braided hair was gray streaked with black. "If it pleases you, janquer lady Denassa asked that I show you to your room."

"Thank you," he said and saw her eyes flicker a wary surprise.

*I'm a courteous demon, by Acrahh!* he railed as he followed her into a hall lined with closed doors. *I know no other life.* But he kept silent, desperate to avoid a repeat of the Shangren nightmare. Ayahn Rahh's welcoming shouts and drums had masked words, not pointing fingers and expressions of horror. They were not completely prepared for him, but he was for them. He had steeled himself for their reactions as best he could.

The hall ended at a kitchen. Denassa turned from the hearth and Kayarra saw dismay flicker across her face. "Alva," Denassa stepped forward, "I'll show janquer lord Kayarra to his room."

The housekeeper dipped her head and nearly leapt aside. Her actions might have been comical had her terror not been so apparent.

Denassa frowned as she turned and passed the hearth, headed for stairs in the far corner of the kitchen.

Kayarra followed. Halfway up the stairs, Denassa stepped sideways, ascending with her shoulder brushing one wall as Yutrenta and Shurna descended.

"We'll be back before abbah," Shurna said as they passed.

Denassa halted and watched them descend. "Are you going to the medical tents?" she asked.

"I am," Yutrenta said. "Shurna's going to Cha-ka."

"Shurna!" Denassa protested.

"I'm riding," Shurna called without looking back. "I'll return in time." She pushed off the bottom step and ran toward the back door. When Shurna jerked open the door, Kayarra caught a glimpse of sunlit yard.

Denassa touched his shoulder and he followed her up the stairs. The floor of the landing creaked under her weight, then creaked louder when he stepped onto it.

They passed moldings and doorframes polished to a sheen by the touch of countless hands, thresholds worn concave, closed doors that intrigued.

"Your room." Denassa pushed open a door and stepped aside that he might enter.

Directly ahead, a lamp burned on a small, ornately carved table situated between two chairs as if his arrival on this day, at this hour, had been expected. *I was expected*, he remembered. *Aya saw to that at the Shangren, hundreds of miles away.*

A heavy bed with a trunk at its foot occupied the left-hand wall and most of the floor space. Kayarra crossed to the chairs, caught movement in his peripheral vision, and jumped away from the blond intruder who appeared without warning at his shoulder. The other's hand reached toward his belt. They drew knives simultaneously.

"No!" Denassa cried.

Kayarra came to his senses in a rush of heat. He whirled and stumbled for the door, knocking its frame with his shoulder as he passed Denassa. He started laughing and covered his eyes with a hand.

He'd been prepared for everything except an encounter with himself.

Denassa reached for his arm but he jerked away from her.

"It's a mirror," Denassa said.

"I know." He stopped in the hall, unable to face her, his laughter gone.

She laid a hand on his arm; had to have felt him shaking. "Have you not seen your reflection in a water's surface?"

"Not so good."

He pressed his temples and then lowered his hand.

"Talk. Please," Denassa urged.

"I see hair." He caught one of her braids, rolled it between his fingertips. "I see Yatren skin." He brushed her cheek. "Every day. I no see Kayarra hair. No see Kayarra—" His throat tightened. "Skin" came out in a strangled whisper. *I scared myself.*

He'd never be accepted.

He jerked away, started toward the stairs.

"Where are you going?"

Denassa's demand hit him in the gut. He stumbled into a wall, heard her start forward, and only then realized he still held a bare-bladed knife. Overwhelmed by anger, he threw the knife on the floor as hard as he could and watched without satisfaction as the blade snapped and ricocheted off the wall.

Denassa stopped. He looked up and she took a step backward.

His courage failed when he saw her retreat. He ran toward her then, and past, and tried to pretend it didn't hurt when she fell against the wall to avoid him.

The slam of his door jarred her taut nerves. She waited breathlessly for the crash of shattering glass. The sound did not come.

Movement at the head of the stairs caught her attention.

"Did you spurn him?" Manerra asked.

"Are *any* manners practiced in Zarthon?" she shouted, whirled, and lunged into a vacant room, slamming the door behind her.

It was Vantrann's room. She threw her back against the wood of the door.

"Denassa, I'm sorry," Manerra called through the door. "Come to me when you can talk. Please."

He waited, but she could not answer him.

"Can you hear me?" he asked.

"Yes!" she shouted so he would leave. But it was awhile before his footsteps retreated.

Only after he was gone did she relinquish control. Then the tears came at once, with a wail of anguish she did not expect. Pain broke forth like a burst floodwall, its source no longer a single grievance. She cried for the loss of Ringgal as much as for Kayarra's pain and her own frustrations, for the shame of a reputation she had no part in creating, for a father she might never see again, for every inadequacy and loss that came together now as anger and hurt and fear.

For a while after the torrent ended, she rested on the floor with her temple pressed against the door, bleak and drained and breathing through her mouth. She briefly considered using Vantrann's washstand, but her strict upbringing asserted the sanctity of others' possessions. She wiped a hand through the tearstains on the floor, rose and, hot-faced, vacated Vantrann's room in favor of her own bedroom down the hall.

# CHAPTER 55

Denassa lifted a heavy kettle of water while Alva guided its handle toward a hearth hook just as the outside door opened. Denassa met Shurna's eye, but hastily returned attention to her task when she spotted the number of women who entered behind Shurna. The kettle's handle clicked into place on the hearth's cooking rod. Denassa left the fire, crossed to the table, and lay the pothook there as an excuse to avert her face from the newcomers.

"Lansa, take over guest services," Shurna instructed. "Alva, I leave you to assign rooms and duties."

A hand slipped around Denassa's waist. "Let's go upstairs," Shurna whispered, released her, and started up the stairs.

Denassa followed without looking back.

"You look terrible," Shurna murmured when Denassa caught up with her on the stairs, "and the evening's not begun. What happened while I was gone?"

Denassa shook her head to delay a response.

Shurna remained silent until they reached the floor landing, then hooked Denassa's arm. "What happened?" Shurna demanded. "Tell me."

Details poured out then, including an admission of her tears shed in Vantrann's room.

Shurna hugged her and brushed new tears from her cheeks. "Where's Kayarra now?"

"He's not come out of his room." Denassa wiped her eyes.

"Vantrann can hardly protest your use of his room. At this late day, I suspect the janquer will serve without its Thurrang representative."

"Any news of him at Cha-ka?"

"None. And no worry about him when Yutrenta's brother—"

"Which brother?" Yutrenta's demand came hollowly up the stairwell. Her head appeared below the landing. "If you'll return downstairs, ears won't strain so hard to catch your words."

Denassa gave a cry of dismay.

"I tease," Yutrenta said, her attention fixed on Denassa's face. Her tone softened, "If your confidence is so personal, you might do well to talk elsewhere."

"Come." Shurna started down the hall. "You, too, Trenta."

"My room," Denassa urged. It was farthest from Kayarra's room.

"Which brother have you seen?" Yutrenta asked as she closed Denassa's bedroom door.

"None seen," Shurna said as they settled, Yutrenta and Shurna in chairs, Denassa on the foot of the bed nearest the chairs. "Next time, pay closer heed to your eavesdropping, lady Trenta."

"In the future." Yutrenta offered a mock bow. "For now, I'll mention that we've moments before we're called to meal."

"Until Benta left the Shangren, no message had been sent inquiring about the status of the negotiations or Vantrann's well-being. Lady Sheron was reluctant to share what she claims are rumors, but the prevalence of tales has become serious. It seems that our Vantrann has taken no spectator's role in the search for Hyranian criminals. Even allowing for embellishments, Aya will not be pleased to hear the rumors of Vantrann's exploits. If any of them have a basis in truth, Vantrann is relying overmuch on the protections afforded members of the janquer."

"What do they say he's done?" Denassa asked.

"Offered rewards for anyone who will name an Hyranian."

Denassa stiffened. "Anyone who hates his brother can call him Hyranian."

"Exactly," Shurna said.

"My feeling before we departed Zarthon," Yutrenta said, "was that Vantrann should not be left to oversee that situation. I know he is older, but Manerra handles himself with greater maturity than Vantrann dreams of possessing."

"Our advice was not asked," Denassa reminded.

"Nor, I think, would it have been heeded if offered," Shurna said. "Manerra's infatuation with Vantrann was too great."

Yutrenta lifted a conch off the table at her elbow.

Denassa's attention followed Yutrenta's hands, more anxious over the safety of the lacy shell than over Vantrann's weary antics. "Manerra's a single child whose only companions are adults," she said.

"Aya was not and is not blind to the situation," Shurna asserted. "He knew what he did by separating those two—what chances he took. Responsibility for punishment is his, if it comes to that."

"Please don't speak of blinding." Yutrenta replaced the conch on the table.

Shurna studied Yutrenta's face. "Did you hear the Kayarran rumors while you were out?"

"What rumors?" Denassa demanded.

"Everything we heard in Zarthon and the Shangren plus embellishments and new tales," Yutrenta replied grimly.

"There is speculation that Kayarra spies out Yatren strengths and weaknesses for a tribe that will take Yatren land."

"The version I heard had the Kayarran intent upon taking control of

Yatra's nation," Yutrenta supplied. "But the one that concerns me more has the demon Kayarra in control of the shecarens. A woman shrieked when I touched her because she thought the demon controlled me. She believed his spirit would blind her soul through my touch. This is what Trini could get from her. She would not speak to me."

Denassa gripped the bedpost so tightly, her knuckles lost color. "Aya must be warned."

Yutrenta's laugh held grim mirth. "Those tales are why the closest we'll get to privacy with Aya will be atop the Altar of Acrahh during abbah. Have you seen the visitors downstairs?"

"I fixed tea while Alva served," Denassa said. Her anxiety peaked. "Has Aya's forewarning failed so completely?"

"No!" Shurna's denial was swift. "The lady Sheron knew the truth of Kayarra's founding and presence and has diffused the more dangerous rumors. But her explanations aren't as dramatic as the threats parents are using to frighten children into obedience."

"The rumors frighten more than children!" Denassa protested. "And the danger to Kayarra—"

Shurna reached to cover Denassa's hand. "I know, Dee. We know. That the tales aren't being laughed away is frightening." Shurna withdrew her hand. "I suggest we not burden Kayarra with this unless he asks."

"He walks into the fire tonight, Shurna. Soon!"

"He came through today's crowd without an arrow in his chest. But we must warn him against leaving the House of Moons without janquer or shecaren escort. After the Shangren, I think he's not anxious to do so, but I won't trust assumptions."

"Any Yatren who believes the shecaren moons have become demon symbols won't stop with one murder." Denassa's mouth went so dry, her tongue added an odd click to her words.

"How does that knowledge protect Kayarra?" Shurna asked.

Denassa could not speak.

"All I ask is that we spare him the knowledge of rumors for as long as we can. Allow him a night's sleep. Acrahh knows, he has little enough security in his life. Why add—"

A knock on the door brought Denassa to her feet, heart pounding.

"Supper, lady Denassa," Alva called through the door.

Yutrenta leapt from her chair and yanked the door open before Alva turned away. Denassa averted her face. *You share your heart with the world*, Shurna told her repeatedly.

"Alva, we're together," Yutrenta said. "I'll inform janquer lord Kayarra. We won't be long."

"Bless you, lady Trenta."

Yutrenta closed the door, returned to her chair, but did not sit. She kept her voice low, "I wish information on any south Ofrann devout in Cha-ka or Ayahn Rahh."

"Are you wanting information on the nomads or the Hyranians?" Shurna asked.

"On Vantrann. His silence is disturbing. Casta should have heard from him before we arrived. His messenger should have been waiting for us in Cha-ka. That we're hearing rumors and nothing from him is upsetting."

"His injury or murder would have outpaced Kayarran rumors," Shurna said. "We're not half a day in residence. Some message may yet reach us."

Denassa ran a hand down the carved bedpost. "We need to attend meal."

"I'll summon Kayarra," Yutrenta offered. "Dee, while I'm gone, collect yourself. All eyes will be upon you, fully half of them Kitarin."

* * * * *

Only a panicked messenger or assassin would have dared breech a meal's silence in the House of Moons, but Shurna found herself anticipating either, so palpable hung the tension. Her heart pounded, scared by the fear she read in their guests' faces, pulses, tense shoulders, stiff stances, furtive glances, arrhythmic breathing, and lackluster appetites.

That three Thurrang lords were present where two would have been unusual in so modest a gathering seemed a serious indication of southern troubles. She wondered if Aya already knew the details surrounding Vantrann's delay and silence.

Shurna watched their guests' scrutiny of Kayarra. That Kayarra wasn't eating did not assuage matters; Yutrenta's calming herbs could not help him if they weren't ingested.

It was odd not being the sole cause of others' discomfort. She had grown so accustomed to others' fears of her that she no longer felt their fear as a personal sting.

She wondered at the person she had become in order to survive. Conversely, she understood how her sister had lost that battle. Poor Aena. Too keen a sensitivity had destroyed her sister's mind.

Aya's signal for the janquer to assemble ended the morbid silence. A table companion lifted her hand, but Shurna leapt to her feet before the woman could snag her sleeve.

"Janquer lady Shurna—" the woman called as Shurna passed rising guests on her way to the outside door.

The youngest Thurrang reached the door ahead of her and held it open that she might precede him. His face seemed familiar, and recognition struck as she passed.

"Lord Tura!" She slowed step until he caught up with her. "The janquer appreciates the service you agreed to perform tonight."

"I was not prepared." He blushed. "I had to borrow a robe from one of my father's men."

A smaller man, Shurna's eye told her. "Your father is lord Sitra of Varaar?"

"Y-yes."

Shurna reached the assembly area, fell into position behind Denassa, and motioned lord Tura to stand beside her. He eyed Kayarra, who fidgeted in place between Denassa and Yutrenta.

"I ask for private audience," he blurted in a hushed whisper.

"With the shecarens?" she asked.

"Not shecaren Manerra." The alarm in Tura's voice refocused Shurna's attention on him. "With you," he pleaded.

Shurna hesitated. "I can speak with you after the ceremonies."

Denassa stepped forward and Shurna hastily followed.

Past the orchard, Aya turned right onto the temple road, where their pace slowed through a crowd that jammed the plaza and spilled into surrounding forest. The only features of the pyramidal Altar of Acrahh visible above the heads of the crowd were the top two steps, the altar, and the altar's upright stone.

The shecarens reached the altar's stairs and started up. Kayarra stumbled on the first step. Denassa's and Yutrenta's hands shot out to steady him, but he neither acknowledged their assistance nor seemed aware of it.

Shurna counted the stairs separating Aya and Kayarra, waited until Denassa was that far ahead of her and then started up. Her foot found the first worn depression in the ancient stone and successive footfalls located others, as if every shecaren and janquer before her matched her step's reach. Gooseflesh prickled arms and legs as she emerged above the heads of the crowd. A final leg push propelled her onto the dais.

She crossed the white stone toward the altar, controlling her pace so it did not appear that she fled to the safety of Acrahh's shadow. She passed behind the line of janquer and emerged at the end position, signaling Tura to stand between Denassa and her as she faced the setting sun.

So great was the roar of welcome, Shurna could almost forget that a stranger stood as Thurrang representative and that Kayarra increased the number of janquer to one never before seen during abbah.

Aya raised both arms for silence, and Shurna's attention strayed past him to the ocean of people beyond: tribal leaders and herders; loose hair and braided; veiled faces and bare; Kitarin tunics and Ofrann robes; young, old; friends, acquaintances and strangers, but all kinsmen, all descendants of the sons and daughters of Yatra.

For a time-stopping moment, she saw their open-mouth shouts and upraised hands as hostile. A hard shudder brought her back from the precipice of panic.

"Acrahh, god and father," Aya shouted into the lessening roar, "and

Crysus, goddess mother, grant health and prosperity to all who come here seeking knowledge and succor. Give them the strength to keep Yatra's promise of goodwill, to approach every encounter with peace, to keep national unity even at the cost of personal sacrifice. Draw that strength now, that each of you may return it measure for measure."

On the south end of the dais, Yutrenta shouted, "Close your eyes!"

"Close your eyes!" Shurna shouted into the masses nearest her before heeding her own warning.

With the temple stone's flare, Shurna recalled her earliest memory of a shecaren's abbah. At three years old, the Kitarin village of Heuay had occupied the edges of her known world, and her parents had traveled for nearly a moon beyond Heuay to stand in the largest crowd she'd ever seen while the hot sun crept endlessly across the sky toward dusk. Crying and wailing had gotten the side of her head smacked. Hitting her older sister had gotten her slapped a second time. Pinching Aena had gotten her bottom whipped and herself jerked into her mother's arms, where finally she could see more than feet, ankles, hems, and Aena's facial contortions. When Parpar lifted Aena, Shurna felt cheated, but the faces of strangers inches from her own distracted her. She reached out to touch the fine stitching on the breast of the man standing behind her mother. Smiling, the man grabbed for her fingers, but she jerked them back before he caught her hand. That reaching and dodging became a game, until people began shouting and Shurna startled in her mother's arms, frightened by the noise.

"That's shon regis Dayla," her mother's excitement confused her. A woman wearing a dazzling white robe, standing high over everyone's head, began shouting. Then she stopped yelling and reached into the pouch hanging at her side, and Aena's hand dropped down over Shurna's eyes.

With an angry "No!" Shurna twisted her head and batted Aena's hand away, only to have her mother's palm cover her eyes and trap her head against her mother's shoulder. Shurna screamed and kicked, wanting to see the amazing light that had flared in shon regis Dayla's hands. No comparable miracle had happened in her brief life—or since—that so captured her imagination. When Marmar told her the light that could have blinded her had come from a stone, she picked up every pebble and stone she could lift for days afterward, managing nothing brighter than a sparkle of mica. She finally reached the unfair conclusion that only the daughter of a god could make rocks glow like the sun. It was a devastating discovery, but a profound revelation. Her imaginings were never dull from that day forth.

Shurna lifted Tura's sweaty hand over her head and stretched her empty palm toward the masses, an invitation of union across distances, drawing them into the keeping of this holy rite performed on their most sacred ground.

"Peace to all the nation through eternity," was an echoing roar that followed the janquer's pledge at the conclusion of abbah.

Aya raised his arms again, as signal, and for silence, then crossed to the northern edge of the dais where he stopped, facing the Temple of Crysus across the packed plaza. Manerra followed, and the janquer shifted until they, too, faced north. Drummers, receiving Aya's signal, beat a call for silence.

"O Crysus, beloved of Acrahh," Aya called into the ebbing roar, "your children have returned to their ancestral cradle. They keep Yatra's promise by honoring this joining of the moons. Judge all faith by the keeping of promises, even as I offer succor and ask it in return."

Shurna looked toward Kayarra, anxious that he respond to that cue. He left the line of janquer, and when he came abreast of Manerra, Manerra matched step with him. They stopped behind Aya.

If Kayarra feared, he had passed beyond fear into resolution. Shurna smiled with pride. She had experienced the breath of his life, and he hers. His demeanor shamed neither of them.

A murmur of unease grew among those standing at the foot of the altar's north steps.

"Generations past," Aya shouted, silencing that murmur, "an Ofrann nomad discovered in canyonlands northeast of the Rahhe, siblings once thought lost forever. The Manteen they were named, after the man who died that his followers should live. Although we cannot imagine their desperation or their sacrifices, their founding is honored in the keeping of abbah, as all lives are honored and respected."

Shurna's anxiety increased over the frowns, the nervous shifting, the exchanged looks and impulsive outbursts she saw among those close enough to hear Aya's words.

"Once again, the Rahhe returns lost children, whose tribe I name Kayarran in honor of their surviving son."

A wail of dismay and shock went up, causing a ripple of alarm through those unable to hear Aya's words. Shurna saw movement even upon the steps of the Temple of Crysus. She only hoped that later repetition of Aya's announcement would bear some resemblance to his actual proclamation.

Aya stepped closer to the crowd. "Lord Kayarra, do you accept Acrahh's service, pledging your life as janquer of the Kayarran tribe?"

"Yes, shon regis," Kayarra's voice sounded faint after Aya's confident boom.

"Then repeat your vow before these witnesses."

Manerra's lips moved, stopped, then Kayarra said, "Blessed Crysus, O great Acrahh." Manerra spoke again, and Kayarra repeated, "I come as Kayarra . . . son of the Kayarran . . . to p-pay—" Manerra spoke rapidly. "To vow my service . . . to Acrahh . . . and the sons of Acrahh . . . before you . . . and this nation . . . . If I am un—unworthy . . . I ask you . . . to strike me down . . . through the power . . . of your stone."

Kayarra cupped his hands and Manerra covered his palms with chamois. Aya turned, approached, and placed the cloaked temple stone in Kayarra's hands.

"Shield your eyes!" Yutrenta shouted and Shurna repeated that warning.

As the temple stone flared, a woman screamed. Shurna kept her eyes closed by force of will.

Aya cloaked the stone and Shurna opened her eyes. Several people crouched beside a woman who lay on the altar's bottommost step.

Yutrenta rushed across the dais and down the stairs.

"Kayarra of the Kayarran," Aya shouted, his hands beneath Kayarra's, the cloaked stone supported between them, "Crysus sanctifies your vow, as Acrahh did upon the sands of the Ofrann Desert when you accepted the promise of the unification prayer. Let this man's witnesses be named."

Shurna stepped forward. "Janquer Shurna, for the Kitarin, twice witnessed," she shouted and then stepped back.

"Lord Tura of Varaar, once witnessed, for the Thurrang."

"Janquer Denassa, for the Ringgangley, twice witnessed."

Yutrenta stood from her crouch over the unconscious woman. "Janquer Yutrenta, of and for the Ofrann, twice witnessed."

"Shecaren Manerra, twice witnessed, before Acrahh, my father, and Crysus, his consort."

"Upon this day," Aya announced, "a new tribe is joined to Yatra's nation. Kayarran destiny now lies in Yatren hands, as Yatren destiny lies in Kayarran hands. In this year of the Ingathering, and in all years following, the sun and moons shall be seen upon the breast of this nation's Kayarran janquer. Know you the Kayarran by these symbols, that weapons be enjoined, and peace bring prosperity to all tribes.

"Peace throughout the nation for eternity."

The repetition by the devout contained a note of uncertainty that caused Shurna's breath to catch.

Drummers on each end of the dais, east and west, began a cadence. Manerra crossed in front of Kayarra to stand beside his brother, giving Aya time to finish securing the temple stone. By the end of the third cadence, the crowd had parted along the white stone path that began at the base of the Altar of Acrahh, passed five upright stone tablets looming above the crowd, and ended at the base of the Temple of Crysus.

As the fourth cadence began, Aya started down the north face of the Altar, Manerra following, and Kayarra trailing them. Shurna stepped sideways and pressed lord Tura toward Denassa, who had started after Kayarra. Yutrenta left the revived woman and fell into step behind Shurna.

Passage through the crowd was slow, then halted when Aya reached the first standing stone. Shurna watched his hand rise, saw him touch six points on the first stone before moving to the second and repeating a different pattern there. Kayarra was slower, had to look at the incised grid and find the impressions to touch, so the gap of a stone's length had opened between he and Manerra by the time he completed the ritual on the fifth stone. Tura, too, hesitated over the patterns, slowed their advance, and opened a second gap between he and Denassa.

By the time Shurna cleared the fifth stone, dusk was deepening, casting the faces of those around her into shadow when the moons passed behind a succession of scudding clouds. Anxiety rose with the knowledge that they passed among people too far away to have heard Aya's explanations, his proclamations, his entreaty and Kayarra's vow; among people who were aware of a disturbance associated with Kayarra's naming but ignorant of its cause. This was the most dangerous segment of their passage, and the janquer were scattered along the length of the white path.

Aya reached the temple steps and the shecarens ascended alone, dwarfed by columns whose pediment seemed to uphold the stars. Tura reached Kayarra and Denassa and stopped behind them. Yutrenta pressed past Shurna to reach Kayarra's side.

Aya and Manerra gained the top of the stairs together and passed from sight into the interior of the temple. Long moments later, the temple stone's light flooded the temple in orange glow, illuminating the carved back wall, transforming the base-relief curls of Crysus's beard into whorls of flame.

Crysus was awake to the presence of her children. The stone of fire and its gifter were reunited, the ancient promises kept and renewed.

The interior of the temple went dark.

Yutrenta slipped her arm through Kayarra's. Shurna reached for Tura's arm, felt him jump, then felt him relax.

Aya and Manerra reappeared between two columns and halted at the head of the stairs. Shurna joined the crowd's roar, raised her hand, palm out, in the symbolic gesture of union. Fresh tears fell, but she had no desire either to staunch their flow or to control her smile.

Men left the shadows of the columns and converged on the shecarens as people surged forward, running up the stairs. Shurna was shoved against Denassa before she had time to take a step sideways, pulling Tura with her. They were pushed partway up the stairs before they reached the corner of the temple and were able to press their way down again, struggling against a mass of people entering the temple. It took longer still to win their way free of the plaza.

Many on the fringes of the crowd were leaving the plaza, crossing through trees, sidestepping tent ropes and smoldering fires as they headed toward whatever spot of ground they called home.

Shurna located a dirt wagon track and walked east toward Cha-ka, watching in the dark for a footpath that branched right. She brought her braids forward to conceal the moons on her shoulder as she strolled at the pace of other eastbound travelers.

"I need to speak tonight," Tura said just as she spotted the dark footpath.

"I've not forgotten," she assured him, although exhaustion pounded along every nerve and muscle. If Vantrann had been present, she could have referred Tura to him, but without Thurrang representation, Tura had the right to choose whomever he wished, and she was duty-bound to hear him.

While they walked, she tried to think where they could speak privately. With the household fully staffed, privacy was a problem.

A log bridge appeared through the gloom. Shurna called ahead, identifying herself and Tura, and saw shadows on either side of the bridge shift. She swept her hair back across her shoulder to reveal the moons.

Despite the symbols of her position, she was aware of intense scrutiny, but no peacekeeper guarding the bridge stopped her.

The trickle of water sounded a lure she would have paused and enjoyed had she been alone. Instead, she stepped from the end of the bridge, continued past a stone bench flanked by night blooming karfa, passed through a cluster of trees, and entered the rear yard of the House of Moons. Their flock occupied the corral on the right; the barn on the left housed shuren. Other buildings held hay and tools. Closer to the kitchen door, they passed gardens, an icehouse, bathhouse, and cold cellar.

Lansa turned from the hearth when Shurna entered the kitchen with Tura close behind.

"Tea for both of us, please, Lansa," Shurna requested, then to Tura, "I'll be right back." She climbed the stairs and returned with two travel robes. One, she hoped, was large enough for Tura. He held a bowl of tea; hers waited on the table. She picked it up on her way toward the door, grateful when Tura opened the door before she reached it.

Rayas's men were reluctant to abandon their guard of the mia, but more reluctant to disobey her command. "Watch at the bridge," she offered them a way to assuage their fear of reprisals. "I'll summon you when we're through."

She saw the sign of acquiescence flashed before the guards left.

"You're herdsman wise," Tura remarked.

"I am herdsman," Shurna said. "I know of no place safer to speak." She sipped her tea and held the warm liquid in her mouth before swallowing. The arm draped with robes, she held out to Tura. "The other one," she said when he reached for her robe. She balanced her bowl atop a fence post then donned the remaining robe. Dew had fallen, the night air, chill.

"Thank you for your thoughtfulness," Tura said after he'd donned the robe.

"Am I correct in believing your news involves the shecaren?" Shurna asked.

Tura's dismayed expression told enough. "What I have to say is not for general hearing," he hedged.

"Do you fear reprisals or exposure of the truth?"

"It's not my intention to deceive!"

She'd raised his ire. Good.

"I made this journey because my father could not. Even now, I worry that I made the wrong decision by leaving him."

"Who is your father?"

Tura appeared dumbfounded. "Lord Sitra of Varaar. You named him tonight. You know him. He speaks highly of you."

"Lord Tura, in audience, I will make no assumptions. Be clear about that, and in whatever you tell me."

He tilted his head. Whether in embarrassment or agreement, she could not tell. "Then I'll be blunt. One of the shon regis's janquer threatens the peace he called for tonight."

"I need details, lord Tura. Names."

Tura's hands shook as he balanced his bowl on the top rung of the fence. "Zarthonian rumor suggests a . . . a close allegiance between shecaren Manerra and janquer Vantrann."

Her heart pounded.

"If the rumors are true, then I risk my life and my father's by speaking with you. I ask, before I say more, if that danger is real, that you say nothing to anyone about what I say."

"I can't make that promise."

Tura stared at her. Even in the inconstant moonlight, she saw his face go rigid, watched him turn, take a step away, stop . . . saw his shoulders tighten before he turned back around.

"I c-can't leave without sharing what I came to tell," he said. He took a breath. "More than my fa—" He touched his brow; brought his hand down hard as if angry. "One of Hyran's followers was taken alive from Varaar field the night Hyran attacked our flocks. I know this. My father's man was involved in the fighting. He's here with me. He was questioned by janquer lord Vantrann." The man's jaw muscles clenched repeatedly. "My father did not expect to be privy to Thurrang-Ofrann negotiations, but he did expect to be consulted on matters of restitution—on the numbers and values of lives lost in that attack.

"When he learned the shecarens had departed Zarthon, he sent me to the capital to inquire after Varaar's interests. Lord Razon told me his son, janquer lord Vantrann, had been appointed by shon regis Aya to oversee the criminal matters, and that I must seek restitution from him.

"Lord Vantrann assured me that restitution would be made, but could not say the kind or amount until he met with lord Casta. He said he would send a man to Varaar with the terms of the settlement."

"Were you displeased by the delay?" Shurna asked when Tura did not continue.

"No. I expected delays. I only wanted to understand the reasons for it. Janquer lord Vantrann anticipated restitution in an amount and kind greater than that my father had asked. My distress began when I was delayed in Zarthon on other errands and learned that the criminal taken alive at Varaar field had died of his wounds."

Shock ran through Shurna. An image flashed to mind of a man close to Denassa's age, alert and defiant when she'd questioned him in Zarthon after the raid.

"Household rumors claimed that lord Vantrann spoke long with the Hyranian, and the man named others before he died. Later, Lord Rayma told me that lord Vantrann had departed Zarthon to investigate the truth of the man's confessions." Tura returned to the corral fence and gripped its middle rung. His free hand shook.

"What house were you guest in during your stay in Zarthon?" Shurna asked.

"Lord Razon's. His garden house. Outside the city."

When Tura did not continue, Shurna asked, "Did you return to Varaar?"

"No, lady," he said as though that decision had been a travesty of judgment.

"Were you in Zarthon when lord Vantrann returned?" She grew impatient with the need to pull information from him.

He tilted his head in affirmation.

Shurna waited. Finally, Tura turned from the fence to face her. "I-I was guest to lord Zimmar when Vantrann returned."

Vantrann's title had dropped so effortlessly from his speech, Shurna realized it had been a conscious effort for Tura to use it.

"He brought a man back with him, bound as one carries the kill from a hunt. I saw this myself.

"After meal that evening, one of the men who had ridden with Vantrann bragged they'd taken a second Hyranian—the man's wife—but she'd fallen upon a knife before they reached Zarthon."

Shurna's mouth went dry. Suicide, among the Ofrann, represented spiritual blinding. It was extremely rare among that tribe. "Did you learn where he had gotten those two, the husband and wife?"

"No one said within my hearing, but I saw the man. He was Ofrann. Or, maybe he wasn't Ofrann," Tura seemed to think better of that claim, "but he wasn't Thurrang. His hair was braided, and his face was the two-toned color of a veil wearer."

"What became of the man?" Shurna asked.

"A six-night after Vantrann's return, he called me to audience. He said the man—Camda, he called him—had confessed his support of

Hyran. As punishment, and in early restitution to Varaar, he was giving Camda to my father for public works labor. He said Camda had agreed to this payment.

"I offered to escort Camda to Varaar since my return was imminent, but Vantrann said he had assembled an escort for Camda and it would be safer if I delayed my departure by two days. At Vantrann's insistence, I agreed.

"When I returned home, Camda's escort had not arrived, and my father had not been told to expect them. I immediately returned to Zarthon, and lord Razon informed me that Camda's party had been attacked on the road. Camda was killed in an escape attempt. Rather than continue on to Varaar with a body, the escorts returned to Zarthon." Tura drew a ragged breath.

"Janquer lady Shurna—" Another ragged breath. "I didn't pass Camda's escort on the road, and in my last audience with lord Vantrann, he asked which road I was taking to Varaar. I laughed at the time, because there's only one road . . . a trail, really. Varaar is grassland and a few houses. We're herders."

"I know, lord Tura," Shurna assured him, "I've been there."

Tura rubbed his face. "Janquer Shurna, my last audience with Vantrann was not private. In that audience, he said Camda had named other Hyranians and given their locations. Camda was to testify against the Hyranians when they were found, concerning other, unpaid crimes. Vantrann begged Lord Sitra and I to keep Camda safe in Varaar." Tura's jaws clenched.

"I did not think to stop Vantrann and ask for a private audience. I thought he must trust the men with us. But there were housekeepers present when Vantrann confided Camda's confessions and promises. And I cannot prove it—I can find no one who admits to being among Camda's escort—but instinct tells me that Camda's body lay in Zarthon before I left for Varaar."

Tura turned his back and his breathing quickened.

Shurna glanced away, across the backs of the drowsing mia. Fires winked through the orchard's trees, and the aroma of cooking blended with the pungent bite of wood smoke and the musky scent of the mia. Somewhere in the distance, a flute's strains trilled faint bird calls. The night's tranquility seemed a cruel affront, a hard glimpse of what they would lose if they didn't come to their senses.

"Has lord Vantrann charged lord Sitra with negligence?" Shurna asked.

Tura reached for the fence rail, gripped it. "Before I left, he had not done so, but I have no idea what has transpired since my departure. All I know is that two men and a woman died under circumstances questioned by more men than me. I made this journey because I'm scared for my father's life. Because I'm scared for Varaar—for Thurra—if bloodlust arises from the blood already spilt." Tura fell to his knees. "Please, lady," he pleaded. "If you cannot find Vantrann capable of crime, then please, I beg you, at least recall him from Thurra, and do not appoint lord Sitra to decide the Ofrann crimes."

Shurna reached toward him. "Lord Tura, please rise."

He confounded her by pressing his forehead to the ground in an obeisance not practiced outside Thurra. Shurna struggled for focus. "The decisions you want are not mine to make," she said over Tura's hunched form. "I can only present your request to shon regis Aya. If remedies are demanded, they will come about through his order, not mine."

# CHAPTER 56

Shurna crossed the audience room's antechamber and reached for the doorframe, jerking her hand back when she encountered bark texture instead of polished wood. Her attention snapped to the carved tree trunk that formed the doorframe and deliberately gripped the trunk, drawing strength from that symbolic contact with her land and tribe.

She halted in the doorway, saw guests' eyes shift toward her, but waited until Aya noticed her before flashing a signal she'd used only once in her life. After that, she withdrew into the antechamber and waited.

Yutrenta was first out of the room, while Aya suggested that they reflect upon the solutions already presented and continue their discussion after morning abbah.

"Is Kayarra all right?" Yutrenta demanded.

"I don't know," Shurna answered before she realized Yutrenta's possible conclusions. She blushed that her brain was so slow, so distracted, so singularly focused. "He's asleep, that I know," she tried to assuage Yutrenta's worries and hoped the Ofrann would not pry into the reasons for the interruption before Aya extracted himself from courtesies.

Aya burst from the room, headed through the house, and Shurna dashed past Yutrenta to catch him.

"A Thurrang lord will not speak before the shecaren," she blurted when she reached Aya's side.

Aya came to an abrupt halt and whirled to face her.

"He has cause," she vouchsafed. "The news involves Ofrann relations." She hoped she made enough sense that he would dismiss Yutrenta's involvement, as well.

"Who is it?" Aya demanded.

"Lord Tura of Varaar. He waits in the kitchen."

She saw the decision in his eyes. "Manerra, Yutrenta," Aya spoke over Shurna's shoulder, "get sleep. This matter may be handled privately. If it cannot, I will send for you. Shurna," he met her eyes, "thank you. Sleep well." Aya turned and strode rapidly toward the kitchen.

Shurna stood frozen, so unprepared for her own dismissal that she had no reaction.

Aya was right, her dulled senses informed her. If his dismissal was not blanket, minor resentments might compound the problems Tura presented.

Shurna glanced aside, into Yutrenta and Manerra's equally stunned faces. If either questioned her, she doubted she could evade through a serious interrogation. She started after Aya. The kitchen allowed the only access to their upstairs rooms.

"Shurna." It was Yutrenta who intended to complicate her retreat. "Your signal was for emergency. What caused our dismissal?"

She could answer that one honestly: "Aya."

Yutrenta's eyes narrowed.

"What forced your interruption?" Manerra countered.

Shurna recalled the few words she'd heard while standing in the doorway. "Learning that the matter you solved our first night home was the problem of waste disposal," came her flippant answer, "but only after a lord begged me for private audience with the shon regis. More than that, it is Aya's choice to share news with the janquer." She turned again to leave.

"You were a long time with this lord not to know his business," Yutrenta called, and Shurna turned because she didn't know how many, if any, remained in the audience room to overhear this exchange. She didn't know why Manerra held back, but was grateful for his restraint.

"You know I was with one lord this whole time when you were otherwise engaged? *You* must teach *me*, Yutrenta!" she transformed fear into anger, so even the tears that sprang unintended to her eyes gave the impression of injury. "I think this day has run too long for all of us and that Aya's gift of sleep should be taken." She whirled and achieved her escape, this time without interruption or redress.

Neither Aya nor lord Tura was in the kitchen when she ran through.

"Lady Shurna!" Lansa's startled cry held concern, but Shurna did not pause to give assurance. Privacy and sleep were her urgent desires. Privacy came easily. Sleep evaded her.

* * * * *

"Shurna. Lady Shurna." Someone shook her shoulder, only a moment after sleep took her. "Lady Shurna, please wake up."

Alva wasn't alarmed, so her message wasn't urgent. Shurna rolled her head to demonstrate her wakefulness, but couldn't summon the energy to lift her head from the pillow.

Light flickered across her closed eyelids and the shaking began anew. "Lady Shurna, it's time to prepare for abbah."

Dawn. Nearly dawn. She forced eyes open, then raised a hand to shield them from the lamplight.

"I'm leaving this lamp and taking yours to fill," Alva said. "Don't go back to sleep now just because I leave. The shecarens are preparing for abbah." The door clicked shut behind her.

Abbah: an honoring of the dead who shared spirit-light with the living . . . an illumination of eyes and mind. Did her ancestors see what the living did in the shadow of closed doors and regret their sacrifices? Were their souls as aggrieved as hers this morning?

Shurna pushed up, but paused with shoulder and head supported by the headboard.

How had honesty become a disassociation from the crime? Vantrann's hands might be bloodless, but the strings he'd cast had snared misguided birds. Foreknowledge could be debated, but that called for an honesty she believed Vantrann lacked.

She slid bare feet over the edge of the bed, crossed the room, and reached for the folded tribal robe Alva had placed on a chair. Dressing, a tremor shook her—from a cold that entered through more than the floor.

She had taught Vantrann. Whatever his crimes, they were no less her own.

* * * * *

Yutrenta pressed a bowl into Shurna's hands even before she sat down at the kitchen table. "Drink it all," Yutrenta ordered.

Shurna's first sip brought a rude shake of her head. "Is this the draught that will finally silence my tongue?" she managed a hoarse demand.

Yutrenta laughed. "If only I'd thought of that earlier," she teased, then sobered. "It will help overcome lost sleep. You'll survive abbah a bit easier."

Shurna took a larger drink, swallowing without allowing the too sweet liquid to linger on her tongue. She looked across the table at Yutrenta and Denassa sitting side-by-side, Kayarra seated across from Denassa. "I apologize for my rudeness last night," she said.

"You were tired and upset," Yutrenta said.

A choke of grief escaped before Shurna could stifle it with a hand.

"Shurna!" Denassa and Yutrenta left their chairs together, but Yutrenta reached her first and slipped a hand around her shoulder. "Shurna, what's wrong?"

"I'm exhausted, Trenta," was all she managed in a husky whisper.

Movement in the hall captured Shurna's attention. She watched Manerra enter the kitchen followed by Aya. Aya's face was haggard, the flesh beneath his eyes dark with fatigue, the corners of his mouth, down turned. His eyes met and held Shurna's as he entered.

As Aya took a seat, Yutrenta squeezed Shurna's shoulder, returned to her chair, and settled into the silence of mealtime.

Shurna sampled the fruit and flatcake Alva placed before her, but could finish neither the food nor Yutrenta's too-sweet tea. Her body craved rest, not food.

When Aya raised a hand, signifying the end of meal, Shurna regretfully separated from the chair that supported her weight.

Later, standing atop the Altar of Acrahh as the spiritual light of her ancestors returned to the world and was greeted by the moons, she completed the tribal link. Yet even as her hands clasped those of her companions, she grieved that their union should ever become empty symbolism.

During their formal retreat, she found herself denying that it would be one of the original tribes, not the Kayarran, who destroyed national unity—and over property damages!

It took the histories to remind her that war had happened among the Ringgangley, and common sense told her this discord encompassed more than property damages. There were issues of pride and injury and restitution, and perhaps revenge and blood feud by now.

*Overreaction is the presence of deep-rooted, unresolved grievances*, her teacher's voice stirred from some long-dormant memory. *The touchstone, no matter how slight, becomes an excuse for action, and the anger expressed can be overwhelming. Certainly, far out of proportion with the nature of the grievance that sparked it.*

*****

Shurna opened her eyes to darkness and reared upright, awake but not alert. For confusingly long moments she wondered where she was until sluggish memory placed her in her bedroom in the House of Moons.

"I have duties, Yutrenta!" she remembered protesting, vexed by Yutrenta's suggestion that she nap. She stood in the shecaren's audience room trying to soak up spilled oil. The accident had happened when she'd tried to refill a lamp and a muscle in her arm shivered.

"Then what are you doing filling lamps?" Yutrenta had demanded. "Why did that drove of housekeepers follow you from Cha-ka if you assume housekeeping duties? Do they perform your tasks?"

"Hush, Trenta, they'll hear you," she tried to hang onto her anger, but like everything else, she lost her grip on it. She had attempted to fill the lamps because the temporary housekeepers were discouraged from this room and its antechamber, and while the shecarens were gone . . . . But it was too late to say so now, and pointless, and in second thought, her actions seemed foolish when the room was vacant and Alva was not overwhelmingly occupied.

"I don't care!" Yutrenta snapped. "You sway on your feet, you ate nothing at breakfast, and you are incompetent even at menial tasks. What possible progress will be made that your presence won't hinder?"

That last hit hard, while the oil-saturated cloth under her fingers only smeared the spill into a wider circle. Tears washed eyes that had been dry half a breath earlier. Again!

"Shurna, *please* sleep," Yutrenta beseeched, this time kindly. "Dee has agreed to inquire into the festival's preparations. It is nothing that requires Kitarin skills."

She had tilted her head in agreement, not trusting her voice. And gotten as far as the kitchen before remembering the slaughter. She didn't know the girl who wielded the knife over the chopping block, but it was that activity that sparked her recall.

"Bring Rayas to me," she told the girl, too dull to frame a gentler request. That knife came down a final time and Shurna winced in anticipation of an injury that did not occur.

"Immediately, lady Shurna." The child abandoned the knife and dashed through the outside door.

Shurna had lowered herself into a chair, unable to stand for longer than necessary.

A man's voice saying "Lady Shurna," woke her, brought her head up from the pillow of her arms. She was disoriented, and momentarily confused by Rayas's presence and attitude of expectation.

*He came at your request; he awaits your command*, came back to her.

She reached up and he graciously helped her rise. The child had resumed her interrupted task.

"Fetch a rope and meet me at the fold," she told Rayas.

"Right away." He nodded and left, never questioning her intentions. Or maybe he knew, his wits not half as addled as hers.

She had not long to wait.

"The two young males, the half-yearlings," she pointed out the ones she meant, easily identified by the short, hard knobs of new horn, "and that female." She pointed out the oldest, whose single gray marking formed a bib-like blaze down her chest. The males were not hard decisions. Whether they were traded or sacrificed made little difference, they could not be kept. Even before their horns broke through they'd butted one another in play. In another three moons, that play would become a serious competition for dominance, and Shurna wanted no injury to their stud.

"Take the female first," she instructed, wanting no irreversible mistake among the females. Except for her exhaustion, she would have caught the animal herself; would have preferred to. The mia knew her and would not be alarmed.

Rayas ducked through the fence and the mia shied from him.

"Where is the slaughter pen?" she asked. He named a location in Cha-ka.

Rayas slowly approached the female. She dodged away from his advance, but his loop fell neatly over her head and a flick of the rope drew the noose snug.

"Tell the lady Denassa that the shon regis's sacrifices have been chosen." She turned away and started back to the house. Rayas would not confuse the males.

Partway across the yard, she stopped cold and stared blindly into a patch of grass combed flat by the recent discard of wash water.

Her mind wickedly identified with the sacrificed female. Because of shared genders? Was she unconsciously worried about the end of her own usefulness?

Not that she knew. Her future was secure in Kita. Was secure beyond Kita, if her heart could consider residence anywhere else.

But personal sacrifice after years of service wasn't the wraith that nudged and haunted her. Trust was entrenched in that mia's blood, where faithfulness and service neither guaranteed longevity nor outcome.

Some duties one performed because tradition or ritual laid clear the choices. Agony had no part in those decisions. Other duties required the painful weighting of gains and losses and still remained unclear. Time was the only sure sieve that separated good decisions from bad, and a person learned from them if her eyes were clear enough to see the truth, all of it, without evasion or slant. Her brain still tried to gauge how one situation was affected, used, and influenced by others. If she could untangle those strings without the unsteadiness of her heart, perhaps there was a solution without bloodshed . . . without additional bloodshed.

In her bedroom, while undressing, she wondered how different were the Kayarran from any of the known tribes. Unique skills and social protocols aside, there were no fundamental differences. Desires for love, safety, happiness, and the need for water and food were the same across all tribes—what she called Yatra's legacy of kinship. Although details of her faith seemed too often in flux, the legacy of kinship—its bedrock—did not waver. And this day, her legacy of kinship consciously expanded to include the Kayarran tribe.

* * * * *

The lamp had either exhausted its fuel or the wick had drowned in its oil for want of trimming. Either way, the event had occurred long enough ago that the rancid smoke from the flame's dying had dissipated. Shurna threw the bed clothes aside and crossed the darkened room, locating the washbasin by familiarity of location and touch. She splashed water on her face and dried with an herb-scented towel before locating her robe and dressing.

The kitchen had become hot enough that Alva had propped open the door with a mica flecked rock. But in the heat of an early summer's midday, there was hardly enough temperature difference to create a cooling draft. Rather did the open door draw outside smoke into the kitchen.

"Are there flatcakes left from breakfast?" Shurna inquired of Alva. She'd spotted tea, already steeped, in a kettle beside the fire. That hunger had awakened at the scent of wood smoke was encouraging.

Alva indicated a cloth wrapped bundle on the table. "The last one."

Shurna carried tea to the table, sat down, and bent to retie a sandal lace improperly wrapped in the dark of her bedroom. When she straightened, Alva stood nearby and offered a damp cloth. Shurna used it to wiped her hands. "Thank you, Alva."

"That—Lord Kayarra ate most what was left."

"I'm glad. He was sick near to death a fortnight north of the Shangren. He's still recovering his strength." Her phrasing was deliberate, and her suspicion confirmed when Alva's eyes hardened, her lips compressed, and she turned aside.

"What were you about to say?" Shurna inquired of the woman's back.

"Nothing that profits anyone," Alva retorted.

"It's not anything that others haven't said already," Shurna coaxed.

Alva turned and stared at her as though weighing her daring.

Shurna added, "The name I've heard him called most often is coranda."

"Aye, he's that, and more," Alva blurted, the trip key found. "He brings a curse upon this valley. Can the shon regis not see it? Can you not make him see it?"

"I could tell him, Alva, if I knew what to tell him."

Alva twisted the cloth she held . . . then seemed to reach a decision. "People outside this house believe he's a demon. They call him cor-anda, Manteen, and worse. They claim his presence will curse the ceremonies, that Acrahh will turn away from his sons. O, lady, please—"

"It's all right, Alva," Shurna interrupted the wail. "You did right by telling me. The shecarens will listen to what I say."

"That's my prayers, lady. Because there are some who won't stay for the joining. They intend to leave before Acrahh cleanses this valley."

Shurna left her chair, closed the distance to Alva, and gripped the woman's thin shoulders. "There was a promise made that has never been broken." Shurna tried not to dig her fingers into Alva's flesh. "This valley is clean. No demon defiles it. If you question that, then attend the abbah this evening, Alva. You will hear shon regis Aya call upon the name of his father. And he will not die, Alva. None of us will die." Shurna loosened her grip, removed her hands. She wanted to slam a wall with her fist. Pointless. She'd only injure her hand. "Where is the janquer lord Kayarra?" she asked, hoping Alva would forgive her terseness.

Alva dropped the cloth and her hands fluttered.

Heat poured through Shurna. Primitive superstitions were experiencing a revival.

"Lord Kayarra—" distaste was audible in that title and name, "is in Cha-ka with the shecarens."

Alarm reared. "Did he go alone?"

"No, lady. The shon regis asked for him."

Shurna did not relax from that announcement. Hatred, fear, superstition, and conceit mistaken for pride. She knew fear herself, but not for Alva's reasons.

# CHAPTER 57

A weak push countered Yutrenta's probing fingers. She drew back, content in a disturbed way to allow the unborn child to return to its oblivious slumber. Additional discomfort to mother and child would change nothing.

Yutrenta studied the mother's face. The thin covering of flesh over bones told its own tragic story, and if pregnancy wasn't a fact, Yutrenta would have suspected the bloating of starvation.

"Is your baby active?" Yutrenta asked, knowing the answer.

The mother's skeletal hands covered that illusion of weight as though to protect the fetal child from words she herself found disturbing. "He's quiet. He's a very good baby."

"Tell me about your trouble on the pilgrimage," Yutrenta invited.

The woman startled, then her eyelids reddened with threatened tears. Her reaction only confirmed what Yutrenta had guessed. A starving woman did not conceive.

"More than halfway here, our guide deserted us. In the middle of the night, he stole everything he could lash onto our horse and fled. My husband tried to stop him, but Granja stabbed him. Three times. He almost died." Tears fell, slithering across lips compressed and stiff with memory.

"Do you know of the meals prepared outside Cha-ka?" Yutrenta asked.

"Yes, lady, but if there is delay getting there, the food is gone. There's not enough to feed everyone."

"Tonight, there will be. But eat slowly. Very slowly."

A scream caused both to look toward a nearby tent. Yutrenta heard, "You lie! I *do* carry Acrahh's son!" before she refocused on her patient. "When you leave here," she said, drawing her patient's attention away from the commotion, "go to the House of Moons. Inquire after Rayas."

"Rayas?" the woman repeated.

"He is a groundskeeper. When he comes, tell him that janquer lady Yutrenta ordered milk for you and your children." The woman stared at her, and Yutrenta realized that in her hopeless trust, in this place where she did not question what she was given or by whom, she had not thought to ask the name of her physician. "And do not give all the milk to your children!" she admonished sternly. "You must eat more. For your unborn baby." She saw the expression of dismay she anticipated. "Have you bowls?"

"Yes, lady."

"Take two bowls with you that Rayas might fill. Make certain they are freshly washed."

"Yes, lady."

Yutrenta lowered the woman's robe to her knees. When she looked back into the emaciated face, it was not difficult to visualize the corpse the woman would become if she died in childbirth. Still, a glint of wonder and hope flickered in those bruised eyes, sparking through the dull will that kept her alive.

"Lady—Thank you, lady." She wrapped her arms around her womb and rocked, and asked the question that begged for another miracle, "Is my baby shecaren?"

This time, Yutrenta's heart wrenched for the child. "Your baby is not likely to come so soon."

Some of the hope left her eyes, but not all.

Yutrenta rose, gripped the woman's hand, and assisted her rise. And held that frail hand a moment longer than necessary, feeling a return grip that wrenched her heart again.

"Lady Yutrenta!"

Both of them looked toward that hail.

Lady Trini abruptly halted her rushed approach.

"Thank you, janquer lady Yutrenta," the woman beside Yutrenta murmured hastily, bobbed her head, and hurried away.

"Lady Trini," Yutrenta acknowledged the physician after her patient left.

Trini closed the gap between them. Yutrenta squatted, plunged her hands into a bowl of water, and rubbed vigorously.

"Lady Yutrenta, if you would—please—there's a woman demanding to see you."

Yutrenta reached for a towel.

"She swears no other physician will touch her."

"You refer to the screaming patient?"

"Yes, lady."

Yutrenta set the towel aside and began gathering her bottles, returning them to her bag. "Is the only problem her refusal—"

"One could wish! Oh." Trini touched her lips. "Forgive me, lady, but this one's not simple. She's convinced she carries Acrahh's son, but there is no child."

Yutrenta stopped collecting her tools and looked up at Trini. "No child?"

"No child."

"The mother does not feel that?"

Trini's hand signal flashed *no.*

Yutrenta broke her stare, convinced of the physician's seriousness. "What have you told her?"

"Only that she does not carry a shecaren. Before I could say more, she screamed that I was ignorant and demanded to be examined by you. She was hysterical."

Yutrenta hastily secured the last of her implements, lifted her bag, and followed Trini across the hard-packed clay to the reddish-brown tent that served as living space and physician's quarters.

The tent was not as neat as Yutrenta would have liked, but she did not brood upon the clutter. Three women awaited her. One crouched alone at the far end of the tent. Trini's assistant. Opposite her, an older woman knelt on the mats holding a weeping girl whose back faced the doorway.

"I am Ofrann janquer lady Yutrenta," she addressed the huddled women. "The lady Trini says you requested my services."

"This woman," the older one waved a dismissive hand at Trini, "told my daughter she doesn't carry Acrahh's child."

Yutrenta swallowed a retort. "Your names?" She stepped around the mat they crouched upon in order to get a better look at the daughter.

"Fava, lady, and my daughter Ura."

Eyes followed her, but not Ura's. Ura kept her face hidden in her mother's lap. In her crouched position, Ura's robe billowed enough that Yutrenta could discern nothing useful about her belly.

Yutrenta bent and smoothed loose hair from the girl's face, shifting enough hair to see the blood pounding through veins in temple and neck. The girl was not crying.

A small shock ran along Yutrenta's arm, but she resisted an impulse to jerk her hand away. "How long have you been with child?" Yutrenta addressed the girl.

The mother answered, "Eleven moons."

Yutrenta blinked at her, then turned toward Trini's cowering assistant and calmly requested that she summon lady Shurna. "Inquire first at the House of Moons," she advised, and with the hand concealed from mother and daughter, signaled the assistant to hurry.

The girl fled.

"You see how I know that my child is Acrahh's, don't you?" Ura grabbed Yutrenta's wrist. Yutrenta jumped in spite of herself. "He delays his birth until the joining of the moons. He waits for that sign from his father."

Yutrenta stared into a young face extraordinarily beautiful beneath a tangle of hair. Despite a high flush, the flesh around the girl's eyes was extremely pale.

"I'm right, am I not?" The girl clung to Yutrenta's hand with both of hers.

"I will know better after I've examined you," Yutrenta answered without shifting her gaze, although she suspected the mother bore watching as well.

Ura released Yutrenta's hand as though it had turned to coals and fell back into her mother's arms. Lips trembled and tears brimmed.

"That other woman already examined her." Fava's jutting jaw indicated Trini, who waited beside the door flap.

"Which is why you called me, according to lady Trini. Perhaps I can learn what she did not understand."

Fava regarded her suspiciously while stroking hair from Ura's face. Then she dipped her head, kissed Ura's brow, and urged her upright with small shoves.

Yutrenta turned her back upon the two women and stepped aside to adjust a lamp wick. Opposite, Trini rushed to trim another lamp, but Yutrenta frowned and Trini stopped. Yutrenta fiddled with lamp wicks in order to give Trini's assistant time to locate Shurna and return. Yutrenta definitely did not want help.

When Yutrenta completed that dalliance, Ura was trembling. The girl wiped her hands across her face and rubbed the tears onto her robe.

"Lady Trini, will you and Fava please wait outside?"

"No!" Fava shouted.

Yutrenta regarded her steadily. When she spoke, it was with utmost patience. "As a physician, Fava, my desire is to protect others' lives and to ease their pain. I will treat Ura with the respect I would offer a daughter. I suspect she may feel more comfortable if we have privacy while I examine her."

"What will you do to her?" Fava demanded.

Yutrenta told her, in detail.

"Lady Trini did not do all those things," Fava objected.

"Perhaps that is why you found her answer unacceptable," Yutrenta suggested. "You inquire after Acrahh's intentions. You know I serve the children of Acrahh. I've assisted a shecaren birth. If I cannot recognize a true child of god, who among us can?"

She half expected a naming of the shecarens. Before Fava could think to do so, Yutrenta asked, "Ura, what is your desire?"

The girl appeared stunned, as if no one had ever asked her preference on any matter.

"I . . ." Her eyes narrowed in a glare of hatred directed at Trini. "I want privacy, if you think that best."

"I do," Yutrenta said, leaving Fava with her mouth open.

Fava closed her mouth and her face wrinkled, reminding Yutrenta of someone who had tasted dysie for the first time, before its sweet aftertaste.

Trini straightened, but made no other move to leave. Yutrenta felt a small relief over Ura's decision. With mother and daughter separated, perhaps the situation would become less volatile. She might learn who inspired whom in this fantasy they kept.

"Lady Trini," Yutrenta said while Fava took an exceedingly long time to gain her feet, "if lady Shurna arrives during my examination of Ura, offer my apology and plead with her to wait until I'm done. I will give word when we're through."

Trini tilted her head.

The exchange had an instant effect on Fava. She suddenly managed to untangle her legs, and hurried from the tent without a backward glance as if whatever happened next was no longer her responsibility. Trini followed her out.

Yutrenta witnessed the transformation and felt distinctly uncomfortable.

"Let's move to the pallet," Yutrenta invited the suddenly wary Ura, careful to keep her voice soothing and confident. "It will be more comfortable than a mat." She offered a hand and Ura hesitantly took it. Then Yutrenta led the beautiful child like a timid and nervous bird. Almost, Yutrenta could believe that Acrahh might bless such a child twice.

"If you haven't done so already, remove your loincloth. Then raise your robe as you sit." Yutrenta turned her back on Ura to peruse Trini's assembled tools. Her skin prickled with the girl behind her.

A quick, encompassing glance at Trini's belongings was enough. She could test each vial and pouch to discover its contents, but doing so diverted attention from Ura. Yutrenta began setting out her own tools.

"I'm ready," Ura whispered hoarsely before Yutrenta finished. Yutrenta turned immediately.

Ura sat on the blanket with bare knees tucked against her chest as close as she could draw them, the bulk of her robe crushed in her lap or pressed around her hips. Yutrenta smiled into Ura's eyes and gently brushed tangled hair from her flushed cheek. Then she slipped a hand to the nape of Ura's neck and pressed Ura's shoulder toward the mat.

"Is this going to hurt?" The girl shivered violently, but allowed herself to be lowered.

"You'll feel the pressure of my fingers and a little discomfort, but if everything's all right, there should be no actual pain." Yutrenta offered that assurance, knowing that everything was not all right and there would be pain. Perhaps the examination itself would tell Ura the things she refused to hear. If Ura understood that she could not give life, perhaps she would accept life for herself instead.

Yutrenta probed below Ura's ears, lingering on the hammering pulse in Ura's neck. She wanted Ura to become accustomed to her touch before she began the more intimate examinations.

Whether Ura feared recriminations, or failure and anonymity, there was danger attached to it. Danger not only in the consequences Ura perceived, but directed toward Trini, and now herself, as the two people who could expose her lie.

Trini had been right to be afraid. Yutrenta still hoped Shurna had been found asleep in the House of Moons.

"Have you told your husband that you may carry a shecaren?"

Ura shifted on the pallet. "In the time of morning abbah, I stood upon a hill above Draka. As the first rays of light pierced the cold, I told him that he had been wed to the Chosen of Acrahh."

Yutrenta carefully slid her hand up the girl's robe to her breast. While doing so, she glanced at the off-center mound of Ura's belly and knew without touching it that the girl was not pregnant.

"I told him that my child would one day lead a nation of tribes and that all Thurrang—all tribes!—would honor me as the blessed vessel of Acrahh."

"How long ago did your husband die?" Yutrenta asked kindly, although the girl's ramblings made her cold.

"I . . ." Ura's eyes filled with tears and overflowed.

Yutrenta waited, but no answer came. She reached for a bit of cloth and pressed the rag into Ura's palm. The girl raised that hand to her eyes.

"It's not important," Yutrenta assured her. "He would not be the one who fathered any child."

"*No*," Ura whispered with hot malice, "no, he didn't."

Yutrenta stared at the girl anew.

Ura stifled cries twice while Yutrenta pressed on and around the bloated, off-centered mound over her abdomen. She gripped the blanket beneath her and squirmed or jerked at the pain that examination caused. Ura fell back panting and sweating when Yutrenta finally turned aside.

"You said it wouldn't hurt," Ura accused while tears dripped from the corners of her eyes.

Yutrenta carefully poured oil into her palm and smeared her fingers through it. "I said it would not hurt if everything was as it should be," she gently reminded.

Ura lay silent, not breathing, as if hearing those words for the first time.

Yutrenta rested her right hand on the girl's side and looked down as she slipped her left hand between the girl's jittery thighs.

A sudden, hard contraction jerked Yutrenta's attention back to Ura. The girl's hand swung toward her, in an arc aimed at her heart. Yutrenta recoiled and pain sliced across breast and arm. She caught Ura's knife wrist in an oily hand and lost it simultaneously. "Trini!" she meant to yell, but the name came out as an inflectionless scream.

Ura rolled away and gained her feet while Yutrenta stared in shock at the gaps in her robe. She reached for her breast as blood colored the fabric.

"You lie!" Ura screamed, face contorted into a carbic's snarl behind a tangle of hair. "I am pregnant!" She backed away as though Yutrenta, seated and lightheaded, still presented the greater threat. "I do carry Acrahh's son! I do!"

Trini burst into the tent, knife drawn.

Ura whirled toward Trini and screamed, "You killed Acrahh's son!" Ura's knife arm jerked and her shoulders lifted. The arm moved again and the knife hit the mat. Blood splattered both.

Fava burst through the door, collided with Trini's shoulder, and both stumbled. Then Fava's scream raked Yutrenta's nerves raw while Ura slumped forward.

From Yutrenta's position, Ura's suicide looked for all the world like a kneel of obeisance.

# CHAPTER 58

People rushed into the tent, blinked, then whirled to leave and collided with others who entered. Soon, more people stayed than left, placing their belongings in danger of trampling.

"Leave!" Yutrenta shouted, while blackness streamed across her vision. "Kara, stay," she stopped that physician from leaving as Kara rose from Ura's body.

Fava's screams, mercifully, had subsided into wails as she rocked Ura's body, oblivious to the blood that soaked them both.

*Knife*, Yutrenta signaled Kara with the hand of her injured arm.

*Hurry, Trini,* Yutrenta silently begged while pain unraveled her control. Trini had ripped away the remnant of her sleeve and nearly completed a hasty binding of her arm. If it weren't for someone holding Yutrenta upright, she might have fallen.

Relief flooded Yutrenta when Kara straightened with Ura's bloody knife in hand. If Fava's shock and grief transformed into rage, better she not have a ready weapon nearby.

Kara circled Fava, knelt beside Yutrenta, and placed the knife in Yutrenta's lap.

"Kara," Yutrenta spoke rapidly, "set a guard at the door. Let no one in who's not been called." Yutrenta wavered again, fought for focus. "Keep watch on Fava. Make certain she doesn't leave. And pick up anything—*anything*—she can use as a weapon. I need—" Too late for Shurna. She must have departed the House of Moons. "—lady Sheron. Summon her from Cha-ka."

"I know lady Sheron," Kara assured her.

Yutrenta was losing trails of thought. Sweat stood out on her skin. "Go, Kara," Yutrenta released her rather than delay longer while she tried to think of everything.

She closed her eyes. Trini's voice drew her back. Yutrenta opened her eyes to a knife poised under her chin and flinched before delayed comprehension told her that Trini intended to cut her robe. Yutrenta lacked the strength to control the violent tremors that shook her while Trini cut away the blood soaked cloth.

Yutrenta kept pressure on her breast wound until Trini indicated readiness to suture it.

*****

A child—a boy—lying in the crook of a low-hanging tree limb caught Kayarra's attention when his head jerked upright. Their eyes locked for a second, then the child reared upright and appeared to lose his balance. Kayarra dashed forward with the thought of catching him, but stopped when the boy landed on feet and hands and then took off running.

Kayarra's attention flashed to Manerra. *He's seen a demon*, Kayarra expected Manerra to say. *Did you think he would wait for your attack?*

That Manerra passed him on the wagon trail with a sidelong glance but no remark was probably due to Aya's presence.

Face burning, Kayarra returned attention to the weedy ground and followed Manerra. Aya had described a meeting in Cha-ka where people wanted to welcome him, but Kayarra would have been happier staying at the House of Moons. He knew Aya had his reasons, but that didn't make the stares and questions, the flinches and other signs of revulsion any easier to take.

An infant's distant wailing alerted Kayarra to the presence of strangers. He glimpsed color among a break in the trees ahead. The baby's crying stopped, replaced by a flutist's solitary notes, and the sudden, screaming laughter of children. As Kayarra neared that gap in the trees, he noticed trails of smoke rising from cookfires, and glimpsed a weaver sitting before her loom, three wood choppers, a pregnant woman nursing a child, men with bows taking aim at a haystack, adults grouped among trees and gathered around fires.

Children chasing each other suddenly veered toward the road, causing adults to look that direction. Kayarra searched the children for Teeka, knowing it more likely that she would find him than he find her. Had she seen him standing among the janquer during abbah? Would Uhle let Teeka approach him?

On the right side of the trail, two women emerged from the trees carrying buckets. A running child swerved to avoid one of the women, knocked her bucket, and showered them both with water. Her cry brought the child's mother running, shouting. Another child, younger, broke her headlong dash against Aya's leg, only to be yanked roughly backward by an older boy. Then they were surrounded by children, shouting questions, staring, touching their robes. The youngest children mimicked the older ones, as if touching robes had become a new game. They were as happy to tag each other's robes as those of the travelers.

"What's wrong with you?" a boy asked, matching Kayarra's pace.

"I am Kayarran," Kayarra answered before realizing that his answer implied that being Kayarran was to be sick or unnatural. The boy dashed away.

Adults shouted names, and some of the children ran back toward the tents, including the girl who strolled hand-in-hand with Manerra. The remainder of their giggling, chattering escort turned back as they reached the edge of the clearing and the forest closed in again. The last child left with a wail of protest when a parent raced after him and, scolding, jerked him aside.

Scattered among the trees stood lean-tos. Near one lean-to, a naked child stood, thumb in mouth, staring as they passed.

After a while, the lean-tos disappeared and the sounds of Yatren activity were replaced by the crunch of their footfalls, the pattering tinkle of a nearby stream, and the chittering and squawking of birds.

Kayarra was trying to glimpse the stream through the trees when he collided with Manerra. Manerra spun and, with the speed of a snake, caught Kayarra's wrist in a painful grip. Kayarra jerked back with an indignant cry, but failed to break free. "Aya!" Kayarra shouted in the second before he spotted an archer in tunic and trousers standing beside a tree. Kayarra stepped back, prevented from retreating by Manerra's grip on his wrist.

"Aya, shon regis . . ."

That hail snapped Kayarra's attention from the archer to a second stranger, this one kneeling amid the weeds in the center of the road, his head bowed. "Manerra, shecaren," that man completed veneration.

The nocked bows and naked blades held by the men standing behind the speaker froze Kayarra's attention. The men wore robes or trousers; wore their hair braided, tied back, or loose; were old and young and ages in between.

"Your souls are forfeit if blood is shed on this ground," Aya said.

Manerra hadn't turned back around. Kayarra looked over his shoulder and saw men standing behind him who hadn't been there seconds earlier. Finally, Kayarra obeyed Manerra's hard tug and stepped forward, letting Manerra direct him by hand pressure until he stood between the shecarens. Only then did Manerra release his wrist.

"None of us wants bloodshed, shon regis," said the kneeling man.

"Then disarm."

"We will lay our weapons at your feet and surrender to your justice, even to death, if you grant us proof that what you said is true."

"Name yourself," Aya demanded.

"Draytel of the Kitarin, shon regis."

"Name the rumor you would die for, Kitarin Draytel."

The man's hands shook, but his voice held firm. "Word of a sixth tribe preceded your arrival, but what you brought with you resembles no tribesman. The legend of Yatra is clear: four tribes descended Mt. Tayenya. There is no lost tribe but the Manteen, and they are Ring-gangley. We fear this thing that travels with you, shon regis. We fear it controls the souls of those who harbor it."

In his stun, Kayarra thought how bizarre Draytel's obeisance appeared . . . until he realized that courtesy, for the moment, kept him alive.

"Janquer lord Kayarra wears the symbol of the sun. His eyes have seen the light of Acrahh. His breath has sustained both the janquer and the children of Acrahh. Those children will not now—or ever—step aside that harm may befall him."

"We only want assurance that our families—that all the tribesmen gathered here—are safe."

"If you attended last evening's abbah, you heard janquer lord Kayarra's vow before Crysus. You know her acceptance of him."

"We heard screams and saw fear among those closest to the altar. Someone besides the demon could have held the uncovered temple stone."

"Demon?" Aya shouted. "You know my father's promise. If a demon stands in Ayahn Rahh, how did it come here?"

"We ask the same question, shon regis. We ask for answers."

Aya took a step forward. Bows lifted. Knuckles whitened on knife hilts. "If my word is insufficient, if my father's promises mean nothing, then I have no proof you will believe."

"You have the temple stone, shon regis. We will believe this . . . man's innocence if he holds the uncovered stone and is not struck down."

"You saw him take the stone last night and yet deny it today."

"Our eyes were closed or we were too far away to see clearly."

"Your eyes will be closed every time janquer lord Kayarra holds the stone or you'll be blinded."

"I and one other have agreed to blinding," Draytel said.

The trickle of the stream filled the silence.

"Janquer lord Kayarra," Aya called without turning, "name the gods you serve."

Kayarra was confused. "Acrahh and Crysus, shon regis," he said, hoping he understood the question correctly.

"Any others?"

Kayarra hesitated. "I serve you, shon regis."

"Any others?"

The repetition made him believe he hadn't given the answer Aya wanted. "No, shon regis," he said rather than risk more guesses, when each answer seemed riskier than the last.

"A demon cannot speak Acrahh's name and live," Aya said.

"There are some who question the speaking of a name. We will believe the temple stone's proof, shon regis," Draytel insisted.

"Manerra," Aya didn't shift his attention, "repeat the litany of the stone."

"The temple stone," Manerra said, "is Crysus's gift to Yatra, carried by the shon regis as proof of Acrahh's life and promise. Never shall blood or unprotected flesh touch the surface of the stone. Its use honors Acrahh and preserves Yatren life. For no other purpose ever is it to be used.

"Light ignites the power within the stone. The stronger the light, the more dangerous its power. The temple stone's use is safe only at sunrise and sunset, or when firelight alone is a source of light," Manerra concluded.

"The stone is not safe for use at midday," Aya admonished. "Even an innocent man can be blinded or killed."

"You may bind his eyes," Draytel offered, "but we insist that he hold the temple stone."

Aya stood so long without speaking, men shifted weight, exchanged glances.

"Produce your bindings," Aya said, at last.

Kayarra swayed, raised a hand to catch himself against Aya's back, but recovered balance without touching him.

A man dug into his belt pouch, withdrew a length of cloth, and advanced toward Aya, extending the offering.

Aya snatched the cloth from his hand. "Find another," he ordered.

Men exchanged glances.

Draytel stood. "Shon regis—"

"And," Aya ordered, his anger cold, "decide who among you is the most godly. For that man shall be the first to hold the uncloaked stone."

The murmuring and shifting halted.

"By Yatra's warning, the temple stone has never been uncovered at midday. If janquer lord Kayarra were struck dead, I would not know whether his death proved him a demon or proved the power of the stone. The man you choose shall be the most virtuous among you. One you all agree is not demon possessed. If he dies, then the stone will burn until dusk, for even I may not touch it. So decide who among you will die this day."

Silence, followed by a muttering that began and swelled.

Aya lifted the temple stone's strap off his shoulder and over his head. "Manerra, step back."

"No!" someone shouted. "No! This use of the temple stone doesn't honor Acrahh or preserve Yatren life. It must not be done. To desecrate the stone will turn the gods from us forever. Draytel, don't force this! Shon regis, don't allow it!"

"The decision to preserve or desecrate the temple stone is Draytel's," Aya said, cradling the pouch in his arms.

Draytel stood unmoving. Then, in slow motion, he drew his knife.

"Draytel, don't do this!" a desperate voice cried.

"My only desire," Draytel spaced his words, "is to preserve the lives of those I love. To know this valley is safe." Draytel sank to his knees.

"As I love you, Aya, shon regis." He stretched his arm out and dropped the knife. All around him, men tossed bows and knives on the ground as if the weapons had suddenly caught fire. "I keep my word, shon regis." Draytel lowered his forehead to the ground and crossed his arms atop his head. Men sank to their knees, then to the ground.

Aya returned the strap to his shoulder and let the temple stone's pouch fall against his hip. "I would have heard you in audience, Draytel," Aya said. "I would have heard any of you!" Aya shouted. "Honorable intentions achieved by violence are little better than murder. I cannot and will not forgive threat to any janquer." Aya crossed the road and circled back, signaling Manerra, and pressing Kayarra's arm in passing.

"Janquer lord Kayarra's vow to Acrahh was not lightly given nor lightly received. There is danger even in the swearing of such a vow. So much so, that failure of my duty to protect him becomes a judgment upon my soul. Yet, knowing that, I would have allowed your test if you had met its conditions, because my duty to Yatra's children and this land precludes even my protection of the janquer. Without a nation, without land, I have no reason to live. But that fact alone does not assuage my anger at being forced to choose among my responsibilities. I demand restitution.

"Sit up. I want to see your faces."

They sat up, their faces grim, resigned, angry, fearful. Only one glared hatred at Kayarra.

"Name yourselves."

Draytel renamed himself, and each man followed, giving his name and tribe. After all eighteen men were named, Manerra renamed them in the order in which they had named themselves, stunning those who must have thought their naming to be a formality.

"As you came together to enforce your will upon me, so will you remain together in restitution. The easiest penalty you will pay is the levy of two offerings: one of food, one of possessions, each one-fourth of what you own. You will make these offerings in the Temple of Crysus, and rename yourselves as each offering is made.

"My second order charges you with protection of the life you nearly took from me. You will begin this charge by attending this evening's abbah. There, you will see janquer lord Kayarra handle the temple stone when it is safe for him to do so, and you will be blinded by that seeing if you fail to shield your eyes, for you will stand at the north base of the Altar of Acrahh.

"Tomorrow, and for as many days as you remain in Ayahn Rahh, you will repeat what you have seen, and tell your listeners that janquer lord Kayarra has no greater power for miracles or possession than you have.

"If your children lie awake frightened in the night, remind them of Acrahh's promise that no demon shall ever walk this valley. If your women fear janquer Yutrenta's touch, tell them also to fear mine, and yours, for no one shall find peace who nurtures baseless fear.

"Janquer lord Kayarra can no sooner change his eye or skin color than you can. Does that mean you are his demons?

"Draytel, Bezan, Laynah, Harra, retrieve your weapons. You four will accompany us to Cha-ka. The rest of you, take up your weapons, return to your kin, and keep this evening's abbah."

Men moved again, some sluggishly as if confused or stunned, some quickly. The few who spoke, did so in murmurs.

Aya signaled and then started forward, weaving through the men, and past them. Manerra shoved Kayarra, who hurried after Aya, his skin crawling.

The four named men hurriedly closed in on either side of Manerra and Kayarra.

# CHAPTER 59

No one spoke, not in words, not in silent speech. The crunch of footfalls on gravel, the crush of brittle weeds, the occasional snap of a rebounding branch sounded loud in the silence.

Kayarra could not keep his attention off Draytel and his companions, off their weapons, off the hands that swung past those knives.

An eternity later, the forest ended. Broad, cultivated fields surrounded a cluster of buildings and shade trees. Trails of smoke rose from cook fires scattered about yards. When they were close enough to discern carcasses of mia spitted over fires, Kayarra's attention shifted to the cultivated crops lining the wagon trail. He didn't recognize the heart-shaped leaves and didn't know if he'd ever eaten in stews or soups the slim, corkscrew pods hanging in clusters below the leaves.

"This is far enough," Aya said.

Kayarra's attention snapped back to Aya even as he halted. Aya and Draytel faced each other, their gazes locked.

"Return to the temple," Aya said, and included Draytel's companions in a sweeping glance. "I expect to see each of you at the base of the altar's north stairs during tonight's abbah."

The men offered hasty veneration, turned, and started back the way they'd come. Draytel was the last to lift his head and depart.

Manerra stepped around Kayarra, but rapidly approaching footfalls shifted their attention to the trail. Kayarra stepped into the weeds bordering the field as a rider overtook Draytel's group at a gallop and passed Aya without slowing.

"Do you recognize the rider?" Manerra asked.

"No," Aya answered, voice tense. He started walking. Manerra fell into step beside him, and Kayarra hurried to catch up.

The rider plunged recklessly through the crowded yard, and for an awful moment, Kayarra thought the rider intended to run the shuren against the wall of the main house. She leapt from the animal before it stopped moving and ran for the door.

"Aya—" Manerra said.

"I know." Aya quickened pace.

They hadn't yet reached the smoke of the nearest cookfire when the house door burst open. A woman with white hair left the building at a run, headed toward the corner of the house. Behind her, slower, stumbled the rider, who reached for the reins of her still-heaving mount.

The white-haired woman collided with a man leading a shuren toward the front of the house. The man caught her waist before she rebounded, lifted her off her feet, and heaved her onto shurenback.

The lady swung around and upright, slapped reins to her mount, and leaned low over the shuren's neck as it bolted.

Aya dodged sideways into the path of the oncoming rider. "Lady Sheron!" he lifted his arms and shouted.

Sheron jerked upright, her face an expression of shock. The shuren brushed past Aya as Sheron fought to halt it. "Shon regis!" she cried, brought the shuren around, and angled toward Aya, who ran to meet her. The shuren danced sideways, spooked by Aya's rush.

Sheron leaned down, speaking rapidly. Kayarra couldn't understand what she said. Manerra started toward them just as Aya reached up, pulled Sheron from her mount, and took her place with a leap. He nudged the shuren toward Manerra, shouted, "Find Denassa and Shurna. Ride with escort. Bring Sheron to the House of Moons." Aya turned the sidestepping shuren toward the forest trail and slapped her hard.

# CHAPTER 60

In deference to the large number of pregnant women attending the Ingathering, Shurna held her shuren to an amble through the tent town. The animal shied from squealing children. She wondered whether the north wagon trail would have been a faster route, but doubted it. Until the joining passed, there'd be no unoccupied ground in the valley.

The density of tents lessened considerably when Shurna reached the finger of forest that divided Cha-ka from the House of Moons. She urged the shuren into a canter on the largely deserted road, but slowed to an amble when she broke clear of the forest. She passed the fields and halted her mount beside one of the open-air fires.

"Where may I find the lady Denassa?" she called to one of the workers. "Do you know?"

The man stirring a huge copper kettle released the handles of a bent wood paddle and approached. Sweat created a sheen on his bare chest. He wiped a forearm across his brow and stared at her bare leg. "Byna. Byna!" the man bellowed to someone behind Shurna. "You know a lady Denassa and where is she?"

"That be the shon regis's Ringgangley," Byna yelled back. "She be at the bake house."

"Thank you," Shurna nodded and nudged the shuren with her heels, but dismounted before she had crossed half the yard. She led her animal through a mill of onlookers and rush of workers, circled the side of the main house, and spotted a child studiously mixing a bowl of mud with a stick. The child startled when Shurna called to her, but finally approached when Shurna motioned and smiled.

"The lady Shurna's animal has the glowing temple stone between its eyes." Shurna pulled the shuren's head down so the girl could see the whorl of white fur on its forehead. "Tie her well, for she would enjoy a sampling from yonder field."

The child grinned, rose on her toes, and eagerly took the reins from Shurna's hand.

"You should have children," a familiar voice remarked from behind.

"Jitta!" Shurna whirled, laughing, and returned the older woman's embrace. "I'm not certain children are part of my future," Shurna replied. "At least, not my own."

"You're still young enough." Jitta released her and stepped back.

"I've patience with children I don't live with," Shurna confessed.

"Lady Sheron was in a tizzy until news of your arrival. And what news you've brought!"

Shurna laughed. "We've more news than you've heard. More than I've time to tell. Do you know where I can find janquer lady Denassa?"

"She was in the bakery for a time, but I just came from there and didn't see her. If you like, visit with Aena and I'll send a child to fetch you when I find her."

Shurna's heart lurched. "Where is Aena?"

Jitta extended an arm. Shurna turned and saw women chopping fruit at a plank table in the shade, none of them Aena.

"In the field," Jitta said.

Shurna's attention left the women and fixed upon a lone figure crouched over bean plants in the field beyond.

"The strangers and confusion make her nervous," Jitta said.

Shurna forced a smile, pressed Jitta's arm, and started away.

"It's pure pleasure having you back," Jitta called.

Shurna turned and walked backwards. "It's wonderful to see you, Jitta. My heart won't behave being this close to home." She turned back around, smiled and nodded at the women working around the makeshift table, then left the shade of the yard for the heat of the field.

The face that lifted and stared as Shurna approached was remarkably unchanged from their childhood days in Kaytron. Suddenly, Shurna felt older and too much changed; felt disconnected from a past that didn't feel like hers.

Wary suspicion flooded the eyes watching her.

Shurna clung to her earlier joy upon seeing Jitta and smiled. "I came to pick beans with you, if that's all right."

"I'm weeding, not picking."

Shurna stopped a body length away and sank to her knees upon the dry leaves that mulched the rows. "Then maybe I can help weed." She breathed deeply of the scent of warm soil and leaf mold as she reached for the wild grass that grew among the beans.

"Why aren't you with the others?" Aena asked, hands resting on her knees, attention unwavering.

"They thought I should work in the field until they can find a job I can do. Jitta said she'd send a girl for me when they do." Shurna pulled a clump of grass, shook soil from its roots, then dropped it in the leaves by her knee.

"This is a job." Aena reached for a leafy weed and pulled. The stem broke. She dropped the leafy portion atop a pile of weeds already pulled and reached for the rooted stem.

"Hot work," Shurna agreed. "But your work assures food for everyone else."

Aena's smile was a shy lift of her lips. "I like you," she said.

Shurna looked up, caught her eye.

"I have water, if you're thirsty," Aena offered.

"I'm fine for now, thank you."

"You're welcome."

They pulled weeds in silence, Aena on one row, Shurna on an adjacent row. Sap stained Shurna's hands green and glued soil to her fingers, while the peace of the field stole into her soul. She yearned for a less hectic life; could welcome back-aching work that produced results one could see and measure. The beans and sun and warm-cool soil were as far as one could get from resentments and jealousies and those who thought that controlling others' actions were as necessary as food and air.

"It's nice here," Shurna said.

"It's nicer when there aren't so many strangers."

"How is your mother?" Shurna controlled the casualness of her tone with difficulty.

"Why do you ask about my mother?" Aena's suspicion returned.

"I was thinking of my mother. I haven't seen her for a very long time. If you told me about your mother, I thought maybe I wouldn't miss mine so much."

"Where have you been?" Aena either forgot Shurna's question or ignored it.

"In Thurra, then in the Ofrann."

"Are you Thurrang or Ofrann?"

"I'm Kitarin."

Aena flashed an unguarded smile, her face lit with the delight of a child. "I'm Kitarin. Cha-ka is near Kita. Maybe your mother came for the joining."

"I think she would have found me by now, or I, her, if she'd come."

"Oh." Aena shifted down her row. Another weed exposed its roots and a new discard pile was begun. "I have a sister. She travels with the shon regis Aya."

Shurna dropped the weed she'd just pulled.

"You don't believe me," Aena said.

"N-no! I do believe you. I know her."

"You do?" skepticism in Aena's voice. "What's her name?"

"Janquer lady Shurna."

Aena looked away, reached for a weed. "What's she like?"

"She tries hard to understand Acrahh's plans for this life, but I don't think she understands it very well."

"She shouldn't try," Aena remarked.

"Why?"

"The gods' plans don't care for individuals."

"Maybe it only seems that way because our understanding is limited. If we can reach into our god force—"

"I don't want to talk about this," Aena interrupted. Another weed gave up its life.

"Did your sister hurt you?" Shurna asked on impulse.

"I don't remember my sister."

"But you know you have one."

"Lady Sheron told me. I think because of the joining, she wanted me to know. You know, with the shon regis coming, she might be with him. I guess she didn't come." Aena pressed a hand against the small of her back and straightened. She stared at Shurna. "Why are you crying?"

"Because I had a sister—" Shurna's throat clamped down on the words and she averted her face.

Aena lurched forward and threw her arms around Shurna's neck. Shurna returned Aena's embrace and cried. Aena was the first to pull away. Shurna let her go.

"Oh dear!" Aena's dismay shifted Shurna's attention to the crushed bean plant Aena lifted and then let fall.

"Is lady Sheron going to scold us?" Shurna asked.

"Lady Sheron doesn't come into the fields."

Shurna laughed despite herself.

Aena smiled, reached across the broken plant, and wiped Shurna's cheek. Her smile vanished. "Oh no!"

"What's wrong?" Shurna demanded.

"I made mud on your face."

Shurna wiped the cheek with her sleeve.

Aena giggled. "You smeared it."

"I'll rinse at the house."

"If you stop crying, the mud will dry and brush off."

"I love you, Aena."

Aena frowned. "Why did you say that?"

"Lady Shurr-naa!" a child's shout interrupted, jerking their attention toward the house. "Lady Shurr-naa!" The child raced along rows, heedless of plants. "You're needed at the house! It's urr-gent!"

Shurna leapt to her feet. "I have to go." She started walking toward the child, then running. The girl stopped to catch her breath. Shurna passed her without slowing. She saw her shuren being led toward the front of the house before she spotted Jitta. People were clustering, walking or running toward the front of the house. Jitta spotted her and pointed the direction everyone else headed. Shurna, full of dread, ran past her without slowing.

Shurna cleared the corner of the house and saw Manerra, mounted, reach a hand down to Kayarra. A man crouched beside Kayarra offered linked hands, prepared to boost Kayarra onto shurenback behind Manerra. Denassa stood nearby, facing the corner of the house. A green rag tied Denassa's braids en mass at the nape of her neck. Rolled sleeves exposed her biceps, and sweat formed a vee shaped stain at the neck of her robe. Denassa lunged forward, intent upon a shuren being lead toward her.

Shurna veered aside and intercepted her own mount. She yanked the reins from its startled handler before the man had an opportunity to identify her. She leapt, got halfway over the shuren's back and started to slide down before a hand caught her foot, stopped her slide, and shoved her higher. She swung a leg over the animal's croup and looked down. "Thank you," she gasped, snatched the reins she'd dropped, and kicked the animal forward, reining in beside Denassa's beast. They locked eyes across the distance separating them, Denassa's eyes wide with fright.

"What's wrong?" Shurna demanded.

"Trenta's hurt."

Shurna's involuntary jerk made her shuren dance backwards. "Are we ready to ride?" she demanded.

"We wait for Sheron. Aya ordered us to ride with escort."

"Why Sheron?" Shurna demanded.

"Yutrenta called for her."

Shurna glanced around, saw four mounted men clear the corner of the house. Warning shouts alerted those who did not see them coming. People cleared a path for the riders.

Shurna fought an urge to slap her shuren into motion. Every muscle tensed. The pounding footfalls of the approaching riders excited her shuren, which started forward under her knees' pressure alone. Shurna hauled on the reins and tried to ease her knee tension.

"Two escorts, come with us," Manerra shouted above the noise of the oncoming riders. "Two, escort lady Sheron."

Before their escorts could arrange a division, shecaren and janquer whipped their mounts and broke for the road.

* * * * *

Three men held Yutrenta while Trini and Kara sutured her wounds. Although Yutrenta wished for the relief of a faint, she could not relinquish control. She wanted to know what Trini did at the same time she wanted Trini to stop. Yutrenta's screams that Acrahh curse them unless they gave her draydine before they continued fell on deaf ears. By the time they finished their butchery and released her, she had no will left to fight them.

"Breathe, Yutrenta," Trini ordered, bending over her. Trini's exhale chilled Yutrenta's sweat-damp skin. "Yutrenta!"

Trini's insistence was a grating irritation. It hurt to breathe. Yutrenta briefly opened her eyes. "Blind you," she cursed, although pain sapped satisfaction.

A warm, damp cloth passed over her face and neck, removing sweat and blood, its warmth incredibly soothing. Remorse for her behavior, though, was forgotten amid the pain of her next breath.

"I may be cursed," Trini retorted, "but not for saving your life. Kara is preparing draydine. If I dared the shon regis's anger, I'd give you dayflower to silence your tongue. But I fear his curses more than yours."

"Don't . . . even jest," Yutrenta whispered.

Trini exchanged the rag for a knife and started slicing through the remainder of Yutrenta's bloody clothing. Even her loincloth was saturated with blood. She was sticky with it.

Yutrenta clamped her jaw to prevent more curses. Each tug on her clothing hurt.

"Lady Yutrenta," an anxious voice intruded. It was Kara. "I have draydine."

Yutrenta opened her eyes. The women's heads touched above her.

"Trini and I are going to lift you so you can drink. We'll bandage you while you're sitting."

They let her lay for a moment while Kara's words sank in. Yutrenta tilted her head. And screamed for them to stop when the weight of her breast shifted, pulling against the sutures. Pain lanced chest and shoulders all the way to her wrists.

Yutrenta reached to support her breast, and gulped the too-hot liquid Kara pressed to her lips, heedless of the way it scorched tongue, pallet, and throat. She swallowed even the dregs of bark and root that had escaped the strainer.

Then Kara supported her while Trini wrapped her arm and chest. When they laid her down, Yutrenta thought that might be the end of the jostling . . . until carriers arrived with a litter to move her to the House of Moons.

* * * * *

It wasn't to her private room upstairs that Yutrenta was taken, but to a hastily vacated bedroom in the housekeepers' quarters downstairs. Rumors had traveled quickly, she realized in a moment when she could think beyond pain. But then, she could not judge how much time had elapsed since Ura's knife had swept toward her and changed her life.

They slid her off the litter and she dropped into the bed from its edge. Despite the draydine, she nearly fainted. Her hand flew to her breast. Despite Trini's snug wrapping, it felt as though the sutures had torn.

"Lady Yutrenta," Kara's voice penetrated the blackness eclipsing her sight, "rest now. You're home. We won't move you again."

If not for her position, she would have told them choice things that no person of power should utter. She had to be content listening to the litter bearers leave.

"Where's Denassa?" she whispered, wanting someone familiar and trusted beside her; someone who would understand Aya's reaction when it came. If Aya had gotten a third- or fourth-hand account of the attack, she hoped the news bearer had had some sense about him in the telling of it.

"I don't know, lady." Kara began loosening the blanket they had wrapped around her before transport. The tugs were a further irritation.

"Find her." She wanted to be left alone, to lie absolutely still until inflamed nerves and flesh quieted.

"You're the housekeeper?" Kara asked.

Yutrenta opened her eyes and saw Lansa—pale, hands clutched at her throat—swaying in the doorway.

"One of them, lady," Lansa answered.

"Warm tea and broth. Bring both as quickly as they can be readied."

Lansa hurried away.

Kara turned back, met Yutrenta's gaze. "Runners have been sent to Cha-ka and throughout the valley. Wherever the janquer and shecarens are, they'll be found." She started tucking the blanket about Yutrenta's neck.

So every pilgrim in Ayahn Rahh learns of the attack—without details, without explanations.

"Kara, take your hands off me!" Yutrenta's tolerance snapped. "Don't touch me. Don't jostle the bed. If you would make me comfortable, bring me another blanket. I'm cold. I hurt. I need to lie still."

"Yes, lady." Kara pulled a blanket off the room's second bed and covered her just as Lansa returned with tea.

"Broth will take a bit longer, lady," Lansa said.

Yutrenta allowed Kara to adjust the pillow, then sipped the tea, although its heat stung the burns in her mouth. The tea's warmth penetrated a little of her chill.

"Leave us!" that roar startled everyone in the room. A credit to Kara that she did not spill the remainder of the tea down Yutrenta's neck. Yutrenta fell back against the pillow with her heart pounding harshly, her eyes fixed on Aya's face.

Kara jumped off the edge of the bed, backed toward the wall, then fled the room as soon as Aya cleared the doorway.

"You've roused Crysus with that shout," Yutrenta protested.

Aya only drew his knife as he advanced. His face was flushed, his expression granite. He panted. He reached the bedside and pulled back the blankets, one at a time.

"Do not do this," Yutrenta whispered, her eyes fixed on his although he wasn't looking at her face.

He neither wavered nor paused. He cut through the fabric that crossed her shoulder, then attacked the material that crossed her breasts.

Yutrenta clamped her teeth against the pain even those small tugs caused. And saw Aya wince as he peeled the fragments of bandage off her breast. He stared at the ugly wound for a long time, then started to slice through the bandage on her arm.

"No!" She cringed away from the knife tip. "There is no point, Aya. The woman who attacked me is dead. Why add to my pain?"

That stopped him. After a momentary pause, he sheathed the knife. "She would have killed you over a lie—a fantasy!" his controlled anger was frightening.

"Being the Chosen of Acrahh is more than a lie."

"And is god-determined, not man-decided."

"Many believe otherwise!" Great Acrahh, it hurt to yell. But she saw his pain and could not abide it. "The Ofrann call it the Month of Divine Conception." She saw him wince and knew she was being cruel, but continued. "Too many believe chance, not divine intervention, determines a shecaren birth, and tribes compete for the status it brings. Ura bet everything she had on it and would have killed me because I forced her to face the truth."

He covered his face with his hands.

"She's not alone, Aya." She calmed. "Look at what Tackta did to Manerra. The lust for power is an illness that never goes away."

When his hands dropped away, his face was wet. "There is proof enough of that with my own brother. With Hyran," he clarified. Then demanded angrily, "Is there nothing sacred that men won't defile?"

Yutrenta stretched a hand toward him, but he stood too far away to reach. Beyond whatever comfort there was in a touch, she had no comfort to offer him. She lowered her hand to the mattress.

When he spoke again, his hands were clenched into fists. "It's not one thing, Trenta, or even two. Why do I uphold laws others ignore? I can't touch the woman I love because I'm half god, so my man needs languish. But laws of god or man make no difference to those who would destroy national unity. Gods *curse* the day of my birth!" Aya whirled and left.

Yutrenta lay against the pillow, stunned for a time, staring at the empty doorway. Eventually, tears blurred her vision, but she wasn't certain whether she cried for Aya or for herself, or simply out of fear and pain.

# CHAPTER 61

Denassa crossed the narrow room, her footfalls, whispers against the tile, her attention fixed on Yutrenta's shockingly pale face. Alarmed by a thought, Denassa's sight darted to Yutrenta's chest, relieved by the faint rise and fall of the blanket.

"Where do you want this?" Lansa's question sounded like a shout in the doorway.

Yutrenta's eyelids fluttered. Her next breath was audible, ending on a moan.

Denassa pointed to the small table at the head of the bed, slipped the strap of her physician's bag from her shoulder, and placed it on the room's spare bed. When she returned, Yutrenta's eyes were open, her brow creased.

"I wanted you," Yutrenta whispered.

Denassa squeezed Yutrenta's wrist through the covers. "Trini and Kara explained what they did to you."

"The attack?"

"Their treatments. Trini didn't know what happened after she left the tent."

"Ura had a knife. I didn't know she had it. I felt a contraction. Looked up. My hands were oily."

"The woman—the mother—has been taken to Cha-ka." Denassa lifted the blankets' edges, removed fragments of bandage, and gazed at the sutured wound. "Trini says you've not been bathed."

Denassa looked into Yutrenta's face. Her eyes were closed again . . . drowsiness being an effect of the draydine.

She reached into the pottery bowl Lansa had placed on the table and squeezed warm water from the rag floating there.

The water darkened with each rinsing, there being dried blood even on the soles of Yutrenta's feet. When Denassa finished bathing her, she lay a dry cloth over Yutrenta's chest and covered her with the blankets. "I'll rinse your hair and back when we're able to move you."

"Tomorrow," Yutrenta said. "For the joining."

"Aya's already asked Benta to take the Ofrann position in abbah."

"Tonight. In the morning. Not tomorrow night," Yutrenta insisted.

"We'll see," Denassa remained skeptical.

A tap sounded at the door and Manerra entered. "Aya asks for High Council as soon as Yutrenta can participate," he announced. "Held in this room."

"Now," Yutrenta whispered.

"Trenta!" Denassa protested.

Manerra inclined his head and left.

Denassa took the bowl of bloody water into the kitchen and found Kara seated at the table.

"Tonight during abbah," she told Kara, "I'll want someone to remain with janquer lady Yutrenta." Denassa passed the bowl to Lansa. "Can you stay, or arrange for another physician?"

"I can do it," Kara offered.

"Thank you, Kara." Denassa smiled her gratitude.

By the time she'd secured a cup of broth and returned to Yutrenta's sick room, Aya was approaching from the audience room. She reached Yutrenta's room ahead of him and slid past Shurna to reach the bedside. Kayarra sat on the room's spare bed. Manerra stood at Yutrenta's footboard and stared at her.

Aya entered the room, closed the door, and Shurna slipped past him to stand beside Kayarra.

"The attack on Yutrenta was not planned as a diversion or an adjunct attack connected with the trail ambush," Aya announced.

Denassa sloshed the broth she lowered onto the table and hastily reached for a rag to soak up the spill.

"Trail ambush?" Shurna asked.

"Eighteen men detained Manerra, Kayarra, and I on the north forest trail. They wanted proof of Kayarra's innocence. As far as I can learn, both attacks were independent of each another."

"What kind of proof?" Denassa asked.

"They demanded he hold the uncloaked temple stone."

Denassa looked toward Kayarra, who appeared uninjured.

"They would not meet my conditions for agreement." Aya gave a brief description of the events, gave the restitution demanded. He paused for a breath. "Shurna, I want you present through Fava's questioning.

"I've asked lady Sheron for peacekeepers. Until they arrive, anyone leaving the House of Moons tonight, except for abbah, will take an escort of house guards.

"Kayarra, tonight's ceremony will repeat last evening's naming but without your vow to Crysus.

"Yutrenta. You treated the Hyranian taken at Varaar field. Were his injuries severe enough to kill him?"

"A man can die from a thorn prick under the right circumstances. But I placed him in a physician's care. None of his wounds were serious enough to worry me."

"Denassa, do you agree?" Aya demanded.

"I do. I helped Yutrenta treat him. But then, you know this. How does—"

Aya lifted a hand for silence. "I've arranged messengers to Zarthon and the Shangren, ordering Vantrann to Tes-Raly and Korrane's representative to Zarthon. Korrane is to negotiate the Hyranian matters himself. Vantrann is to be divested."

Denassa's gasp was the last sound heard until Shurna asked, "Will you not hear Vantrann's explanations before deciding?"

"If Vantrann's innocent of wrongdoing, he's not innocent of incompetence. His retention on the janquer weakens us. I will hear him, but only to decide if additional intervention is necessary. This is his second offense in half a year."

Denassa stared at Manerra, who stood with head bowed.

"What offense?" Yutrenta demanded.

Aya described Tura's accusations and added, "I heard and questioned Tura's corroborator, and others in his company. I located another Thurrang, independent of Tura's influence, who knew something of the matter. All others I spoke with left Thurra before we did, or came from areas far removed from Zarthon and Varaar."

"There's danger in Vantrann's divestment," Shurna warned. "The shame may be enough to drive him to an Hyranian allegiance, and Hyran's criminals need no such ally in Thurra."

"Do you propose that I retain him, disempowered, on the janquer, and give false sanction to his actions?" Aya asked.

"No," Shurna denied. "I ask only that you be aware of the possibility."

"Lord Razon's reactions are no less a concern," Aya said, "but we lose more by delaying consequences than by facing them. We cannot fight a northern and southern conflict at the same time. But even that threat will not prevent me from doing what is right."

"A northern conflict?" Shurna and Denassa asked together.

"Rumors claim the Hyranians are searching for Kayarran presence with the intention of provoking them to violence."

"*Why?*" Denassa demanded.

"You tell me what they gain by it," Aya challenged.

Manerra answered, "They keep us out of the southlands, perhaps long enough to seize land and assemble enough followers to hold it against us."

"If they secure our deaths by Kayarran hands," Shurna offered, "whatever they do can go largely unchallenged."

"Hyran didn't want me dead," Aya said. "He wanted me discredited, my effectiveness broken. He wanted me to live with shame. His attacks were upon national unity. In the resulting chaos, the arentas—he and Myra—were to restore order and thereby usurp my power."

"Hyran's dead," Shurna said. "Do we have any assurance that his followers—even Myra—shared his scruples enough to enforce his intentions?"

"Myra might, but I question whether she has the respect of Hyran's followers or his powers of persuasion. But enough conjecture. Locating Kayarra's tribe remains my greatest need. Afterwards, we will sail from Bana and join Vantrann in Tes-Raly. Do you agreed to Vantrann's disempowerment until his divestment?"

The legacy of the Manteen hung huge in Aya's mind. Mante's followers did not flee with the foreknowledge that they would eat the flesh of their kin in order to survive. Unintended consequences. That's what frightened Aya. It could freeze his ability to act if he thought too long.

"Yes, shon regis," Yutrenta whispered, her voice hoarse but firm. He stared at her, his staunchest supporter, and knew that she was likely to be hurt the deepest by his orders before these conflicts were resolved. The hard part was knowing that she suspected it and gave him that power anyway.

Manerra surprised him by agreeing next with the sign of acquiescence. Aya studied his brother's face, wondering if Manerra's agreement was motivated by feelings of use and betrayal or by an obligation to the nation. Of anyone, Aya had hoped Manerra might offer a different solution to the problem of Vantrann, but the shecaren said nothing, and his face remained unreadable.

Shurna and Kayarra signaled acquiescence nearly together, Kayarra, without knowing Vantrann, likely agreeing because the others did. Shurna, stolid and resolute, knowing nearly as much as he did about Vantrann's misguided fervor, still troubled by an action that undermined the janquers' unity and violated the bonds pledged in the ritual of unification.

Denassa wept, and for a long time did not reply.

"Denassa," Aya urged.

She tilted her head, then choked on a sob as if that agreement sealed her betrayal.

"Agreement is given by the shecaren and all janquer members present.

"Tomorrow night is the joining. Is a shecaren birth imminent?" Aya asked.

"At the time of Ura's attack," Yutrenta answered, "I had received no such report, but there are a few possibilities. I will know tomorrow."

"If the news is positive, then Denassa will deliver the child," Aya said.

Denassa's response was still only a head tilt.

"Let's pray for this miracle," Aya said, but both Yutrenta's "Month of Divine Conception" and the adage, "When a shecaren is born, another dies," lay like loadstones upon his spirit.

*Please, Acrahh, Father*, he prayed, *if a shecaren must die, let it not be Manerra.*

# CHAPTER 62

Whether all eighteen men who had ambushed them on the forest road were present at abbah, Kayarra could not tell, but he locked eyes with the man who had shot him the glare of hatred. That one stood beside another man Kayarra recognized. Their presence made his hands sweat, his movements clumsy, as he accepted the cloaked temple stone from Aya's outstretched hands.

Both shecarens stepped back and Shurna shouted for the devout to protect their eyes. Kayarra closed his eyes and removed the stone's cover.

Every other time he'd held the ignited stone, either Manerra or Aya had cloaked it. But Aya had insisted that he handle the stone alone this time so there could be no question of his acceptance by the gods. How ironic if he injured himself by accidentally touching the uncovered stone.

After two failed attempts, the sack part of the cover finally snagged the crystal's curve and Kayarra pulled the fabric over and down. Then, just as he'd practiced with an ordinary rock and the temple stone's spare cover, he rolled the god-made crystal into the sack and flipped its flap over, extinguishing the light.

He opened his eyes, turned and, hands wet with perspiration and shaking, offered the cloaked stone to Aya.

Kayarra's knees wobbled as he returned to his position among the janquer, thankful for the concealing robe. His eyes swept the faces of his companions, disturbed by the strangers among them. Vextra, familiar only from the Shangren's abbahs, stood where Tura had been, and Benta, whom Kayarra did not remember meeting at the Shangren, stood in place of his sister. Two men, two women, and one demon, came that self-deprecating tally.

Aya concluded abbah and retreated to the east edge of the dais, where mats, cushions, and bowls lay arrayed. Kayarra trailed Denassa, taking his cues from her actions.

The janquer sat with their backs to the crowd on cushions placed along the edge of the dais. The shecarens settled on cushions in front of them.

Music drifted up the stairs, and crowd noises began to abate. Denassa lifted a tiny marble bowl and leaned close so Kayarra could hear, "No more than a sip. Eat before you taste it." She set the bowl down beside her supper bowl.

Silence was never fully achieved during mealtime.

Over the heads of the crowd, Kayarra watched food being distributed to the thousands who filled the plaza, leaf-wrapped packages and whole fruit passed hand-to-hand toward those in the center of the square.

Denassa nudged him and held out a bowl of sliced fruit. He took a piece, looked past her, and stared into the face of a woman watching him. Kayarra lowered the hand gripping the fruit to his knee and regarded the bowls arrayed before him. When the stranger's attention shifted away, he ate the fruit, then reached for a bronze utensil laying beside one of the bowls. The handle was a snake entwined around a branch. The snake's split tail formed a two-pronged fork. It's fangs created an ornamental brace for the bowl of a spoon. Twirling the utensil caused the snake's emerald eyes to glint in the day's fading sunlight.

Denassa touched the rim of a bowl and signed *water*.

Kayarra traded the fork-spoon for the bowl of water, holding it suspended above the cross of his legs while he watched Aya and Manerra eat, then watched the wagons at the edges of the crowd leave when their loads of food were exhausted. More wagons arrived. He finished drinking the water and declined Denassa's offer of additional fruit. Another wagon rolled away into the gathering dusk. Were they expected to sit there until the thousands filling the plaza finished eating?

He looked toward Denassa, but was distracted by a glowing disk beyond her shoulder. The globe of milky glass, lit within, was carried above the heads of the crowd by a woman covered, head to sandal, by a black robe. Kayarra searched for eye slits but saw none.

The globe bearer walked the white stone path from the Temple of Crysus. When she reached the altar steps, she started up, moving with a sensuous grace that kept the globe stationary above her head.

When the globe bearer reached the dais, musicians began strains of a strange, foreign music—the song Manerra had played after the unification prayer—music attributed to Yatra.

The dancer angled toward the shecarens then slid away, inscribing a circle atop the dais. She passed temporarily from sight behind the upright stone each time she completed a loop.

Kayarra, mesmerized by the simple beauty of the globe and the grace of the dancer, wondered whether the globe represented the temple stone. So spellbound was he that he missed the approach of a second dancer until the smaller globe entered his peripheral vision. Comprehension struck at once. The first dancer represented Ryna; the newcomer gliding the length of the bottommost step was Trys, her lover.

Ryna crossed the dais toward the shecarens then circled away in steps fantastically joined to the unworldly music. Trys climbed a step and slid along its length, passing Ryna across the distance that separated them as she completed a loop and started back.

The dance progressed with Trys rising a step at alternating ends of the dais while Ryna circled large and alone above him, each pass a little higher, a little closer.

Trys reached the platform as Ryna completed the farthest reach of her orbit. He glided after her as she slid toward the shecarens. Her next orbit narrowed with Trys beside and behind her, and their steps slowed as the music changed. Their courtship developed a more complicated wooing as they inscribed circles around each other. Finally, Ryna slid to a stop in front of the shecarens while Trys raised his globe to the level of hers and completed a slow circle of her body. When the circle was complete, a baby's nearby cry made Kayarra jump. So intent had he been upon the movement of the globes that he failed to notice a third person scurry across the dais and lay an infant beside Aya's knee.

A cheering roar from the crowd startled the infant anew. It wailed as Aya lifted it to his cheek, then held it out for Manerra's blessing. Manerra pressed his cheek to the baby's forehead but was prevented from withdrawing by the infant's grip in his hair. Aya laughed while Manerra gently opened the tiny fist and freed his braids.

Aya carefully returned the distraught child to its kneeling mother, who lifted the baby to her cloth-covered shoulder, gave veneration, then scurried away to calm her twice-honored, wailing infant.

When Kayarra's attention returned to the moon dancers, Ryna had extinguished her globe and was circling Trys, sweeping her darkened globe past his, taking Trys through the lunar phases: waning, eclipsed, waxing, full. Twice she circled him, then both dancers turned toward Aya, knelt, and placed their globes on the stone in front of him. Their cloth-covered heads dipped in grave nods, then they sidled sideways, slipped over the edge of the dais, down the stairs, and disappeared among the crowd.

Drum rolls started and the crowd roared, drowning out the flutes and even the drummers for a time. When Kayarra could hear the flutes again, they played a livelier tune, having quit Yatra's heavy, sorrowful music.

"We're free to go or stay," Denassa shouted into Kayarra's ear.

"You leave?" he shouted back.

"Soon."

"I wait," he told her and stopped trying to talk above the crowd's jubilant shouts.

Denassa dipped her finger into one of the marble cups and sucked the liquid from her fingertip. Kayarra did the same before he remembered that she'd told him to eat before taking any of the amber liquid. He reached for another slice of fruit.

Even the little bit he'd taken on his finger coated his tongue and mouth in an unpleasant way. When the fruit didn't cut through the coating, he signaled for water. Denassa reached for a distant bowl, passed it to him, and smiled.

"What is?" He pointed to the marble cup.

Her reply was incomprehensible.

He had meant his question to elicit an explanation, as if he'd asked, *What does it do?* But that's not what he'd asked, and Denassa had answered literally, and he wasn't willing to continue a conversation that made him feel like they argued.

Several women among the crowd had raised their hands above their heads, and nearby men circled them, thrusting their hips forward. Kayarra watched until his arousal became uncomfortable, then looked toward the shecarens. What he could see of Aya's face was a fleeting profile when the shon regis leaned close to speak to Manerra.

"I leave," Denassa yelled, gave veneration neither shecaren noticed, then thrust her legs over the edge of the dais and started down the stairs in a crouch. Kayarra followed. From the corner of his eye, he saw Shurna touch Aya's shoulder.

Kayarra felt exposed on the stairs; felt safer after they entered the gyrating crowd, although he looked over his shoulder to see whether any of the men from the trail ambush followed.

A bowl was shoved under his chin, and a woman's finger dipped into the amber liquid. He followed the finger back to her mouth, and watched her lips purse as she slowly withdrew the finger. She laughed when he flinched back, then laughed harder when someone's hand passed over his groin. He knocked the hand away and lunged after Denassa, his face burning, his anger sparked.

Just as he reached her, Denassa whirled and collided face-to-chest with him. He grabbed her shoulders as she rebounded.

"We must not separate," she gasped breathlessly, caught his hand, and held tightly until they broke free of the pressing crowd. When she tried to release his hand, he held onto it, craving the warmth and familiarity of her touch.

Denassa whirled, yanked free, and took hasty steps backward.

"Dee?" He halted and watched the distance between them increase.

She turned and walked hastily away. He followed because he didn't have a choice.

"Is hand touch bad?" he shouted after her when her pace slowed. He caught up with her when she stopped walking. "I am sorry, Denassa."

"What you did followed the moons' dance."

He knew she wasn't saying that because she thought him too stupid to understand what he'd seen. "I not understand."

"The moons bring the shecarens," she said, avoiding his eyes.

"Denassa, I not Yatren."

She gasped and looked over her shoulder. Too late, he realized his mistake in saying that where he could be overheard. Denassa started walking again, her attention on the ground. "When the moons join, we are given a shecaren," she said. "Men can only duplicate that event with the birth of a child. Will you tell me that you did not feel the power in the dance and the effects of the itenyan?"

The amber syrup. An aphrodisiac? He felt as violated as he had when that hand fell upon his crotch. "I not love you. I not sex you. Why iten—" his pronunciation fell apart in his anger. He started past her, angry at what felt like trickery, angry at all the things he didn't understand.

"It's tradition that we participate," Denassa called after him, following him, because she didn't have a choice in what she did, either.

He stopped and turned. "How—" Distress shredded what vocabulary he had, brought him face-to-face with a concept he had no way to express. *How do you cope?* he wanted to demand, when the question was better asked of Aya. "I want you," he confessed what she could see by looking at him. "I love you."

"Please stop," she begged.

"Touch me." He held out his hand in entreaty.

She turned and started away.

He followed, careful to keep an arm's length of distance between them. "I not say love because I drink drink," he informed her.

They entered the grove of trees that separated the plaza from the orchard. Intertwining branches cast shadows across her face.

"Tell me you have no wife, no children," she demanded.

"You know I not know," he said. "You say I love you. You now hatred me?"

She stopped and turned. He stopped walking. "There are too many things we don't know, too many things I do know. None of them have anything to do with hatred. That I love you only confuses me."

His heart pounded.

"I know what Aya and Yutrenta suffer," she said.

He took a step toward her. She retreated. "I need to look upon Yutrenta," she said.

*****

Kayarra retrieved his belt from the table in the audience room where he'd left it and used the excuse of buckling it on to keep his eyes averted from the kitchen workers. He only looked up when he reached the stairs. His physical ache would require relief if he hoped to sleep.

The floor of the landing creaked its familiar complaints, sounding unusually loud in the silent hall. He passed Shurna's vacant room on the right and Aya's closed door on the left. He was halfway to his own room when a stranger with unbraided hair, wearing a sleeveless robe, stepped through the open doorway ahead of him.

Kayarra gave a startled cry and jumped backward, shoulder colliding with the wall. The stranger's hand moved and Kayarra reached for his own knife. He was staring at the point of the stranger's blade even as his knife hand swung up and around.

"That knife isn't yours," the dark giant growled.

Kayarra glanced at his knife hand only to have that wrist slammed against the wall. The knife fell from suddenly numb fingers.

"Vantrann!" Denassa screamed. "Release him."

Vantrann chuckled and stepped back. "So this is my demon brother," he remarked.

Kayarra cradled his bruised hand. His eyes swept Vantrann's hands and he realized with a secondary shock that the knife Vantrann had held seconds earlier was now sheathed. Denassa would see only the damning evidence of his own knife—Manerra's damned knife—on the floor while Vantrann stood barehanded. A chill swept him.

"Kayarra, are you all right?" Denassa grabbed his forearm and pulled his wrist toward her.

He tilted his head.

Vantrann bent, retrieved the knife, and offered it hilt-first to Kayarra's hand. "I'd like to hear the story of how this knife came into your possession," Vantrann remarked, "and how you haven't lost it to another before now."

Denassa gasped and looked up. "You'll bring complaint against him?" she demanded.

Vantrann hesitated as though considering the idea. "No," he said, "there was no harm done. I startled him, after all. And I hear from the housekeepers that you've reason to be nervous."

Denassa rubbed Kayarra's bruised hand before releasing it. "Come downstairs," she urged. "Both of you come downstairs. Lansa's made tea, and our companions will return from the ceremony soon."

Vantrann eyed Kayarra. "Go ahead. I would free the twigs from my hair first. I only came out because I thought Manerra might have returned." Vantrann gave a cursory nod—the first Kayarra had seen that managed to be devoid of regard or respect—reentered his room, and closed the door.

"Come." Denassa tugged Kayarra's sleeve. "Let me look at your hand in better light. It's time you met our Thurrang janquer."

But Kayarra had met him and suspected there wasn't much more he cared to know about Vantrann. He tilted his head though and followed Denassa downstairs, his blood pumped with so much adrenaline, sleep was now impossible.

* * * * *

Shurna preceded Benta through the audience room, its antechamber, and started down the hall before she noticed Kayarra and Denassa seated at the kitchen table. The tension in Kayarra's shoulders drew her past Yutrenta's closed door and into the kitchen. She watched Denassa's head jerk up at the sound of her footsteps, saw the lines of tension around Denassa's eyes, and cringed at the thought of anything else going wrong.

"Janquer lady Shurna, lord Benta." Denassa's smile stretched her lips.

Kayarra pulled his hand from Denassa's, and Shurna glimpsed an unusual redness across his knuckles before his hand disappeared into his lap.

"Janquer lady Denassa," Benta returned her acknowledgement. "Janquer lord Kayarra."

"If you've time for tea," Denassa said, "janquer lord Vantrann will be joining us soon."

Shurna's heart began thumping.

"A gracious invitation," Benta answered, "but in the few moments I have, I'd hoped to look upon my sister. I hope you understand."

*No wishes for good health extended to our long-time-absent Thurrang janquer?* Shurna mused.

"Certainly," Denassa replied. "Walk safely, lord Benta."

Benta nodded in leave taking, and Shurna escorted him back down the hall to the door of Yutrenta's room.

By the time she returned to the kitchen, Lansa had set bowls of tea upon the table. However, Shurna's attention went to the stairs in disbelief of Denassa's news. *Vantrann! Here.*

"Lansa, give us privacy, please," Denassa said. "I'll take over service. If the shecarens need you when they return, I'll call for you." And as Lansa started toward the hall, Denassa voiced a heartfelt, "Thank you."

A door opened and shut in the hall. Shurna looked back and saw Benta signal *asleep*, offer veneration, then hasten toward the audience room. Gods, if she could run, she'd do the same. She looked back in time to see Vantrann descend the stairs. His attention fixed on her and he grinned.

He'd lost weight.

"You've cut a thin slice off the shon regis's orders," Shurna said before Vantrann could speak.

He reached the base of the stairs and started toward her. "I live for your praises." His arms encircled her shoulders, drew her close, and she rested her hands on his waist. The leather of his shoulder belt mingled with the odor of his sweat. She pulled back, but he held his embrace. When he released her, she was interested to see the perfunctory nod he offered Denassa, how he ignored Kayarra. He circled the table and settled in a vacant chair near the wall—the chair opposite her customary seat. She considered sitting at the other end of the table, beside Denassa, but such a move would be too obvious a slight.

"When did you arrive?" She slid into the seat opposite him.

"I saw the beginning of the moon dance," Vantrann said, "but was too dirty from the trip to force my way through that crowd. I sent my men to find tent space and came on to the house. I suspected lady Denassa would not stay for the wilder festivities." He winked at Denassa.

"Have you spoken to Trenta?" Denassa inquired.

"She was asleep. I didn't wake her." Vantrann's attention shifted to Kayarra. "Who was that in the Thurrang position?"

"Vextra of Duric."

Vantrann's attention snapped back to her. "Who in Acrahh's ass is he?"

"Vantrann!" Denassa protested.

"Sorry, sweet sister," Vantrann's apology lacked contrition.

"Vextra served us at the Shangren. Aya asked for him when we arrived," Shurna said.

"Did lord Tura refuse service?"

"He's served us, as well." *Yes, he's here, Van. Were you chasing Tura across the Ofrann? Is that why you're here?* "Did you see lord Sitra before you left Thurra? Tura says he was ill." *Pray Acrahh he's alive, Van, and still is.*

Vantrann's attention returned to her with surprise. "Lord Sitra's old, not infirmed. Likely, he'll outlive us all. I'm surprised Tura inquired after him. Sitra suggested that Tura's sudden departure was the result of a quarrel."

Shurna spread her fingers on the tabletop. "Guilt may have driven him to inquire." *Guilt. That emotion you've never suffered.*

Vantrann's attention returned to Kayarra. "Do you speak?" he asked.

"Yes," Kayarra answered.

"Then tell me what you are, and how you secured the unification prayer faster than any supplicant in Yatren history."

"Vantrann!" Denassa protested.

Shurna caught Kayarra's confused glance and intervened. "Manerra came upon Kayarra in the borderlands. The Manteen held him atop a plateau. Manerra took him from them."

"And Kayarra cannot tell me this himself?"

"No, he can't. He still learns our words."

"So he's Manteen."

"No."

Vantrann frowned. "So he *is* a demon."

Denassa stood so suddenly, her chair clattered to the floor. "He's not a demon!"

"Then what is he?" Vantrann shouted back. "Can no one answer a simple question?"

"Aya believes him to be a member of a lost tribe," Denassa retorted. "You will do well to remember that in Aya's presence."

"And in yours," Vantrann remarked. "My apologies for the insult to your demon lover."

Denassa lifted her tea bowl and threw it on the floor. Tea splattered Shurna's robe and a pottery fragment hit the wall by the door. Denassa whirled, ran to the kitchen door, yanked it open, and slammed it as she left.

Vantrann started laughing. Shurna saw Kayarra's fist clench and leapt from her chair even as he stood.

"No, Kayarra. No." Shurna reached a hand to his chest. "Aya will not abide fighting among the janquer. Go to your room. No one will bother you there."

"Don't go, Kayarra." Vantrann rubbed a knuckle across one eye, his laughter bringing tears. "I would hear more about this wonder of the lost tribe."

Kayarra's jaw clenched. "I go," he said, turned, and headed for the stairs.

"Oh, Kayarra, I'm sorry." The laughter in Vantrann's voice made a mockery of the apology.

Shurna folded her arms. "That ingratiated you to no one," she observed.

"I only teased," he said. "How could I know my little Ringgangley sister was in love with a . . . whatever." He shook his head.

"You don't know, do you?"

"Know what?" He sobered.

"The attack on Yutrenta came from one of your too-often-teased Thurrangy sisters. If I were you, I would not presume upon Aya's tolerance for Thurrang humor right now. His patience has been sorely tested."

"You must pity me tonight. Has our separation made you appreciate my better qualities, or is it only the itenyan you swallowed?"

Shurna laughed. "Vantrann, you have no better qualities. Perhaps my humor is only grateful for the reprieve of your absence. In another day, I will recall everything I despise about you."

"Then take me as husband. Tonight."

"Van—" She couldn't say what she thought.

He stood and leaned both hands upon the table. "More than a year in Zarthon has reminded me of the stupidity of Thurrangy women. I don't think I've sinned enough to warrant lifelong boredom. With you as wife, I would willingly honor banishment to Kaytron."

Her laugh held scorn. "Within a seven-night, I would be a widow."

"But what a glorious seven-night. And I think you would not kill me."

"It's my Kitarin sisters whose tolerance I doubt."

Vantrann smiled and started around the table.

Shurna crossed to a towel rack in the corner near the yard door. She listened for a splash or crunch of broken pottery that warned of Vantrann's approach. He didn't follow.

"Are there no women left unbeaten in Thurra?" she asked as she selected a towel. When she turned, Vantrann stood at the corner of the table nearest the hall door.

"Many," Vantrann replied.

Shurna grabbed the midden basin on her way back to the table. Halfway across the room, she bent and picked up a shard of pottery.

"Thurrang men do not compare stories of wife beatings," Vantrann said. "And despite rumor, beatings are not as prevalent as outsiders assume."

"Siblings are outsiders?" Shurna asked, then said before he could answer, "If you men don't talk, you don't know. There is danger in ignorance." She dropped the towel into the puddle of tea and bent to reach more pottery fragments.

"I did not travel so far and so hard to argue customs with my Kitarin lover."

She snorted.

"I am, however, curious about this lost creature. Has he flown or set metal aflame?"

"No, nor can he. He's really too ordinary for your tastes." She wrung the dripping towel over the basin, then again dropped it into the tea spill.

"How can you say that? Look at his hair, skin, eyes. Listen to him speak. He's quite extraordinary."

"He'll be pleased you approve . . . once his hand heals and he's recovered from your insults."

"I only thought to preserve my skin intact."

She had been right about Kayarra's hand.

"As for the insult, how was I to know he was smitten with little Dee? I spoke in jest. I told them so."

"You'd do well to offer them a formal apology."

"If you will not wed me, perhaps you will introduce me to some of your unwed Kitarin sisters."

A large chunk of pottery hit the basin with a clang. "This nation is not prepared for such an unholy alliance."

"You never said that about Hyran."

She whipped her head around, all jest forgotten. "There is something about Hyran you would emulate?"

"Only an appreciation for his choice in mates."

"Why this sudden interest in marriage? Are you weary of Acrahh's service?"

Movement in the doorway caught her eye. Vantrann's attention shifted and he dropped to hands and knees, his hair brushing the floor tiles.

Shurna rose smoothly to her feet, a pottery fragment in one hand, the dripping towel in the other. "Lord Vantrann joins us after all," she told Aya, quite unnecessarily.

# CHAPTER 63

"I expected you sooner," Aya said over Vantrann's bowed head. He had halted inside the kitchen door, Manerra behind him.

"Shon regis, there were complications," Vantrann answered without lifting his face from the floor. "The delay was unavoidable."

"Look at me," Aya ordered.

Vantrann settled back upon his heels.

"I will hear your explanations, but not tonight. High Council will meet in the morning after abbah. Shurna, spread word to the others. It's the only obligation I place upon you tomorrow." Which was as close as he came to apologizing for calling them to duty on their holiest day. Even the housekeepers did not work except by personal choice. Aya looked at her. "Where is Denassa?"

"With the mia, I believe."

"Send her to my room when she returns." Aya looked back at Vantrann. "Your return is ostentatious. Do not expect tomorrow to be leisurely. You'll do well to take what rest you can now. Good night to you both." He nodded to each of them, then headed toward the stairs.

Manerra did not follow him.

"Shecaren." Vantrann's grin returned. He rose from obeisance with unexpected grace and closed the distance between them. They met in embrace, Manerra's enthusiasm less apparent than Vantrann's.

Manerra pulled back. "A day later and you'd have missed the joining."

"Lady Shurna was gracious enough to say as much." Vantrann's grin wilted. "It was a hard trip."

Manerra started toward the hearth. Shurna squatted to pick up the midden basin, heard the crunch of pottery, and watched Manerra lift a foot to inspect his sandal. "What went on here?" He plucked a fragment of pottery from the leather sole and dropped it into Shurna's bowl.

"Ask your Thurrang friend to describe his homecoming," Shurna suggested.

Vantrann shrugged. "Dee was offended by a jest."

"More than that," Shurna countered. "Kayarra would have hit him if I'd not intervened."

Manerra's eyes widened. "How long have you been here?" he

demanded.

"I saw part of the moon dance from the edges of the crowd when I arrived."

"Who flung the bowl?"

"Denassa."

"Why?"

"I stumbled upon her love affair with the . . . lost janquer."

Shurna saw Manerra's shock. "There is no affair," she assured. "They would not desecrate their vows in such a way." She silently cursed Vantrann. That rumor was the kind of weapon he would never relinquish.

"The man's name is Kayarra," Manerra said.

"You rescued him alone?" Vantrann's grin returned. "Our year of hunting netted interesting game."

Shurna's attention snapped to Vantrann's face. His grin disappeared. Beside him, Manerra missed a breath.

If Vantrann was dismayed by that slip, his imagination was severely limited.

"Those days are gone," Manerra said. "A lot has changed."

"So I'm learning."

Manerra poured a bowl of tea. Unattended, the hearth fire had burned down to a scattering of coals. Manerra turned, the tea bowl cupped in both hands. "I suppose Korrane told you about our Shangren stay."

"I didn't take the Shangren trade route," Vantrann said.

"What about restitution?" Manerra demanded, obviously shocked. "That's why Aya left you in Thurra."

Shurna interrupted, "Aya means to discuss these matters tomorrow," but Vantrann spoke over her: "I sent men to invite Casta's representative to Zarthon in order to settle Sitra's complaints, but they didn't arrive before I left. I appointed my father to stand in my stead."

"You don't know about Casta's death," Manerra said.

"What?" Vantrann gasped. "What happened to Casta?"

"His heart failed. Aya revived him, but he survived less than a day. Aya accepted Korrane's vow of homage."

"Yutrenta didn't take the position?" Vantrann was aghast.

"Not everyone is seduced by position and power," Shurna said.

The expression Vantrann shot her made her understand that he considered such individuals fools.

"If you didn't come by the Shangren trade route, how did you come?" Manerra asked.

"Across the interior basin."

"One foolish action doesn't compensate another!" Shurna gasped.

"We arrived without loss of man," Vantrann protested, "and before the joining."

"Barely, to both, I wager," Shurna countered.

Vantrann's flush, combined with his phrasing, alarmed her. "What loss to animals?" she demanded.

"The mia and two shuren."

She flung up both hands but was too late to prevent Manerra from asking, "How many mia?"

"Twelve." Vantrann did not look at her.

Shurna stepped aside, sat down, and covered her face.

"Aya expected me at the joining," Vantrann argued. "I could not keep my vows with clear conscience if I disappointed him."

Shurna bit into her lip to prevent a retort she would absolutely regret. She stood. "I cannot stay," her tone let them know she was anything but sorry. "This day has gifted too many shocks. If I don't—"

A frantic banging reverberated eerily through the silent house. Shurna stared with disbelief toward the audience room. "Gods, no!"

A door beyond Yutrenta's room opened and Rayas lurched out with a lamp in hand, headed toward the front door. Overhead, floorboards creaked. Manerra started after Rayas, Vantrann following. Shurna hugged herself and lowered her head.

Moments later, the banging stopped and a woman's shrill, frantic voice was heard, then Rayas's baritone trying to calm her hysteria.

Shurna pushed away from the table, crossed to the outside door, and opened it. She saw Denassa hurrying across the moonlit yard toward her. As the kitchen light fell on Denassa's face, Shurna saw it was still flushed.

"What now?" Denassa demanded at nearly the same time Aya asked from behind, "What's wrong?"

"A woman asks for a physician and shecaren," Shurna told them together.

"Manerra?" Aya asked.

Until Shurna glanced toward the hall door, she thought he asked whether Manerra could handle the task, but the shecaren stood in the kitchen doorway.

"Five men experimented with dayflower," Manerra reported. "This woman's husband is one. She begs for a shecaren and physician."

"Shurna, come with us," Aya ordered and strode toward the door. "Manerra, stay here."

Shurna glanced at the stairwell. Everything she desired resided upstairs.

Kayarra stood on the stairs and must have seen her desperation but said nothing. What could he do, after all? She envied his innocence.

She turned and followed Aya through the hall, conscious of the housekeepers' somber stares as they passed.

*****

Although it was nearly moonset by the time they returned, Lansa had waited for them. She had rekindled the hearth fire, cleaned up the remaining shards of broken pottery and spilt tea, and heated water.

It had rained while they were out, a brief, sudden downpour that soaked everyone and everything and turned hard-packed ground into red mud.

Shurna crossed to the hearth, reached for the fire's warmth, and only then noticed the mud soiling her robe and caking her sandals.

Aya and Denassa passed, headed for the stairs, but Shurna was too cold and exhausted to make that ascent. She closed her eyes and considered the empty bed in Yutrenta's room, but supposed Kara slept there. Aya and Denassa politely refused Lansa's offers of tea and food. Shurna listened to her companions' footfalls as they ascended the stairs.

"I'll bring a dry robe, lady," Lansa offered.

By the time Shurna realized that Lansa had spoken to her and opened her eyes, Lansa was gone.

Shurna stared into the steaming kettle of water.

Aya had requested her assistance with the emergency because dayflower enhanced fear. Any physician who knew how to prepare and administer the herb did not abandon an individual who had consumed it. Reassurances were as much a part of treatment as the tea itself. Aya had thought her skills might be necessary, but their summons had come too late. One man lay dead when they arrived; the others screamed and convulsed. Denassa's only recourse had been to mix exceptionally strong draydine into the remaining poison. Aya had administered the draught.

That camp was a slaughter ground when they left.

Great Acrahh, could there be a worse heralding of the joining?

Yes, if Yutrenta had died.

In her twelve years with the shecarens, she'd not seen such carnage. First in Varaar field, then at the Shangren, now here. What was happening to their nation?

Hyran had wanted to prove that Aya could not control national disorder even with janquer support. Yet Hyran had not been strong enough to maintain control if Aya had failed. Had Hyran's hatred no logical hope, after all—only the rationale that if he had no chance at power, Aya should have none either?

No fire in the world was hot enough to warm her.

Lansa hurried back. "Here's a blanket, lady."

Shurna reached for the ties at the nape of her neck, loosened the cords enough to slip the fabric over each shoulder, and let the robe fall with a sodden plop. Lansa draped the blanket over her bare shoulders, then knelt to unfasten her sandals. Shurna felt like an infant in Lansa's care.

Lansa freed both sandals, then scooped warm water into a washbasin and bathed Shurna's feet and legs. Droplets sizzled and hissed where they splashed too close to the flames.

When Shurna's feet and legs were clean and the wash water was its own umber blood, Lansa beseeched, "Let me help you to bed, lady."

"Thank you, Lansa," Shurna mumbled and felt the housekeeper take her arm. And next knew Alva waking her with insistences that she prepare for abbah, unaware of how she had made it to bed or how long she'd been there.

* * * * *

A single lamp burned with a low flame, its light not bright enough to sear Yutrenta's eyes when she opened them. Aya knelt at her bedside, face uplifted, eyes closed in an attitude of prayer.

Her eyelids drooped shut of their own accord, her will still governed by the draydine she'd consumed. She sluggishly pondered the image impressed upon her retinas: Aya's haggard face defined in the stark contrasts of lamplight and shadow.

Yutrenta slid her hand beneath the covers, reaching for his hand, but fell asleep before touching him.

* * * * *

The bowl on the table beside Yutrenta's chair in the audience room remained untouched. The presence of the bowl and its contents was the compromise she had agreed to in order to gain the privacy of the audience room, but it wasn't one she intended to use.

Sitting in the audience room when the shecarens and janquer returned from abbah was her private test of strength and fortitude in anticipation of the evening's rituals. She could not—dared not—allow another to take her place in the rituals of the joining. Fear and rumors were evoking a revival of the superstitious practice of warding, which indicated serious problems that demanded a strong demonstration of unity. The nation's leaders could not show weakness tonight, of all nights.

Yutrenta had been told of Vantrann's arrival, but seeing him walk through the audience room door was still a shock. He'd lost weight—most obvious in his face—and his hair was longer. He advanced upon her chair and offered Ofrann veneration. She wondered whether he intended mockery by offering a form of veneration he did not recognize as proper. "Janquer lord Vantrann," she acknowledged him.

He raised his head. "Janquer lady Yutrenta, know that Thurra grieves the loss of lord Casta."

"Thank you, lord Vantrann," she said, unprepared for the grief that reminder brought to the fore.

Aya crossed to the chairs by the unlit hearth, but Shurna sank onto the table nearest the door as if she hadn't the strength to take a step farther. Kayarra and Denassa chose seats nearby, and Manerra lingered near the wall as if undecided where he should sit.

"Taycra," Aya called to a housekeeper waiting inside the ante-chamber door, "bring tea. Then make certain no one enters the antechamber so long as this door is shut. Go, please."

Taycra hurried away.

"Are peacekeepers guarding the front door?" Yutrenta asked.

"There are no audiences today," Aya said. "But yes, they are. And I urge each of you to nap today, but not at the expense of your cleansing. I remind anyone who has obligations in Cha-ka or elsewhere to keep an escort. Our peacekeepers have volunteered their services today, as have Rayas and some of the house staff . . . . Thank you, Taycra. Come in."

Heads turned toward the door as Taycra entered carrying a tray laden with bowls. She approached the shecarens first, then circled the room with her offerings. Only Vantrann refused tea. Manerra closed the door after Taycra left the room.

Their privacy assured, Aya sat down, said, "I would conclude this meeting quickly. Vantrann—"

Vantrann hastened toward Aya's chair, dropped upon elbows and knees, and pressed his forehead to the floor.

"I want only the factual information you learned regarding the Hyranian attack at Varaar field. Van, sit up."

The Thurrang settled back upon his heels and remained there, like an overgrown child kneeling at his father's feet.

"Where shall I start?" Vantrann asked.

"With Ouban," Aya suggested.

"He clarified the question of the arentas, shon regis."

"Then enlighten me."

"As we've heard before, according to Ouban, Acrahh first visited Hyran as he was falling asleep one night. Acrahh spoke Hyran's name and called him arenta, blessed child. That's when Acrahh supposedly told Hyran that the children of Yatra had grown too many, their needs too great, for his sons to attend. Acrahh ordered Hyran to offer you his services. What we haven't heard before is that Acrahh supposedly told Hyran that he feared his sons had grown arrogant. That in their pride, they would likely scoff at Hyran's message and spurn his offer."

"Then Acrahh would have done better to have visited his sons, don't you think?" Manerra demanded.

"Settle, Manerra," Aya ordered. "So, how does this vision justify wonton destruction?" Aya asked.

"Acrahh is supposed to have told Hyran, 'Do not shed the blood of any man; only show my sons how they may no longer rule north, south, east and west alone. They break their hearts trying and I will not have them sent to me prematurely when the arentas are able to share their burden.'

"Apparently, Acrahh also instructed Hyran to wed only another arenta, and he was given a power for miracles that other men would recognize the truth of his claims."

"What power for miracles?" Aya demanded.

"What Ouban described as miracles were kindnesses visited upon the poor. The things not so easily explained sounded like Kitarin tricks Myra would have taught him.

"According to Ouban and others I questioned, Acrahh's predictions came true when you refused your half-brother's services."

Manerra snorted.

"Is there more?" Aya asked.

"Very little. The husband and wife Ouban named to corroborate his story said only that Hyran's staunchest followers were nomads and nearly impossible to locate. Other sources said there are poor farmers and even some of Myra's friends in Kita who support Hyran's efforts. However, they would not name other Hyranians."

"Silence has been their greatest weapon," Manerra remarked.

"What do his followers gain by their support?" Aya asked.

"If you ask what promises he made, that I can't say. I've heard only general promises of a better life—an easier life—where their complaints would be heard. They envisioned Hyran overseeing local problems while you attended intertribal disputes.

"Ouban and the farmer both said Hyran anticipated your arrival in Thurra at the conclusion of Manerra's training. Hyran's slaughter of the mia was intended to force a meeting with you. But Hyran underestimated Varaar's defenses, and his murder threw his followers into confusion. Thus, you were able to leave Thurra before they recovered from the blow."

"Does Myra lead in his stead?"

"While Hyran lived, she did not, although, apparently, he converted her with his tale of divine blessing and purpose. She actively aided in the care of the poor, so her position as his supporter is well established. I think that only since Hyran's death has she been seen as the arenta who will fulfill Acrahh's prophecy, and your lengthy absences from the south makes the idea of her leadership appealing."

"A woman leader in the south?" Shurna asked incredulously.

"Who supports her leadership?" Aya asked.

"Mostly, southern Ofrann, but I've been told there are those in northern Thurra who secretly support Myra, and supported Hyran before her."

"The southern nomads bring only their most persistent problems to Ofrann leaders," Aya mused. "I can understand their support of Hyran, but can't imagine their acceptance of a foreign leader. But it interests me that Thurrang are so sympathetic to the Hyranian cause. Do they mean to set Myra up as a local power answerable to Korrane and Razon, or equal to them?"

"The criminals I questioned were unclear about boundaries of power. They thought Myra would hold a position equivalent to janquer and yet remain in south Ofrann to either force Cas— *Korrane* and my father to greater attention to their complaints, or usurp their power and independently govern some portion of the Ofrann, answerable only to you."

"Myra recognizes my authority?" Aya's skepticism was audible through his surprise.

"Probably not," Denassa remarked.

"I don't know," Vantrann confessed. "I know only what Hyran's followers have been led to believe . . . or fabricated. Their support is being won by a claim of divine decree and the vision of arentas, janquer, and shecarens holding joint rule."

"And Mante's promise of an idyllic life," Yutrenta offered.

Aya drummed his fingertips on the chair's armrest. "I am sorely tempted to test Myra's allegiance."

"A meeting with her would appear to legitimize her claims to a position she doesn't hold," Shurna said.

"I will not meet with her," Aya assured. "There is nothing I can say that will not be twisted to her benefit. Rather, I would order her return to Kita and have lady Toma deal with her. Or, if she's foresworn her birth tribe, have her appear before Korrane. But I think she will not risk Korrane's mercy after all that Hyran has burdened the Ofrann government."

"Aya, proceed with caution on this," Yutrenta begged. "I've seen the extremes to which one woman will go to maintain a lie. The power Myra risks losing is far greater than what Ura sought."

Aya met her eyes. "Your warning is heeded, Yutrenta. I'm willing to let Toma deal with her so long as Myra cooperates. My greater concerns are the problems that underlie southern unrest. Hyran would not have gained the power he did if those problems did not exist. If we can solve local complaints, I think Hyran's claim that my father champions the arentas' cause will not withstand a revision.

"I will meet with Ofrann and Thurrang alike at the conclusion of the joining and hear their grievances. If some matters can be resolved here, or even identified, our work may be less in Thurra and the Ofrann, where distances and travel are troublesome."

“I wonder,” Yutrenta said, “whether Thurrang and Ofrann criminals are using the animosity between tribes to shift blame for their thefts onto the Hyranians."

"Likely," Aya said, "but you cross into speculation, which I didn't want to do."

"But resolutions that don’t halt the raids will appear to be failures. The raids are the crux of Thurrang complaints against the Ofrann."

Aya raised a hand. "I must end this council," he said. "Not because your concerns aren't valid, but simply because I can't deal with anything more without sleep. I ask that each of you remain available to private audiences. Bring me any new information that has bearing on these matters. I will be available before every abbah, but few other matters cannot be interrupted if the news is important enough.

"Vantrann, I would meet with you privately, but not today. I would hope to have some sense about me when we speak. Make yourself available to me tomorrow.

"Manerra, please handle what you can while I sleep. None of you forget your cleansing." Aya stood, and Manerra pushed away from the wall.

Before Aya reached the door, Yutrenta said, "The janquer wish longevity to the sons of Acrahh on this day of their birth."

Both shecarens turned. Aya's smile twitched his lips. "My thanks and gratitude to each of you for your unfailing service. Right now, longevity will seem more appealing with sleep. Wake me if there is a need." He left.

* * * * *

Kayarra reached to stop Shurna before she passed. "What is clean-sing?" he asked.

"Manerra will show you," she said and stepped around him, leaving him in dismay. He thought about asking Denassa, but she assisted Yutrenta.

Kayarra hung back, hoping Vantrann would leave, but the Thurrang seemed to have plans that included Manerra.

"Kayarra?" Manerra inquired.

"Shurna say I ask what is clean-sing."

Vantrann laughed.

Kayarra didn't want to know whether it was his speech or his question that Vantrann thought amusing.

"Get a clean robe and loincloth. Meet us in the kitchen. We'll go now," Manerra said, glancing at Vantrann, who tilted his head. "Wear a travel robe."

Kayarra left the audience room. The thought of going anywhere with those two made his stomach clench. If Aya hadn't stressed the importance of this thing, he'd go to his room and stay there until evening abbah.

Alva was alone in the kitchen when Kayarra returned with the required items. For fifteen minutes, he sat at the table and ignored her covert glances. Finally, she located a vegetable, turned her back, and bent over the cutting block. Not that he wanted her attention while she held a knife, but acknowledgement of his existence would have been a courtesy.

He began to believe that Manerra and Vantrann had played him for a fool by ordering him to wait and then leaving without him.

Heavy footsteps on the stairs brought his attention around. He watched Manerra and Vantrann descend. They reached the kitchen's floor tiles and headed toward the outside door as if they'd forgotten he was to accompany them. Kayarra followed, hating the feeling of being at their mercy.

Two armed men lounging on a door-side bench leapt to their feet and flanked them as they started across the yard.

Manerra and Vantrann crossed the guarded log bridge, then turned left toward the plaza and the Temple of Crysus. Only the presence of escorts prevented Kayarra from turning back. Manerra wasn't likely to harm him in front of witnesses. If the guards were ordered away, he'd leave with them. Facing Aya's anger for disobeying Manerra was better than suffering anything Manerra had in mind.

The plaza teemed with people standing, sitting, sleeping, eating, or weaving through the thinned crowd. Manerra and Vantrann, in their plain robes, passed unnoticed. Kayarra lifted the hood of his robe, drew his hands inside his sleeves, kept his attention on the flagstones, and still felt exposed and vulnerable.

At the far corner of the Temple of Crysus, a dirt path entered trees bordering the lake's north shore. Children walked the trunk of a fallen tree, arms outstretched, whooping and shouting when a playmate fell. Farther down the trail, with sounds from the plaza muted, they startled a boy and girl in embrace. The girl darted into the trees. The boy, flushed, stolidly watched them pass. One of their guards ordered the boy to return to the plaza.

Glimpses of water through the trees showed reflections of mountain and sky, and shorelines softened by shade. Beyond the distant shore, the ground rose sharply skyward, the base of the mountain they'd crossed to reach this valley. Gazing at the towering ridge, Kayarra found it difficult to believe that he'd walked that mountain's slope. He glimpsed the outcropping where he'd caught first sight of the lake, temple, and valley.

"Here," Manerra said, snapping Kayarra's attention back to the trail and his companions. *Here* was a break in the brush and trees that lined the lake's shore, and a path that wound down between boulders to water-lapped pebbles. Thirty feet offshore rose a tiny island with its own water-lapped boulders and a dozen trees.

Kayarra remained on the trail with their escorts while Manerra and Vantrann descended to the pebbled beach. His suspicion of purpose was confirmed when they tossed the clothing they carried onto a boulder and began loosening the laces of their robes.

"Is a . . . 'nother way . . . clean-sing?" he called down to them.

Manerra and Vantrann looked back and up.

"What do you hide beneath that skirt?" Vantrann shot back.

Manerra slapped his arm. "There is a bathhouse at the House of Moons. You can use that, but you'll have to heat your own water."

"I heat water," Kayarra answered with forced civility, wondering why that option had not been offered earlier.

Manerra turned away, drew his knife, and began cutting off the tips of braids, dropping the loose ends onto the ground. Vantrann began unraveling the shortened braids.

"No Thurrang would waste so much time on vanity," Vantrann grumbled.

"No?" Manerra challenged. "How long do you spend untangling your hair after a mounted hunt?"

Vantrann ignored the question, asked instead, "The Kayarran do not perform domestic tasks?"

"Stop!" Manerra ordered, and Vantrann dropped his hands to his sides. "Kayarra, stay where you are," Manerra warned, although Kayarra hadn't moved. "I would not set you two so close together. Matters have grown too serious for jest."

Vantrann turned around, bowed to Kayarra. "I embrace my demon brother."

Manerra's face showed his anger. "Kayarra is janquer. You'll do more than embrace him before our stay is through. Your gesture of acceptance is expected." Manerra turned his attention onto Kayarra, as if he expected Kayarra to meet Vantrann halfway.

*Gesture of acceptance.* Kayarra shuddered, almost certain he understood Manerra's reference. Vantrann's revulsion substantiated his guess.

"No more of this," Manerra said and reached for another braid.

Kayarra caught Vantrann's eye before he turned away and knew that nothing Manerra said softened Vantrann's feelings. If anything, Manerra's warning drove Vantrann's hatred underground, where it would wage a more dangerous war.

Kayarra thought he knew where Manerra had learned his tactics, and in no way welcomed a battle with Vantrann.

Kayarra left the trail, crossed to a shaded rock and sat down, where he gazed at the temple's columns and pediment visible above the trees. He tried to imagine the strength and skill needed to shape and lift such massive stones but his imagination failed.

At long last, a splashing dive broke the quiet of the forest, and he shut his ears to the splashes, hoots and shouts that followed. He wasn't part of their camaraderie, only part of their problems. And yet, Aya fought even his brother-successor to assure his safety.

Why?

That was the one question whose answer he'd never understood.

# CHAPTER 64

Denassa jerked awake, heart pounding, and reared halfway to sitting before awareness asserted control. She dropped back onto an elbow before she realized she smelled smoke, then swung her feet to the floor, crossed to the table, and adjusted the lamp wick until the flame burned clean.

She wasn't convinced the guttering flame had awakened her, but any dream remnant had disappeared.

Barefooted, she crossed the room, passed along the hall, and padded down the stairs, her passage silent except for the creaking floorboards.

Alva worked in the kitchen. The outside door stood open, inviting a breeze, and the beginnings of soup rested on a tripod over the hearth flames. The much larger cookpot suspended on the hearth hook contained water.

"Alva, this is your rest day!" Denassa scolded.

"My rest days happen when the shon regis travels," Alva answered, "and number many more than yours. Besides, Rayas and I must eat. It's a small matter to fix a little extra."

Denassa hugged Alva awkwardly from the side and won a smile.

"There's water aplenty for bathing," Alva added.

Denassa laughed. "Is my need so obvious? First, I want to check on Yutrenta."

"Lady Yutrenta's in the audience room."

That news caused Denassa to pause. "She's with someone?"

"No, lady. The guests left, but lady Yutrenta asked to sit. Said she's tired of being bedridden."

Denassa pressed Alva's arm and headed down the hall toward the audience room. She found Yutrenta sitting alone in one of the hearth chairs. Faint light from neglected lamps placed the room in dusk. Denassa paused beside a lamp and raised its wick.

"There will be a new shecaren," Yutrenta said as though she remarked upon a breeze.

Denassa stood stunned. Tears sprang and spilled in the course of a blink and she turned, laughing, toward the impassive woman. "You're not thrilled?" Denassa demanded incredulously.

"I would be more hopeful if things were settled." She looked up.

"What do we bring this child into, Denassa? Or any child, for that matter."

Denassa could not feel Yutrenta's pessimism. She wiped tears from her face. "That may be Acrahh's reason for sending this child now, Yutrenta, for hope. Is a divine birth not a promise?" Then a new wonder struck Denassa, "Does Aya and Manerra know?"

"Aya sleeps. Manerra, Kayarra, and Vantrann haven't returned. You're the first to know. And," Yutrenta offered a wane smile, "you'll be pleased. The mother is Ringgangley."

A second shock, as great as the first. Her shoulders shook with weeping. *Silly tears!* She tried to control both her laughing and crying.

"I will attend the ceremonies tonight," Yutrenta stated, "but you must deliver the child. Trini is with the mother now and will keep us apprised of her progress. Trini will also assist you with the birth."

"Great gods, Yutrenta, I've never delivered a shecaren."

Yutrenta chuckled, winced, touched her breast. "Few have. Pretend it's a Yatren birth. You might wish to meet and examine the woman before you deliver her child."

"Yes. Oh! Yes."

Yutrenta chuckled again despite her obvious pain. "Her name is Ammira. This child is her first."

"How old is she?" Denassa's brain finally focused.

"Nineteen."

"Is the pain such that you can attend tonight's ceremonies?" Denassa demanded, suddenly full of doubt.

"I will attend tonight's abbah," Yutrenta stated. "Tonight, as no other night, it's imperative that the janquer be whole in its show of unity."

*Show.* The word nearly slapped her. "What of your pain?" Denassa persisted.

"I'll carry a vial of draydine."

"Have you completed your cleansing, then?"

"No. I hoped you would assist me."

"I will if you'll rest afterwards."

"Resting has become a chore, Dee. My body refuses more sleep. It's cruel of you to place conditions upon your help."

"Nothing you've argued moves me; not when you intend to perform duties tonight that will tax the strength you have. You lost a lot of blood."

"Before you lecture, remember who taught you."

"That recollection is my pride." Denassa nodded veneration.

"Enough! You have agreement."

"Then come." Denassa offered a hand.

*****

"What does Kayarra do in company with Vantrann and Manerra?" Denassa inquired of Yutrenta while she mixed an antiseptic in the kitchen, safely away from Alva's food preparations.

"They bathe in the lake."

Denassa's head snapped up, her disbelief complete. "Kayarra agreed?"

"Apparently."

Denassa looked down only to finish counting out the measures of powder. "I've set some of the herbs from the garden to dry," she said, unwilling to speculate upon Kayarra's fate in Manerra and Vantrann's care after last night's fiasco. She wondered what drove Vantrann to such cruelty, and why Aya forgave his disrespect. Not all Thurrang lords were so crass that they must tolerate Vantrann's crude humor. If Vantrann was the best Thurra offered, there really was no hope for the south.

Alva located Rayas and bullied him, as only a wife dared, into carrying water for them. Yutrenta carried a lamp to the bathhouse, and Denassa carried the antiseptic, her physician's bag, and clean clothes. At the bathhouse, Rayas lit a brazier from Yutrenta's lamp then left them.

"Shurna shared with me Vantrann's remarks about you and Kayarra," Yutrenta said while Denassa unfastened the laces of Yutrenta's robe.

"Do you mention it to discover the truth of the accusation?" Denassa asked tightlipped.

"I already know where the anger lies."

Denassa sent Yutrenta a frowning glance. "Vantrann charged us with love, not anger." Denassa gingerly freed Yutrenta's wrist from the belt sling that held her arm immobile.

"Razon nurtured bitter resentment over shon regis Dayla's choice of janquer. He coveted that position."

"You think enough, even now, to encourage his son to mischief?" She freed Yutrenta's belt and hung it over a peg.

"Perhaps not that."

Denassa returned. "Then what?" She pulled the robe's yoke wide enough to slip it over Yutrenta's shoulders.

"Perhaps Vantrann is too much like Razon."

"You believe Aya was wrong to accept Vantrann?" Denassa untied the arm bandage and began unwinding it.

"I believe that injured Thurrang sensitivities don't mend."

"Why are you telling me this?" Uneasiness crept in.

"I told Ouban he would not die of his wounds. I was wrong."

Denassa stopped, the bandage dangling from one hand, and searched Yutrenta's face. "An uninjured man also died in Vantrann's care."

Yutrenta's alarmed glance toward the door reminded Denassa too late of their uncertain privacy. Denassa strode to the door, through it, and circled the bathhouse.

"There's no one nearby," she announced upon her return.

"Let's be done here," Yutrenta urged.

Denassa started unfastening the bandage that bound Yutrenta's chest. "How do you intend to withstand tonight's abbah?" she asked.

"If you will lift my hand—"

"I meant the fear, Yutrenta."

Yutrenta didn't answer immediately. "The plaza will be easier to face than my imagination. Shurna's in a more dangerous position right now than I will be."

Denassa's heart thumped. "Where's Shurna?"

"In Cha-ka."

"They question Fava?"

"There was worry if they waited she would fabricate a tale."

Denassa bent, tugged the robe that lay on the river stones, and Yutrenta obligingly stepped from its circle. Denassa tossed both robe and bandage over a peg, then shifted a bucket of water closer. A wooden bowl, rim battered, bobbed on the surface like a child's toy. She used the bowl to pour water over Yutrenta's shoulder, then cautiously applied scrub leaves in a rag to the tender area. The wounds' immediate flesh was swollen, flushed and warm to the touch. Dried blood ran the length of the slashes, some of it crusted in the suture's dimples. Ugly as they appeared, they were clear of infection. Unquestionably, Yutrenta would bare scars.

"It's likely you'll live," Denassa offered her opinion.

"Then what argues otherwise?" Yutrenta demanded. "Denassa, I'm scared of what we do."

"And you accuse me of pessimism!" Denassa protested in an attempt to lighten Yutrenta's mood.

"This is different."

"How so?"

"Shurna claims a madness grips people when the moons ride the same sky. Until this year, I scoffed at her superstition. Men clash wherever they meet, whether both moons ride the sky or not. But consider the joinings' influences upon Ringgal's tides and the earth tremblings in the Smoking Mountains."

"One of Mante's fables concludes that women, who suffer in bringing forth life, are less anxious to take a life than are men who experience pleasure from conception," Denassa offered a variation.

Yutrenta said nothing.

The water Denassa poured over Yutrenta's hair ran red with blood.

"Is Ammira in Trini's tent?" Denassa changed the subject in order to engage Yutrenta again, but Yutrenta's head tilt was her only answer.

* * * * *

A pale blue robe lay folded in the center of Kayarra's bed. He assumed it was the tribal robe he was expected to wear tonight, and started to unfold it, to give the creases an opportunity to relax. An abundance of beadwork and embroidery captured his attention. He lifted the robe and held it at arm's length.

The only similarity between this robe and his first tribal robe was the sun's central position on the breast. High on the right shoulder, the shecarens' moons glistened in dark blue abalone. Erupting in a vee from the hem stretched a twining of branches, leaves, and tendrils. Tucked among that flora like flowers were the tribal symbols of the Ofrann, Kitarin, Thurrang, and Ringgangley.

Still lying on the bed was a quilted circlet with tie cords, its function obscure.

Kayarra left the garments spread across the mattress and went in search of Denassa. She wasn't in her bedroom.

"She's with the physicians," Alva told him, not using his name so she didn't have to apply his titles.

"Where is lady Shurna, lady Yutrenta?" Kayarra asked.

"Lady Shurna's in Cha-ka. Lady Yutrenta sleeps."

His frustration peaked. "Shecaren said clean-sing here. Where?"

"The shon regis uses the bathhouse."

The woman did not intend to be helpful. "I hot water?" he asked.

"You didn't bathe in the lake?"

He flushed. "No," he said and turned away.

Kayarra located Manerra and Vantrann seated in the audience room, Manerra surrounded by women braiding his hair. It was Manerra, incredibly, who interrupted the women and showed Kayarra where the bathhouse was, and Aya who demonstrated the bathing process.

Kayarra carried bucketfuls of water across soggy ground, washed his hair, then scrubbed with the used water and rinsed with the clean.

"Janquer lord Kayarra!" that greeting startled him when he entered the kitchen. It came from Denassa, who assisted Alva with the braiding of Aya's hair. The radiance of her smile stopped him. "Acrahh blesses this night's joining with the birth of a shecaren."

*When a shecaren is born, another dies*—Shurna's saying—collided with Denassa's obvious joy. "Birth is good?" he asked. If Manerra died, he might agree, although fantasies of Vantrann's death had taken over first place.

"It's glad news," Aya confirmed. "Thirty-two sun years I awaited Manerra's birth. The shecaren is spared my insecurities."

"Acrahh's promise is stronger than Hyran's," Denassa boasted.

Yutrenta's anxious plea came from the doorway, "Don't name Acrahh and Hyran together." She entered the kitchen, rubbing her arm.

"There is no blasphemy in doing so," Aya said.

"Does your arm hurt?" Denassa asked, her smile gone.

"Not unbearably."

Aya twisted, yanking a partially completed braid from Denassa's fingers. "I'm concerned about your intentions."

"As long as I'm not crushed in the crowd, I'll be fine."

"Approach is formal and retreat will be arranged," Aya answered. "You will not go unescorted."

She rested a hand over the wound on her arm. "Someone needs to attend the hair of our Kayarran member."

"Shurna must be recalled, too," Aya added.

Alva set aside the quartz bead she was about to thread into Aya's hair. "I'll send someone." She hurried from the kitchen.

*****

Sitting in the audience room, Shurna swirled her soup, less to cool it than to occupy her hands. The few sips she'd taken were a show of respect for Alva's labor on a holy day. Nervous energy was enough to sustain her for days.

Blessedly, Aya signaled an early release from supper. Shurna shot to her feet before his, "I'd like a report of Fava's questioning," halted her intended flee.

"You might wish a more ostentatious tale," Shurna demurred.

"Truth jinxes only liars," Aya countered.

Shurna flashed a wry smile and shifted attention to Yutrenta, who pretended not to have heard Aya's request. She sighed and sat down.

"Fava is the mother of Yutrenta's attacker," she said for Vantrann's benefit. "She related descriptions of Ura's beauty, even as an infant. Because of that beauty, Ura was courted young, well before her age allowed considerations of marriage. Nevertheless, one man, a metal smith named Bidek, won parental favor, and Ura was promised in marriage as soon as menses came upon her. She wed at the age of twelve.

"From onset, Fava claims that Ura railed against marriage. Fava believes that Ura was accustomed to lavish attention and refused the secluded demeanor of a Thurrang wife. Fava thought this haughtiness brought on her daughter's beatings, but Ura's brother described perversions in the marriage bed that he claims Ura confided to him.

"A year and a half after his marriage, Bidek took to bed after supper, complaining of illness. Ura found him dead the next morning. Soon afterward, Ura announced her pregnancy.

"Fava claimed no reason to doubt her daughter's honesty, and only questioned the baby's slow development. That's when Ura proclaimed her child to be Acrahh's son, and said she had been told in a vision to attend the joining.

"Fava insists she was convinced by Ura's descriptions of the conception and vision, and so agreed to the journey.

"The brother says there were rumors that Bidek's death had been by poison, and he believes his mother's decision to accompany Ura to Ayahn Rahh was as much to escape the inquiries as to settle this matter of the unborn child.

"I think Fava truly believed her daughter's innocence, and trusted the child's birth would prove it.

"Unfortunately, by the time Ura reached Ayahn Rahh, she had run out of lies, time, and places to run. She was desperate when she refused Trini's diagnosis and demanded examination by Yutrenta. It was her final delay tactic, which exploded when Yutrenta was called to Trini's tent. I believe she expected her demand to be refused. She could not know the interest Yutrenta takes in the health of the devout, nor that Yutrenta was one of the physicians present that morning. Ura lost much more than a child when Yutrenta exposed her lie."

The audience room lay silent until Aya asked, "Has Fava other children?"

"Yes. A married son who remains in Draka, and the son I questioned today. Fava's husband refused the journey. Ura made claims that her father laid with her after her marriage to Bidek, so they were estranged at the time the journey was proposed. But with the lie of her pregnancy, it's impossible to know what is truth or lie in anything Ura claimed."

Aya shook his head. "I would have lady Sheron retain Fava in Chaka, and have her intervene with the son, as well."

"Vantrann," Denassa asked, "where is Draka?"

"Far south and east, among the Orada's lower slopes. Farther even than Ancower in the foothills. Its principle trade is copper ore."

"Isolated, with little need for female children," Aya mused.

Vantrann shrugged. "Mining forces a hard livelihood."

"Yutrenta," Aya said, "have you comment upon the sentencing?"

"Ura is beyond my anger," she stated. "Whatever she suffered, I cannot feel pity for her, but I won't find satisfaction in prolonging her family's suffering. I place guilt and blame solely upon Ura."

"Shurna," Aya said, "tell lady Sheron that Fava and her son are not to leave Ayahn Rahh without my permission."

"Do you require my presence at the interventions?" Shurna asked.

"If other duties permit. This is still a crime against the janquer. I will not readily turn away from it."

Shurna signed acquiescence.

"But now, everyone dress for abbah," Aya ordered. "Denassa . . . thank you," he said as Denassa reached for his bowl, ". . . bring your drum."

# CHAPTER 65

The quilted circlet, Denassa demonstrated, was a collar to be worn underneath the new robe. Kayarra understood its usefulness as soon as he donned the robe and realized the robe's weight. Knotted threads would have abraded his shoulder if not for the padded collar.

For the first time, Kayarra regretted the removal of the mirror. He would have liked to see himself as others would see him. He had seen no robe more beautiful . . . until Aya and Manerra joined them in the audience room.

The shecarens' black robes bore white moons. A constellation of stars glittered across their chests and sleeves and illusionally continued into the quartz beads scattered throughout Aya's hair. Fantastical plants and creatures adorned the hems of their robes. Above the highest claws and blooms arched the symbols of the major tribes, Kayarra's sun beside the Ofrann's palm and circle. With that stunning discovery, he searched for the sun on other robes and found it on everyone's except Vantrann's.

He was struck dumb that his companions wore that symbol in defiance of the nation's condemnation. Before he could trust his voice or discover adequate words to express his gratitude, Aya strode toward the door. His companions rose and followed.

As had happened before their Shangren approach, Aya paused after they assembled and held each member's eye. Kayarra tried to convey gratitude in his silent exchange. Aya smiled, such an expression of confidence and pride that Kayarra forgot his fears of failure and mistake and momentarily believed he did belong as who and what he was. Then Denassa's drum resonated and the company began their formal approach to the Altar of Acrahh.

Their robes were not the only finery in evidence, only the most richly adorned. A wall of hands vied to touch their robes in passing, apparently without discrimination. Kayarra felt an unaccustomed brush and tug against his robe. Only Yutrenta escaped that hope for blessing or luck, protected by Shurna and Vantrann on one side and Kayarra and Denassa on the other. A route remained open to the steps of the altar and did not close as they ascended the dais.

In deference to his coming of age, Manerra performed abbah while Aya looked on. After abbah and before moonrise, while final sunlight drenched the sky with slowly changing colors, Manerra related first the legend of Acrahh, then the story of Ryna and Trys. He told how two tribal leaders met and fell in love but chose service to their tribesmen over personal fulfillment. Even when animosities escalated between their tribes, Ryna and Trys kept secret alliance and labored long to end the hostilities. At the conclusion of their lives, they died childless, but their tribes had achieved peace and their members prospered.

"After death, their spirits rose to the threshold of Acrahh's world but were denied union with the sun.

"'How did we so displeased you that our spirits are denied this tribute?' they cried in one voice.

"'It is not in punishment that I deny you union with the spirits of your ancestors,' Acrahh replied. 'If that were my intention, you would be blind to this world and left to wander the sky without purpose. Lo, I know the sacrifices you made to preserve the lives of my son's descendants. No child of Yatra should suffer as you have suffered in the keeping of his promise.

"'On this day, I place your spirits in the sky where they shall light the world's darkness. For those children who question their strife, your spirits shall serve as proof of my benevolence. And because you sacrificed earthly unions to restore tribal harmony, your heavenly union shall bring forth my sons and daughters to guide the descendants of Yatra.'"

Kayarra saw torchbearers advancing through the crowd.

"Thus saying, Acrahh set the spirits of Ryna and Trys into the night sky, where they keep witness to this night of Acrahh's divine promise."

"Tonight," Aya shouted, "the shecaren Manerra comes of age to be called shon regis."

A roar of approval precluded speech. Aya waited for the cheering to abate.

"As Acrahh's wishes will be made known through Manerra, so too shall Acrahh's line continue with the birth of a shecaren."

Deafening roars, while litter bearers became visible behind the torchbearers. The torchbearers reached the steps of the Altar of Acrahh and started up.

Yutrenta and Denassa separated from the janquer, met the litter bearers at the altar, and supervised Ammira's placement upon the raised and draped stone. Trini, who concluded the procession, circled to Denassa's side.

Unlit torches were rammed into holes in the standing stone that backed the altar, were lit, then the men who were neither shecaren nor janquer departed.

The shecarens approached the altar side-by-side. When they stopped, Vantrann and Kayarra crossed to positions at Ammira's head. Shurna flanked Denassa at Ammira's feet. Yutrenta knelt at Ammira's shoulder and gripped her hand, but their exchange was lost amid the crowd's roar.

Kayarra marveled at Ammira's fortitude until he realized that pain narrowed her focus of concern. He saw her one fearsome look past Yutrenta's shoulder at the crowd before a hard contraction drew her knees up. After that, her attention did not shift from Yutrenta.

A low humming began as a faint undertone that swelled and eventually replaced the shouts. The tune was slow and monotonous, its repetition, nearly hypnotic.

Aya turned toward the crowd, raised his hands, and the crowd reached toward the sky, linked hands, and began swaying in time to the rise and fall of the hum.

Kayarra looked at the night sky. Trys and Ryna's full discs clearly touched at the points of greatest curve.

Aya began a chant joined to the undulation of the humming, phrases that rotated like the stanzas of an endless song. Even standing as close as Kayarra did, he listened through several repetitions before he began to understand the words, and still could not distinguish all of them. Aya beseeched his father to provide strength through all crises; to never forsake Yatra's children. He asked Acrahh's guidance in maintaining unbroken peace, gave gratitude for the earth's bounty, and blessed the fruitfulness of sexual unions. What he said about the tribes and the imminent birth were among the words Kayarra did not understand.

Ammira sweated, strained, and cried out as labor advanced. Trini joined Yutrenta at Ammira's shoulder, applied oil to Ammira's lips, and spoke encouragement between Yutrenta's instructions, but Ammira was clearly tiring as the moons advanced and her child resisted birth. Torches sputtered and smoked overhead but no one moved to replace them.

Yutrenta retreated to Denassa's shoulder and their heads touched as the physicians conferred. Denassa indicated affirmation, faced Kayarra's position and signaled, although he didn't understand the signals she used.

Ammira's head lolled in pleading denial when Vantrann and Manerra closed upon either shoulder.

Upon Denassa's signal, the men lifted Ammira until she knelt upon the altar. Trini shouted instructions, while Ammira struggled between cooperation and pain. With the next hard contraction, Trini threw her arms around Ammira, who screamed, clutched Trini's arms, and was delivered of the child.

Trini, Vantrann and Manerra lay Ammira back upon the draped and blood-soaked altar.

A baby's cry pierced the humming.

Manerra began weeping.

*A sister*, Denassa mouthed, then concentrated on the baby's cleansing. Trini and Yutrenta concentrated on Ammira's care.

Aya, jolted from his trance by the baby's cry, continued the words of joining, although his attention fixed upon the altar.

When, at last, Denassa proffered the infant, Aya advanced, cupped her in both hands, and studied her. Finally, he turned toward the humming crowd and lifted her skyward.

"Raena," he named her, "behold the unity of the nation you will rule. That unity is your divine trust. What is of Acrahh is for all people."

Shouts burst from thousands of throats, startling the infant. She wailed until she trembled, although her cries were lost amid the greater jubilation.

Aya brought her face below his, exhaled over her lips, and inhaled the breath she expelled by her cries. When he straightened, Manerra advanced and gingerly accepted the precious gift Aya offered.

Manerra held the infant with extreme care, fearful of dropping her while he repeated Aya's ritual of unity. His hands trembled while the Yatren nation looked on. *A sister.*

When he could shift his attention from her wrinkled, red face, Aya's glittering shape shimmered through an excess of tears.

He held his prayers' answer.

Carefully, he shifted Raena to his arm.

Ammira, weak and spent as she was, plaintively reached toward the infant and Manerra's heart nearly broke over the desperation in that gesture. Harder still to return the infant to Denassa for swaddling before Ammira received her for suckle. As Denassa's hands brushed his arm during the transfer, a part of Manerra's heart departed with the infant. When he looked back around, Ammira was weeping.

For a moment, he thought she wept for his reasons, then he realized she wept in grief. The child she had conceived, carried, and borne in public humiliation was not hers to keep or even to name. Raena belonged to Acrahh and to the nation of Yatra, even to the janquer, before she belonged to her mother.

Manerra flashed upon Matera's face and realized that Ammira could as well have been his mother during her time. The Chosen's bond of grief continued unbroken. And with intimate shock, Manerra realized the tremendous trust between the shecarens and the Chosen of Acrahh, and how hard trust was for him. For two years, Ammira would raise his sister, then be expected to relinquish her forever. He knew intimately the shecaren's pain and suffering when that agreement failed. Now, he understood the grief of the Chosen of Acrahh in the keeping of that covenant.

"What is of Acrahh is for all people," Aya shouted, and Manerra attempted to lead the response but his voice failed. He could only mouth, "And what is of Acrahh is this world and everything upon it," while his true response came from the excruciating pain in his throat and heart.

"As the firstborn of Acrahh, Yatra swore a sacred promise to preserve Axxord in trust for all generations," Aya stated. "That oath of stewardship is the Oath of Yatra—the vow and charge of every shecaren who has followed. Tonight, shecaren Manerra will pledge that vow before Crysus and Acrahh as his age, position, and training demand, just as Raena, in her time, shall swear the same oath."

Manerra glanced back. Kayarra had caught his cue and advanced to Aya's shoulder. They descended the stairs side-by-side.

Devout pressed back and aside to open a pathway along the white stones that joined the Altar of Acrahh with the Temple of Crysus. Manerra's oath would be sworn at the Temple of Crysus before the gods and janquer with the nation as witness.

Aya's black robe shifted in stark contrast to Kayarra's pale blue robe, the gemstones on each, glittering in the moonlight. One dark robe, one light; two crescent moons, two full. The power in the symbolisms wove a spell that kept Kayarra's shoulders squared and his head erect, not focused on the pathway at his feet.

They reached the standing stones midway across the plaza and Kayarra waited while Aya touched the depressions on the first stone then passed to the second stone before he reached for the first depression. Kayarra was touching the third stone when Aya completed the last stone.

Shurna advanced to stand at Manerra's shoulder as soon as Aya and Kayarra entered the crowd. They waited at the edge of the dais, their cue to descend when Kayarra passed the last standing stone.

Dressed in black, Aya blended with the shadows. Only the beads on his robe and in his hair glittered like a small bit of the heavens passing among men, vastly insubstantial and temporal. Manerra resisted an impulse to look upon his own chest to see if he appeared any more or less substantial than Aya did in that moment. An urge to look over his shoulder was also squashed, hoping that Raena's sudden silence meant she nursed.

Through all the years of his childhood, through this latest, long trek to Ayahn Rahh, Manerra had resisted and railed against this moment. Once his oath was heard, he was shon regis upon Aya's death or infirmity. He had thought to be scared, resentful and angry, but what he felt in this moment was calm. Acrahh had granted his prayer for a shecaren. The second half of his prayer had a chance to be fulfilled.

Manerra pressed his hands against his thighs.

He had a shecaren. A half-sister.

Full of pride, almost in shock, but finally without fear, Manerra stared back at the sea of faces that had witnessed this miracle his father had wrought.

"Blessed are the children of Acrahh," someone shouted and that cry spread. Manerra dipped his head in mute gratitude, not alone for himself.

Kayarra cleared the standing stones.

Manerra started down the stairs, Shurna matching him step-for-step. Three-fourths of the way down, the stone stair dropped away without warning and returned with a shock that jarred Manerra's leg to the hip.

He fell, with time only to shield his face before he collided with a body and then struck pavement.

Screams deafened him. Men, women, and children struck the flagstones and bounced. An incredible sight.

A crack like strangled thunder rolled across the screams, followed by screams more terrible than the earlier cries.

His own fall wouldn't quite end—like falling onto the back of a galloping shuren when he had expected solid stone and pain. He collided with someone, the world's laws, as he understood them, defied.

When, at last, the ground lay firm, he didn't quite believe it. He raised his head from his arm. A stranger raised her head and stared into his eyes, first in blank stun, then with flooding terror. He saw her scream build and her mouth open before sound erupted.

Manerra lurched to his feet and staggered, his equilibrium shaken. Others were stirring, but the plaza looked like a ripe grain field felled by harvesters. Manerra saw clearly the Temple of Crysus, and midway across the plaza, a gap in the standing stones. That significance was slow to register. Then he remembered the thunder.

Manerra stumbled forward a step, which was all the clear pavement that existed between him and Aya's last location. Then he whirled, relief paralyzing him, seeing the altar's standing stone intact. He ran up the stairs, two and three at a time.

Ammira lay curled at the base of the altar as if her naked body were a shield protecting her screaming infant. At Ammira's shoulder, Yutrenta lay motionless. Denassa applied pressure to Yutrenta's breast. Trini, crouched on hands and knees, appeared stunned. Bloody water covered the dais, shaken into bizarre patterns across the white stone. A torch had fallen into the water and burned with a hiss, sending up smoke that smelled of burnt flesh.

Vantrann. Vantrann wasn't visible. Manerra circled Denassa and the altar and saw him lying in water, hidden by the altar, contributing his own blood to that menacing stain.

Manerra felt Vantrann's neck for broken bones, then rolled him over. Blood covered his face and leaked into his closed eyes. Manerra grabbed for the pouch at his waist. His hand struck embroidered cloth. He wasn't wearing a belt. None of them were.

"Trini, I need a cloth," he shouted, certain the physician must have one. Even the hem of his robe was too heavily beaded to use.

Beyond the physicians' shoulders, a stranger rushed toward Ammira and Raena. Manerra leapt to intercept him.

"He's my husband," Ammira wailed. "Please, lord shecaren."

Manerra stepped aside, turned, and froze. Flames flickered through the trees from the direction of the tent city. Not the contained glimmer of cook fires, but a blaze fed upon ample fuel. He remembered the unattended lamps in the House of Moons and panic tried to seize him.

Who was there to extinguish flames? Or any fire? He turned and spotted other fires.

Manerra snatched up the overturned bucket and ran for the stairs. Most people were on their feet again, or aiding those who were not. A dense crowd encircled the fallen standing stone, the place from which horrible screams still came.

Aya had passed the standing stones before the earthquake struck. Manerra knew that, although Aya's black robe now made him impossible to spot. Kayarra should have been easier to locate, but there were too many gray robes—too similar to blue in the graying wash of moonlight. There were bodies and severe injuries where the stone had fallen. In this dense crowd, there could be no other outcome. Trini and Denassa were the only physicians whose locations he knew, and he could not order them there when Yutrenta and Vantrann were unconscious and Ammira still bled from childbirth. Pray Acrahh neither Raena nor Ammira sustained injuries in their fall.

Manerra reached the lower steps. "The tent city's burning!" he yelled into dazed faces. "You," he shoved the bucket into the arms of the nearest man standing, "organize a fire line. Find more buckets. It's your homes and the forest you save. Your lives. *Run!*" He shoved another man toward the first. "Follow him!" He looked into faces bewildered and terrified, numb and stunned. Some started moving. With a purpose, they would recover quickly; hopefully, enough of them to avert the panic presently contained by shock. Panic and hysteria grew around the fallen standing stone.

Manerra whirled and leapt for the stairs. An aftershock shook his feet out from under him and his shin hit the edge of a step. Numbing fire paralyzed him for a moment. He gained his feet, limped, and then ran up the stairs. "Move away from the altar!" he shouted. The Chosen of Acrahh and her daughter were already safe. Ammira's husband had seen the danger, or simply moved his wife out of the watery blood into which she'd fallen. "Trini, take your bag to the standing stone," Manerra shouted. He crouched beside Yutrenta, forced his arms under her shoulders and knees, lifted her away from Denassa's ministrations, and felt his leg start to fold. He shifted balance, locked his knee, then lurched sideways, afraid of falling despite his efforts. Somehow, he cleared the stone's line of fall. Denassa helped lower Yutrenta.

Vantrann, now conscious, crawled to safety. Trini frantically stuffed items into her bag.

Denassa grabbed Manerra's sleeve. "Where's Aya and Kayarra?" she yelled above the crowd's unending roar.

"Safe," he said because he'd seen Kayarra clear the last standing stone.

"Shurna?"

"I don't know." Odd that he'd not seen her since their fall. He'd assumed she'd survived with bruises because he had. He rose to find her but froze when the dais vibrated.

An explosion turned all faces toward the Temple of Crysus as rock fragments burst skyward, then rained across the pediment and onto the crowd below.

Screams as people were hit and crushed by falling rock.

But it was the fireball rising from the temple that delayed panic. A tremendous boom drowned out all cries and vibrated in Manerra's chest.

"Crysus! Crysus!" demotic screams were terror-laden.

"Crysus?" Denassa asked.

Manerra took a step in the direction of the fireball's arc. "*Aya*!" he screamed.

# CHAPTER 66

The earth had become a dog shaking itself dry. Twigs and sand grains jumped on the flagstones before Kayarra's face. He reached for Aya's foot, desperate for contact. Then an explosive crack deafened him and he whipped his head around. Wet spray struck his face. He jolted away, then looked back. Screams drowned out the ringing in his ears. Someone grabbed his robe, pulled hard, tried to climb him. Kayarra grabbed the woman's wrists and tore her hands from his robe. She screamed in his face.

A hand swung from nowhere, slapped the woman so hard, her head snapped back and aside. She fell away from him. Aya grabbed the back of Kayarra's robe and pulled him to his feet by strength alone.

Kayarra looked back at the massive stone that lay where he'd stood seconds earlier. A dark stain spread beyond the stone's edge, filling cracks between paving stones, spreading past feet that protruded beneath the fallen stone, past the person who reared up on both hands, head thrown back, mouth open in a scream, whose legs and hips were pinned beneath that stone. Bodiless hands protruded.

Men were gripping the edge of the stone, trying to lift it, slipping in blood.

"No!" he screamed and tried to reach them, terrified they might succeed in opening that door to hell. Aya pulled his arm, pulling in the wrong direction. Denassa knelt at the altar. Once that door opened, she'd be trapped on the other side. He had to get to her before the fire, to escape the fire.

But he stumbled backwards, pulled by a force too powerful to resist. He stepped on something round that shifted like raw meat under his sandal.

He leapt away, whirled and ran, ran with Aya toward the Temple of Crysus, ran from the devils men were about to free. He tripped, stumbled, fell, was hit. Aya dragged him up, made him run, pulled him faster.

He stepped on the hem of his robe going up the temple stairs, stumbled, yanked up the hem and ran after Aya, past huge fluted columns.

Temple offerings were strewn everywhere. A hide-wrapped bundle blazed with breeze-whipped flames beside an overturned lamp. Bells tinkled like falling rain. He shrank from the carven image of Crysus in that living fire and roiling smoke, but Aya pulled him past the burning offering and into the shadows beneath the image on the wall.

A stone block lay askance across a hole's black maw. A cold, damp breeze wafted from the hole.

"Help me," Aya shouted and grabbed an edge of the stone, straining to shift it.

Kayarra joined him, lifted and pushed, although he didn't know what Aya intended with the stone. The block moved—was lifted high enough that Aya had to shift his grip. Although the block's lower corner was snagged on something, Kayarra couldn't support the weight by himself. The block's top corner lost elevation before Aya secured a new grip, threw his weight and strength against the block, and it rose to square over the hole. Kayarra felt an audible click. Aya grabbed Kayarra's arm and jerked him back as he sprang away. The hinged stone began a slow swing shut. Aya leapt forward, grabbed the edge and stopped its close.

"In," Aya ordered through gasping pants.

Kayarra stepped back. An image of that other door, limbs protruding beneath its crack, brought a rush of vertigo. He'd be entering the backdoor to hell if he entered Aya's crawlspace.

"Kayarra!" Aya shouted, then lunged forward, ducking low, stepping high to enter that tunnel. The stone block started to swing shut, and Kayarra stumbled after Aya.

Cold, moisture-thick air shocked his laboring lungs, made breathing difficult. "Aya!" he shouted into the dark when his body and the closing door blocked the firelight from the temple. The back of a hand struck his shoulder, reversed, gripped the fabric and pulled. Water seeped through Kayarra's robe, wetting his knees and shins and coating his hands with slime. The stone he crawled over was smooth, rounded, slippery. The tug on his robe assumed an upward angle. Kayarra jerked his robe hem clear of his feet as he stood and rose to full height in claustrophobic darkness.

Aya's hand slid down Kayarra's arm, closed around his wrist, and pressed his knuckles against a leather strap. Kayarra gripped the temple stone's strap, and stretched his right hand toward a non-existent wall. A water drop struck his head. The strap tugged and he followed.

Their shuffling footfalls awakened sounds, their passage remarked upon in whispers by the ghosts of Aya's ancestors.

"We climb," Aya warned. "Keep your head low."

Aya's warning repeated, whispered by the ghosts in eerie voices.

Advance was up an incline, progress achieved bent over, one hand gripping Aya's strap, one lifting the hem of his robe, feet blindly locating footholds on the slick stone.

The incline leveled and the echoes of their panting changed, giving the impression of immense space. Kayarra straightened, dropped his robe, and swung his arm out. His fingers struck a wall of stone as smooth and cold as the air.

Aya stumbled, and the toe of Kayarra's right sandal struck a solid surface on his next step. He raised his left foot too high and nearly fell bringing it down. A faintly hollow clang answered his stomp, but Aya was walking again, left, up another incline almost as steep as the first, and nearly as smooth as the right-hand wall they'd left behind. Air blew up from below, giving the impression of a drop-off. Kayarra's hand sweated against the leather of Aya's strap. He feared aftershocks in this place because of the unknown depth they paralleled and the weight of the mountain rising above them.

"Why here?" he demanded, fighting panic.

"Crysus," Aya said and stopped walking.

Kayarra felt a hard tug on the belt he gripped but didn't release his hold. Leather brushed leather. Aya was removing the temple stone.

If Aya could draw light from the temple stone, why had he not done so earlier?

Kayarra listened to each whisper of sound, heard a thunk-click, then a scraping unrelated to leather, stone, or wood.

Aya's sudden cry held notes of shock and panic. Kayarra's heart lurched and he gripped the strap tighter. Aya slapped a wall with the flat of his hand.

A hollow boom behind Kayarra made him jump.

Aya whirled, tearing free of Kayarra's grip.

Light flared, blinding. Kayarra yelled, threw an arm over his eyes, staggered sideways, stuck a wall, and slid to his knees.

Aya bolted.

Kayarra dropped his arm, blinked frantically, saw shadows and shapes and . . . recognition, then confusion.

They were trapped in a metal room. The temple stone's light poured from the ceiling, illuminating body-shaped couches. Aya, on the far side of the couches, reached toward a ladder rung.

"Where is?" Kayarra shouted, and lunged through the opening that separated his alcove from Aya's circular room. Aya didn't slow his frantic, scrambling climb toward a hole in the ceiling.

There were no doors. No other way out. No other way in.

Kayarra passed the first couch when a rumble sent a signal of nausea and disorientation through stomach and brain. He reached for the nearest couch, but an explosion collapsed his legs, and the floor came up to meet his head.

* * * * *

A headache woke him. The pain became a throb when he shifted his head off his arm. An unpleasant vibration passed through the floor. He blinked against light, squeezed his eyes shut, pressed a hand against his forehead, and willed away the pain.

Afterimages started registering, and the memory of a nightmare got tangled up with memories. He squinted across the floor, through a grove of poles, at a heap of heavily embroidered black fabric. A paw, claws extended, rose above a tangle of leaves, reaching toward a circle-enclosed sun.

Aya. Aya was hurt.

He had regained consciousness. Aya would wake soon. Aya would know where they were and what had happened. Aya would know how they could leave this place. Denassa was in danger.

Kayarra pressed both palms against the floor, drew his legs up, and with infinite care, gained hands and knees.

He slid one hand forward, then one knee. Then the other hand. Then the other knee, careful of balance between shifts, because balance felt oddly off, as though he was lightheaded and listed at the same time. The explosions might have injured his eardrums, affected his equilibrium. It took an eternity to reach Aya's side.

Aya remained unconscious. He'd fallen with his head turned sideways and tucked toward one shoulder. Kayarra reached out to straighten Aya's head. His cheek was frighteningly cold. When Aya's head moved, bones grated.

Kayarra jerked his hand back, an electric shock running the length of his arm. He gasped air to begin resuscitation, but a wailing cry came instead. He drew back and back and back, until something solid halted his retreat.

* * * * *

Sleep. Food. Water.

Sleep, when he attempted it, was nightmare.

Food . . . there was none. Nor water. This place was metal and dust and death, and he would die of thirst before he resorted to the Manteen's method of survival.

Was this the price one paid for waking a goddess? Or had Crysus killed Acrahh's son for desecrating her temple . . . for bringing a demon here?

Black holes in Kayarra's memory sucked away time. He might have passed out, but if so, he'd passed out repeatedly.

He remembered—or hallucinated about—pressing his hands against thick black glass, behind which burned four fist-sized suns. The temple stone and three others. He was certain of it. Although, how Aya had placed the temple stone there, he didn't know. Actions were possible in total darkness that were impossible in light.

He huddled against the juncture of wall and floor, well away from

Aya's body, fading in and out of awareness. He'd stared at the dark hole at the top of the rung ladder, too fear-paralyzed to explore. Crysus had killed Aya for attempting to go there.

Kayarra shouted for help, but only ghosts answered.

* * * * *

The room was growing colder, or he was sickening.

A metallic clank and a tremor felt through floor and wall made him whip his head around. He dropped a hand to the floor, poised to move, with nowhere to go, and waited for the sound and vibration to repeat. *Willed* them to repeat. Maybe Manerra knew where they were. Manerra would want the temple stone—want Aya—for abbah.

Nothing happened. Kayarra heard only faint noises that he recognized as part of this place, hardly audible now above the pounding of his heart. Since he'd gained consciousness, the life, the pulse of this room had been broken only by the sound of his voice—an impossibility now, with his throat and tongue drying.

He drew his knees to his chest and tugged on the cloth of his robe until the Kayarran tribal symbol rested atop one knee. The shell had broken in one of his falls. Fragments were missing, so even when he pressed the edges together until the fracture lines disappeared, there were gaps in its rippled surface. It would never be whole again.

*Pang.*

He jumped. That sound was closer than the last. Out of habit, he looked toward the hole in the ceiling, but nothing emerged. The sound seemed to come from his right, on the other side of the alcove's wall. He scurried across the floor to the nearest couch and crouched behind it. The couch offered no real barrier, but having something between himself and the noise felt safer than sitting exposed against the wall.

A snake hissed a long, dark warning.

Kayarra shifted, trying to hide behind the couch's narrow pedestal. The sounds came, unmistakably, through the recessed area near the temple stones.

His heart pounded so hard that its beat interfered with hearing. He hoped desperately to see Manerra. The shecaren would not challenge the goddess for him, but he would for Aya. Was Manerra strong enough without the temple stone to win their freedom?

Nothing made sense. Not this room, not Aya's death, not his value as a pawn in some hoped-for war, not the gods' involvement.

The wall in the recessed area suddenly, simply vanished. What stood there were demons. Demons with wrinkled, metallic hides and mirrored heads.

Kayarra didn't cry out only because his throat was too raw and dry for sound. He clamped his teeth together as the demons advanced cautiously into the room. If they violated Crysus, then Acrahh was dead.

*Denassa!*

Could Crysus defend her captive?

Kayarra screamed to Crysus for help. He watched the demons' progress through the metal supports beneath the couches and realized with horror that they had seen Aya. When a metallic hand descended toward Aya's chest, something within Kayarra snapped. He bounded over the couch, his only intention, to stop that touch. How dare a demon touch Aya when he could not, who loved him?

A sickening tingle constricted his chest. He lost consciousness in mid-air.

# CHAPTER 67

Shurna dropped her basket on the ground beside a shorn limb and began picking unripe fruit. Vantrann had complained that her skills were wasted in labor a child could perform, but he didn't understand how desperate she was to exhaust memories and relieve tension. One more blow and she'd join her sister in Cha-ka. She wanted to, now.

Neither Aya's nor Kayarra's body had been found when the broken standing stone was lifted.

Tears streamed down Shurna's face as she shoved against branches that kept several clusters of fruit just beyond reach.

No one present at the lifting of the stone would ever be free of that memory: of the sight of crushed bodies, of the stench, of the horrific wails of living relatives. Heads had been crushed by the stone's fall. Identification of the dead had been by clothing or not at all.

Shurna backed away from the branches that kept her from the fruit and reached for easier pickings. When the basket filled, she lugged it through the orchard toward the cookpot set up in the backyard of the House of Moons. Their housekeepers stewed the unripe fruit with honey, berries, and sweet herbs to feed the masses who had lost everything they owned in the fires.

She emptied her basket into a feed trough and started back to the orchard. The earthquake had devastated their fruit-laden trees.

Children helped with the picking, warned to stay clear of hanging limbs. Rayas' work crew was cutting down broken limbs and sawing them into firewood.

Ironic to need or want firewood after the night and daylong effort to dowse the wildfires. The worse damage to the House of Moons had been upstairs in their private chambers, where stairs and smoke had impeded firefighting efforts. The funeral fires afterward convinced Shurna that her lungs would never again be free of smoke. Today was better. A steady breeze blew away the haze of cookfires, without replacing wood smoke with the fecal and urine stench of the middens.

Shurna dropped to her knees beside a limb so she could reach up and out instead of down for the remaining fruit. Her back appreciated the reprieve. It took remarkably little time to fill the basket. Then came the trudge back to the yard and the feed trough. What fruit they couldn't cook would be used as fodder to replace the hay stockpiles that had burned.

She detoured toward the groundskeepers who struggled with a tangle of broken limbs and branches. "Chelis," she called, "if you can spare a rope and man, there's another stray mia breaking fast on our fruit." She pointed the direction, then left Chelis to decide whether animal chasing was worth the increased risk to the men left struggling with the broken limbs. Half the tree they worked on was down.

"Lady Shurna!" Lansa shouted, halting Shurna as she turned away from yet another visit to the feed trough. "The shon regis asks for counsel."

Shurna's heart skipped a beat, then pounded in compensation. *Manerra*, Lansa meant, not Aya. She still had trouble with that change. Not because of incompetence or resentment. The janquer had finally administered the Oath of Yatra that Aya had intended when he . . . disappeared? left?

The absence of a body kept alive a hard core of hope that denied the need to mourn.

*Manerra, shon regis*, Shurna practiced in her head, a chant intended to lessen the shock she kept experiencing over Lansa's innocent messages.

*Great Acrahh, why did Crysus flee Ayahn Rahh and her children? What does she say about the things we do? Is any of it true, as Denassa believes, that her and Yutrenta's love for Kayarra and Aya—in violation of their vows—brought on this end? Is Manerra's assumption so critical that he must gain that position on the very day he can? Please, Acrahh, help me understand.*

The smell of burnt timbers assailed her nostrils as she entered the kitchen and headed toward the audience room. No number of pine boughs and herbs could mask that smell.

Shurna stopped, hesitant and confused, inside the antechamber doorway. Manerra stood alone, his back to the door.

"Shon regis?" She bowed her head.

"Shurna." His voice was faint, lost.

She raised her head and saw his conflict and discomfort over her use of that title. The less sleep he got, the freer his emotions.

"Enter. I asked Lansa to call you first. She goes now to summon Denassa."

Denassa was in Cha-ka. That gave them a lengthy time alone. Why?

"I've been speaking with lady Sheron," he said, "trying to understand."

She experienced a twinge of . . . jealousy? resentment?

Did Manerra distrust her?

That was crazy. It would have benefited no one, least of all her, to be privy to Manerra's fears, grief, and anger. He was shon regis now, not the child she had helped raise. His decision to confide in Sheron left her unburdened by unnecessary knowledge, and worries she would have no way to share. Shurna's estimation of him rose and she nodded again, gravely, respectfully, while wondering if this was Aya's training or Manerra's own sensibilities, but knowing a distinction made no difference.

His eyes flashed gratitude for her understanding, then clouded. "I wanted private counsel with you. Yutrenta's asked for divestment."

The shock of that news was offset by its expectation.

"It's my right to refuse, but I want your opinion before I give my decision."

Yutrenta's spirit died with Aya's disappearance. As much as Yutrenta loved Manerra, Shurna did not believe Yutrenta could accept Manerra in the position Aya had held. Such a transition would seem a desecration of Aya's memory, and to force Yutrenta to admit and accept Aya's death seemed a cruelty Shurna could not advocate, no matter who it supposedly benefited.

Love. The one physical expression denied the shecarens and janquer, but the single emotion, stronger than kinship, that transcended differences. Were they sensible to deny love's physical comfort to anyone—no matter the rationale—who had the chance to discover it?

"What service can she provide if you deny her release?" Shurna asked, not expecting an answer. "You already have one serious weakness in the janquer. Yutrenta would not intend a second, but do intentions make a difference when it comes to loss? Consider the answers in personal counsel, Manerra. It's all the insight I can give."

Grief spread across his face and he looked at the ceiling. "I prayed for a shecaren," he said, and she recognized his burden of guilt.

*When a shecaren is born, another dies.*

"That was only half my wish." His shoulders shook. "I miss him, Shurna." Manerra covered his face and wept for the first time before a witness since that miraculous and terrible night.

* * * * *

When, at last, Manerra reentered the audience room, Shurna saw in him a pride worn to elemental simplicity, near humility, by exhaustion . . . and in his eyes, a pathway worn to his soul by grief. Now, weary decision burned there, too. In the hard and exhausting days since Aya's disappearance, the shecaren had made astonishing progress to come this far.

"Manerra, shon regis," Shurna murmured for her companions' benefit as well as his.

The expression Manerra turned upon her held none of his earlier flinch. He appeared to understand her intentions, and she saw him fight back the grief that resided so close to the surface in him.

"Janquer lady Shurna. Janquer lord Vantrann." Manerra halted before the ring of their chairs and formally named each of them in turn—

his abbreviated company—with no immediate hope of replacing Kayarra in either abbah or in fact. "I've made decisions that affect each of you. You need to know that I intend to enact them as quickly as possible." He stared at Yutrenta for longer than was comfortable, but Yutrenta's head had remained bowed after veneration and Shurna wasn't certain the Ofrann was aware of Manerra's scrutiny. Yutrenta had taken draydine and had been difficult to rouse for council. Her question's answer, Shurna suspected, would be the most upsetting news Manerra shared.

"You knew Aya's intentions to identify and resolve the problems contributing to southern unrest. It's my intention to follow those plans until it is shown they have no hope for success. He confided the details, rationale, and contingencies of those plans, so I don't assume his intentions or guess at his methods." Manerra paused and swallowed hard, as he did when discussing the assumption of a power that had always been Aya's alone. He was his brother's usurper, his interloper. If Aya had been infirm, or they'd found a body whose spirit required release, he could more easily reconcile himself to his duty and his actions. But Aya had been alive when last they'd seen him. Manerra recalled likening Aya's robe to the star-studded sky, and anything that insubstantial could not be harmed. A hand or weapon would pass through him without touching the substance or soul of him. Aya had to be alive. And while Aya lived, these decisions were not his to make. What would Aya think of his presumptuous, upstart shecaren when he returned?

Tears spilled down Manerra's cheeks and he had to accept the fact he would not get through this meeting dry-eyed. He only waited until he thought his voice would remain steady before continuing.

"The issues involving the sixth tribe have become critical. We can't know that everyone who left Ayahn Rahh heading north after the earthquake was Kitarin. Right now, we have more to fear from Hyranians locating the Kayarran than we have to fear from the Kayarran themselves . . . as long as we don't delay. Kayarra's gift of his language is a more powerful weapon than our enemies boast."

Denassa's hand flew to her mouth to cover a sob.

"As soon as the meetings with the southern lords conclude, I'm taking Vantrann to Timeon Valley.

"Shurna and Denassa, you will remain in Ayahn Rahh and conclude the work I don't finish. During my absence, you will have full power for decisions."

He paused for breath before taking the next step. How did one release a part of life as dependable and constant as the moons? Yutrenta had been more mother to him than had the woman whose body had nurtured him.

*Forgive me, Matera. This is a day of hard truths.*

Irrationally, he wanted to be angry at Yutrenta for loving Aya more than him, but that was because anger was easier to face than the pain of rejection and separation. In the privacy of his room, late one night, he had railed against Aya and their father for setting him up in a birth he'd never wanted, then forcing upon him a power and responsibility he wasn't prepared to wield. If tribal unity collapsed, it would do so under his rule, the shame attached to his name.

Emotional extremes were the most grueling part of what he'd faced so far. Lady Sheron had helped; helped by being unafraid of a boy's cries coming from the mouth of the nation's ruler. And Shurna's forgiveness for not confiding in her did much to close the wounds he felt he created by not being Aya and not having Aya's experiences, wisdom, and presence.

"Yutrenta has asked for release from service," he said.

"No!" Denassa jumped up with that wail and lunged toward Yutrenta, but Shurna caught her. "Out of my way!" Denassa struggled against Shurna's hold. "Yutrenta, why?"

"I have to," Yutrenta answered hoarsely.

"You don't. You don't. They're alive. They'll come back. Gods, Trenta, don't go. *Please* don't go." Denassa ceased struggling, clung to Shurna, and sobbed.

Yutrenta sat with head bowed, one thumb ceaselessly stroking the wrist of her injured arm.

"Yutrenta," Manerra said, then louder, "Yutrenta."

Her head lifted.

"I've thought long about your request. I've been able to think of little else since you asked. I've weighted the merits of your arguments against the questionable benefits of an imposed service. My decision must be to deny your request."

Gasps came from Shurna and Denassa. Yutrenta covered her face with a hand. Vantrann made no sound, didn't move.

"However," Manerra raised a hand before reactions could escalate from stun, "I order your service continued at the Shangren. You will leave here as soon as you can travel safely. That determination will be made by lady Trini, not yourself, not Denassa. I will ask Benta to delay his departure long enough to escort you home."

Yutrenta lowered her hand from her face but did not look at him.

"Your first duty will be to pledge homage to Korrane. The janquer's occupation of the Shangren shall not become a contest of powers. Nor shall you accept his hospitality without service, regardless of kinship. Your dedication will be to the problems of the homesteaders and nomads of south Ofrann. If that duty requires restitution, the apprehension and punishment of criminals, or a residence in the south Ofrann, you will negotiate those requirements with Korrane and abide by his law.

"Meanwhile, I will need a tribal representative to answer in your stead until you resume diplomatic and religious duties, or until I dismiss you from service. Impress upon Korrane the seriousness of this appointment. If anything happens to you, his representative must be able to accept the unification prayer."

The longer he talked, the more dazed Yutrenta appeared, until finally Manerra wasn't certain she heard him. "Korrane will receive confirmation of my orders through a separate messenger," he added, thinking that Korrane, at least, should understand what his sister was doing at the Shangren even if that sister did not fully comprehend it.

"Shon regis," Yutrenta spoke for the first time and shaped the sign of acquiescence. Tears streamed down her cheeks, but they did not appear to be of resentment or accusation. It simply was too soon for recovery. Too soon to let go the hope offered by denial. Crysus might yet return those she'd taken.

* * * * *

The day of Manerra's departure dawned cool and overcast. Rayas, with escorts and three burdened shuren in tow, left for their rendezvous point as Manerra led the janquer in abbah—a futile-seeming gesture without a clear definition of sun on the one hand and a flaming firebrand on the other, a poor substitute for the omnificence of the temple stone. The devout who remained in Ayahn Rahh, however, were faithful in their devotions, adhering to the rites with desperate fervor.

After abbah, Manerra and the janquer met Rayas on the Kitarin road north of the temple. Manerra and Vantrann donned travel robes over their tribal robes, clothing removed from a bulging pack lashed to one shuren's fly-irritated flank. The shuren stamped and tossed her head, anxious to move, as though walking could provide escape from the winged pests.

Manerra turned from the animal. Dressed in a gray robe and youth, he appeared no different from any sixteen-year-old about to journey to Kita, until one observed his eyes and wondered what hardships had befallen this particular youth.

Vantrann, older, taller, impulsively wrapped an arm around Manerra's shoulders. "Don't worry about our young shon regis," he boasted. Manerra freed himself from that condescending arm with a duck and an ease that left Vantrann frowning.

"Shon regis, a word?" Shurna requested. Vantrann's thwarted familiarity reminded her of an unasked question.

Manerra motioned and walked away down the road he was prepared to take. Shurna followed.

"What is it?" he asked, his back to their companions so there could be no lip reading.

"I request permission to send Aena to Kaytron if the Hyranians bring trouble to Cha-ka."

Manerra regarded her.

"She is the only weapon they may use against me without attacking Kaytron itself," Shurna explained in his silence.

"I understand your reasons," he assured. "I only question why you ask permission. You command Ayahn Rahh in my absence."

"Because I swore an oath not to use my position for personal benefit. This falls uncomfortably close to that purview. I ask that the decision be yours."

"Yes, Shurna. Do what you must to assure Aena's safety. I need your head and conscience clear in the moons ahead." Manerra suddenly smiled over her shoulder and started past. Shurna turned and saw Ammira cradling a carefully swaddled bundle in her arms.

Greetings were formal, even though Ammira and her family now resided in the House of Moons. They would live there until they departed Ayahn Rahh, or Raena reached her second sun year. At that time, the child would be given over completely into her half-brother's care for the preparations that would allow her acceptance of the Oath of Yatra.

Manerra lifted his sister and smiled with a pleasure only she could evoke. Care vanished from his face and, in those fleeting moments, he was a young man crooning over the only girl who could ever command his heart.

Finally, he pressed a cheek to each of Raena's cheeks. Then, with tears sparkling his eyes, he returned the bubbling infant to her mother's steady arms. "Thank you," he told Ammira with grave solemnity. *Keep her safe*, his eyes begged Shurna—words he couldn't speak aloud. "Acrahh's watchcare to all of you, and in your journey to Tes-Raly," he wished them.

When heads straightened from veneration, they saw only his back as he strode away.

Shurna stopped beside Denassa and watched Manerra, Vantrann, and their escorts retreat. Nearly two years ago, her stomach had knotted with anxiety over a naive shecaren left in Thurra when their company departed Zarthon. Today, the demigod who walked away had learned more about life and trust in the last four moons than their rhetoric had taught him in ten years. He was immensely stronger, with Aya's wisdom—and grievously hurt by the loss of his brother. That was his vulnerability, once again entrusted into Thurrangy care. That was the basis of her misgivings. She urgently wanted to shout, *Don't! Take someone else*, but knew that was a far worse solution. There could be no shielding him if he was to become the leader Yatra's children desperately needed. The janquer's final parental responsibility must be the assurance that Manerra's pain became compassion and not vengeance. Vantrann, who loved no one more than himself, was not the one to achieve that.

Shurna hooked Denassa's arm in hers. Denassa looked up, her eyes wide with fear.

"Strength, Dee," Shurna whispered. "Vantrann is powerless. Do not wish it otherwise." But she had the distinct impression that she spoke to herself as much as to Denassa.

# CHAPTER 68

Import/Export was a warehouse on the edge of the landing field, protected from trespass by a divider fence that separated the landing field and warehouse from the base's main compound. Export occupied most of the building, separated from Import by a single yellow line spanning the concrete floor. Weeds edged the open bay doors, the same dusty, blade-sharp grass and nettle-bearing weeds that grew wherever foot traffic failed to compact the soil.

Gavin Christoph stood with one foot in Import and one in Export simply because that location offered the best view of the lone shuttle standing on the outside tarmac. Heat waves from atmospheric entry shimmered across its skin, borrowed energy not yet reclaimed by the breeze that puffed through the open doors.

After what seemed like an eternity, Gavin glimpsed movement on the far side of the shuttle and started toward the doors.

A man wearing the blue of Security stepped into his path, bringing him up short, reminding him that he wasn't alone. Many more security personnel than usual, warehouse workers, medical personnel, two women wearing Orbital staff insignia, and others he didn't recognize occupied warehouse space with him.

"I have to ask that you remain here, Sir, until the shuttle's cleared for boarding."

"I'm booked on that shuttle," he told the man.

"I'm sorry, Sir. Special circumstances. Governor's orders. No exceptions."

Gavin squinted against the sunlight pouring past the man's shoulder, trying to get a clear look at his face. "Do I know you?"

"William Scott, Sir. We've not been introduced, but I know who you are. D.A.A. regulations are required study for all field security officers."

The Department of Alien Affairs. His oversight agency. Only Governor Roode ranked higher. "Then we both know why I'm booked on the shuttle?"

"I'm sorry, Dr. Christoph, I can't let you board."

"I'll wait." Out on the landing field, a sausage-shaped balloon now hovered under the nose of the shuttle, four feet above the tarmac. The balloon was tethered by white-suited handlers who waited for members of a security detail to flank them. When Security assumed positions, the entourage moved en masse, and Gavin was startled to see Security draw weapons.

"Goddamn, Roode!" he breathed.

"Sir?"

A second jar. His uninvited Security attachment had no intention of leaving. "Nothing." Gavin shook his head. "Nothing."

Gavin's attention remained on the bubble-enclosed gurney. Activity and conversations around him ceased when others noticed its approach. *If I were sneaking him in, Roode, I'd have assigned another two dozen men. Maybe included a missile launcher. Alerted even the blind.*

Warehouse Security, with the exception of Gavin's newfound friend, ordered people back toward the walls and grounded pallets, clearing the area around the bay doors. Gavin, with William Scott beside him, stood far enough away that he was not asked to move. Which provided a front-line view of the entourage when it entered the warehouse.

There were too many bodies in the way for Gavin to get a clear look inside the balloon. Those who escorted the containment unit were approached by those waiting to receive it. Gavin was jostled by someone behind him straining for a better look. He didn't have a clear direction to step to get out of the woman's way. Then the armed officer in front of him stepped aside and the medic standing beside the c-unit turned and Gavin caught a two-seconds-long look at the face of the man inside.

Justin Reids was young, and unconscious, and nearly unrecognizable from the pictures Gavin had seen of him. His head lay sideways on the pillow, held in position by straps. Tubes entered nostrils and mouth, which explained the drool that dampened the pillow. Then the medic turned back around and Gavin lost his glimpse of the boy. Gavin was left to reflect in afterthought that the wrap covering Reids' hair was a bandage and not a turban as first impression gave. The boy had appeared ill beneath the tan that darkened half his face. Gavin suspected that Reids should be lying in a recovery room, not flying between Orbital and Base. Whoever had authorized his transfer was an idiot.

"Come this way, Sir," said the now-familiar voice at Gavin's shoulder.

Gavin scanned nearby warehouse walls for a data link . . . spotted an occupied work counter instead.

"Dr. Christoph?"

"I'll be right with you." Gavin pressed between two men on his right as he drew a computer from his breast pocket. Depressing the power button, he brought the mike to his lips. "Send to James Matley, OAL2. Jim, I want J. Reids' placement contract sent to this unit." Then, as an afterthought, "If you can." Reids' records had been sealed after the crash. Access to them now depended upon what new clearances had been assigned to the reopened case. Governor Roode might explain the security restrictions even if he couldn't share the files, but Gavin couldn't make that request over Base channels. Jim's success or failure would tell him enough.

Gavin stopped opposite the man leaning over the work counter's embedded screen. "Is there a data link I can use?" he asked before the man looked up. Gavin spotted the link the same instant the man raised a hand to point.

Gavin touched his handheld's contact to the metallic pad and waited seconds longer than should have been necessary for the in-use transmission light to turn green. He didn't want incoming work. The shuttle's flight time wasn't long enough to complete all the work he presently carried.

Half a day later, when Jim's terse, "Reids' records show Restricted Access," came back, Gavin had been at Orbital for four hours and had finally concluded the arrangements for his examination of the sentient. Jim's setback lost importance the moment Gavin halted beside the examination table and drew back the sheet that covered the body.

For three minutes, Gavin stared, until his assistant's arrival drew his attention away from the body. For a confusing moment, the monitor readouts on the faceplate distracted him, until he forced his attention past the faceplate and onto the face visible through that other contamination suit's helmet. Katherine was her name. Kariack, he thought she'd said, or something close to it.

"No autopsy," he said, not sure whether the suit's audio pickup had an on-off switch or voice activation.

"If you're basing that order on his dress, Dr. Christoph, you should know that Reids wore similar attire when they were picked up."

"Where's Reids' clothing?"

"It was treated as personal property. It went groundside with him."

"Describe it."

"The beadwork, embroidery, and motifs on the skirt are similar to what you see here, only worked on light blue wool. A marked difference is in this area." She circled the chest with a gloved finger. "On Reids' garment, the chest motif appears to be a sunflower or starburst, and this symbol," Katherine's gloved hand hovered flat above the chest, "is reproduced in miniature on Reids' right shoulder, here."

The shoulder she pointed to lay under a tangled mass of narrow braids. Gavin lifted the braids off the dead man's shoulder. The fabric underneath was unadorned, but a glint in the braids made Gavin peer closer at what he held. He spotted a faceted bead woven into one plait. Then, looking for them, he spotted others.

"I think we're in deep shit," Gavin said.

"Pardon?"

"This man is no commoner. And we've got his body. Try explaining that to anyone who comes looking for him."

"His time of death was estimated at thirty-two hours before the boarding team gained entry."

"Katherine, Reids is alive. This man is dead. I'm not sure that anything Reids can say—the truth or a lie—is going to matter a hell of a lot to any sentient searching for this man." Then he added, "Let's hope to hell I'm wrong." He tried to rub his temple and knocked the faceplate of his helmet. "No autopsies," he repeated. "I want that order placed on record."

"We're being recorded, Dr. Christoph."

"Shit."

He had three days for tests and analyses. Then he wanted to talk to Reids. By that time, he'd have a hell of a lot of questions for Reids.

*****

Stomach and intestinal samples; nail scrapings; dentin, skin, and hair samples; fiber and dye analyses; eyes . . . .

Gavin, his own eyes closed, head heavy against the shuttle seat's headrest, saw in his imagination the dark, haunting eyes of the sentient and wondered just how far their animal similarities went. An amazing adaptation, sparked by what evolutionary dictate, he couldn't guess without knowing their functional properties. He could wish for the sophisticated equipment of a medical or pharmaceutical research lab, but that would only get him transported to someplace he didn't want to be, working a job he hated.

Although he'd never been able to sleep on a shuttle flight, overstimulation accounted for his current inability to relax. All he could hope was that adrenalin would carry him through his meeting with Roode, and a miracle would allow him to focus. Because right now, his brain kept reviewing information, grouping and regrouping facts, remembering details, and running through test lists to determine whether he'd overlooked any avenue of investigation.

As it was, he'd be receiving test results and query replies for a week or more. His only regret was that he couldn't return with the body, but Base didn't have the facilities for long-term storage and, if what he suspected was true, the body was too valuable to risk further deterioration.

*****

Archson's head jerked up as Gavin burst into the reception area. The secretary's eyes followed Gavin's progress across the room. "He expected you an hour ago," Archson said.

"Boarding was delayed," Gavin said. "Again."

"He knows."

"Get in here," a voice ordered through the open door at Archson's back.

The door closed as soon as Gavin crossed the threshold. However, for all of Roode's impatience, his eyes didn't shift from his monitor as Gavin crossed the room.

"I know how many times you and Matley have tried to access the Reids file," Roode said as if speaking to himself, "but restrictions aren't coming off this one."

Roode touched the screen, stood, then stepped past the corner of his desk. "Sit down." Roode gestured toward his vacated seat. "I'll be right back." He left the office.

Gavin circled the desk, his attention on the lit monitor, eyes darting to the heading on the open file. The Reids file. He touched the medical tab before he was seated.

Among the file's cross-referenced reports was one on Thurman that Gavin began scanning, then reading word-for-word.

The door opened and Roode entered carrying a mug. "Want coffee?" he asked.

Gavin stood and circled the desk. "No. Thanks." He turned to sit in the visitor's chair and saw Roode's attention go to the monitor.

Shit! He'd left the file open on the Thurman report. Thurman had been one of Roode's closest friends. "The rumors are amazingly accurate," Gavin broke the silence.

Roode touched the screen, closing the report. "There was no gag order," he said, finally turning his attention to Gavin. "And a lot of people were involved. Pieces got connected."

"What's the boy's story?"

"The boy's not talking. Did you hear that he attacked the boarding party? Of course, you did. You came straight from Orbital."

Gavin leaned forward. "I want to be placed in quarantine with Reids."

Roode's lips twitched and he tapped the desk's edge with a fingertip. "Don't tempt me. To be free of you for thirty days . . . ."

"I've been in a stinking contamination suit for three days. What's the difference?"

"Then you're asking for access rather than confinement?"

"No. I want confinement. I want to live with him for twenty-six days, without a C-suit."

"You've got greater confidence in our medical staff than I do."

"Reids is alive." Too late, Gavin realized his mistake. Silence started to lengthen. "I'm sorry, Roode."

"Don't be. The majority of blood in the transport's cabin was Thurman's. Opinions vary on whether he survived the crash. All safety devices operated according to manufacturers' specifications, but that doesn't protect a pilot from crumpled metal, broken fiberglass, shattered plastics . . . ."

Gavin had learned from the report that Thurman's leg had been amputated in order to remove him from the transport. So, sentient cannibalism could be more pragmatic—more opportunity-based—than hostile aggression. Reids might have burned his hands trying to pull Thurman from the fire.

Aloud, Gavin said, "I'll sign legal papers stating that my commitment is voluntary, and was aggressively sought."

Roode laughed. "Thanks for the warning." He met Gavin's eyes, and Gavin saw the pain that lingered there despite the laugh.

"On psych reports alone, I can argue a case for purview," Gavin said. "Attacking his rescue party, identification with the dominant native life form—"

Roode tapped the monitor screen three times. "You can stop trying to convince me. I'm granting your wish."

# CHAPTER 69

"Ka'rra," Gavin said.

The boy pushed up from the mattress on the floor and spun around. Gavin saw distrust in the eyes that locked onto his. The boy drew back against the wall. His hospital gown crinkled when he moved. Paper.

Gavin saw no recognizable indication that the boy had been asleep.

The room's single furnishing was that mattress. Toilet facilities were located in a doorless closet at the rear of the room. The head bandage he'd worn in the containment unit was gone, making it hard not to stare at the shaved portion of his scalp. A plate had been surgically implanted to replace the skull's missing bone.

"I'm Gavin Christoph," he introduced himself. "I understand you speak our language."

No answer.

"Is it okay if I sit?"

The boy looked down at the mattress.

Gavin crossed to the wall opposite and sat on the floor with his back against the wall. When his attention returned to Justin, the boy glanced away.

*I'm the first person he's seen without quarantine gear*, Gavin realized. *God, what humans do to their own kind!*

"What do you want?" The boy's attention returned.

Gavin noticed the accent. "To meet you. To get to know you."

"Why?" Strong suspicion.

Gavin wondered how complete the amnesia was and how far the boy had assimilated. Doctors had found some organic brain damage, but claimed Reids' amnesia was psychogenic—so-called hysterical amnesia. Not hard to guess its roots, if the diagnosis was accurate. Gavin suspected the suicide watch had been ordered on the basis of the same report. During quarantine prep, the base's psychiatrist had cautioned Gavin against inadvertent references either to the accident or the subsequent "incident" involving Thurman.

"Because I think there's a lot you can teach me," Gavin answered Justin's *why*.

"I don't know anything. Nobody will answer me. Where am I? Who are you?"

That gave Gavin pause. "You're at Culver Base," he said. "I'm with the Office of Alien Liaison."

"I don't know what the fuck 'Culver Base' is! I want out of here." Justin gripped the edge of the mattress, and Gavin saw clearly the reddish-brown discolorations on those hands. Burn scars.

Gavin drew his feet in and rested both elbows atop folded knees. "Culver Base is a supply station for science exploration ships. We supply water, oxygen, and food for long-range, long-term expeditions."

Gavin waited, but Justin didn't move, didn't speak. "Tell me about the man they found with you. Was he a friend?"

Justin's shoulders drew up until the wavy hair behind his ears brushed the hospital gown. "I want to go outside. I want to touch the ground," Justin said without looking at him.

Stalemate.

"We can't leave this room."

Justin's head jerked around. "You can leave. Why can't I?"

"You'll be able to leave before I can," Gavin said.

That head turned away.

"You stared when I came in because I wasn't wearing a contamination suit. This is a quarantine unit. I was contaminated the second I came through the airlock. You're here for twenty-five days, I'm here for thirty."

The boy shifted away, leaned his shoulder and head against the wall, and held that position without speaking until Gavin's belongings arrived: an inflatable mattress, a paper gown identical to Justin's, and a computer. The computer had been Gavin's hardest won concession.

Justin watched Gavin inflate the mattress, break away the inflator, and drop the device into the recycle chute, but turned away every time Gavin looked directly at him. Was that aversion to eye contact a native custom or Justin's answer to injured pride?

"What is your name for this world?" Gavin asked, trying again for conversation.

"Axxord," Justin said.

"I like that better than Culver." Silence stretched out. "You speak the local language, don't you?"

"Why are you here? What do you want from me?"

*Personal questions set him off*, Gavin realized. *He trusts no one.*

"I'm here because I examined the man they found with you," Gavin said, then answered the alarm in the boy's eyes: "The body was handled with respect."

Justin rubbed his face.

"What's the man's name?"

"Aya."

For a moment, Gavin thought the boy had voiced a murmur of grief. "What's his name?"

"*Aya*," Justin spoke louder, with a touch of anger.

"Who was he?"

"I don't want to talk about this."

*It's what you most want to talk about*, Gavin guessed. "What will you talk about, then?"

"Nothing. Leave me alone."

Gavin scooped his computer from the floor, crossed to the bathroom, sat on the lidless toilet, and balanced the computer across his knees. "When you want to talk," he raised his voice, "we can discuss your future."

Gavin activated the machine, opened the directory, scanned the computer's contents, and spotted a file that set his heart racing.

"I want to leave."

Gavin looked up. Justin stood in the doorway in bare feet and legs, the pale blue gown a fashionless cover that stuck out at odd angles where the paper had creased.

"Neither of us can leave," Gavin told him.

"In twenty-five days. I want to leave."

"Justin, it's not—"

The boy's fist slammed the doorframe. "My name's Kayarra!"

Gavin closed the computer while assessing his maneuverability in the tiny space. "Then tell me about Ka'rra," he shouted back, "because your skin cells identically match Justin Reids' DNA." Gavin shoved the computer into a corner with his foot as he stood.

"Learn who I am before you call me names."

Gavin took a step forward, which was all the space separating them. "You won't *let* anybody know you!" he shouted into the boy's face. "And what I've seen so far, I don't like."

The boy's fist hit his stomach.

Trained reflexes caught Justin's wrist, whipped the arm over the boy's head, and Gavin caught him in a vice grip as Justin spun around. "I can call you Shithead," Gavin panted in Justin's ear, "and if you know who you are, it won't matter."

Kayarra jerked against Gavin's hold, the boy stronger than he looked. Gavin shoved him away and stepped clear of the door, relieved to be free of that confining space. Kayarra spun and faced him, right arm raised defensively. Both hands were fists.

"I can't leave," Gavin yelled at the boy. "If we attempt to kill each other, all they can do is lock us in separate rooms. Whether you believe me or not doesn't change fact."

"Stay away from me!" Justin shouted. "Leave me alone!" He backed up.

Gavin saw a reddening of the flesh around Justin's eyes. "I'll be in the bathroom." Gavin returned to the toilet and reached into the corner for the computer. Then he stood with his back to the wall listening. The only sound at the other end of the room was the low crinkling rustle of paper and then silence.

Gavin sat down on the toilet and reactivated the computer. The surprise file titled with Justin Reids' code name contained a single line of nonsense symbols fifteen characters long.

* * * * *

Gavin stared at the floor beside the boy's mattress, at the paper plate containing breakfast remnants. No wonder the boy was so skinny. He didn't eat enough to sustain an ant.

Maybe toilet water was more nutritious than any of them suspected.

Gavin shuddered. The loss of taste had its drawbacks—and benefits, he supposed.

"Who was I here?"

That question shifted Gavin's attention from the plate to Justin's face. "You were a senior geology intern assigned to Dr. George Thurman."

Not even a blink over that name.

"What did I do?"

"Cartography. Sound wave tests." Gavin shrugged. "Whatever geologists do. I have very little contact with the geology department. I can't tell you more than that."

"Why was I in the desert?"

Gavin hesitated. He was being tested. Roode had authorized his review of Justin's briefing files. Did the boy hope for different answers, or did he compare one person's story with another's? "You were on a field trip when a transport malfunctioned."

"Was I alone?"

"Dr. Thurman piloted the craft."

Justin blanched and his attention shifted away.

Gavin leaned forward. "What happened that day?"

"I don't know."

"You know something about it."

"I wasn't there!" Justin shouted, then appeared confused by his own denial. "If I was, I don't remember. All I remember is a tent, and my hands, and *ilan* Denassa."

"What is 'ill-and' . . .?" Gavin trailed off, the other word escaping him.

Justin's attention snapped back. His face revealed confusion. "It's . . . a title. For a woman."

"Teach me more."

Silence.

Gavin lifted his empty plate and stood. Kayarra sipped from the paper cup of water he held.

"Are you going to eat anything else?"

The cup came down. "If I leave without touching anyone, without getting near anyone, will you let me go?"

"Ka'rra, I'm not in a position to authorize anything like that."

"Who is? Governor Roode?"

"Even Governor Roode can't allow it. There are laws—"

Justin's arm rose, came down hard, and the cup of ice water burst against the floor at Gavin's feet, spraying him. Gavin didn't flinch.

Justin jammed the heels of his hands against his eyes and rocked.

Gavin's anger sparked. "Be glad those laws are there, because it protects them from us. Humans would swarm this planet and suck it dry if not for those laws. Instead of railing against them, planning ways around them, be damned glad they're there. Those people saved your life. The least you can do is protect them."

He stopped rocking, pressed both fists against his forehead. "How?"

"By helping me understand them. By convincing me they're worth protecting. Because there are damned huge corporations waiting in line to claim Culver's resources. Timber, oxygen and water alone are worth the price of a court battle. Forget minerals, biologicals, and everything else."

*While you're at it, tell me how the hell you were pulled from a UFO going God knows where. Are there more races here than we've discovered? Where the hell are they? Shit, what a mess!*

"If I help, will you leave? All of you?"

"Leave what?"

"Go back to wherever you came."

'We' didn't exist in his vocabulary. "You're one of us."

Justin's head jerked up.

*Good!* "What happens to us, happens to you. You can call yourself Ka'rra until you're blue, but your DNA seals your fate in any court of law."

"What if the Yatren attack?"

Gavin flashed back upon the male with the quartz beads in his hair. *We're in deep shit.* "We're here," he said. "If every one of us is killed, our backers will rebuild with stronger defenses. Probably secure authorization to use lethal force in their defense of the new base. And my successor will have a hell of a time convincing anyone that we should respect indigene rights to either their resources or their lives."

"We *are demons.*" Justin folded his arms across his knees and buried his face in their juncture.

*We are* were the only words Gavin understood. He stared at the top of the boy's head, at the incision line where the plate had been inserted.

Justin Reids had graduated *summa cum laude.* Ka'rra shocked the medics by proving he could neither read nor write.

How much of Justin Reids had they recovered with Ka'rra? How thoroughly had Justin suppressed everything human in his need to deny the accident and its outcome? How much of his memory loss was attributable to organic damage? A notation in Justin's file said he'd drunk out of the toilet and urinated in the sink, as though he'd never seen either fixture.

# CHAPTER 70

From the mattress in the corner by the bathroom, shallow half-snores sounded with rhythmic regularity.

Kayarra shifted on his mattress, turned his head on his arm, opened his eyes, then shut them. Opening his eyes to escape the vision of Aya felt like a rejection of him, when Kayarra's only wish was to undo everything that had happened after the earthquake. Even in his imagination, though, he couldn't keep the hinged stone closed, couldn't prevent Aya from entering the tunnel in the wall below the fearsome depiction of Crysus.

Aya. Firelight reflecting in his eyes like liquid motion, smoke rising between them like a gauze veil. Aya after supper one night, describing the placement of a single fate within each child at birth. Describing how an adult could resist Acrahh's plan, but resistance was a snow-burdened branch. The branch might break, or the snow might melt and the branch return to its original position. But as long as the branch knew burden, so did the spirit. A body did not die as long as birth-fate remained unfulfilled.

*Was your sole birth-fate to escort me home? Then Acrahh's plan makes no sense. I'm no one. Why didn't Crysus kill me? If you knew Manerra was right about me, why did you protect me?*

"It is Acrahh's gift that man not know his purpose," Aya said, his face alight with fire-glow, his back shaded by trees, the cacophony of night creatures rising. "It is a man's responsibility not to rail against Acrahh's gifts or lack of gifts, but to find a way to accept and use what he has been given."

"How does a person recognize tools she's never seen to complete a task she doesn't know?" Denassa had asked.

"The same way a newborn knows to suckle."

Kayarra rubbed his face hard. *Are you still protecting me?* he sent that question into the sky, into that room he thought of as Crysus where Aya had last lain. *I heard you that night, but I was groping. I still am. It's taken me this long to understand what you said.*

* * * * *

Kayarra reared up, surprised to realize he'd slept. Real sleep, not the eyes closed, mind roiling, nightmare-broken thing that had passed for sleep since well before the joining. He let an arm and the wall support his weight while he looked for Gavin.

Gavin sat cross-legged on his mattress, the computer wedged in the cross of his legs, his fingers motionless on the keyboard while he stared at the monitor.

"Aya died bringing me here," Kayarra said, not because he expected Gavin to understand the significance of that statement, but because he needed to say it.

Gavin's attention shifted from the monitor. Gavin's eyes were brown. Dark enough that Kayarra felt a pang while looking into them.

"Aya thought—" *I was someone important.* Kayarra shifted attention to the wall behind Gavin. Blank. Featureless. Windowless. As similar to and different from Yatren construction as two walls could be. It was the similarities—the absence of windows—that made the differences so frighteningly foreign. And there was no one to tell him whether abbah was anticipated or past.

It took tremendous effort to look back into Gavin's face, to meet the intensity of his stare. "Was Justin Reids a criminal?" he asked.

"No. Justin was well liked. I didn't know him personally, but I know people who did."

"Was whatever happened my fault?"

"There was an accident. A machine failed to operate properly. None of what happened was your fault. It's only a miracle that you survived."

Kayarra looked at the wall.

"I found a reading program," Gavin said, "if you're interested in learning how to read."

"*You are batok*," Kayarra said, hands shaking.

"Pardon?" Gavin's brow creased.

"It means, 'You are my family,'" Kayarra told him.

* * * * *

A moan broke Gavin's concentration. He looked over at Kayarra. The boy's face was turned away from the bathroom light, toward the wall. The only part of him visible above the blanket was the back of his head.

Gavin squeezed his eyes shut for a moment of relief from the monitor's eye-tiring glow. When he looked back at the monitor, he noticed that the date in the lower right-hand corner of the screen had changed.

Kayarra's release date.

CELL BLOCK 1, DAY 24, he titled yesterday's report, stood, and crossed the room to the data link. He waited through the transfer of information and saw the date blink red. *Ahh, celebration, at last*, he thought, although the blinking date merely indicated newly received data.

Curiosity won out over sleep. Among the new mail, 'James Matley' appeared twice, 'Gov. C. Roode,' once. Roode won out over Matley.

*Governor Roode is holding*
*1400 hours open for*
*a meeting with you on the*
*day of your release.*
*—R. Archson*

Gavin scanned Jim's mail to see whether his assistant could shed light on the governor's summons, but Jim's messages were forwarded confirmations of approval for Justin's temporary assignment to the Office of Alien Liaison, and release instructions from Justin's doctor.

Gavin looked back at Justin's head. Gavin suspected that Justin withheld permanent assignment agreement because he planned to run. Gavin had warned both Roode and Jim of that likelihood, and wasn't surprised that Roode had issued a security alert before he received Gavin's warning.

Gavin closed the computer, returned to his mattress, and sat down. In five days, he'd have a chair again. God, he couldn't wait.

*****

A nurse wearing a contamination suit arrived to escort Justin from the room, although neither Gavin nor Justin had exhibited symptoms of illness during their confinement. Justin started toward the nurse before Gavin intercepted him. He caught Justin's hand and pressed his arm. "*Walk well*," he said in Yatren, staring into Justin's eyes. *Don't do anything rash.* "Jim is waiting for you in the lounge. I'll see you in five days." He let go his grip and stepped aside.

Justin followed the nurse from the room, his attention on the floor.

*****

Archson rose from his desk and started around its corner when Gavin walked into the governor's suite five days later.

"Don't leave," Gavin joked. "I've served my time and repented."

A polite smile and a, "He's waiting for you," were all he got before Archson left the office.

Gavin stared at Roode's back when he entered the governor's private office. "I'm losing my touch," Gavin remarked as a way of announcing his presence.

Roode blanked his monitor and swiveled around. "You may lose more than that. Have a seat."

"I've had neither breakfast nor lunch, so my cookies are safe." Gavin sat down in the nearest chair.

Roode shut the door from the control panel on his desk. "The trace report on the ship came in. So did test results on the body in Orbital's freezer."

"And?"

"We're occupying an Earth colony."

"Huh?" Gavin grunted before he realized that Roode wasn't referring to Culver Base. "That's not possible."

"Initial biochemical results support the ship's trace report."

"What's the trace say?"

"Earth manufacture. Hard records don't exist on our specific ship, but the design matches one of five commissioned by a fanatic religious cult involved in an 'Adam and Eve' project. They sent shiploads of believers off Earth in advance of an Armageddon prediction. Our ship is the only one that's surfaced. And we've got recordings on everything from seismic to radar to visual establishing its launch point. That data coincides with what Reids told you."

An irrational anger burst through Gavin's stun. "Was visuals part of the package?"

"You knew Reids was under suicide watch before you went in," Roode reminded him.

Gavin gripped the chair's armrests. "I'm sorry. You're right. I knew. It's just . . . this changes so many things."

"It changes everything."

"Does Matley know?"

"No. There'll be no staff announcement until legal avenues are exhausted and our charter's declared illegal."

"God."

"How close are you to a breakthrough with the boy?"

"He hasn't committed yet, but I think he will."

"It's imperative that we keep him."

"He wants to stay. On Culver, that is. Just not at the base. I explained the restrictions on indigene-human contact. But this . . . ."

"They're indigenes until the courts rule otherwise."

"We don't have another option," Gavin said. "This discovery doesn't change how they view us."

"We need legal contracts in place before the charter challenges are decided. Our future depends on whatever you and Reids can negotiate."

"Our success or failure has a lot to do with who the iced man is."

"Keep me informed," Roode said.

Gavin recognized the dismissal and stood.

"Christoph," Roode added, "I won't authorize travel for Reids until he's not an escape threat."

"That makes contact rather tricky."

Roode shrugged. "Work it out. At the moment, losing Reids is more of a threat to our legal placement than that goddamn ship."

# CHAPTER 71

Kayarra stood in front of the Office of Alien Liaison's only window while beads of water slid erratic paths down the outside glass. Rain struck gravel in the yard beyond the window, beat against weeds that bordered the diamond meshed fence, and dulled the greens of distant trees.

It was the fence he had been staring at when Gavin walked in, but he shifted attention to the reflection of the room behind him when greetings began. There was genuine pleasure in the exchange between Jim Matley and Gavin.

"Ka'rra," Gavin's voice rose, "good to see you again. Are you settling in? Learning your way around?"

He glanced over his shoulder. "Yes," he said, then turned back to the window. In the glass, he saw Gavin sit down at the left hand desk and poke at the large computer monitor there. Jim Matley hovered over him, back to the window, speaking in murmurs too low to distinguish. He wondered what Jim Matley was saying about him.

Kayarra looked back out the window, past the fence to the tree line. He was only vaguely aware, by a flicker of motion in the reflection, when Jim Matley left Gavin's desk and crossed to the desk on the opposite side of the room.

Gavin hadn't lied to him. Today was the fifth day after his release, and the first time he'd seen Gavin since they parted in 'the cell block,' as Gavin called it. Jim Matley, the only person who worked with Gavin in the Office of Alien Liaison, had met Kayarra after his release and shown him to a private room that was 'his.' Jim Matley had secured clothes for him, shown him where meals were served, and set tones to sound on a computer when meals were being served. He'd also introduced him to strangers, whose reactions, although subtle, were reminiscent of the Shangren's citizens' reactions. And he couldn't grow accustomed to the differences in their hair, eyes, and skin coloring . . . their clothing . . . their speech. Gavin, with his brown eyes and hair, was closer to Yatren normal than others, although there were two black-haired men who snagged Kayarra's attention every time he glimpsed one. One of the black-haired men had seen him in the dining hall, dropped his plate, and shouted "Justin!" with such emotion it had startled Kayarra. Jim Matley later explained that the man had been a close friend of Justin Reids. The incident had been unnerving.

Kayarra pulled back from the window far enough to see his reflection in the glass. The uncut hair at the back and sides of his head was longer than that worn by Base men, but far shorter than any adult Yatren wore. Long hair and braids conflicted with human clothing; pale hair and skin belied Yatren robes. On either side of the line, he wasn't quite right, he didn't quite fit.

"Have you thought about my offer?" Gavin asked.

Kayarra turned from the window, but it was Jim Matley who asked, "Are you talking to the machine, yourself, or one of us?"

"You've grown way too cocky in the director's chair," Gavin retorted, grinning. "I was speaking to Ka'rra, if you don't mind."

"I've thought about it," Kayarra answered. He'd thought about little else. Justin Reids' internship contract mandated his removal from Axxord/Culver if he failed to perform certain duties in accordance with standards set forth in that document. Gavin's explanation of contracts made Kayarra realize that Justin had been owned by people who didn't live on Axxord. If he agreed to Gavin's proposal, he would be owned again, first by Gavin, but ultimately by the Department of Alien Affairs, the same people who owned Gavin.

Kayarra had tried to reconcile his participation in the unification prayer with Gavin's offer and failed. All he knew for sure was which agreement held his loyalty in the event of conflicting interests.

"Have you reached a decision?" Gavin asked, his attention unwavering.

"*I work with you*," Kayarra answered.

"Pardon?" Jim Matley asked.

"You answered in Yatren," Gavin explained what Kayarra hadn't realized he'd done.

Kayarra stared at the floor, embarrassed by the transparency of his distress. "I want to stay on Axxord," he said, meeting Gavin's eyes. "I will work with you."

Gavin stood, his smile broad. He crossed the room with a hand extended. "This position will give you a chance to look out for Yatren interests." His fingers closed around Kayarra's. "You won't regret it."

Kayarra looked down at their clasped hands even as he pulled away.

Gavin's smile wavered. "Come on. Let's talk to Professional Management. If we start today, the transfer will be complete by the end of the week."

Kayarra nodded numbly.

* * * * *

Translations were what Gavin had him working on—with Jim's

help—because his reading skills were still so poor. Jim read words and Kayarra spoke the Yatren equivalent. The computer produced a phonetic spelling of Kayarra's word beneath Jim's printed word. It was an intensely disturbing exercise that highlighted Kayarra's limitations with the Yatren language and gave the humans knowledge he'd rather not hand them.

"Leader," Jim said.

Kayarra stopped, unable to answer.

"Do you know this one?" Jim asked.

"The word's too vague."

"Which word?"

"The human word."

"How would they make an inquiry about a leader? Do they have leaders?"

"They have leaders."

"Name all of them and we'll work through the list."

*"Shon regis, shecaren, tribal leader, janquer."*

Jim laughed. "They like structure, don't they? What do the words mean?"

"Acrahh's sons, family ruler, family representative to Acrahh's sons."

"What are the other three?"

"They use compound words." Kayarra hesitated. Manerra was shon regis now, and the baby was shecaren, which destroyed the security of his known world. "Shon regis and shecaren are both Acrahh's children."

"Who's Acrahh?"

They worked through an explanation of the gods; that the differences in titles distinguished—not the sex of a child—but which child ruled, and that there were two of them. Jim questioned Kayarra's 'family' interpretation. "Do you mean 'tribe'?" Jim finally asked.

"Yes," Kayarra said, desperate to change the subject, although Jim's word didn't have the right feel. Kayarra's emotions were fraying more the longer they discussed the distinctions of leadership.

Jim typed something into the computer.

"What level of leader comes next, below the shecaren?"

"Janquer." *I was janquer.*

"What are—"

"Security," the computer blared, "to Dr. Christoph. Report to Gate Three immediately. Repeat—"

Jim froze their program and pushed a button. "This is OAL, James Matley. Dr. Christoph is in Professional Management or Communications."

"OAL, why don't you and your new employee meet Dr. Christoph at Gate Three?"

"Under whose authority, Security? Request rationale and identification."

"Governor Roode. Native contact. ID—"

Kayarra left his chair and reached the hall before Jim could sign off. Jim caught up to him before Kayarra reached the building's main entrance.

"You don't leave without me!" Jim shouted when he caught up at a run.

Kayarra couldn't reply. Yearning and anxiety overwhelmed him. He paused while Jim manipulated the door's locking mechanism, glimpsed his reflection in the glass, and almost turned away. He wore the foreigners' clothes. His ceremonial robe hung in the closet in his room, but to wear it for any purpose other than ritual felt blasphemous. To face any Yatren now was to present himself as a cor-anda.

The door opened and Jim dashed down the stairs, Kayarra following. Gravel crunched underfoot as they jogged across the compound, passing buildings and shade trees. The chest-high fence surrounding the base appeared like a mockery of protection, but Gavin had warned that the physical barrier was only a visual indication of the security perimeter. He'd demonstrated its effectiveness with a thrown rock. "It won't kill," Gavin had explained, "but you won't be standing if you touch it."

The location of Gate Three was apparent the moment they cleared the corner of the building that blocked its view. Peacekeepers—*security guards*, Kayarra corrected himself—were clustered there.

Jim hooked Kayarra's arm and dropped back to a walk. "Gavin's not here yet," he said.

Beyond the blue of security uniforms, Kayarra glimpsed a flutter of gray cloth. He quickened pace, then halted abruptly when he caught sight of a Yatren face.

Manerra turned at the same time as if he sensed Kayarra's presence. Their eyes locked.

An eternity passed in those seconds. Manerra's expression shifted from stun to hope to dismay before Vantrann stepped between them. Jim tugged Kayarra's arm, but Kayarra pulled back.

"Where is Aya?" Vantrann shouted.

Manerra circled Vantrann and started forward. Guards stepped in front of him. Vantrann's knife flashed into his hand, and the guards pulled weapons.

"No!" Jim shouted, raising both hands. "No guns!"

Manerra sidestepped the guard in front of him but did not advance. "Where's Aya?" Manerra repeated Vantrann's demand.

"Aya—" Kayarra's throat clenched so hard it hurt.

Manerra dipped his head.

"Answer!" Vantrann shouted.

"Sheathe your knife," Manerra said without looking up. "Wait with the shuren."

"Shon regis—" Vantrann protested.

"Do it," Manerra said.

"What's going on?" Jim demanded at Kayarra's side, his voice tense. The crunch of gravel gave warning of a new arrival, but Kayarra kept his attention on Manerra.

Vantrann's retreat was stiff, grudging, tense.

"What's going on?" the new inquiry was Gavin's. "Do you know these men?"

"Manerra, shon regis, I show you Gavin Christoph of the *human* tribe," Kayarra said.

"Gavichristo," Manerra repeated a close approximation of Gavin's name, "peace from the children of Yatra."

"Gavin Christoph, I show you Manerra, shon regis," Kayarra said and heard Jim's sharp intake of breath.

"Janquer lord Kayarra," Manerra said, "I would speak with you alone."

Kayarra looked back at Gavin. "Shon regis Manerra wants to talk to me alone." Then added when Gavin hesitated, "I won't try to escape."

"The guards have to stay," Gavin said. "They don't understand Yatren. You'll have privacy." Gavin motioned Jim to accompany him and retreated to the shade of a tree.

"Peacekeepers stay," Kayarra told Manerra. "They not know Yatren talk."

"You are not trusted," Manerra said.

"They know I not want to stay."

"Your eyes tell me things I don't want to hear, but must. Was Aya's spirit released?"

"I not know where is Aya."

"You were with him." Manerra's voice rose, "Will you tell me Crysus didn't take you when she took him? How do you live when he does not? Where's the temple stone?"

Guards shifted. Some glanced across at Gavin.

With words and hand signals, Kayarra described as best he could what happened from the moment the standing stone broke until the demons arrived, although the word description damned him. "I not know how I come here," Kayarra insisted, needing Manerra to believe him. "I know Crysus. I know here. I not know where is Aya."

Manerra stared over Kayarra's left shoulder as if looking at him had become too painful. "I want to hate you," Manerra said. "For coming to me. For taking away everything I loved . . . for taking away my brother. But how do I hate my father for using me when I was born to be his voice and his tool? I thought myself clever enough to escape my birthright." Manerra dipped his head, his fists pale-knuckled balls at his sides.

Manerra lifted his head and met Kayarra's eyes, his face flushed with anger and grief, his eyes, too bright. "In the end, the gods have used us both and set us apart. I'm as alone as you are. I have a shecaren, but for two years, she's not mine. You have a tribe, but you have no past with them."

"I go with you," Kayarra said.

"Make peace with your tribe, Kayarra. It's not safe for you where I go." Manerra signaled Vantrann.

"Where is janquer?" Kayarra blurted as Vantrann started back. *Is Denassa safe?*

"In Ayahn Rahh, overseeing what I cannot."

Vantrann carried a coiled belt with an attached sheath and pouch, and a narrow, drawstring bag. He offered them to Manerra. Manerra pointed at Kayarra, and Vantrann turned, holding out the items.

Kayarra approached, casting nervous glances at the guards. None made a move to stop him. He approached close enough to take the items from Vantrann, then stood holding them, stroking a thumb over the leather of the belt: the precious, final remnants of the life he'd lost.

Gravel grated behind Kayarra but he didn't turn.

"Is everything okay?" Gavin glanced at the sheathed knife but said nothing.

"Gavichristo," Manerra said, the syllables separated and accented strangely, "my broth-or walk Kayarra. You know my broth-or?"

Gavin turned toward Kayarra. "Who is his brother?"

"Aya."

"Tell him that his brother is not here, but I can have his body brought here. It will take at least three days to arrange the transfer. While he's waiting, I'd like to talk to him. I have questions about his people. I'm sure he has questions about us."

Kayarra translated.

"I talk to Gavichristo," Manerra answered. "I talk Yumen. We talk . . . ." Manerra pointed to the line of trees twenty yards from the security fence.

"Fair enough," Gavin said. "Let's go. Ka'rra, you're coming, too. The guards stay here."

* * * * *

Manerra led them to a cluster of trees at the base of an outcropping, where fallen rocks provided natural seating. Twigs dangling from branches and trampled plants indicated this wasn't the first time the place had been used as a rendezvous. That Manerra knew about it made Kayarra wonder how long Manerra had been in these woods, watching the base, searching the area.

Using a mixture of languages, hand motions, and drawing in the dirt, Manerra warned Gavin of the Hyranian danger. Gavin let him know there'd been sightings of Yatren in the woods, but only one incident where a Yatren had approached close enough to throw a rock at the fence. He warned Manerra about the dangers of the fence, and apologized for laws that did not allow Yatren visitors inside their houses or their compound. Manerra asked about the temple stone, but Gavin, once he understood the object and the question, denied knowledge of it.

The second day, they exchanged food. Gavin was allowed to examine Manerra's knife, and Manerra agreed to allow Jim and Gavin to observe abbah the next morning, provided Kayarra participated in the rite. Manerra asked where they came from, why they were there, what they wanted, and if there were more who would follow. Gavin's answers grew murky, then untranslatable. Manerra's answers were similarly vague and confusing when Gavin asked for information about the Yatren.

Where Manerra and Vantrann slept, Kayarra never learned. The only fire or smoke he saw was on the second day when Vantrann built a fire in their meeting circle so Manerra could steep tea, and again when Manerra built a small fire to ignite the end of the stick he used in abbah.

On the third day, in the dew-heavy gray of predawn, Manerra met them in the meeting circle and led them to the top of the hill, out of sight of the compound, and there, he performed abbah. At the conclusion of abbah's refrain, Vantrann jerked his hand down so hard, pain lanced Kayarra's wrist before he could let go. When they returned to the meeting circle, Vantrann positioned himself between Manerra and Kayarra.

It was nearing noon when Manerra stood from his rock seat. Vantrann lunged to his feet and stepped toward Manerra before a signal from the shon regis stopped him. "Kayarra, I would speak with you," Manerra said. "Alone."

Kayarra, alarmed by Vantrann's scowl, watched Vantrann's heavy-footed retreat with trepidation.

"Gavichristo, Jaymah," Manerra stumbled over Jim Matley's name, dipped his head, and started away, opposite the direction Vantrann had taken.

"What's wrong?" Gavin demanded.

"Manerra wants to talk to me in private," Kayarra explained.

Gavin frowned, glanced at Jim, but nodded.

Kayarra caught up with Manerra, who had stopped within sight of the humans.

"I will not dismiss you from Acrahh's service unless you request it," Manerra said, and in the lengthening silence, Kayarra realized that Manerra awaited his decision.

"What you order me?" Kayarra asked, keenly aware of the tenacity of his position.

"That you remain with the Yumens and encourage them to wisdom in their dealings with Yatra's children."

Kayarra felt his face heat. "I no man," he said, hating that truth.

"You're wrong, Kayarra. I've watched Gavichristo with you. He watches your lead and hears what you say. Even if he will not heed your recommendations, he will hear them. Do not allow Hyranians to use the power of your people against their siblings. Do not allow any Yatren to turn the goodwill of your tribe into anger. Keep the stewardship that is your trust. It is your vow as much as mine."

Kayarra stood overwhelmed, and distrustful of Manerra's generosity. He glanced back at Gavin and Jim, wanting to believe Manerra, but unable to.

"I cannot force you to stay," Manerra said, "but know that I cannot protect you if you leave. The nation witnessed Crysus's leave-taking. They know she took the temple stone from shecaren hands. They believe your presence tainted the rites and angered the gods. Your death by Yatren hands need never be over insults given. Even among the janquer, beware Vantrann."

Kayarra stared at Manerra, struggling to believe and trust the changes in him. "Why—" he got out before he lost thought direction amid his vast confusion.

"The nation's problems are no longer assuaged by reminders of kinship and history. Hyran recognized that truth years before Aya did. Even Crysus told us that when she reclaimed the temple stone. That's why I separated the janquer and gave them more than a symbolic trust. They now have the power that Aya once held. My prayers go to Acrahh that their love for one another will temper their passions and zeal."

In the meeting circle, Gavin stood up, and Kayarra searched the direction of Gavin's sudden attention. He spotted movement through the trees. Vantrann approached.

Manerra brushed Kayarra's arm. "One day you will have Yumen memories and Yumen trust, and you will not be so anxious to leave them."

Kayarra's attention returned to Manerra. "How I tell you . . . of change."

Manerra started back toward the circle.

Kayarra matched step with him. "They not let me leave."

"The fence does not restrict your view of the north hill," Manerra pointed to the next hill over, "and the silent speech is a tradesman's skill."

They reached the meeting circle at the same time Vantrann did. Vantrann held out Manerra's wrapped flute, but their eyes remained locked even after Manerra took it.

* * * * *

The notes of Manerra's flute came light, playful, quick, while Vantrann's dark tones held to the extreme of endurance. Played together, the effect was at once dark and light, bitter and sweet, heartfelt and angry.

Kayarra heard a distant snap of deadfall through the agony of the song and opened his eyes, startled to see a stranger approach. The man was obese. Sight of him jarred loose a memory flash of his first sighting of Denassa in the tent in the desert . . . a memory blurred and buried by sickness and time. He had the impression that his life was starting anew from a pivotal point that he thought he'd passed . . . a moment that defined his mental birth.

The obese man crouched beside Gavin, his back to the group, and their heads nearly touched as the man whispered in Gavin's ear.

Manerra and Vantrann played without pause. By the time their notes merged and joined midway of the extremes, the stranger was on his way back to the compound.

Gavin offered a seated bow. "Manerra, shon regis, janquer lord Vantrann, your musical skills are breathtaking. Thank you. Shon regis, I just received the news we've been waiting for. Aya's body has arrived."

Manerra paled, then reached for a cloth lying in his lap and began wiping his flute. "Vantrann, fetch the shuren," Manerra said. Cloth and flute disappeared inside the flute's cover. Manerra looked at Gavin. "Take me to him."

Gavin led them to a fenced enclosure at the rear of the compound. A shuttle rested on the tarmac, heat waves shimmering along its contours. But the shuttle was not their destination. The vehicle's principle cargo awaited claiming in a grassy patch at the edge of the tarmac, well away from the nearest building.

Kayarra spotted the black bag atop the silver gurney flanked by two men and suddenly didn't want to advance closer. He halted beside the shuren's shoulder while Manerra and Gavin approached the bag and its escorts.

"Are you ready to see him?" Gavin asked.

Manerra's "Yes" was tense.

One of the humans reached for the bag's zipper and Kayarra looked away. His only memory of a days-old corpse was the maggot-infested carcass he'd seen beside the mountain trail. A similar sight could not be his last memory of Aya.

The grate of the zipper ended. Silence deepened. Kayarra looked at Manerra, who stared at the bag's contents without the look of revulsion and horror Kayarra anticipated. He drew enough strength from Manerra's courage to dare a glance at the open bag.

Aya lay there, as Kayarra never thought to see him again, with sunlight glinting so strongly off the beads in his hair and robe that Kayarra's eyes watered. Aya, son of Acrahh . . . so miraculously unchanged that Kayarra awaited the rise and fall of his chest in a breath that didn't come. The only breath finally taken was his own, in a sob, as grief denied reality.

"Is this Aya?" Gavin's tone was somber.

"Yes." Manerra's voice was that of a stranger. He reached into the body bag, removed the temple stone's empty pouch, and slipped its strap over his arm and head.

Gavin motioned to one of the attendants, took a palm-sized box from the man, depressed buttons, then returned the device. As if on signal, the attendants stepped away, heading toward the shuttle.

Manerra gripped Aya's cloth covered arm. "Van," he said, and Vantrann thrust the shuren's reins into Kayarra's hand.

"The body's been frozen," Gavin warned, but Kayarra didn't know how to translate the warning.

Manerra and Vantrann lifted Aya, while Kayarra shortened his grip on the reins and grabbed the shuren's cheek strap. Gavin caught the plastic bag and pulled it free of Aya's body.

Aya's transfer to shurenback happened quickly. But when Aya's hands dropped past the shuren's ribcage and swung above the ground, Manerra's fingers curled into fists. He buried his face between his up-raised arms and his gasping breaths became sobs.

The facade of control broken, Kayarra averted his face as tears came in response to Manerra's grief.

Manerra lowered his arms once he was able to reassert control, but remained facing the shuren.

"Is there anything I can do?" Gavin asked.

"The funeral pyre," Manerra said in his own language, "will be built on the crest of the north hill."

It took a moment for Kayarra to realize that Manerra spoke to him. "I can't," he whispered hoarsely, remembering too vividly Casta's cremation.

Manerra risked a glance at him, then dipped his head. Then he turned and faced Gavin. "Gavichristo, thank you for my broth-or's spirit." Manerra dipped his head again, this time in haste, and reached for the shuren's reins.

Gavin gripped Kayarra's arm as Manerra turned the shuren, but images of a white robe catching fire, flames illuminating and then blackening the leg beneath, prevented Kayarra from following Manerra.

* * * * *

That evening, Gavin accompanied Kayarra to their office building's main door, released the lock, and held the door open. Kayarra stepped through before Gavin turned away.

Kayarra caught the closing door. "Are you coming?" he asked.

"Go ahead," Gavin told him. "I forgot something in the office."

Kayarra released the door, which swung shut with an audible click. He stood in the fading sunlight and stared at the locked door, alone for the first time since his arrival.

The release from supervision was so sudden, he waited minutes for

Gavin's return before turning from the door, descending the stairs, and walking the compound's gravel path. Where the footpath veered toward staff quarters, Kayarra kept straight across the yard, past shade trees and shrubbery, past the guards at the locked Gate Three.

A twenty-yard swath around the compound's perimeter fence afforded a clear view of the river valley's northern ridge.

Kayarra halted facing the ridge, and read in the sun's position the final preparations for abbah: the rinsing away of dirt and the donning of tribal robes.

Kayarra closed his eyes and saw again Manerra walking away with the empty tooled pouch over his shoulder, but memories superimposed images of Aya performing abbah, Aya handling the fiery temple stone. Kayarra finally recalled Manerra, dressed in black in honor of his second birthday, performing abbah atop the Altar of Acrahh. Once again, colored jewels glittered against the backdrop of Kayarra's eyelids, and the words of abbah came to him.

"Great Acrahh, god and father . . ." Kayarra repeated the words aloud, his voice a weak imitation of the confident voices inside his head. When he opened his eyes at the conclusion of abbah, his arms were raised. He lowered them slowly.

"Thank you, Aya," he whispered to the sun's setting rim, aware that tears streaked his face.

A flicker of light on the ridge pinpointed Manerra and Vantrann's location. Kayarra watched smoke rise and firelight brighten while the sun bled color far and wide across the sky.

"Beautiful, isn't it?" a voice commented nearby—Kayarra's first indication that he wasn't alone.

"Is that fire on the ridge?"

"A cremation," the first speaker answered in a tone meant to discourage questioning.

Footsteps moved away, but Kayarra's attention remained unswervingly focused upon the distant pyre. His main grief had been shed earlier. The tears that trickled down his cheeks now were the beginnings of a painful recovery.

For a while longer, he watched the fire brighten against the deepening sky, then wiped his face dry on his sleeve and walked back toward staff quarters. Gavin had offered him a tentative trust. He went now to keep it.

###